December 2015

January 2016

February 2016

March 2016

April 2016

May 2016

Billionaire BOSSES

HIRED FOR HIS PLEASURE

CAROLE MORTIMER
ANNA CLEARY
SUSANNE JAMES

First Published in Great Britain 2016
By Mills & Boon, an imprint of HarperCollins*Publishers*
1 London Bridge Street, London, SE1 9GF

ISBN: 978-0-263-91794-9

24-0516

Our policy is to use papers that are natural, renewable and recyclable products and made from wood grown in sustainable forests.
The logging and manufacturing processes conform to the legal environmental regulations of the country of origin.

Printed and bound in Spain
by CPI, Barcelona

THE TALK OF HOLLYWOOD

CAROLE MORTIMER

Carole Mortimer was born and lives in the UK. She is married to Peter and they have six sons. She has been writing for Mills & Boon since 1978, and is the author of almost 200 books. She writes for both the Mills & Boon® Historical and Modern™ lines. Carole is a USA Today bestselling author, and in 2012 was recognised by Queen Elizabeth II for her 'outstanding contribution to literature'.

Visit Carole at www.carolemortimer.co.uk or on Facebook.

CHAPTER ONE

'IT WOULD appear that your guest has finally arrived, Gramps,' Stazy said as she stood stiffly beside one of the bay windows in the drawing room, facing towards the front of Bromley House and watching the sleek black sports car as it was driven down the gravel driveway of her grandfather's Hampshire estate. She was unable to make out the features of the driver of the car behind the tinted windows; but, nevertheless, she was sure that it was Jaxon Wilder, the English actor and director who for the past ten years had held the fickle world of Hollywood in the palm of his elegant hand.

'Don't be so hard on the man, Stazy; he's only five minutes late, and he did have to drive all the way from London!' her grandfather chided indulgently from the comfort of his armchair.

'Then maybe it would have been a good idea on his part to take into account the distance he had to travel and set out accordingly.' Stazy had made absolutely no secret of her disapproval of Jaxon Wilder's visit here, and found the whole idea of his wanting to write and direct a film about the life of her deceased grandmother totally unacceptable. Unfortunately, she hadn't been able to persuade her grandfather into dismissing the idea as readily—which was why Jaxon Wilder was now parking that sleek black sports car on the driveway outside her grandfather's home.

Stazy turned away before she saw the man in question alight from the car; she already knew exactly what Jaxon Wilder looked like. The whole world probably recognised Jaxon Wilder after he had completely swept the board at every awards ceremony earlier in the year with his recent film, in which he had once again acted and directed.

Aged in his mid-thirties, he was tall and lean, with wide and powerful shoulders, slightly overlong dark hair, and piercing grey eyes set either side of an aristocratic nose. His mouth was sculptured and sensual, his chin square and determined, and the deep timbre of his voice had been known to send quivers of pleasure down the spines of women of all ages. Jaxon Wilder was known to be the highest paid actor and director on both sides of the pond.

His looks and appeal had often led to his being photographed in newspapers and magazines with the latest beautiful woman to share his life—and his bed! And his reason for coming here today was to use that charm in an effort to persuade Stazy's grandfather into giving his blessing—and help—to the writing of a screenplay about the adventurous life of Stazy's grandmother, Anastasia Romanski. A woman who, as a young child, had escaped the Russian Revolution with her family by fleeing to England, and as an adult had been one of the many secret and unsung heroines of her adopted country.

Anastasia had died only two years ago, at the age of ninety-four. Her obituary in the newspaper had drawn the attention of a nosy reporter who, when he had looked deeper into Anastasia's life, had discovered that there had been far more to Anastasia Bromley than the obscure accolades mentioned. The result had been a sensationalised biography about Anastasia, published six months ago, and the ensuing publicity had caused her grandfather to suffer a mild heart attack.

In the circumstances, was it any wonder that Stazy had been horrified to discover that Jaxon Wilder intended to make a film of Anastasia's life? And, even worse, that the film director had an appointment with her grandfather in order to discuss the project? Stazy had decided it was a discussion she had every intention of being a part of!

'Sir Geoffrey.' Jaxon moved smoothly forward to shake the older man's hand as the butler showed him into the drawing room of Bromley House.

'Mr Wilder.' It was hard to believe that Geoffrey Bromley was a man aged in his mid-nineties as he returned the firmness of Jaxon's handshake. His dark hair was only lightly streaked with grey, his shoulders still stiffly erect in his tailored dark three-piece suit and snowy white shirt with a meticulously tied grey tie.

'Jaxon, please,' he invited. 'May I say how pleased I am that you agreed to see me today—?'

'Then the pleasure would appear to be all yours!'

'Stazy!' Geoffrey Bromley rebuked affectionately as he turned towards the woman who had spoken so sharply.

Jaxon turned to look at her too as she stood in front of the bay window. The sun shining in behind her made it hard for him to make out her features, although the hostility of her tone was enough of an indication that she, at least, wasn't in the least pleased by Jaxon's visit!

'My granddaughter Stazy Bromley, Mr Wilder,' Sir Geoffrey introduced lightly.

Jaxon, having refreshed his memory on the Bromley family before leaving his London hotel earlier that morning, already knew that Stazy was short for Anastasia—the same name as her grandmother. Information that had in no way prepared him for Stazy Bromley's startling resemblance to her grandmother as she stepped out of the sunlight.

About five-six in height, with the same flame-coloured hair—neither red nor gold, but a startling mixture of the two—and a pale and porcelain complexion, she had a wide, intelligent brow above sultry eyes of deep emerald-green. Her nose was small and perfectly straight, and she had full and sensuous lips above a stubbornly determined chin.

The hairstyle was different, of course; Anastasia had favoured shoulder-length hair, whereas her granddaughter's was stylishly cut in an abundance of layers that was secured at her nape and cascaded down to the middle of her back. The black, knee-length sheath of a dress she wore added to the impression of elegant chic.

Other than those minor differences Jaxon knew he might have been looking at the twenty-nine-year-old Anastasia Romanski.

Green eyes raked over Jaxon dismissively. 'Mr Wilder.'

Jaxon gave an inclination of his head. 'Miss Bromley,' he returned smoothly.

'That would be *Dr* Bromley,' she corrected coolly.

Stazy Bromley had the beauty and grace of a supermodel rather than the appearance of a dusty doctor of Archaeology, as Jaxon knew her to be. Maybe, faced with her obvious antagonism towards him, Jaxon should have had Geoffrey Bromley's granddaughter investigated more thoroughly than simply making a note of her age and occupation…

'Stazy, perhaps you would like to go and tell Mrs Little we'll have tea now…?' her grandfather prompted, softly but firmly.

Those full and sensuous lips thinned. 'Is that an unsubtle hint for me to leave you and Mr Wilder alone for a few minutes, Gramps?' Stazy Bromley said dryly, those disapproving green eyes remaining firmly fixed on Jaxon.

'I think that might be best, darling,' her grandfather encouraged ruefully.

'Just try not to let Mr Wilder use his reputed charm to persuade you into agreeing to or signing anything before I get back!' she warned, with another cold glance in Jaxon's direction.

'I wouldn't dream of it, Dr Bromley,' Jaxon drawled. 'Although I'm flattered that you think I have charm!' Mockery perhaps wasn't the best line for him to take when Stazy Bromley was obviously so antagonistic towards him already, but then Jaxon couldn't say he particularly cared for being treated as if he were some sort of trickster, trying to dupe her grandfather into selling off the family jewels!

Obviously the subject of her grandmother's past was a sensitive one to Stazy Bromley.

'I don't know you well enough as yet to have decided exactly what you are, Mr Wilder,' Stazy Bromley assured him distantly.

But she obviously didn't number his 'charm' as one of his more obvious attributes, Jaxon recognised ruefully. That was a pity, because her physical similarities to her grandmother were already enough to have him intrigued. Similarities that she seemed to deliberately downplay with her lack of make-up and the confinement of her riotous red-gold hair.

If that really was Stazy's intention then she had failed miserably. As if those sultry green eyes and that poutingly sensuous mouth weren't enough of an attraction, her curvaceous figure in that fitted black dress certainly was!

Stazy had only ever seen Jaxon Wilder on the big screen before today, where he invariably appeared tall and dark and very powerful. It was an image she had believed to be magnified by the size of that screen. She had been wrong. Even dressed formally, in a tailored black suit, snowy-white silk shirt and silver tie, Jaxon Wilder was just as powerfully charismatic in the flesh.

'That really is enough, darling,' her grandfather rebuked. 'And I have no doubt that Mr Wilder and I will manage perfectly well for the short time you're gone,' he added pointedly.

'I have no doubt you will, Grandfather.' Her voice softened as she smiled affectionately at her aged grandparent before leaving.

Her grandfather was now the only family Stazy had, her parents having both died fifteen years ago, when their light aeroplane had crashed into the sea off the coast of Cornwall.

Despite already being aged in their early eighties, Anastasia and Geoffrey had been wonderful to their traumatised granddaughter, taking fourteen-year-old Stazy into their home and their lives without a second thought. As a result Stazy's protectiveness where they were both concerned was much stronger than it might otherwise have been.

To the point where she now saw Jaxon Wilder's plans to make a film about her deceased grandmother as nothing more than Hollywood sensationalism—no doubt inspired by that dreadful biography, in which her grandmother had been portrayed as the equivalent of a Russian Mata Hari working for British Intelligence!

No doubt Jaxon Wilder also saw the project as a means of earning himself yet another shelf of awards to add to his already considerable collection. That was a pity—for him!—because Stazy saw it as her mission in life to ensure that film was never made!

'I'm afraid Stazy doesn't approve of your making a film of my late wife's life, Jaxon,' Sir Geoffrey murmured wryly.

He gave a rueful smile. 'One would never have guessed!'

The older man smiled slightly. 'Please, sit down and tell me exactly what it is you want from me,' he invited smoothly as he resumed his seat in the armchair beside the unlit fireplace.

'Shouldn't we wait for your granddaughter to return before we discuss this any further?' Jaxon grimaced as he lowered his lean length down on to the chair opposite, already knowing that Stazy Bromley's attitude was going to be a problem he hadn't envisaged when he had flown over to England yesterday with the express purpose of discussing the details of the film with Geoffrey Bromley.

Jaxon had first written to the older man several months ago—a letter in which he had outlined his idea for the film. The letter he had received back from Geoffrey Bromley two weeks later had been cautiously encouraging. The two men had spoken several times on the telephone before Jaxon had suggested they meet in person and discuss the idea more extensively.

In none of those exchanges had Sir Geoffrey so much

as hinted at his granddaughter's antagonism to the film being made!

Sir Geoffrey smiled confidently. 'I assure you that ultimately Stazy will go along with whatever I decide.'

Jaxon had no doubt that when necessary the older man could be as persuasive as his wife was reputed to have been, but in a totally different way—the part Geoffrey Bromley had played in the events of the previous century were even more shrouded in mystery than those of his now deceased wife. But from the little Jaxon knew the other man had held a very high position of authority in England's security at the time of his retirement twenty-five years ago.

Was it any wonder that Stazy Bromley had the same forceful determination as both her grandparents?

Or that his own visit here today promised to be a battle of wills between the two of them!

A battle Jaxon ultimately had every intention of winning…

'I trust the two of you didn't discuss anything of importance during my absence…?' Stazy said softly as she came back into the room, closely followed by the butler. He was carrying a heavily laden silver tray, the contents of which he proceeded to place on the low coffee table in front of the sofa where Stazy now sat, looking enquiringly at the two men seated opposite.

Her grandfather gave her another of those censorious glances as Jaxon Wilder answered. 'I'm sure that neither of us would have dared to do that, Dr Bromley…' he said dryly.

Stazy was just as sure that the forceful Jaxon Wilder would pretty much dare to do anything he damn well pleased! 'Do you care for milk and sugar in your tea,

Mr Wilder?' she prompted lightly as she held the sugar bowl poised over the three delicate china cups.

'Just milk, thanks.'

Stazy nodded as she added two spoonfuls of sugar to her grandfather's cup before commencing to pour the tea. 'No doubt it becomes more difficult, as you get older, to maintain the perfect bodyweight.'

'Darling, I really don't think this constant bickering with Jaxon is necessary,' her grandfather admonished affectionately as she stood up to carry his cup and saucer over to him after handing Jaxon his own cup.

'Perhaps not,' Stazy allowed, her cheeks warming slightly at the rebuke. 'But I'm sure Mr Wilder is equally capable of defending himself if he feels it necessary.'

Jaxon was fast losing his patience with Stazy Bromley's snide comments. She might appear delicately beautiful in appearance, but as far as he could tell, where this particular woman was concerned, that was exactly where the delicacy ended.

'Undoubtedly,' he bit out abruptly. 'Now, if we could perhaps return to discussing *Butterfly*...?'

'"Butterfly"...?' his adversary repeated slowly as she resumed her seat on the sofa before crossing one silkily elegant knee over the other.

'It was your grandmother's code name—'

'I'm aware of what it was, Mr Wilder,' she cut in crisply.

'It's also the working title of my film,' Jaxon explained tersely.

'Isn't that rather presumptuous of you?' She frowned. 'As far as I'm aware,' she continued warily, 'there has been no agreement as yet to there even *being* a film, let alone it already having a working title!' She turned enquiring eyes to her grandfather, her tension palpable.

Sir Geoffrey shrugged. 'I don't believe there is any way in which we can stop Mr Wilder from making his film, Stazy.'

'But—'

'With or without our co-operation,' Sir Geoffrey added firmly. 'And personally—after the publication of that dreadful biography!—I would rather be allowed to have some say in the content than none at all.'

Stazy Bromley's eyes glittered with anger as she turned to look at Jaxon. 'If you've dared to threaten my grandfather—'

'Of course Jaxon hasn't threatened me, darling—'

'And Jaxon resents the hell—excuse my language, sir—' Jaxon nodded briefly to the older man before turning his chilling gaze back to the bristling Stazy Bromley '—out of the implication that he might have done so!'

Stazy had the good sense to realise that she just might have been out of line with that last remark. It was really no excuse that she had been predisposed to dislike Jaxon Wilder before she had even met him, based purely on the things she had read about him. Especially when he had been charm itself since his arrival. To her grandfather, at least. Stazy was pretty sure, after her barely veiled remarks, that the antagonism now went both ways!

But exactly what had Jaxon Wilder expected to happen when he had arranged to come here? That he would meet alone with a man aged in his mid-nineties who had recently suffered a heart attack? That the two of them would exchange pleasantries before he walked away with Geoffrey's complete co-operation? If that was what he'd thought was going to happen then he obviously didn't know Stazy's grandfather very well; even twenty-five years after his supposed retirement Geoffrey was a power to be reckoned with! And Stazy considered herself only one step behind him…

Not only was she a highly qualified London university lecturer, it had been hinted at by the powers that be that she was in line to become head of the department when her professor stepped down next year—and Stazy hadn't put herself in that position at only twenty-nine by being shy and retiring.

'I apologise if I was mistaken,' she murmured softly. 'Mr Wilder's use of the term "working title" seemed to imply that things had already been settled between the two of you.'

'Apology accepted,' Jaxon Wilder grated, without even the slightest lessening of the tension in those broad shoulders. 'Obviously I would rather proceed with your blessing, Sir Geoffrey.' He nodded to the older man, at the same time managing to imply that he didn't give a damn whether or not he had Stazy's!

'And his co-operation?' she put in dryly.

Cool grey eyes turned back in her direction. 'Of course.'

Stazy repressed the shiver that threatened to run the length of her spine—of alarm rather than the pleasure she imagined most women felt when Jaxon Wilder looked at them! As his icy gaze raked over her with slow criticism Stazy knew exactly what he would see: a woman who preferred a no-nonsense appearance. Her lashes were naturally long and dark, requiring no mascara, and in fact her face was completely bare of make-up apart from a pale peach lipgloss. Her hands, throat and ears were completely unadorned with jewellery.

Certainly Stazy knew herself to be nothing in the least like the beautiful and willowy actresses in whose company Jaxon Wilder had so often been seen, photographed for newspapers and magazines during the last dozen years or so. She doubted the man would even know what to do with an intelligent woman…

What on earth—?

Why should she care what Jaxon Wilder thought of her? As far as Stazy was concerned there would be absolutely no reason for the two of them ever to meet again after today—let alone for her to care what he thought of her as a woman…

She straightened determinedly. 'I believe you are not only wasting your own time, Mr Wilder, but also my grandfather's and mine—'

'As it happens, I'm willing to give Jaxon my blessing and my co-operation. I will allow him to read letters and personal papers of Anastasia's.' Geoffrey spoke firmly over Stazy's scathing dismissal. 'But only under certain conditions.'

Stazy's eyes widened as she turned to look at her grandfather. 'You can't be serious!'

Her grandfather gave a slight inclination of his head. 'I believe you will find, darling, that it's called controlling a situation that one knows is inevitable, rather than attempting a futile fight against it.'

Jaxon felt none of the exhilaration he might have expected to feel at Sir Geoffrey not only giving his blessing to the making of the film, but also offering him access to certain of Anastasia's personal papers in order to aid in the writing of the screenplay. Inwardly he sensed that whatever Geoffrey's conditions were, Jaxon wasn't going to like them…

Stazy Bromley obviously felt that same sense of unease as she stood up abruptly, a frown between those clear green eyes as she stared down at her grandfather for several long seconds before her expression softened slightly.

'Darling, remember what happened after that awful book was published—'

'I'm insulted that you would even *think* of comparing the film I intend to make with that sensationalised trash!' Jaxon rose sharply to his feet.

She turned to look at him coolly. 'How can I think otherwise?'

'Maybe by giving me a chance—'

'Now, now, you two.' Sir Geoffrey chuckled softly. 'It really doesn't bode well if the two of you can't even be in the same room together without arguing.'

Jaxon's earlier feeling of trepidation grew as he turned to look down at the older man, not fooled for a moment by the innocence of Sir Geoffrey's expression. 'Perhaps you would care to explain your conditions...?' he prompted slowly, warily. Whatever ace Geoffrey Bromley had hidden up his sleeve Jaxon was utterly convinced he wasn't going to like it!

The older man gave a shrug. 'My first condition is that there will be no copies made of my wife's personal papers. In fact they are never to leave this house.'

That was going to make things slightly awkward. It would mean that Jaxon would have to spend several days—possibly a week—here at Bromley House in order to read those papers and make notes before he was able to go away and write the screenplay. But, busy schedule permitting, there was no real reason why it couldn't be done. Over the years he had certainly stayed in infinitely less salubrious places than the elegant comfort of Bromley House!

'My second condition—'

'Exactly how many conditions are there?' Jaxon prompted with amusement.

'Just the two,' Sir Geoffrey assured him dryly. 'And the first condition will only apply if you agree to the second.'

'Fine.' Jaxon nodded ruefully.

'Oh, I wouldn't give me your agreement just yet, Jaxon,' the older man warned derisively.

Stazy didn't at all like the calculating glint she could clearly see in her grandfather's eyes. His first condition made a certain amount of sense—although there was no guarantee, of course. But at least Jaxon Wilder having access to her grandmother's personal papers might mean there was a slight chance his screenplay would have some basis in truth. Not much, but some.

That only left her grandfather's second condition…

'Go ahead, Gramps,' she invited softly.

'Perhaps you should both sit down first…?'

Stazy tensed and at the same time sensed Jaxon's own increased wariness as he stood across the room from her. 'Do we need to sit down…?'

'Oh I think it might be advisable,' her grandfather confirmed dryly.

'I'll remain standing, if you don't mind,' Jaxon Wilder rasped gruffly.

'Not at all,' Geoffrey chuckled. 'Stazy?'

'The same,' she murmured warily.

'Very well.' Her grandfather relaxed back in his chair as he looked up at the two of them. 'I have found your conversation today highly…diverting, shall we say? And I assure you there is really very little that a man of my age finds in the least amusing!' her grandfather added ruefully.

He was playing with them, Stazy recognised frustratedly. Amusing himself at their expense. 'Will you just spit it out, Gramps!'

He smiled slightly as he rested his elbows on the arms of the chair before linking his fingers together in front of his chest. 'Stazy, you obviously have reservations about the content of Jaxon's film—'

'With good reason!'

'With no reason whatsoever,' Jaxon corrected grimly. 'I am not the one responsible for that dreadful biography—nor have I ever written or starred in a film that twists the truth in order to add sensationalism,' he added hardly.

'I doubt most Hollywood actors would recognise the truth if it jumped up and bit them on the nose!' Those green eyes glittered with scorn.

Jaxon wasn't sure which one of them had closed the distance between them—was only aware that they now stood so close that their noses were almost touching as she glared up at him and Jaxon scowled right back down at her.

He was suddenly aware of the soft insidiousness of Stazy's perfume: a heady combination of cinnamon, lemon and—much more disturbing—hotly enraged woman…

Close to her like this, Jaxon could see that those amazing green eyes had a ring of black about the iris, giving them a strangely luminous quality that was almost mesmerising when fringed with the longest, darkest lashes he had ever seen. Her complexion was the pale ivory of fine bone china, with the same delicacy of appearance.

A delicacy that was completely at odds with the sensual fullness of her mouth.

Her lips were slightly parted now, to reveal small and perfectly straight white teeth. Small white teeth that Jaxon imagined could bite a man with passion as easily as— What the…?

Jaxon stepped back abruptly as he realised he had allowed his thoughts to wander way off the reservation, considering the antagonism the two of them clearly felt towards each other. Not only that, but Stazy Bromley was exactly like all the buttoned-down and career-orientated women he knew who had clawed themselves up the professional ladder so that they might inhabit the higher echelons of certain film studios. Hard, unfeminine women, whom Jaxon always avoided like the plague!

He eased the tension from his shoulders before turning back to face the obviously still amused Geoffrey Bromley. 'I agree with Stazy—'

'How refreshing!' she cut in dryly.

'You may as well just get this is over with,' Jaxon finished ruefully.

'Let's hope the two of you are in as much agreement about my second condition.' Sir Geoffrey nodded, no longer smiling or as relaxed as he had been a short time ago. 'I've given the matter some thought, and in view of Stazy's lack of enthusiasm for the making of your film, and your own obvious determination to prove her suspicions wrong, Jaxon, I feel it would be better for all concerned if Stazy were to assist you in collating and researching Anastasia's personal papers.'

'What…?'

Jaxon was completely in agreement with Stazy Bromley's obvious horror at the mere suggestion of the two of them working that closely together even for one minute, let alone the days or weeks it might take him to go through Anastasia Bromley's papers!

CHAPTER TWO

STAZY was the first to recover her powers of speech. 'You can't be serious, Gramps—'

'I assure you I am perfectly serious.' He nodded gravely.

She gave a disbelieving shake of her head. 'I can't just take time off from the university whenever I feel like it!'

'I'm sure Jaxon won't mind waiting a few weeks until you finish for the long summer break.'

'But I've been invited to join a dig in Iraq this summer—'

'And I sincerely doubt that any of those artifacts having already been there for hundreds if not thousands of years, are going to disappear overnight just because you arrive a week later than expected,' her grandfather reasoned pleasantly.

Stazy stared down at him in complete frustration, knowing that she owed both him and her grandmother so much more than a week of her time. That if it wasn't for the two of them completely turning their own lives upside down fifteen years ago she would never have coped with her parents deaths as well as she had. It had also been their encouragement and support that had helped her through an arduous university course and then achieving her doctorate.

Stazy's thoughts came to an abrupt halt as she suddenly became aware of Jaxon Wilder's unnatural silence.

Those silver-grey eyes were narrowed on her grandfather, hard cheekbones thrown into sharp prominence by the clenching of his jaw, and his mouth was a thin and uncompromising line. His hands too were clenched, into fists at his sides.

Obviously not a happy bunny, either, Stazy recognised ruefully.

Although any satisfaction she might have felt at that realisation was totally nullified by her own continued feelings of horror at her grandfather's proposal. 'I believe you will find Mr Wilder is just as averse to the idea as I am, Gramps,' she drawled derisively.

He shrugged. 'Then it would appear to be a case of film and be damned,' he misquoted softly.

Stazy drew in a sharp breath as she remembered the furore that had followed the publication of the unauthorised biography six months ago. The press had hounded her grandfather for weeks afterwards—to the extent that he had arranged for round-the-clock guards to be placed at Bromley House and his house in London. And he had suffered a heart attack because of the emotional strain he had been put under.

Stazy had even had one inventive reporter sit in on one of her lectures without detection, only to corner her with a blast of personal questions at the end—much to her embarrassment and anger.

The thought of having to go through all that again was enough to send cold shivers of dread down Stazy's spine. 'Perhaps you might somehow persuade Mr Wilder into not making the film at all, Gramps?' Although her own behaviour towards him this past hour or so certainly wasn't conducive to Jaxon Wilder wanting to do her any favours!

Probably she should have thought of that earlier. Her grandmother had certainly believed in the old adage, 'You'll catch more with honey than with vinegar...'

The derision in Jaxon Wilder's piercing grey eyes as he looked at her seemed to indicate he was perfectly aware of Stazy's belated regrets! 'What form of...persuasion did you have in mind, Dr Bromley?' he drawled mockingly.

Stazy felt the colour warm her cheeks. 'I believe I referred to my grandfather's powers of persuasion rather than my own,' she returned irritably.

'Pity,' he murmured softly, those grey eyes speculative as his gaze moved slowly over Stazy, from her two-inch-heeled shoes, her curvaceous figure in the black dress, to the top of her flame-coloured head, before settling on the pouting fullness of her mouth.

She frowned her irritation as she did her best to ignore that blatantly sexual gaze. 'Surely you can appreciate how much the making of this film is going to upset my grandfather?'

'On the contrary.' Jaxon deeply resented Stazy Bromley's tone. 'I believe that a film showing the true events of seventy years ago can only be beneficial to your grandmother's memory.'

'Oh, please, Mr Wilder.' Stazy Bromley eyed him pityingly. 'We both know that your only interest in making this particular film is in going up on that stage in a couple of years' time to collect yet another batch of awards!'

Jaxon drew in a sharp breath. 'You—'

'Enough!' Sir Geoffrey firmly cut in on the conversation before Jaxon had chance to finish his blistering reply. Eyes of steely-blue raked over both of them as he stood up. 'I believe that for the moment I have heard quite enough on this subject from both of you.' He gave an impatient shake of his head. 'You'll be staying for dinner, I hope, Jaxon...?' He raised steel-grey brows questioningly.

'If you feel we can make any progress by my doing so—yes, of course I'll stay to dinner,' Jaxon bit out tensely.

Sir Geoffrey gave a derisive smile. 'I believe it will be up to you and Stazy as to whether any progress will or can be made before you leave here later today,' he said dryly. 'And, with that in mind, I am going upstairs to take a short nap before dinner. Stazy, perhaps you would like to take Mr Wilder for a walk in the garden while I'm gone? My roses are particularly lovely this year, Jaxon, and their perfume is strongest in the late afternoon and early evening,' he added lightly, succeeding in silencing his granddaughter as she drew in another deep breath with the obvious intention of arguing against his suggestion.

Jaxon was reminded that the older man had once been in a position of control over the whole of British Intelligence, let alone one stubbornly determined granddaughter! 'A walk in the garden sounds...pleasant,' Jaxon answered noncommittally, not completely sure that Stazy Bromley wouldn't use the opportunity to try and stab him with a garden fork while they were outside, and so put an end to this particular problem.

'That's settled, then,' Sir Geoffrey said heartily. 'Do cheer up, darling.' He bent to kiss his granddaughter on the forehead. 'I very much doubt that Jaxon has any intention of attempting to steal the family silver before he leaves!'

The sentiment was so close to Jaxon's own earlier thoughts in regard to Stazy's obviously scathing opinion of him that he couldn't help but chuckle wryly. 'No, Sir Geoffrey, I believe you may rest assured that all your family jewels are perfectly safe where I'm concerned.'

The older man placed an affectionate arm about his granddaughter's slender shoulders. 'Stazy is the only family jewel I care anything about, Jaxon.'

'In that case, they're most *definitely* safe!' Jaxon assured him with hard dismissal.

'And on that note…' Sir Geoffrey smiled slightly as his arm dropped back to his side. 'I'll see both of you in a couple of hours.' He turned and left the room. Leaving a tense and awkward silence behind him…

Stazy was very aware of the barely leashed power of the man walking beside her across the manicured lawn in the warmth of the late-afternoon sunshine, and could almost feel the heated energy radiating off Jaxon Wilder. Or perhaps it was just repressed anger? The two of them had certainly got off to a bad start earlier—and it had only become worse during the course of the next hour!

Mainly because of her own less-than-pleasant attitude, Stazy accepted. But what else had this man expected? That she was just going to stand by and risk her grandfather becoming ill again?

She gave a weary sigh before breaking the silence between them. 'Perhaps we should start again, Mr Wilder?'

He raised dark brows as he looked down at her. 'Perhaps we should, Dr Bromley?'

'Stazy,' she invited abruptly.

'Jaxon,' he drawled in return.

He obviously wasn't going to make this easy for her, Stazy acknowledged impatiently. 'I'm sure you are aware of what happened five months ago, and why I now feel so protective towards my grandfather?'

'Of course.' Jaxon gave a rueful smile as he ducked beneath the trailing branches of a willow tree, only to discover there was a wooden swing chair beneath the vibrant green leaves. 'Shall we…?' he prompted lightly. 'I resent the fact,' he continued once they were both seated, 'that you believe he might need any protection from me.'

That was fair enough, Stazy acknowledged grudgingly. Except she still believed this man was in a position to cause her grandfather unnecessary distress. 'He and my grandmother were totally in love with each other until the very end…'

Jaxon heard clearly the pain of loss underlying her statement. 'I'm not about to do anything to damage either Geoffrey's or your own treasured memories of Anastasia,' he assured her huskily.

'No?'

'No,' Jaxon said evenly. 'On the contrary—I'm hoping my film will help to set the record straight where your grandmother's actions seventy years ago are concerned. I don't believe in making money—or in acquiring awards—' he gave her a pointed look '—by causing someone else unnecessary pain.'

Stazy felt her cheeks warm at the rebuke. 'Perhaps we should just draw a veil over our previous conversation, Jaxon…?'

'Perhaps we should.' He chuckled wryly.

Stazy's eyes widened as she saw that a cleft had appeared in Jaxon's left cheek as he smiled, and those grey eyes were no longer cold but the warm colour of liquid mercury, his teeth very white and even against his lightly tanned skin.

Stazy had spent the past eleven years acquiring her degree, her doctorate, and lecturing—as well as attending as many archaeological digs around the world as she could during the holidays. Leaving very little time for such frivolities as attending the cinema. Even so, she had seen several of Jaxon Wilder's films, and was able to appreciate that the man in the flesh was very much more…*immediate* than even his sexy screen image portrayed. Mesmerisingly so…

Just as she was aware of the heat of his body as he sat beside her on the swing seat—of the way his lightly spicy aftershave intermingled with the more potent and earthy smell of a virile male in his prime.

That was something of an admission from a woman who over the years had eschewed even the suggestion of a personal relationship in favour of concentrating on her career. And now certainly wasn't the time for Stazy to belatedly develop a crush on a film star!

Even one as suavely handsome as Jaxon Wilder…

Especially one as suavely handsome as Jaxon Wilder! What could a London university lecturer in archaeology and an award-winning Hollywood actor/director possibly have in common? *Nothing*, came the clear answer!

Was she disappointed at that realisation? No, of course she wasn't! Was she…?

Stazy got abruptly to her feet. 'Shall we continue with our walk?' She set out determinedly towards the fishpond, without so much as waiting to see if he followed her.

Jaxon slowly stood to stroll along behind Stazy, not quite sure what had happened to make her take off so abruptly, only knowing that something had. He also knew, after years of spending time with women who were totally fixated on both their career and their appearance—and not necessarily in that order!—that Stazy Bromley was so much more complex than that. An enigma. One that was starting to interest him in spite of himself, Jaxon acknowledged ruefully as he realised he was watching the way her perfectly rounded bottom moved sensuously beneath her black fitted dress as she walked…

Even Stazy's defence of her grandparents, although an irritation to him, and casting aspersions upon his own character as it undoubtedly did, was still a trait to be admired. Most of the women Jaxon was acquainted with would sell their soul to the devil—let alone their grandparents' reputations!—if it meant they could attract even a little publicity for themselves by doing so!

Stazy Bromley obviously did the opposite. Even that inaccurate biography had only fleetingly mentioned that Anastasia had had one child and one grandchild, and any attempt to talk to Stazy after the publication of that book had been met with the response that 'Dr Stazy Bromley does not give personal interviews'.

'So,' Jaxon began as he joined her beside a pond full of large golden-coloured fish, 'what do you think of your grandfather's idea that the two of us meet here in the summer and research your grandmother's personal papers together…?'

She gave a humourless smile as she continued to watch the fish lazing beneath the water in the warmth of the early-evening sunshine. 'If I didn't know better I would say it was the onset of senility!'

Jaxon chuckled appreciatively. 'But as we both do know better…?'

She gave a shrug. 'You really can't be persuaded into dropping the film idea altogether?'

He drew in a sharp breath. 'Stazy, even if I said yes I know for a fact that there are at least two other directors with an interest in making their own version of what happened.'

Stazy turned to look at him searchingly, knowing by the openness of his expression as he returned her gaze that he was telling her the truth. 'Directors who may not have your integrity?' she questioned flatly.

'Probably not.' He grimaced.

'So, what you're saying is it's a question of going with the devil we know, or allowing some other film director to totally blacken my grandmother's name and reputation?' Stazy guessed heavily.

Jaxon nodded abruptly. 'That about sums it up, yes.'

Damned if they did—double damned it they didn't. 'You do realise that if I agree to do this I would be doing so under protest?'

His mouth twisted derisively. 'Oh, I believe you've made your feelings on that particular subject more than clear, Stazy,' he assured her dryly.

She shot him an irritated glance before once again turning to walk away, this time in the direction of the horses grazing in a corner of the meadow that adjoined the garden. One of those horses, a beautiful chestnut stallion, ambled over to stretch its neck across the fence, so that Stazy could stroke absently down the long length of his nose as she continued to consider the options available to her.

There really weren't any.

She either agreed to help Jaxon Wilder in his research or she refused, and then he'd go ahead and make the film without any input from her grandfather or Anastasia's private papers.

Her uncharacteristic physical awareness of this man was not only unacceptable but also baffling to Stazy, and even now, standing just feet away from him as she continued to stroke Copper's nose, she was totally aware of Jaxon's disturbing presence. Too much for her not to know that spending a week in his company was simply asking for trouble.

It was all too easy for Jaxon to see the riot of emotions that flashed across Stazy Bromley's expressive face as she considered what to do about this situation: impatience, frustration, anger, dismay—

Dismay…?

Jaxon raised dark brows as he wondered what *that* was all about. Obviously Stazy would rather this situation didn't exist at all, but she didn't appear to be the type of woman who would allow anything to get the better of her… And exactly *why* was he even bothering to wonder what type of woman Stazy Bromley was? Jaxon questioned self-derisively.

Her physical resemblance to her grandmother had aroused his interest initially, but this last hour or so of being insulted by her—both for who and what he was—had surely nullified that initial spark of appreciation?

Jaxon studied Stazy from beneath lowered lids. That wonderful hair gleamed fiery-gold in the sunlight, her eyes were a sultry and luminescent green, and there was a slight flush to her cheeks from walking in the sunshine. Her full and sensuous lips curved into an affectionate smile as the stallion nudged against her shoulder for attention.

He drew in a deep breath. 'It must have been a difficult time for you after your parents died—'

'I would rather not discuss my own private life with you, if you don't mind,' she said stiffly.

'I was only going to say that this must have been a wonderful place to spend your teenage years,' Jaxon murmured as he turned to lean his elbows on the fence and look across at the mellow-stoned house.

'It was—yes,' Stazy confirmed huskily. She looked up at him curiously. 'Whereabouts in England are you from?'

'Cambridgeshire.'

'And do you still go home?' she prompted curiously.

'Whenever I can.' Jaxon nodded. 'Which probably isn't as often as my family would like. My parents and younger brother still live in the small village where I grew up. But it's nowhere near as nice as this.'

It really was idyllic here, Jaxon appreciated, with horses gently grazing behind them, birds singing in the trees in the beautiful wooded area surrounding Bromley House and the coastline edging onto the grounds. The slightly salty smell of the sea was just discernible as waves gently rose and fell on the distant sand.

'I had forgotten that places like this existed,' he added almost wistfully.

'Nothing like it in LA, hmm?' Stazy mocked as she turned to look at him.

He shot her a rueful smile. 'Not exactly, no.' The place he had bought on the coast in Malibu several years ago was too huge and modern to feel in the least homely. 'Although I do own a place in New England—very rustic and in the woods—where I go whenever I get the chance.' Which, he realised, hadn't been all that often during recent years…

He had been busy filming and then editing his last film most of the previous year, then caught up in attending the premieres and numerous awards ceremonies since—including those that Stazy had mocked earlier! All of that had left him little time in which to sit back and smell the roses. Here at Bromley House it was possible to do that. Literally.

But the serpent in this particular Eden appeared to be the tangible antagonism of the beautiful and strangely alluring woman standing beside him…

Jaxon breathed deeply. 'For your grandfather's sake, couldn't we at least try to—?' He broke off as Stazy gave a derisive laugh. 'What?' he prompted irritably.

'My grandfather has taught me never to trust any statement that begins with "for whoever or whatever's sake"!' she revealed. 'He assures me it's usually a prefix to someone imposing their will by the use of emotional blackmail!'

Jaxon gave a rueful shake of his head. 'I would have thought you were old enough to make up your own mind about another person's intentions!'

Stazy felt the sting of colour in her cheeks at this obvious challenge. 'Oh, I am, Jaxon,' she assured him derisively.

He arched dark brows. 'And you decided I was going to be trouble before you even met me?' he guessed easily.

'Yes.' A belief that had been more than borne out these past few minutes as Stazy had become more physically aware of this magnetically handsome man in a way she wasn't in the least comfortable with! 'Shall we go back to the house?' It was a rhetorical and terse suggestion on Stazy's part, and she gave Copper one last affectionate stroke on his velvet-soft nose before walking away.

Jaxon fell into step beside her seconds later. 'And is that your final word on the subject?'

Stazy eyed him derisively. 'Don't be misled by my grandfather's social graciousness or his age, Jaxon. If you do come here to stay for a week to do your research then I believe you will very quickly learn that he always has the last word on any subject!'

Jaxon Wilder wouldn't be here at all if Stazy had her way!

A fact he was well aware of if his rueful smile was any indication. He shrugged those impossibly wide shoulders. 'Then I guess the outcome of all this is completely in your grandfather's hands.'

'Yes,' she acknowledged heavily, knowing her grandfather had left her in no doubt earlier as to what he had already decided…

Geoffrey was his usual charming self when he returned downstairs a short time later, obviously refreshed and alert from his nap. He took charge of the conversation as they all ate what on the surface appeared to be a leisurely dinner together.

Beneath that veneer of politeness it was a different matter, of course: Stazy still viewed Jaxon Wilder with suspicion; and on his part she was sure there was amusement, at her expense, glittering in those mercurial grey eyes every time he so much as glanced her in her direction!

By the time they reached the coffee stage of the meal Stazy could cheerfully have screamed at the underlying tension in the air that surrounded them.

'So.' Her grandfather finally sat back in his chair at the head of the table. 'Did the two of you manage to come to any sort of compromise in my absence?'

Jaxon gave a derisive smile as he saw the way Stazy's mouth had thinned into stubbornness. 'I believe my conclusion is that all the talking in the world between the two of us won't make the slightest bit of difference when you are the one to have the final say in the matter!'

'Indeed?' the older man drawled. 'Is that what you believe, too, Stazy?'

She shrugged slender shoulders. 'You know that I will go along with whatever you decide, Gramps.'

'I would rather have your co-operation, darling,' Geoffrey prompted gently.

Jaxon watched Stazy from beneath lowered lids as he took a sip of his brandy, knowing her initial antagonism towards him hadn't lessened at all over the hours. That if anything Stazy seemed even more wary of him now than she had been earlier—to the point where she had avoided even looking at him for the past half an hour or so, let alone making conversation with him.

Could that possibly be because she was as physically aware of him as Jaxon was of her…?

Doubtful!

She grimaced before answering her grandfather. 'Mr Wilder has very kindly pointed out to me that he isn't the only film director interested in making a film about Granny.' The coldness of Stazy's tone implied she considered Jaxon anything but kind.

'So I believe, yes.' Geoffrey nodded.

Stazy's eyes widened. 'You knew that?'

'Of course I knew, darling,' her grandfather dismissed briskly. 'I may not be in the thick of things nowadays, but I still make it my business to know of anything of concern to my family or myself.'

Jaxon frowned. 'In my defence, I would like you to

know that I have every intention of giving a fair and truthful version of the events of seventy years ago.'

'You wouldn't be here at all if I wasn't already well aware of that fact, Jaxon.' Steely-blue eyes met his unblinkingly. 'If I had believed you were anything less than a man of integrity I would never have spoken to you on the telephone, let alone invited you into my home.'

His respect and liking for the older man deepened. 'Thank you.'

'Oh, don't thank me too soon.' Sir Geoffrey smiled. 'I assure you, you've yet to convince my granddaughter!' he drawled, with an affectionate glance at Stazy's less than encouraging expression.

Jaxon grimaced. 'Perhaps the situation might change once we've worked together…?'

'Stazy…?' Geoffrey said softly.

Stazy was totally aware of being the focus of both men's gazes as they waited for her to answer—her grandfather's encouraging, Jaxon Wilder's much more guarded as he watched her through narrowed lids.

But what choice did she have, really…?

Her own feelings aside, her grandfather might have said he would have to accept Jaxon's film and 'be damned', but Stazy wasn't fooled for a moment. She knew of her grandfather's deep and abiding love for her grandmother, and of how much it would hurt him—perhaps fatally—if the film about Anastasia were to be in any way defamatory. And the only way to guarantee that didn't happen was if she agreed to work with Jaxon Wilder.

'Okay,' Stazy agreed heavily. 'I can give you precisely one week of my time at the beginning of my summer break.' She glared across at Jaxon as she recognised the triumphant gleam that had flared in his gaze at her capitulation. 'But only on the condition.'

'Another condition?' Jaxon grimaced.

She nodded. 'My grandfather has to give his full approval of the screenplay once it's been written,' she added firmly.

Working here with the prickly Stazy Bromley for a week was far from ideal as far as Jaxon was concerned. But not impossible when he considered the alternative…

'Fine.' He nodded abrupt agreement.

The tension visibly left Sir Geoffrey's shoulders, and Stazy saw this as evidence that he hadn't been as relaxed about this situation as he wished to appear. 'In that case, shall we expect to see you back here the first week of July, Jaxon?'

'Yes.' Even if that would involve reshuffling his schedule in order to fit in with Stazy Bromley's.

She still looked far from happy about the arrangement…

Her next comment only confirmed it. 'A word of warning, though, Jaxon—if anything happens to my grandfather because of this film then I am going to hold you totally responsible!'

Great.

Just great!

CHAPTER THREE

'WHAT'S with all the extra security at the front gates?'

Much as six weeks previously, Stazy had been prowling restlessly up and down in the drawing room of Bromley House as she waited for Jaxon Wilder. Her stomach had tightened into knots when she'd finally seen their visitor had arrived. Not in the expensive black sports car she had been expecting, but on a powerful black and chrome motorbike instead.

Convinced Jaxon Wilder couldn't possibly be the person riding that purring black machine, and confused as to why the guards had let a biker through the front gates at all, Stazy had continued to frown out of the window as the rider had brought the bike to a halt outside the drawing room window, before swinging off the seat and straightening to his full, impressive height.

The man was completely dressed in black—black helmet with smoky-black visor, black leathers that fitted snugly to muscled shoulders and back, narrowed waist and taut backside, and long, powerful legs. Black leather gloves. And heavy black biker boots.

He—it was definitely a he, with that height and those wide and muscled shoulders—had had his back turned towards her as he'd removed his gloves, before unfastening and removing the helmet and shaking back his almost shoulder-length dark hair as he placed the helmet on top of the black leather seat.

Stazy had felt the colour drain from her cheeks as the rider had turned and she had instantly recognised him. Jaxon Wilder. Almost instantly he had looked straight up into the window where she stood staring down at him, leaving her in absolutely no doubt as to his knowing he was being watched.

Staring?

Gaping at him was probably a more apt description!

All her defences had gone—crumbled—with the disappearance of the sophisticated man she had met six weeks ago, wearing a discreetly tailored suit, silk shirt and tie, with his dark hair slightly long but nevertheless neatly styled. In his place was a rugged and dangerous-looking man who looked as if he would be completely at home at a Hell's Angels reunion!

Stazy had left all the details of Jaxon's visit to her grandfather, knowing from conversations with Geoffrey that the two men had been in contact by telephone on several occasions during the last six weeks, and that the date for Jaxon to arrive at Bromley House had been fixed for today—the day after Stazy had driven herself down from London.

That initial meeting with Jaxon, the sizzling awareness she had felt, had seemed like something of a dream once Stazy had been back in London. So much so that she hadn't even mentioned her encounter to any of her friends at the university. Besides, she very much doubted that her work colleagues would have been interested in knowing she had spent part of the weekend with the famous Hollywood actor and director Jaxon Wilder.

But that didn't mean Stazy hadn't thought about him.

About the way he looked. The aura of male power that was so much a part of him. The mesmerising grey of his eyes. The sensual curve of those chiselled lips. The deep and sexy timbre of his voice…

That aura was even more in evidence today—dangerously so!—as he looked up at her and gave her a slow and knowing grin.

Stazy had been completely flustered at being caught staring at him. Damn it, just because the man had arrived today looking like testosterone on legs, it didn't mean she had to behave as though she were no older than one of her students. She was virtually drooling, with her tongue almost hanging out, and she found it impossible to look away from how hot Jaxon looked in biker's leathers!

He had become no less imposing when the butler had shown him into the drawing room. Those leathers fitted Jaxon's muscled body like a second skin, the black boots added a couple of inches to his already considerable height, and that overlong dark hair fell softly onto his shoulders.

Already feeling something of a fool for being caught staring out of the window at him in that ridiculous way, Stazy was in no mood to repeat the experience.

'And a good afternoon to you, too, Jaxon,' she drawled pointedly.

Humour lightened his eyes. 'Are we aiming at playing nice this time around?'

'I thought we might give it a try, yes.' The tartness in her voice totally belied that.

Jaxon grinned, totally appreciative of how good Stazy looked in a white blouse that fitted snugly to the flatness of her abdomen and the fullness of her breasts, with faded denims fitting just as snugly to her curvaceous bottom and long and slender legs. Her glorious red-gold hair tumbled in loose layers over her shoulders and down the slenderness of her back today. And those sultry green eyes glowed like twin emeralds in the sun-kissed beauty of her delicately beautiful face.

She looked far younger and sexier today than the twenty-nine Jaxon knew her to be. In fact if any of his own university lecturers had ever looked this good then he doubted he would ever have been able to concentrate on attaining his degree. 'In that case, good afternoon, Stazy,' he drawled.

She gave him a slow and critical perusal, from the soles of his booted feet to his overlong hair. 'Are you on your way to a fancy dress party?'

He raised derisive brows. 'Whatever happened to playing nice…?'

She shrugged. 'It seems a perfectly reasonable question, considering the way you're dressed today. Or not, as the case may be.' She grimaced.

After the way she had stared wide-eyed at him out of the window earlier, Jaxon wasn't at all convinced by Dr Stazy Bromley's condescending tone in regard to the way he was dressed. He returned her shrug. 'I keep an apartment for my use when I'm in London, and the car and the bike are kept there too. As it's such a beautiful day, and I've been stuck on a plane for hours, I decided a ride down on the bike was called for.' He gave an appreciative smile. 'Have you ever been on a bike before, Stazy?'

'No,' Stazy answered huskily, her cheeks blazing with colour as she was assailed with the idea of wrapping her legs around that monstrous machine, feeling its vibration between her legs even as her arms were tightly clasped about the strength of Jaxon's waist, her breasts pressed against the warmth of that muscled back—

'Would you like to...?'

Stazy straightened abruptly, completely nonplussed at the way her thoughts kept wandering down a sensual path that was totally alien to her. Especially as she had managed to convince herself these last six weeks that she had imagined finding this man in the least attractive! 'No, thanks,' she dismissed coolly.

'You only have to say so if you should change your mind...'

'I won't,' she assured firmly. 'Is the bike also the reason for the long hair?' she prompted abruptly, fighting the uncharacteristic longing to run her fingers through those silky dark locks...

She had dated very little during the past eleven years, and the few men she had been out with had always possessed intellect rather than brawn. She had never particularly cared for long hair on men—had always thought it rather effeminate.

Jaxon had shown on the last occasion they had met that he was a man of intellect as well as brawn. And as for his being effeminate—the man was so blatantly male there was no possibility of ever doubting his masculinity!

'The long hair is for a pirate movie I start filming next month.' He ran his fingers ruefully through the length of that hair.

In exactly the same way Stazy's fingers itched to do!

She clasped her wayward hands firmly together behind her back. 'I'd always assumed actors wore a wig or extensions for those sorts of roles?'

He grimaced. 'I've always preferred to go with the real thing.'

Just the thought of Jaxon as a pirate, sweeping his captive—*her*!—up into his arms, was enough to make Stazy's palms feel damp. 'Whatever,' she snapped.

What on earth was wrong with her?

She'd never had fantasics about being swept off her feet by a marauding pirate before, so why now?

The disturbing answer to that question unfortunately stood only feet away from her…

'So, you didn't answer me—what's with the added security at the front gates?' Jaxon prompted lightly.

'I'm afraid it's all over the estate—not just the front gates.' Stazy shrugged. 'My grandfather arranged it.'

That didn't sound good. 'To keep the two of us in or other people out?' he asked.

'Very funny.' Those full and sensuous lips thinned at his teasing. 'Gramps received a telephone call late last night and the security guards arrived almost immediately afterwards. I believe he did attempt to call you and give you the option to postpone your visit until a later date, but he couldn't reach you on any of the telephone numbers you'd given him…' She arched red-gold brows.

'As I said earlier, I only arrived in England a few hours ago. I was probably in transit,' Jaxon dismissed distractedly. 'Any idea what the problem is?'

'Gramps never discusses matters of security with me.' She shook her head. 'Unfortunately you won't be able to discuss it with him either,' she added unapologetically, 'because he left for London very early this morning.'

Meaning that, apart from the household staff, the two of them were currently alone here together.

Probably not a good idea, when Jaxon was totally aware of Stazy's femininity today in the fitted blouse and tight denims. And that glorious unconfined red-gold hair was a temptation he was barely able to resist reaching out and touching.

What would it feel like, he wondered, to entangle his fingers in that silky hair? Or, even more appealing, to have the length of that gorgeous hair tumbling sensuously about his thighs as a naked Stazy knelt between his parted legs, her fingers curled about his throbbing shaft as she bent forward to taste him…?

'He did say he would try to telephone you later today to explain,' she added dismissively.

'Fine,' Jaxon accepted tersely, aware that his erotic imaginings had produced a bulge of arousal beneath the fitted leathers. Something Stazy was going to become aware of too if he didn't get out of here soon!

'I'm sure he'll understand if, under the circumstances, you decide you would rather leave the research for now and come back another time…'

Was that hope he heard in Stazy's voice? Probably, Jaxon acknowledged ruefully. Despite her casual appearance, she didn't seem any more pleased to see him this time around than she had six weeks ago. 'Sorry to disappoint you, Stazy, but I don't have any other time free.'

'I assure you it makes absolutely no difference to me whether you stay or go,' she dismissed scathingly.

Nope, Stazy wasn't pleased to have him here at all. 'In that case, I'm staying,' he drawled.

Stazy nodded tersely. 'Gramps left all the necessary papers in the library for us to look through, if you would like to get started?'

Jaxon shook his head. 'I've been travelling for almost twenty-four hours. What I would really like to do is shower and change out of these leathers.' All of that should give enough time for his wayward arousal to ease!

Unfortunately Jaxon's request instantly gave Stazy an image of Jaxon stripped out of those decadent leathers, standing naked beneath a hot shower, the darkness of his hair wet and tousled as rivulets of soapy water ran down his hard and tanned torso—

'Would you like some tea before you go upstairs?' she bit out abruptly, inwardly cursing the way her breasts felt fuller just at her thinking about a naked Jaxon in the shower.

This was ridiculous, damn it! She had never been a sensual being—had certainly never—*ever*!—reacted like this in her life before, let alone found her imagination wandering off into flights of fantasy about a man whose reputation with women was legendary!

'Just the shower and a change of clothes, thanks.'

She nodded. 'I'll have Little take you up to the suite of rooms my grandfather has had prepared for your arrival.'

'Why put the butler to all that trouble when you're already here…?' Jaxon asked huskily.

Stazy stilled, her finger poised over the button that would summon the butler back to the drawing room, before slowly turning to look at Jaxon. The mockery in those assessing grey eyes and the challenging expression on his ruggedly handsome face indicated that he was aware of exactly how much his suggestion had disconcerted her.

Her mouth thinned. 'Fine.'

Jaxon realised this was going to be a long week if the two of them were going to get into a battle of wills over something as small as Stazy showing him up to his suite of rooms!

'I trust you didn't have too much of a problem rearranging your departure for Iraq to next week instead of this?' He attempted conversation as the two of them walked up the wide staircase together.

She gave him the briefest of glances from those emerald-green eyes. 'Would it bother you if I had?'

'Honestly? Not really.' He grimaced, only to raise surprised brows as she gave a laugh. A husky laugh that brought a warm glow to those sultry green eyes. A dimple appeared in her left cheek as the parted fullness of her lips curved into a smile.

Strangely, Jaxon had found himself thinking about those sensuous lips more often than he would have liked these past six weeks. Full and luscious lips that were at odds with the rest of Stazy's buttoned down, no-nonsense appearance… The sort of lips that would be delicious to kiss and taste, and to have kiss and taste him in return…

Something he probably shouldn't think of again when he was already so hard his erection waxs pressing painfully against the confines of his leathers!

'Which isn't to say I don't appreciate your having—'

'Oh, don't go and spoil it by apologising, Jaxon.' Stazy still chuckled softly as they reached the top of the stairs and she turned right to walk down the hallway ahead of him. 'If we're to spend any amount of time together then you need to know that I'll appreciate your honesty much more than I would any false charm.'

'My charm is never false,' he snapped irritably.

Stazy turned to quirk a teasing brow. 'Never? Be warned, Jaxon, I'm guilty of having watched film awards on television in the past!'

'Guilty…?'

She snorted. 'Oh, come on, Jaxon—it's all so much glitzy hype, isn't it?'

'I believe the newspapers praised me for the shortness of my acceptance speech this year,' he drawled.

'I'm not surprised; I thought your co-star was never going to get off the podium!'

'She can be…a little emotional,' Jaxon allowed reluctantly.

'A little…?' Stazy raised mocking brows. 'She thanked everyone but the man who sweeps the studio floor!'

His eyes narrowed. 'You really can be a—' He broke off with an impatient shake of his head. 'Never mind,' he muttered tersely.

Stazy pushed open the door to the suite of rooms she knew her grandfather had allocated to his guest. The green and cream decor and dark furniture there was more obviously masculine than in some of the other guest suites, as was the adjoining cream and gold bathroom visible through the open doorway. But it was the massive four-poster bed that dominated.

'The sitting room is through here.' She turned away from the intimacy of the bedroom to walk through to the adjoining room with its green carpet and cream sofa. A mahogany desk placed in front of the bay window looked out over the gardens at the back of the house, with the blue of the sea visible above the high wall that surrounded the grounds.

'This is very nice,' Jaxon murmured evenly.

Stazy eyed him derisively. 'You seem a little…tense?'

Those grey eyes narrowed. 'I wonder why!'

She shrugged. 'Can I help it if the much publicised Wilder charm doesn't work on me?'

Jaxon's mouth thinned at the deliberate insult. 'You

shouldn't believe everything you read in trashy magazines!'

Her eyes flashed deeply green. 'I've never read a trashy magazine in my life, thank you very much!'

'Too lowbrow for you?' he taunted.

She drew in a sharp breath. 'My grandfather made it clear to me before he left that he expected me to be polite to a guest in his home during his absence—'

'I hate to be the one to tell you—but so far today you've failed. Miserably!' Jaxon bit out.

Stazy eyed him coolly. 'Being polite doesn't mean I have to be insincere.'

'If you wouldn't mind…?' He began to unzip those body-moulding leathers. 'I would like to take my shower now.' He arched mocking brows.

Stazy had no doubt that Jaxon's challenging attitude now was in return for her earlier scathing comments about 'the much-published Wilder charm'. But as he continued to move that zip further and further down his hard muscled chest she knew it was a challenge she simply didn't have the sophistication—or the experience!—to meet.

'Come downstairs when you're ready and I'll show you the library where we're to work,' she said stiltedly, before turning sharply on her booted heels and hurrying over to the doorway.

Totally aware of the sound of Jaxon's throaty laughter behind her…

'Where do you want to start?'

'I have absolutely no idea.' Jaxon looked down in some dismay at the copious amount of documents and notebooks Geoffrey Bromley had left neatly stacked on the desktop in the library for him to look through.

Jaxon wasn't sure he would be able to get through them all in just the week Stazy had agreed to give him.

The library itself was full of floor to ceiling mahogany bookcases stacked mainly with leather-bound books, although some of the shelves near the door seemed to be full of more modern hardbacks that he might like to explore another time.

Jaxon felt somewhat refreshed after a long cold shower and a change of clothes, and thankfully had succeeded in dissipating the last of his erection as well as washing off the travel dust.

The erection was something—despite their sharp exchange in his suite earlier—that was guaranteed not to stay away for very long if Stazy was going to continue bending over the desk in that provocative way, her denims clearly outlining the perfect curve of her bottom.

'Maybe we should just sort them out year by year today, and start looking through them properly tomorrow?' he prompted tersely.

'Sounds logical.' Stazy nodded.

Jaxon regarded her through narrowed lids. 'And are you big on logic?'

She looked irritated by the implied criticism. 'I've always found it's the best way to approach most situations, yes.'

'Hmm.' He nodded. 'The problem with logic is that it leaves no room for emotion.'

'Which is precisely the point,' Stazy reasoned shortly.

No doubt—but Jaxon didn't work that way. 'Are these Anastasia's diaries?' He ran awed fingers lightly over a pile of a dozen small notebooks.

'They certainly look like them, yes…' Stazy frowned down at them as if they were a bomb about to go off.

He glanced up as he sensed her tension. 'You didn't know there were diaries?'

She gave a pained wince. 'No.'

Jaxon breathed deeply. 'Stazy, as much as you may choose not to think so, I *do* appreciate that none of this can be easy for you—'

Those green eyes flashed in warning. 'I doubt you have any idea how much I hate doing this!'

'Obviously Anastasia was your grandmother, and you only knew her during her latter years, but—'

'But even then she would still have known exactly how to deal with someone like *you*!' Stazy assured him dismissively. Even that red-gold hair seemed to crackle with her repressed anger.

'Like me?' he said softly.

'You know exactly what I mean!'

'I do,' he acknowledged, with that same deceptive mildness. 'I'd just like to hear you say it,' he added challengingly.

She glared her frustration. 'Jaxon, you've known from the first that nothing is going to make me like you *or* your damned film!'

'Nothing...?'

Stazy stilled as she looked up at him guardedly. The darkness of that overlong hair was still damp and slightly tousled from his shower. His jaw was freshly shaven, and he had changed out of the black leathers into a tight-fitting white short-sleeved tee shirt that revealed the tanned strength of his arms and black denims that rested low down on the leanness of his waist.

He looked, in fact, every inch Jaxon Wilder—sex symbol of both the big and little screen. A stark reminder—if Stazy had needed one—of just how little it actually mattered to this man whether or not she liked or approved of him and what he was doing.

Her chin rose determinedly. 'I'm sorry to disappoint you, Jaxon, but I have absolutely no interest in… in providing you with a—a romantic diversion to help while away your leisure time during your week-long stay here,' she assured him derisively.

'What on earth makes you think I would be in the least interested in having you as "a romantic diversion"—now or at any other time…?' His expression was amused as he leant back against the desk and looked down at her with mocking grey eyes, his arms folded across the powerful width of his chest, revealing the bulge of muscle at the tops of his tanned arms.

Stazy's cheeks heated with embarrassed colour at this deliberate set-down. What on earth had she been thinking? Of *course* Jaxon's challenge hadn't been hinting he was in the least interested in her in a personal way!

'But just to set my mind at ease, if things *should* go that way between us I'd be interested to know whether or not you're involved with someone at the moment…?'

When had Jaxon moved so that he now stood only inches away from her? Stazy wondered warily. He was pinning her as he looked down at her with piercing grey eyes.

She moistened her lips with the tip of her tongue. 'I don't see what that has to do with anything…'

'Humour me, hmm?' he encouraged gruffly.

The more immediate problem for Stazy—the whole root of the problem between the two of them—was that from their first meeting she had realised his magnetism was such that she wanted to do so much more than humour this man!

It was totally illogical. Ridiculous. Not only that, but it went totally against everything she had said and thought about this man!

And yet at this moment she literally *ached* to curve her body into his as she ran her hands lightly up the warmth of that muscled chest, over the broad expanse of his shoulders, before allowing her fingers to become entangled in the heavy thickness of that overlong dark hair to pull his head down and have those sensually chiselled lips claim hers…

This wasn't just ridiculous—it was dangerous!

And so completely out of character that Stazy barely recognised herself. Damn it, she didn't even *want* to recognise herself as this woman who couldn't seem to stop fantasising about the two of them in one clinch or another!

She had taken precisely two lovers in her twenty-nine years. The first had been one of her university lecturers, twenty years her senior, on a single night ten years ago. The second one had been a man on a summer dig in Tunisia four years ago—a man who had a wife and children back home in England. Admittedly that was something Stazy had only learnt *after* spending the night with him, when his wife had telephoned to inform him that one of his three children was in hospital and he was needed back home immediately!

Neither of those experiences had resulted in Stazy feeling any warmth or pleasure in the act, let alone having an orgasm. They certainly hadn't prepared her for the seductively lethal charm and good looks of Jaxon Wilder!

She stepped back abruptly. 'As it happens I'm not involved with anyone at the moment. Nor do I wish to be,' she added with cold dismissal.

It was a coldness so at odds with the quickened rise and fall of her breasts, the deepening in colour of those sultry green eyes and the soft swelling of poutingly moist lips, that Jaxon wanted nothing more than to take Stazy in his arms and prove her wrong!

That need hovered in the air between them for several long, tense seconds.

Stazy's chin rose as she deliberately tilted her head back in order to meet his gaze.

Did she have any idea how tempted Jaxon was by that challenge? Of how he wanted nothing more at that moment than to pull her into his arms and kiss the hell out of her?

Stazy was a beautiful woman in her late twenties, and as such she had to be aware of exactly what she was doing. Which begged the question—did she actually *want* him to kiss the hell out of her…?

CHAPTER FOUR

STAZY took a step back as she saw the look of sexual interest that had entered Jaxon's narrowed eyes. 'Perhaps you would like to concentrate on the papers and I'll sort out the diaries?' To her dismay she sounded slightly breathless, and Jaxon was still standing close enough that she was aware of the heat of his body and the tantalising smell of his aftershave.

'Fine,' he agreed huskily, that smoky-grey gaze unblinking.

She continued to eye him warily, very aware that something—she wasn't quite sure what—hung in the balance in these tension filled minutes. Something deep and almost primal. Something so nerve-tinglingly huge that Stazy feared it threatened to tear down the structured life of academia that she had so carefully surrounded herself with these past eleven years!

Jaxon felt as if he could have reached out and touched the sudden and obvious panic that spiked through Stazy as her eyes widened and the slenderness of her body trembled. The very air between them seemed to shimmer with that same emotion.

The question was *why*? What was so wrong with a man finding Stazy attractive enough to want to kiss her? Maybe even make love to her?

Had she been hurt in the past to the extent that it had made her wary of all men? Or did she only feel that wariness where Jaxon was concerned? She had certainly seemed to imply as much earlier!

Admittedly the newspapers had seemed to take great delight in photographing him with the beautiful actresses he'd been involved with during the past ten years; but in reality they really hadn't been that numerous—and a lot of the photographs that had appeared had actually been publicity shots, usually for the film he was currently working on.

Even so, he didn't feel that was any reason for Stazy to look at him in that wary and suspicious way. Almost as if she feared that at any moment he might rip her clothes off before throwing her across the desk and having his wicked way with her!

It was an idea that might merit further investigation, but certainly wasn't something Jaxon thought was likely to happen in the next few minutes!

He eased the tension from his shoulders. 'Shall we make a start then…?'

'Why not?' Stazy felt as if she were emerging from a dream as she forced herself to reply with the same lightness of tone, before ignoring him completely to concentrate all her attention on the piles of papers.

On the surface, at least. Inwardly, it was a different matter!

What had happened just now?

Had *anything* happened…?

Maybe she had just imagined the physical tension that had seemed to crackle briefly in the air between Jaxon and herself? Or—worse—maybe that physical awareness had only been on her side?

No, Stazy was sure it hadn't been. But, as she had

assured him earlier, she certainly knew better than to take seriously any emotional or physical games a man as experienced as Jaxon might decide to play. He was only here for a week, and then he would depart to commence making his pirate film, at which time he would probably forget Dr Stazy Bromley even existed.

As long as she kept reminding herself of that fact she should escape from their week's confinement together unscathed…

'Geoffrey seemed more than a little…evasive as to his reason for the need for extra security when I spoke to him on the telephone earlier…?' Jaxon looked across the dinner table at Stazy. The butler had served them their first course of prawns with avocado before once again leaving them alone together in the small and sunlit family dining room.

Stazy looked extremely beautiful this evening, having changed into a knee-length red sheath of a dress that should have clashed with that red-gold hair and yet instead somehow managed to add vibrancy to the unusual colour. Her legs were long and shapely in high-heeled red sandals, and her sun-kissed face was once again bare of make-up except for a red gloss on the fullness of her lips. A light dusting of endearing freckles was visible across the bridge of her tiny nose.

It had only taken one look at her when they'd met up in the drawing room before dinner for Jaxon to once again become aroused, quickly bringing him to the conclusion that suffering a whole week of this torment might just be the death of him.

'I did try to warn you that until Gramps has something he thinks we should know he'll play whatever this is pretty close to his chest,' Stazy answered unsympathetically.

Jaxon arched dark brows as she continued to eat her prawns and avocado. 'You seem to be taking it all very calmly?' It 'all' included those security guards at the main gates, as well as half a dozen more he had seen patrolling the grounds when he'd looked out of his bedroom window earlier—several of them accompanied by dogs.

She shrugged slender shoulders. 'I lived here with Granny and Gramps for almost ten years.'

'And you've had other security scares in the past?'

'Once or twice, yes,' Stazy said lightly.

'But—'

'Jaxon, if you're that worried about it you always have the option of leaving,' she reasoned softly.

Great—now she'd managed to make him sound like a complete wuss! 'I'm happy where I am, thanks,' he dismissed—or at least he would be if he didn't feel so on edge about his constant state of arousal whenever he was in Stazy's company!

Admittedly Stazy was beautiful, but she was nowhere near as beautiful as some of the women Jaxon had been involved with in the past. Nor did she make any attempt to hide her distrust of him. In fact the opposite.

Which was perhaps half the attraction…?

Maybe—although somehow Jaxon doubted it. Stazy was like no other woman he had ever met. For one thing she didn't even seem aware of her own beauty. Add that to her obvious intelligence and it was a pretty potent mix.

Jaxon had never been attracted to a woman simply on her looks alone, and he liked to be able to talk to a woman out of bed as well as make love with her in it. Stazy Bromley obviously ticked all the boxes as far as his raging libido was concerned.

Stazy wasn't sure she particularly cared for the way in which Jaxon was looking at her from between those hooded lids—almost as if he were thinking of eating *her* for his dinner rather than the food on his plate!

She had deliberately put on her favourite red dress this evening, in order to give herself the boost in confidence she had felt she lacked earlier. After those tension-filled minutes in her grandfather's library she had felt in need of all the armour she could get where Jaxon Wilder was concerned, and feeling confident about her own appearance was definitely a good place to start.

Or at least it would have been if the moment she'd seen him again she hadn't been so completely aware of how dangerously attractive Jaxon looked this evening, in a loose white silk shirt and those black denims that fitted snugly to the leanness of his muscled thighs and long, long legs…

His shirt was unbuttoned at his throat to reveal the beginnings of a dusting of dark hair that no doubt covered most of his chest. And lower. That 'lower' being exactly where Stazy had forced her thoughts to stop earlier today. Unfortunately she didn't seem to be having the same success this evening!

This just wasn't *her*, damn it. Those two attempts at taking a lover had not only proved completely unsatisfactory but had also firmly put an end to any illusions she might have had where she and men were concerned. She certainly didn't indulge in erotic fantasies about movie stars—or any other man, come to that!—and the sooner her grandfather returned from London and put a stop to this cosy intimacy for two the better!

'So...' Jaxon waited until the butler had been in to clear away their used plates before leaning forward. 'Have I told you how lovely you're looking this evening...?'

That air of intimacy between them became even cosier—in fact the temperature in the room seemed to go up several degrees! 'No, you haven't—and I would prefer that you didn't do so now, either,' Stazy bit out determinedly.

He raised dark brows. 'I thought you asked me for honesty earlier...?'

'Not that sort of honesty!' Her eyes flashed a deep disapproving green. 'We're work colleagues, Jaxon, and work colleagues do not comment on each other's appearance if they are to maintain a proper working relationship.'

'You sound as if you're speaking from experience...?'

Colour warmed her cheeks. 'Perhaps.'

'Feel like telling me about it...?'

Her mouth firmed. 'No.'

Pity, because Jaxon would have liked to know more—a lot more!—about Stazy's personal life. 'Most of the actresses I've worked with would be insulted if I didn't mention their appearance at least once a day.'

Stazy shot him an impatient frown. 'Well, I assure you in my case it isn't necessary. Or appreciated.'

He smiled ruefully. 'I thought all women liked to receive compliments?'

'I would rather be complimented on my academic ability than the way I look,' she stated primly.

Jaxon might have been more convinced of that if Stazy's hand hadn't trembled slightly as she picked up her glass and took a sip of the red wine. 'That's a little difficult for me to do when I know next to nothing about your academic ability—other than you're obviously good at what you do—but I can clearly see how beautiful you look in that red dress.'

Those green eyes darkened. 'We aren't out on a date, Jaxon, and no amount of compliments from you is going to result in the two of us ending up in bed together at the end of the evening, either— Damn, damn, *damn*!' she muttered, with an accusing glare in his direction as the butler returned to the dining room just in time to hear that last outburst.

Jaxon barely managed to keep his humour in check as Stazy studiously avoided so much as looking at him again as Little hastily served their food before beating an even hastier retreat. 'Guess what the gossip in the kitchen is going to be about later this evening…' he murmured ruefully.

'This isn't funny, Jaxon,' she bit out agitatedly. 'Little has worked for my grandfather for years. I've known him all my life. And now he's going to think that I— that we—' She broke off with a disbelieving shake of her head.

'Oh, cheer up, Stazy.' Jaxon smiled unconcernedly. 'Look on the bright side—at least I now know where I stand in regard to the possibility of sharing your bed tonight. With any luck, after hearing your last remark, Little will decide to put lighted candles on the dinner table for us tomorrow evening, in an attempt to heat up the romance!'

Much as she hated to admit it, Stazy knew she didn't need any 'heating up' where this man was concerned! And considering it was now July, and the evenings stayed light until after ten o'clock at night, she didn't think there was much chance of any candles appearing on the dinner table—tomorrow night or any other. In fact it was still so light at the moment that the curtains hadn't even been drawn over the floor-to-ceiling windows yet, and the view of a beautiful sunset was certainly adding to the air of romance.

Whatever cutting reply Stazy might have wanted to make to Jaxon's suggestion was delayed as Little returned with a laden tray, his face completely expressionless as he served their main course without meeting the gaze of either one of them before quietly departing again.

'You're enjoying yourself, aren't you?' Stazy eyed Jaxon impatiently as he grinned across the table at her.

Jaxon chuckled softly. 'So would you be if you would just lighten up a little. Oh, come on, Stazy—just think about it for a minute and then admit it *was* funny,' he cajoled irritably as she continued to frown.

'I'll admit no such thing! You—'

'Ever heard the saying about the lady protesting too much…?' He raised mocking brows. 'I've been told that when a lady does that, it usually means she wants you to do the opposite of what she's saying.'

'Whoever told you that was an idiot!' She gave an impatient shake of her head. 'And if you weren't my grandfather's guest I would ask you to leave!'

'Pity about that, isn't it?' he murmured dryly.

Stazy threw her napkin down on the tabletop before standing up and moving away from the table. 'If you will excuse me—'

'No.'

She stilled. 'What do you mean, no?'

'Exactly what I said—no.' The humour had gone from Jaxon's voice and expression, and there was a dark scowl on his brow as he threw down his own napkin before standing up to move purposefully around the table towards her.

Stazy raised a protesting hand even as she instinctively took a step backwards—only to find herself trapped between a looming Jaxon in front of her and a glass cabinet containing china ornaments behind her. ‘Stop this right now, Jaxon—’

‘Believe me, I haven’t even started yet,’ he growled, a nerve pulsing in his tightly clenched jaw as he towered over her. ‘In fact I think maybe we should just get this over with and then maybe we can move on!’ he muttered impatiently.

Stazy looked up at him with startled eyes. ‘Get what over with…?’

He gave a shake of his head and lifted his arms to place them either side of her head so that his hands rested on the doors of cabinet behind her, his body almost, but not quite, touching hers. ‘For some reason you seem to have decided that at some time during my stay here I’m going to try and seduce you into my bed, so I thought we might as well make a start!’

‘You—’ Stazy’s protest came to an abrupt end as she realised that lifting her hands and placing them against Jaxon’s chest, with the intention of pushing him away from her, had been a bad idea. A *very* bad idea…

Her hands lingered. His chest felt very warm to her touch through the soft material of his shirt—like steel encased in velvet as his muscles flexed beneath her fingers. The smell of his cologne—cinnamon and sandalwood—combined with hot, hot male was almost overwhelming to the senses.

Almost?

Stazy ceased to breathe at all as she stared up at Jaxon with wide, apprehensive eyes. Was he right? *Had* she been 'protesting too much'? When in reality she had been longing for this to happen?

God, yes…!

Much as it pained her to admit it, Stazy knew she had thought about Jaxon far too often for comfort in the last six weeks. Damn it, she had even fantasised earlier about what it would be like to be naked with Jaxon, making love with him…

But wanting something and getting it weren't the same things, were they? For instance she had wanted an expensive microscope when she was ten years old—had been convinced at the time that she intended to be a medical doctor when she was older. Her parents had bought her a less expensive microscope, equally convinced that it was just a fad she was going through, with the promise of buying her the more expensive microscope one day if she ever *did* become a doctor.

Maybe not the best analogy, but Stazy no more needed Jaxon in her bed now than she had really needed that very expensive microscope nineteen years ago.

In other words, allowing Jaxon Wilder to kiss her would be an extravagance her emotions just didn't want or need!

Stazy liked her life ordered. Structured. Safe!

Most of all safe…

She had learnt at a very young age that caring for someone, loving them, needing a special someone in your life, was a guarantee of pain in the future when that person either left or—worse—died. As her parents had died. As Granny had died. As her grandfather, now in his nineties, and with that heart attack only a few months ago behind him, would eventually die.

Stazy didn't want to care about anyone else, to need

anyone else—couldn't cope with any more losses in her life.

'Don't do that!' Jaxon groaned huskily.

She raised startled lids. 'Do what?'

'Lick your lips.' The darkness of his gaze became riveted on the moistness of those lips as Stazy ran her tongue nervously between them. 'I've been wanting to do exactly the same thing since the moment we first met,' Jaxon admitted gruffly.

Her eyes were wide. 'You have…?'

He rested his forehead against hers, his breath a warm caress across her already heated cheeks. 'You have the sexiest mouth I've ever seen…'

She gave a choked laugh. 'I thought it was universally acknowledged that that was Angelina Jolie?'

'Until six weeks ago I thought so too.' Jaxon nodded.

He had fantasised about Stazy's mouth these past six weeks. Imagined all the things she could do to him with those deliciously full and pouting lips. Grown hard with need just thinking of that plump fullness against his flesh, kissing him, tasting him. As he now longed to taste her…

'I'm going to kiss you now, Stazy,' Jaxon warned harshly.

'Jaxon, no…!' she groaned in protest.

'Jaxon, yes!' he contradicted firmly, before lowering his head and capturing those full and succulent lips with his own, groaning low in his throat as he found she felt and tasted as good as he had imagined she would!

If Jaxon's mouth had been demanding or rough against hers then Stazy believed she might have been able to resist him. She *hoped* she would have been able to resist him! As it was he kissed her with gentle exploration, sipping, tasting, as his mouth moved over and against hers with a slow languor that was torture to the senses. Taste as well as touch.

Those chiselled lips were surprisingly soft and warm against her own, his body even hotter as Jaxon lowered himself against her with a low groan, instantly making her aware of the hardness of his arousal pressing against her own aching thighs.

Unbidden, it seemed, her hands glided up his chest and over his shoulders, until her fingers at last became entangled with the overlong thickness of that silky dark hair.

He pulled back slightly, and Stazy at once felt bereft without the heat of those exploring lips against her own.

'Say so now if you want me to stop…'

'No…' She was the one to initiate the kiss this time, as she moved up onto her tiptoes, her lips parting to deepen the kiss rather than end it as she held him to her.

It was all the invitation Jaxon needed. He pressed himself firmly against the warm softness of her body as his hands moved to cup either side of her face so that he could explore that delicious mouth more deeply, tongue dipping between her parted lips to enter and explore the moist and inviting heat beneath.

Her taste—warmth and the sweetness of honey, and something indefinably feminine—was completely intoxicating. Like pure alcohol shooting through Jaxon's bloodstream, it threw him off balance, ripping away any awareness of anything other than the taste and feel of Stazy's mouth against his and her warm and luscious body beneath him.

He could only *feel* as Stazy wrapped her arms more tightly about his shoulders and arched her body up and into his, her soft breasts against the hardness of his chest, the heat of her thighs against the hot throb of his arousal. His hands moved down to her waist before sliding around to cup the twin orbs of her bottom to pull her up closer to him.

Jaxon kissed her hungrily, his arousal a fierce throb as Stazy returned the hunger of that kiss, lips hot and demanding, tongues duelling, bodies clamouring for even closer contact.

As Stazy had expected—feared—the tight control she usually exerted over her emotions had departed the moment Jaxon began to kiss her. Her nipples had grown hard and achingly sensitised, and the heat from their kisses was moving between her thighs—a feeling she hadn't experienced even when fully making love with those two men in her past.

She didn't want Jaxon ever to stop. Every achingly aroused inch of her cried out for more. One of his hands moved to cup the fullness of her breast, sending hot rivulets of pleasure coursing through her as his thumb grazed across the aching nipple. Stazy pressed into the heat of his hand, wanting more, needing more, and Jaxon lifted her completely off the floor to wrap her legs about his waist.

She no longer cared that they were in her grandfather's family dining room, or that Little could walk back into the room at any moment to remove their dinner plates.

All she was aware of was Jaxon—the heat of his arousal pressing into her softness, the pleasure that curled and grew inside her as he squeezed her nipple between thumb and finger, just enough to increase her pleasure but not enough to cause her pain, the hardness of him sending that same pleasure coursing through her.

She whimpered in protest as Jaxon broke the kiss, that protest turning to a low and aching moan of pleasure as his mouth moved down the length of her throat, his tongue a hot rasp against her skin as he tasted every hot inch of her from the sensitivity of her earlobe to the exposed hollow where her neck and shoulder met. And all the time his thighs continued that slow and torturous thrust against her.

Stazy still felt as if she were poised on the very edge of a precipice, but no longer cared if she fell over the edge. She wanted this. Wanted Jaxon. He felt so good, so very, very good, that she never wanted this to end…

Jaxon pulled back with a groan, his forehead slightly damp as it rested against hers. 'Lord knows I don't want us to stop, but Little is sure to come back in a few minutes…'

Stazy stared up at him blankly for several seconds, and then her face paled, her eyes widening with dismay as she took in the full import of what had just happened. 'Oh-my-God…!' Her expression was stricken as she struggled to put her feet back onto the floor, her face averted as she pulled out of Jaxon's arms to hastily straighten and pull her dress back down over the silkiness of her thighs.

'Stazy—'

'I think it's best if you don't touch me again, Jaxon,' she warned shakily, even as Jaxon would have done exactly that.

His arms dropped back to his sides as he saw the bewilderment in her eyes. His tone was reasoning. 'Stazy, what happened just now was perfectly normal—'

'It may be "normal" for you, Jaxon, but it certainly isn't normal for me!' she assured tremulously.

'Damn it, I *asked* you if you wanted me to stop!'

'I know…!' she groaned. 'I just— This must never

happen again, Jaxon.' She looked up at him with tear-wet eyes.

'Why not...?'

'It just can't,' she bit out determinedly.

'That isn't a reason—'

'I'm afraid it's the only one you're going to get at the moment,' she confirmed huskily, giving him one last pleading look before turning to hurry across the room to wrench open the door, closing it firmly behind her several seconds later.

Leaving Jaxon in absolutely no doubt that the passionately hot Stazy—the woman he had held in his arms only minutes ago—would be firmly buried beneath cool and analytical Dr Anastasia Bromley by the time the two of them met again...

CHAPTER FIVE

'IF YOU had let me know you were going out riding earlier this morning then I would have come with you, rather than just sat and watched you out of the window as I ate my breakfast...'

Stazy's gaze was cool when she glanced across at Jaxon as he entered the library the following morning. 'To have invited you to accompany me would have defeated the whole object.' Having to accept one of her grandfather's security guards accompanying her, and in doing so severely curtailing where she rode, had been bad enough, without having Jaxon trailing along as well!

After last night he was the last person she had wanted to be with when she'd got up this morning!

Neither of her two experiences had prepared her in the least for the heat, the total wildness, of being in Jaxon's arms the previous evening.

It had been totally out of control. *She* had been out of control!

Her two sexual experiences had been far from satisfactory, and yet she had almost gone over the edge just from having her legs wrapped around Jaxon's waist while he thrust against the silky barrier of her panties!

Having escaped to her bedroom the previous

evening, Stazy had relived every wild and wanton moment of being in Jaxon's arms. The thrumming excitement. The arousal. And—oh, God!—the pleasure! She had trembled from the force of that pleasure, the sensitive ache still between her thighs, her breasts feeling full and sensitised.

She had been so aroused that she dreaded to think what might have happened if Jaxon hadn't called a halt to their lovemaking. Would Jaxon have stripped off her clothes? Worse, would she have ripped off her own clothes? And would he have made love to her on the carpeted floor, perhaps? Or maybe he would have just ripped her panties aside and taken her against the cabinet? Having either of those two things happen would have been not only unacceptable but totally beyond Stazy's previous experience.

'Am I wrong in sensing the implication that you much preferred to go out riding rather than having to sit and eat breakfast with me…?' Jaxon prompted dryly.

She looked across at him. 'Is that what I implied…?'

He eyed her frustratedly. Knowing that beneath Stazy's exterior of cool logic was a woman as passionate as the fiery red-gold of her hair, a woman who had become liquid flame in his arms as she absorbed—*consumed*!—the blazing demand of his desire before giving it back in equal measure didn't help to ease that frustration in the slightest.

'Besides which,' she continued briskly, 'I was up at six, as usual, and breakfasted not long after.'

Jaxon closed the door behind him before strolling over to sit on the edge of the table where Stazy sat. 'I'll have to remember that you're an early riser if I ever want the two of us to breakfast together.'

Stazy could think of only one circumstance under

which that might be applicable—and it was a circumstance she had no intention of allowing to happen! That didn't mean to say she wasn't completely aware of Jaxon's muscled thigh only inches away from her where he perched on the edge of the table…

He looked disgustingly fit and healthy this morning for a man who had flown over from the States only yesterday: the sharp angles of his face were healthily tanned, that overlong dark hair was slightly damp from the shower, his tee shirt—black today—fitted snugly over his muscled chest and the tops of his arms, and faded denims outlined the leanness of his waist and those long legs. There was only a slightly bruised look beneath those intelligent grey eyes to indicate that Jaxon suffered any lingering jet lag.

'I shouldn't bother for the short amount of time you'll be here,' she advised dryly.

He gave a relaxed smile. 'Oh, it's no bother, Stazy,' he assured her huskily.

She shifted restlessly. 'Considering your time here is limited, shouldn't we get started…?'

Jaxon didn't need any reminding that he now had only six days left in which to do his research. Just as he didn't need to be told that it was Stazy's intention to keep her distance from him for those same six days…

There had been a few moments of awkwardness the previous evening, when he'd told Little that Stazy wasn't feeling well enough to finish her meal and had gone upstairs to her bedroom. The knowing look in the older man's eyes, before he'd quietly cleared away her place setting had been indicative of his scepticism at that explanation. But, being the polite English butler that he was, Little hadn't questioned the explanation—or Jaxon's claim that *he* didn't want any more to eat either.

Food, at least…

Jaxon's appetite for finishing what he and Stazy had started had been a different matter entirely!

Once upstairs, despite feeling exhausted, he had paced the sitting room of his suite for hours as he thought of Stazy's fiery response to his kisses, his shaft continuing to throb and ache as he remembered having her legs wrapped about his waist, the moist heat between her thighs as he pressed against her.

A virtually sleepless night later he only had to look at her again this morning to recall the wildness of their shared passion. The fact that her appearance was every inch the prim and cold Dr Anastasia Bromley again today—hair pulled back and plaited down the length of her spine, green blouse loose rather than fitted over tailored black trousers, and flat no-nonsense shoes—in no way dampened the eroticism of last night's memories.

In fact the opposite; if anything, that air of cool practicality just made Jaxon want to kiss her until he once again held that responsive woman in his arms!

'Fine.' He straightened abruptly before taking the seat opposite hers and concentrating on the pile of papers Geoffrey Bromley had left for him to look through.

That was not to say he wasn't completely aware of Stazy as she sat opposite him. He could smell her perfume—a light floral and her own warm femininity—and the sunlight streaming through the window was turning her hair to living flame. A flame Jaxon wanted to wrap about his fingers as he once again took those full and pouting lips beneath his own…

'Have you heard from Geoffrey this morning?' he prompted gruffly after several minutes of torturous silence—minutes during which he was too aware of Stazy to be able to absorb a single thing he had read.

She shook her head. 'As I've already told you, my grandfather has become a law unto himself since Granny died.'

Jaxon sat back in his chair. 'And before that…?'

Her gaze instantly became guarded. 'What exactly is it you want to know, Jaxon?'

He shrugged. 'All my own research so far gives the impression their long marriage was a happy one.'

'"So far"?'

Discussing Stazy's grandparents with her had all the enjoyment of walking over hot coals: one wrong step and he was likely to get seriously burned! 'You know, we're going to get along much better if you don't keep reading criticism into every statement I make.' He sighed.

It wasn't in Stazy's immediate or long term plans to 'get along' with Jaxon. In fact, after her uncharacteristic behaviour last night, she just wanted this whole thing to be over and done with. 'Sorry,' she bit out abruptly.

'So?'

'So, yes, their marriage was a long and happy one,' she confirmed evenly. 'Not joined at the hip,' she added with a frown. 'They were both much too independent in nature for that. But emotionally close. Always.'

'That's good.' Jaxon nodded, making notes in the pad he had brought downstairs with him.

Stazy regarded him curiously. 'You mentioned your own parents when you were here last…are they happily married?'

'Oh, yes.' An affectionate smile curved Jaxon's lips as he looked up. 'My brother, too. One big happy family, in fact, and all still living in Cambridgeshire. I'm the only one in the family to have left the area and avoided the matrimonial noose,' he added dryly.

Stazy doubted that he was in any hurry to marry, considering the amount of women reputedly queuing up to share the bed of Jaxon Wilder. Something she had been guilty of herself the previous evening…!

'I don't suppose your lifestyle is in any way…conducive to a permanent relationship,' she dismissed coolly.

Jaxon studied her through narrowed lids. 'Any more than your own is. An archaeologist who travels around the world on digs every chance she gets…' he added with a shrug as she looked at him enquiringly.

She smiled tightly. 'That's one of the benefits of being unattached, yes.'

'And what do you consider the other advantages to be?' he prompted curiously.

She gave a lightly dismissive laugh. 'The same as yours, I expect. Mostly the freedom to do exactly as I wish *when* I wish.'

'And the drawbacks…?'

A frown creased the creaminess of her brow. 'I wasn't aware there were any…'

'No…?'

'No.'

He raised dark brows. 'How about no one to come home to at the end of the day? To talk to and be with? To share a meal with? To go to bed with?' He smiled ruefully. 'I suppose it can all be summed up in one word—loneliness.'

Was she ever lonely? Stazy wondered. Probably. No—definitely. And for the reasons Jaxon had just stated. At the end of a long day of teaching she always returned home to her empty apartment, prepared and ate her meal alone, more often than not spending the evening alone, before sleeping alone.

That was exactly how she preferred it! Not just preferred it, but had deliberately arranged her life so it would be that way. Apart from her grandfather, she didn't want or need anyone in her life on a permanent basis. Didn't want or need the heartache of one day losing them—to death or otherwise.

She eyed Jaxon teasingly. 'I find it difficult to believe that you ever need be lonely, Jaxon!'

He gave a tight smile. 'Never heard the saying "feeling alone in a crowd"?'

'And that describes you?'

'Sometimes, yes.'

'I somehow can't see that…' she dismissed.

'Being an actor isn't all attending glitzy parties and awards ceremonies, you know.'

'Let's not forget you get to escort beautiful actresses to both!' she teased.

'No, let's not forget that,' he conceded dryly.

'And you get to go to all those wonderful places on location too—all expenses paid!'

Jaxon smiled wryly. 'Oh, yes. I remember what a wonderful time I had being in snake and crocodile infested waters for days at a time during the making of *Contract with Death*!'

Her eyes widened. 'I'd assumed you had a double for those parts of the film…'

And from the little Stazy had said during that first meeting six weeks ago Jaxon had assumed *she* was far too much the academic to have ever bothered to see a single one of his films! 'I don't use doubles any more than I do hair extensions.'

'You must be a nightmare for film studios to insure.'

'No doubt.'

'What about the flying in *Blue Skies*...?'

He shrugged. 'I went to a village in Bedfordshire where they have a museum of old working planes and learnt to fly a Spitfire.'

A grudging respect entered those green eyes. 'That was...dedicated. What about riding the elephant in *Dark Horizon*?'

He grinned. 'Piece of cake!'

'Riding a horse bareback in *Unbridled*?'

He gave her a knowing look. 'A blessed relief after the elephant!'

'Captaining a boat in *To the Depths*?'

So Stazy obviously hadn't seen just one of his films, but several. Although Jaxon was sure that Stazy had absolutely no idea just how much she was revealing by this conversation. 'I used to spend my summers in Great Yarmouth, helping out on my uncle's fishing boat, when I was at university.'

Her eyes widened. 'You attended university?'

Jaxon was enjoying himself. 'Surprised to learn I'm not just a pretty face, after all?'

If Stazy was being honest? Yes, she *was* surprised. 'What subject did you take?'

He quirked a teasing brow. 'Are you sure you really want me to answer that?'

She felt a sinking sensation in her chest. 'Archaeology?'

'History and archaeology.'

She winced. 'You have a degree in history and archaeology?'

He gave a grin. 'First-class Masters.'

'With what aim in mind...?'

He shrugged. 'I seriously thought about teaching before I was bitten by the acting bug.'

'Why didn't you tell me that before?' Before she'd made a fool of herself and treated him as if he were just another empty-headed movie star. That, in retrospect, had not only been insulting but presumptuous…

Jaxon shrugged wide shoulders. 'You didn't ask. Besides which,' he continued lightly, 'you were having far too much fun looking down your nose at a frivolous Hollywood actor for me to want to spoil it for you.'

Because it had been easier to think of Jaxon that way than to acknowledge him as not only being a handsome movie star but also an intelligent and sensitive man. Which he obviously was…

A dangerous combination, in fact!

Stazy straightened briskly. 'Shall we get on?'

In other words: conversation over, Jaxon acknowledged ruefully. But, whether she realised it or not, he had learnt a little more about Stazy this morning; it was a little like extracting teeth, but very slowly he was learning the intricacies that made up the personality of the beautiful and yet somehow vulnerable Stazy Bromley.

And finding himself intrigued and challenged by all of them…

'Time for lunch, I believe…'

Stazy had been so lost in reading one of her grandmother's diaries that she had momentarily forgotten that Jaxon sat across the table from her, let alone noticed the passing of time. Surprisingly, it had been a strangely companionable morning, that earlier awkwardness having dissipated as they both became lost in their individual tasks.

She gave a shake of her head now. 'I rarely bother to eat lunch.'

'Meaning that I shouldn't either?' Jaxon teased.

'Not at all,' she told him briskly. 'I'll just carry on here, if you would like to go and— What are you doing…?' She frowned across at Jaxon as he reached across the table to close the diary she was reading before rising to his feet and holding out his hand to her expectantly.

'Ever heard the saying "all work and no play…"'

Her mouth firmed as she continued to ignore his outstretched hand. 'I've never pretended to be anything other than dull.'

'I don't find you in the least dull, Stazy,' Jaxon murmured softly.

She raised startled eyes. 'You don't?'

'No,' he assured her huskily; having spent the past three hours completely aware of Stazy sitting across the table from him, how could he claim otherwise? She was a woman of contradictions: practical by nature but delicately feminine in her appearance. Her hands alone seemed proof of that contradiction. Her wrists were fragile, her fingers slender and elegant, but they were tipped with practically short and unvarnished nails. He had spent quite a lot of the last three hours looking at Stazy's hands as she turned the pages of the diary she was reading and imagining all the places those slender fingers tipped by those trimmed nails might linger as she caressed him…

'Let's go, Stazy,' he encouraged her now. 'I asked Little earlier if he would provide us with a lunch basket.'

She frowned. 'You expect me to go on a picnic with you?'

'Why not?' Jaxon asked softly.

Probably because Stazy couldn't remember the last time she had done anything as frivolous as eating her lunch *al fresco*—even in one of the many cafés in England that now provided tables for people to eat outside. When she was working she was too busy during the day to eat lunch at all, and when she came here her grandfather preferred formality. Occasionally Granny had organised a picnic down on the beach at the weekends, but that had been years ago, and—

'You think too much, Stazy.' Jaxon, obviously tired of waiting for her to make up her mind, pulled her effortlessly to her feet.

Stazy couldn't think at all when she was standing close to Jaxon like this, totally aware of the heat of his body and the pleasant—*arousing*—smell of the cologne he favoured. 'Aren't we a little old to be going on a picnic, Jaxon?'

'Not in the least,' he dismissed easily. Not waiting to hear any more of her objections, his hand still firmly clasping hers, he pulled her along with him to walk out into the cavernous hallway. 'Ah, Little, just in time.' He smiled warmly at the butler as he appeared from the back of the house with a picnic basket in one hand and a blanket in the other. 'If Mr Bromley calls we'll be back in a couple of hours.'

Jaxon handed Stazy the blanket before taking the picnic basket himself, all the time retaining that firm grasp on Stazy's hand as he kept her at his side. He strode out of the front doorway of the house and down the steps onto the driveway.

The warm and strong hand totally dwarfed Stazy's, and at the same time she was tinglingly aware of that warmth and strength. The same strength that had enabled him to ride an elephant, go bareback on a horse, to handle the controls of a Spitfire and captain a fishing boat, and do all of those other stunts in his films that Stazy had assumed were performed by someone else.

Making Jaxon far less that 'pretty face' image she had previously taken such pleasure in attributing to him…

If she were completely honest with herself Jaxon was so much more than she had wanted him to be before meeting him, and as such had earned—albeit grudgingly!—her respect. It would have been far easier to simply dismiss the pretty-faced Hollywood actor of her imaginings; but the real Jaxon Wilder was nothing at all as Stazy had thought—hoped—he would be. Instead, he had a depth and intelligence she found it impossible to ignore.

Add those things to the way he looked—to the way he had kissed her and made her feel the previous evening—and Stazy was seriously in danger of fighting a losing battle against this unwanted attraction.

That was why it really wasn't a good idea to go on a picnic with him!

He turned to look down at her from beneath hooded lids. 'Beach or woody glade?'

'Neither.' Stazy impatiently pulled her hand free of his. 'I really don't have time for this, Jaxon—'

'Make time.'

She eyed him derisively. 'Did you need to practise that masterful tone or does it just come naturally?'

Jaxon grinned unconcernedly. 'Just getting into character for next week, when I become captain of a pirate ship and need to keep my female captive in line.'

'Seriously?'

The look of total disbelief on Stazy's face was

enough to make him chuckle out loud. 'Seriously.' He grinned. 'That's before I have my wicked way with her about halfway through the movie, of course.'

She winced. 'After which she no doubt keeps *you* in line?'

'I seem to recall I then become her willing slave in the captain's cabin, yes,' Jaxon allowed dryly, enjoying the delicate blush that immediately coloured Stazy's cheeks; for a twenty-nine-year-old woman she was incredibly easy to shock. 'So, Stazy—beach or woody glade?' He returned to their original conversation.

Stazy's thoughts had briefly wandered off to images of herself as Jaxon's captive on his pirate ship, where he swept her up in his arms. Her hair was loose and windswept, and she was wearing a green velvet gown that revealed more than it covered as he lowered his head and his mouth plundered hers.

Just imagining it was enough to cause her body to heat and her nipples to tingle and harden inside her bra as the warm feeling between her thighs returned.

Good grief…!

She gave a self-disgusted shake of her head as she dismissed those images. 'I think you'll find that my grandfather's security guards might have something to say about where we're allowed to go for our picnic.' She grimaced as she recalled how her ride this morning had been decided by one of those attentive guards.

'Let's walk down to the beach and see if anyone tries to stop us.' Once again Jaxon took a firm hold of her hand, before walking towards the back of the house and the pathway down to the beach.

Dragging a reluctant Stazy along with him…

CHAPTER SIX

No one tried to stop them, but Jaxon noted the presence of the two black-clothed men who moved to stand at either end of the coved beach that stretched beyond the walled gardens of Bromley House, positioning themselves so that they faced outwards rather than watching the two of them as he and Stazy spread the blanket on the warmth of the sand.

The sun was shining brightly and a breeze blew lightly off the sea.

'Little seems to have thought of everything,' Jaxon murmured appreciatively as he uncorked a bottle of chilled white wine before pouring it into the two crystal glasses he had unwrapped from tissue paper.

'Years of practice, I expect.' There was a wistful note in Stazy's voice as she knelt on the blanket, arranging the chicken and salad onto plates.

His expression was thoughtful as he sipped his wine. 'You used to come here with your grandparents.' It was a statement rather than a question.

She nodded abruptly. 'And my parents when they were still alive.'

'I hadn't realised that.' He winced. 'Would you rather have gone somewhere else?'

'Not at all,' she dismissed briskly. 'I'm sure you

know me well enough by now, Jaxon, to have realised I have no time for sentimentality,' she added dryly.

No, Jaxon couldn't say he had 'realised' that about her at all. Oh, there was no doubting that Stazy liked to give the impression of brisk practicality rather than warmth and emotion; but even in the short time Jaxon had spent in her company he had come to realise that was exactly what it was—an impression. Even if she hadn't responded to him so passionately—so wildly—the evening before he would still have known that about her. Her defence of her grandparents, everything she said and did in regard to them, revealed that she loved them deeply. And as she had no doubt loved her parents just as deeply…

'Where were you when your parents died…?' He held out the second glass of chilled wine to her.

Her fingers trembled slightly as she took the glass from him. 'At boarding school.' Her throat moved convulsively as she swallowed. 'My father was flying the two of them to Paris to celebrate their twentieth wedding anniversary.'

'Do you know what went wrong…?'

Her eyes were pained as she looked up at him. 'Are you really interested, Jaxon, or are these questions just out of a need for accuracy in your screenplay—'

'I'm really interested,' he cut in firmly, more than a little irritated that she could ask him such a question. Admittedly they had only met at all because of the film he wanted to make about her grandmother, but after their closeness last night he didn't appreciate having Stazy still view his every question with suspicion. 'I've already decided that neither you nor your parents will feature in the film, Stazy.'

She raised red-gold brows. 'Why not?'

Jaxon shook his head. 'There's only so much I can cover in a film that plays for a couple of hours without rushing it, so I've more or less decided to concentrate on the escape of Anastasia's family from Russia, her growing up in England, and then the earlier years of the love story between Anastasia and Geoffrey.'

Her expression softened. 'It really was a love story, wasn't it?'

Again there was that wistful note in Stazy's voice. Jaxon was pretty sure she was completely unaware of it. An unacknowledged yearning, perhaps, for that same enduring love herself…? Yet at the same time Stazy was so determined to give every outward appearance of not needing those softer emotions in her life.

She seemed to recognise and shake off that wistfulness as she answered him with her usual briskness. 'There's no mystery about my parents' deaths, Jaxon. The enquiry found evidence that the plane crashed due to engine failure—possibly after a bird flew into it. One of those one in a million chances that occasionally happen.' She shrugged dismissively.

It *was* a one in a million chance, Jaxon knew, and it had robbed Stazy of her parents and completely shattered her young life. A one in a million chance that had caused her to build barriers about her emotions so that her life—and her heart?—would never suffer such loss and heartache again…

He was pretty sure he was getting close to the reason for Stazy's deliberate air of cold practicality. A coldness and practicality that he had briefly penetrated when the two of them had kissed so passionately the evening before…

He reached out to lightly caress one of her creamy cheeks. 'Not everyone leaves or dies, Stazy—'

He knew he had made a mistake when she instantly flinched away from the tenderness of his fingers, her expression one of red-cheeked indignation as she rose quickly to her feet.

'What on earth do you think you're doing, Jaxon?' She glared down at him, her hands clenched into fists at her sides, her breasts rapidly rising and falling in her agitation. 'Did you really think all you had to do was offer a few platitudes and words of understanding in order for me to tumble willingly into your arms? Or is it that your ego is so big you believe every woman you meet is going to want to fall into bed with you?'

Jaxon drew his breath in sharply at the deliberate insult of her attack, his hand falling back to his side as he rose slowly to his feet to look down at her gloweringly. 'It's usually polite to wait until you're asked!'

'Then I advise you not to put yourself to the trouble where I'm concerned!' she bit out dismissively, two bright spots of angry colour in her cheeks, green eyes glittering furiously as she glared up at him. 'I may have made the mistake of allowing you to kiss me last night, but I can assure you I don't intend to make a habit of it!'

Jaxon gave a frustrated shake of his head. 'You kissed me right back, damn it!'

Stazy knew that! Knew it, and regretted it with every breath in her body. At the same time as she wanted to kiss Jaxon again. To have him kiss her. Again. And again…!

She ached for Jaxon to kiss her. To more than kiss her. Had been wanting, aching for him to kiss her again ever since the two of them had parted the night before. So much so that right now she wanted nothing more than for the two of them to lie down on this blanket on the sand—regardless of the presence of those two guards!—and have him make love to her.

That was precisely the reason she wouldn't allow it to happen!

Jaxon was only staying here at Bromley House for a week. Just one week. After which time he would leave to make his pirate movie, before returning to the States and his life there. It would be madness on Stazy's part to allow herself to become involved with him even for that short length of time.

Why would it? The only two relationships she'd previously had in her life had been with men she had known were uninterested in a permanent relationship. Surely making Jaxon the perfect candidate for a brief, week-long affair…

No, she couldn't do it! She sensed—knew—from the wildness of her response to him yesterday evening that Jaxon represented a danger to all those barriers she had so carefully built about her emotions. So much so that she knew even a week of being Jaxon's lover would be six days and twenty-three hours too long…!

'Where are you going?' Jaxon reached out to firmly grasp Stazy's arm as she would have turned and walked away.

'Back to the house—'

'In other words, you're running away?' he scorned. 'Again,' he added, those grey eyes taunting.

Just the touch of his fingers about her arm was enough to rob Stazy of her breath. For her to be completely aware of him. Of his heat. His smell. For her fingers to itch, actually ache to become entangled in the long length of his hair as his lips, that sensuously sculptured mouth, claimed hers.

What was it about this man, this man in particular,

that made Stazy yearn to lose herself in his heat? To forget everything and everyone else as she gave in to the rapture of that sensuous mouth, the caresses of his strong and capable hands?

Danger!

To her, Jaxon represented a clear and present danger.

Physically.

Emotionally.

At the same time Stazy knew she had no intention of revealing her weakness by running away from the challenge of his taunt. She pulled her arm free of his steely grasp. 'I happen to be *walking* away, Jaxon, not running. And I'm doing so because I'm becoming bored by the constant need you feel to live up to your less than reputable image!'

The hardness of his cheekbones became clearly defined as his jaw tightened harshly. 'Really?'

'Really,' she echoed challengingly.

Jaxon continued to meet the challenge in those glittering green eyes for several long seconds as he fought an inner battle with himself, knowing the wisest thing he could to do was to let Stazy go, while at the same time wanting to take her in his arms and kiss her into submission. No—not submission; he wanted Stazy to take as much from him as he would be asking of her.

In your dreams, Wilder!

Stazy might have had a brief lapse in control the evening before, but he had no doubt it was that very lapse that made her so determined not to allow him to get close to her again. If he even attempted to kiss her now she would fight him with every part of her. And he didn't want to fight Stazy. He wanted to make love to her…

He also had no doubt that at the first sign of a struggle

between the two of them those two watching bodyguards would decide that Stazy was the one in need of protection. From him…

He stepped back. 'Then I really mustn't continue to bore you any longer, must I?' he drawled dryly.

Stazy looked up at him wordlessly for several seconds, slightly stunned at his sudden capitulation. What had she expected? That Jaxon would ask—plead—for her not to go back to the house just yet? To stay and have lunch with him here instead? That he would ask her for more than just to have lunch with him? If she had thought—hoped for—that then she was obviously going to be disappointed. Jaxon Wilder could have any woman he wanted. He certainly didn't need to waste his time charming someone who continued to claim she wasn't interested.

'Fine,' she bit out tautly. 'Enjoy your lunch.' Her head was held high as she turned and walked away.

Jaxon watched her leave through narrowed lids, knowing that he had allowed Stazy to get to him with those last cutting remarks, and feeling slightly annoyed with himself for allowing her to do so. And, damn it, what 'less than reputable image' was she referring to?

Okay, so over the past ten years or so he'd had his share of relationships with beautiful women. But only two or three in a year. And only ever one at a time. He certainly wasn't involved with anyone at the moment.

He was allowing Stazy's remark to put him on the defensive, when there was nothing for him to feel defensive about!

Jaxon turned slightly as he saw the nearest guard had moved off the headland and was now following Stazy back to the house. His smile became rueful as he watched the second guard leave his position in order to follow behind them, nodding curtly to Jaxon as he passed by several feet away, at the same time letting him know *he* wasn't the one being protected.

Just watching the way the two men moved so stealthily told Jaxon they were attached to one of the Special Forces, and even though neither man carried any visible weapon Jaxon was certain that thcy were both probably armed.

That knowledge instantly brought back the feelings of unease Jaxon had felt when he had arrived yesterday…

'Ready to call it a day…?'

Stazy had been wary of Jaxon's mood when he'd returned to the house an hour after she had left him so abruptly on the beach, but her worries had proved to be unfounded. Whatever Jaxon felt about that heated exchange, it was hidden beneath a veneer of smooth politeness she found irritating rather than rcassuring; either Jaxon had a very forgiving nature, or her remarks had meant so little to him he had totally dismissed them from his mind!

She glanced at the plain gold watch on her wrist now, as she leant against the back of her chair, surprised to see it was almost half past six in the evening.

'Jaxon, I—' She drew in a deep breath before continuing. 'I believe I owe you an apology for some of the things I said to you earlier…'

'You do?' Jaxon raised dark brows as hc flexed his shoulder in a stretch after hours of sitting bent over the table, the two of them having only stopped work briefly when Little had brought in a tray of afternoon tea a couple of hours ago.

Stazy had been just as distracted by Jaxon's physical

proximity this afternoon as she had this morning, and now found herself watching the play of muscles beneath his tee shirt as he stretched his arms above his head before standing up. His waist was just as tautly muscled above those powerful thighs and long legs. Damn it, even that five o'clock shadow looked sexy on Jaxon!

And she was once again ogling him like some starstruck groupie, Stazy realised self-disgustedly.

'My grandfather would be…disappointed if he were to learn I had been rude to guest in his home,' she said.

'I'm not about to tell him, Stazy.' Jaxon gave a rueful shake of his head. 'And technically we weren't *in* your grandfather's home at the time.'

'Nevertheless—'

'Just forget about it, okay?' he bit out tautly, no longer quite as relaxed as he had been. 'But, for the record, that disreputable image you keep referring to is greatly overstated!'

Obviously she had been wrong. It hadn't been a case of Jaxon having a forgiving nature *or* her remarks meaning so little to him he had dismissed them at all; Jaxon was just better at hiding his annoyance than most people!

'I only said that because—' She broke off the explanation as she remembered exactly why she had felt defensive enough to make that less than flattering remark earlier. Because she had once again been completely physically aware of Jaxon. Because she had been terrified of her own aching response to that physical awareness, of the danger Jaxon represented to her cool control…

She gave a shake of her head. 'Did you find anything interesting in my grandmother's papers?'

Stazy's attempt at an apology just now had gone a

long way to cementing the fragile truce that had existed between the two of them this afternoon, and in the circumstances Jaxon wasn't sure this was the right time to discuss anything he might or might not have read in Anastasia's private papers.

'A couple of things I'd like to discuss with Geoffrey when I see him next.'

'Such as?'

'It can wait until Geoffrey comes back,' he dismissed.

Stazy's mouth firmed. 'I thought the whole reason for my being here was so that you didn't need to bother my grandfather with any questions…?'

Jaxon gave a rueful smile. 'And I thought the reason you had decided to be here was to make sure I didn't decide to run off with any of any of these private papers!'

'I'm sure the security guards would very much enjoy ensuring you weren't able to do that!' she came back dryly.

'Thanks!' Jaxon grimaced.

She gave him a rueful smile of her own. 'You're welcome!'

That smile transformed the delicacy of her features into something truly beautiful: her eyes glowed deeply green, there was a becoming flush to her cheeks, and her lips were full, curved invitingly over small and even white teeth.

An invitation, if Jaxon should decide to risk taking it up, that would no doubt result in those teeth turning around and biting him.

Now, *there* was a thought guaranteed to ensure he didn't sleep again tonight!

Stazy's smile slowly faded as she saw the flare of

awareness in the sudden intensity of Jaxon's gaze fixed on her parted lips. 'I think I'll go upstairs for a shower before dinner,' she said briskly.

'I'd offer to come and wash your back for you if I didn't already know what your answer would be,' he finished mockingly.

Stazy looked up into that lazily handsome face—warm and caressing grey eyes, those sculptured lips curved into an inviting smile, that sexy stubble on the squareness of his chin—and briefly wished that her answer didn't have to be no. That she really was the sophisticated woman she tried so hard to be—the woman capable of just enjoying the moment by separating the physical from the emotional.

The same woman she had succeeded in being during those other two brief sexual encounters in her past...

But not with Jaxon, it seemed.

Because her reaction to him was frighteningly different...

He quirked one expectant dark brow. 'You seem to be taking a while to think it over...?'

'Not at all.' Stazy shook herself out of that confusion of thoughts. 'I'm just amazed—if not surprised!—at your persistence in continuing to flirt with me.'

He gave an unconcerned shrug. 'It would appear I have something of a reputation to live up to.'

Stazy gave a pained wince. 'I have apologised for that remark.'

'And I've accepted that apology.' He nodded.

'But not forgotten it...?'

No, Jaxon hadn't forgotten it. Or stopped questioning as to the reason why Stazy felt the need to resort to insulting him at all...

Did he make her feel threatened in some way? And,

if so, why? Once again he acknowledged that Stazy Bromley had to be one of the most complex and intriguing women he had ever met. On the outside beautiful, capable and self-contained. But beneath that cool exterior there was a woman of deep vulnerability who used that outer coldness to avoid any situation in which her emotions might become involved. Including physical intimacy. *Especially* physical intimacy!

Not that Jaxon thought for one moment that Stazy was still a virgin. But she would have chosen her lovers carefully. Coolly. Men who were and wished to remain as unemotionally involved as she was.

Had she found enjoyment in those encounters? Had she managed to maintain those barriers about her emotions even during the deepest of physical intimacy?

The cool detachment of her gaze as she looked at him now seemed to indicate those relationships hadn't even touched those barriers, let alone succeeded in breaching them.

As Jaxon so longed to do…

Last night he had briefly seen a different Stazy—a Stazy who had become a living flame in his arms as she met and matched his passion, her fingers entangled in his hair as she wrapped her legs about his waist to meet each slow and pleasurable thrust of his erection against the moist arousal nestled between her thighs.

Jaxon's hands clenched at his sides as he fought against taking her in his arms and kissing her until she once again became that beautiful and intoxicating woman.

'I think I'll go outside for a stroll before dinner.' And

hope that the fresh air would dampen down his renewed arousal!

If not, there was always the coldness of the English Channel he could throw himself into to cool off…!

CHAPTER SEVEN

'I'VE invited an old friend of my grandfather's to join us for dinner this evening,' Stazy informed Jaxon when he came into the drawing room an hour later.

'Really?' He strolled further into the room. He was wearing a black silk shirt unbuttoned at the throat this evening, with black tailored trousers. His hair was once again damp from the shower, the square strength of his chiselled jaw freshly shaven.

Stazy was quickly coming to realise that Jaxon used that noncommittal rejoinder when he was less than pleased with what had been said to him. 'I thought you might be getting a little bored here with just me for company,' she came back lightly as she handed him a glass of the dry martini she now knew he preferred before dinner.

'Did you?' he drawled softly.

She felt the warmth of colour enter her cheeks at his continued lack of enthusiasm. 'Obviously you're used to more sophisticated entertainments—'

'All the more reason for me to enjoy a week of peace and quiet.' Jaxon met her gaze steadily.

'I was only trying to be hospitable—'

'No, Stazy, you weren't,' he cut in mildly.

She stiffened. 'Don't presume to tell me what my motives are, Jaxon.'

'Fine.' He shrugged before strolling across the room to sit down in one of the armchairs, placing his untouched drink down on a side table before resting his elbows on the arms of the chair and steepling his fingers together in front of his chest. 'So who is this "old friend" of your grandfather's?'

Stazy's heart was beating so loudly in her chest she thought Jaxon must be able to hear it all the way across the room. He was right, of course; she hadn't invited Thomas Sullivan to dinner because she had thought Jaxon might be bored with her company—she had invited the other man in the hope he would act as a buffer against this increasing attraction she felt for Jaxon!

For the same reason she was wearing the same plain black shift dress she had worn six weeks ago, when she and Jaxon had first met, with a light peach gloss on her lips and her hair secured in a neat chignon.

She moistened dry lips. 'He and my grandfather were at university together.'

Jaxon raised dark brows. 'That *is* an old friend. And your grandfather's…outside employees are okay with his coming here this evening?'

'I didn't bother to ask them,' she dismissed.

'Then perhaps you should have done.'

Stazy frowned. 'We aren't prisoners here, Jaxon.'

He gave a slight smile. 'Have you tried leaving?'

'Of course not—' Her eyes widened as she broke off abruptly. 'Are you saying that you tried to leave earlier and were prevented from doing so…?'

Jaxon wasn't sure whether Stazy was put out because he might have tried to leave, or because he had been stopped from doing so. Either way, the result was the same: it appeared that for the moment neither of them were going anywhere.

'I had half an hour or so to spare before dinner and thought I would go for a ride—enjoy looking at some of the scenery in the area. I was stopped at the main gate and told very firmly that no one was allowed in or out of Bromley House this evening. Which probably means your grandfather's old friend isn't going to get in either,' he added derisively.

'But that's utterly ridiculous!' She looked totally bewildered as she placed her glass down on a side table before turning towards the door. 'I'll go and speak to one of them now.'

'You do that.' Jaxon nodded. 'And while you're at it maybe you can ask them what that flurry of activity was half an hour or so ago.'

Stazy stopped in her tracks and turned slowly back to face him. 'What flurry of activity?'

He shrugged. 'Extra chatter on the radios, and then about half a dozen more guards arrived fifteen minutes or so later—several of them with more dogs.'

Her cheeks were now the colour of fine pale porcelain. 'I wasn't aware of any of that…'

'No?' Jaxon stood up abruptly, frowning as Stazy instinctively took a step backwards. 'I think you have a much bigger problem here to worry about than me, Stazy,' he said harshly.

She looked even more bewildered. 'I'll telephone my grandfather and ask him what's going on—'

'I already tried that.' A nerve pulsed in Jaxon's clenched jaw. 'I even explained to the woman who answered my call that I was staying here with you at Bromley House at Sir Geoffrey's invitation. It made absolutely no difference. I was still politely but firmly told that Sir Geoffrey wasn't able to come to the telephone at the moment, but that she would pass the message along.'

Stazy gave a slow shake of her head. 'That doesn't sound like my grandfather…'

'I thought so too.' Jaxon nodded tersely. 'So I tried calling him on the mobile number he gave me. It was picked up by an answering service. Needless to say I didn't bother to leave another message— Ah, Little.' He turned to the butler as the other man quietly entered the drawing room. 'Dr Bromley and I were just speculating as to the possible reason for the extra guards in the grounds…'

To his credit, the older man's expression remained outwardly unchanged by the question. But years of acting, of studying the nuances of expression on people's faces, of knowing that even the slightest twitch of an eyebrow could have meaning, had resulted in Jaxon being much more attuned than most to people's emotions.

Even so, if he hadn't actually been looking straight at the older man he might have missed the slight hardening of his brown eyes before that emotion was neatly concealed by the lowering of hooded lids. Leaving Jaxon to speculate whether that small slip might mean that Little was more than just a butler.

'It seems that several teenagers were apprehended earlier today, trying to climb over the walls of the estate with the idea of throwing a party down on the beach,' Little dismissed smoothly.

'Really?' Jaxon drawled dryly.

'Yes,' the older man confirmed abruptly, before turning to Stazy. 'Dinner is ready to be served, Miss Stazy. Mr Sullivan telephoned a few minutes ago to extend his apologies. Due to a slight indisposition he is unable to join the two of you for dinner this evening after all.'

'What a surprise!' Jaxon looked across at Stazy knowingly.

To say *she* was surprised by all of this was putting it mildly. In fact she had been more than willing to dismiss Jaxon's earlier claims as nonsense until Little came into the room and confirmed at least half of them. That made Stazy question whether or not Jaxon might not be right about the other half too…?

'Little, do you have any idea why my grandfather might be unavailable this evening?'

The butler raised iron-grey brows. 'I had no idea that Sir Geoffrey was unavailable…'

She had known Little for more years than she cared to acknowledge, and had always found him to be quietly efficient and totally devoted to the comfort of both her grandmother and grandfather. Never, during all of those years, had Stazy ever doubted Little's word.

She doubted it now…

There was something about Little's tone—an evasiveness that caused a flutter of sickening unease in the depths of Stazy's stomach. 'Could you please ask Mrs Harris to delay dinner for fifteen minutes or so?' she requested briskly. 'I have several things I need to do before we go through to the dining room.'

This time she was sure that she wasn't imagining it when Little's mouth tightened fractionally in disapproval. 'Very well, Miss Stazy.' He gave her a formal bow before leaving.

But not, Stazy noted frowningly, before he had sent a slightly censorious glance in Jaxon's direction!

'Not a happy man,' Jaxon murmured ruefully as he stood up.

'No,' Stazy agreed softly.

She was obviously more than a little puzzled by this strange turn of events—to the point that Jaxon now felt slightly guilty for having voiced his concerns and causing Stazy's present confusion. Maybe he should have just kept quiet about the arrival of the extra guards and his not being allowed to leave the grounds of Bromley House earlier? And the fact that Geoffrey had been unable to come to the telephone when he'd called. Whatever that obscure statement might mean…

Jaxon certainly regretted the worry he could now see clouding Stazy's troubled green eyes, and the slight pallor that had appeared in the delicacy of her cheeks. 'I'm sure there's no real need for concern, Stazy—'

'You're sure of no such thing, Jaxon, so please stop treating me as if I were a child,' she dismissed. 'Something is seriously wrong here, and I intend to find out exactly what it is!'

After only two days of being in close proximity to Stazy he knew better than to argue with her. Or offer her comfort. He was only too well aware that she was a woman who liked to give the outward appearance of being in control of her emotions, at least.

'And how do you intend to do that…?' he prompted softly.

'By telephoning my grandfather myself, of course.' She moved to where her handbag lay on the floor beside one of the armchairs, taking her mobile from its depths before pressing the button for one of the speed dials. 'I've never been unable to talk to my grandfather—Is that you, Glynis…?' She frowned as the call was obviously answered not by Geoffrey, as she had hoped, but probably the same woman Jaxon had spoken to earlier. 'Yes. Yes, it is. Where—? Oh. I see. Well, do you have any idea when he will be out of the meeting?' She shot Jaxon a frowning glance.

Jaxon gave her privacy for the call by strolling across the room to stand in front of one of the bay windows that looked over the long driveway. The same window, he realised, where Stazy had been standing six weeks ago, and again two days ago, as she had waited for him to arrive…

He had certainly been aware of the existence of Geoffrey and Anastasia Bromley's granddaughter before coming here, but he had in no way been prepared for Stazy's physical resemblance to her grandmother. Since his return to Bromley House he had become aware that that resemblance was more than skin deep; Stazy had the same confidence and self-determination that his earlier research had shown Anastasia to have possessed in spades.

It appeared that the only way in which the two women differed was emotionally…

Not even that self-confidence and strong outer shell were able to hide Stazy's inner emotional vulnerability. A vulnerability that for some reason brought forth every protective instinct in Jaxon's body…

That was pretty laughable when Stazy had made it clear on more than one memorable occasion that he was the last person she wanted to get close to her—emotionally or otherwise!

He turned back into the room now, as he heard her ending the call.

'Everything okay?' he prompted lightly.

She seemed preoccupied as she slipped her mobile back into her bag before straightening. 'My grandfather is in a meeting,' she explained unnecessarily; Jaxon had already ascertained that much from listening to the beginning of Stazy's telephone conversation. 'Glynis will get him to call me back as soon as he comes out.'

'And Glynis is…?'

The frown deepened between Stazy's delicate brows. 'She was his personal secretary until his retirement twenty-five years ago…'

Considering the speed with which those guards had appeared outside Bromley House following the late-night telephone call that had taken Geoffrey up to London two days ago, Jaxon would be very surprised if Geoffrey had ever fully retired.

He gave a shrug. 'Then we may as well go and have dinner while we wait for him to return your call.' He held his arm out to Stazy.

Stazy didn't move, more than a little unsettled by everything that had happened this evening. Those extra guards and her grandfather's unavailability. Little's careful evasion of her questions. Her own feelings of unease at Glynis's claim that her grandfather couldn't speak to her because he was in a meeting. Not once in the fifteen years since Stazy's parents had died had her grandfather ever been too busy to talk to her on the telephone. And why would Glynis be answering Geoffrey's personal mobile at all…?

'It's probably best if you try not to let your imagination run away with you, Stazy.'

She drew herself up determinedly as she realised Jaxon had moved to stand in front of her—so close she could see the beginnings of that dark stubble returning to the squareness of his jaw, and each individual strand of dark hair on his chest revealed by the open neck of his black silk shirt. She could feel the heat of his body, smell the lemon shampoo he had used to wash his hair, and the sandalwood soap he had showered with, all overlaid with a purely male smell that she had come to know was uniquely Jaxon. A smell that always succeeded in making Stazy feel weak at the knees…!

Unless that was just a result of the tensions of these past few minutes?

Who was she trying to fool with these explanation? Herself or Jaxon? If it was herself then she was failing miserably; once again she found it difficult even to breathe properly with Jaxon standing this close to her. And if it was Jaxon she was trying to convince of her uninterest, then the simple act of accepting his arm to go through to the dining room would reveal just how much she was shaking just from his close proximity.

She nodded abruptly as she chose to ignore that proffered arm. 'I'll just go and tell Little we're ready to eat now—if you would like to go through to the dining room?'

Another moment of vulnerability firmly squashed beneath that determined self-control, Jaxon thought ruefully as he gave a brief nod, before lowering his arm and following her from the drawing room. Except Jaxon didn't consider it a vulnerability to acknowledge concern for someone you loved as much as Stazy obviously loved her grandfather…

'Sir Geoffrey is on the telephone,' Little informed them loftily as he came in to the dining room an hour and a half later to remove their dessert plates. 'I took the liberty of transferring the call to his study.'

Stazy stood up abruptly. 'I'll go through immediately—'

'It was Mr Wilder that Sir Geoffrey asked to speak with.' The butler straightened, his gaze fixed steadily on Jaxon rather than on Stazy.

'Mr Wilder?' she repeated dazedly. 'You must be mistaken, Little—'

'Not at all,' the butler assured her mildly. 'I believe you telephoned Sir Geoffrey earlier this evening, sir…?'

Jaxon had to admire the other man's stoicism in the face of Stazy's obvious disbelief of his having correctly relayed the message from Geoffrey Bromley. At the same time he recognised that Stazy's reaction was completely merited; what possible reason could Geoffrey have for asking to speak to Jaxon rather than his own granddaughter? Whatever that reason was, Jaxon doubted it was anything good!

'I did, yes,' he acknowledged lightly as he placed his napkin on the table before standing up. 'If you could just show me to Sir Geoffrey's study…?'

'Certainly, Mr Wilder.'

'Jaxon!'

His shoulders tensed as he turned slowly back to face an obviously less than happy Stazy. Justifiably so, in Jaxon's estimation. Geoffrey had to know that his granddaughter wouldn't just accept his asking to speak with Jaxon rather than her without comment.

'I'm coming with you,' she informed him determinedly.

'I believe Sir Geoffrey wishes to speak with Mr Wilder alone,' Little interjected—bravely, in Jaxon's estimation.

Stazy looked ready to verbally if not physically rip anyone who stood in the way of her talking with her grandfather to shreds. And at the moment Little was definitely attempting to do just that!

Her eyes flashed deeply green as she turned to the butler. 'Sir Geoffrey can wish all he likes, Little,' she assured him firmly. 'But I'm definitely accompanying Mr Wilder to the study!'

Jaxon managed to stand back just in time as Stazy swept past him and out of the room. 'I think that was a pretty predictable reaction, don't you?' he drawled ruefully to the watching butler. 'And, on the positive side, at least I actually got to eat this time before she walked out on me!' The food had been untouched when he had handed the picnic basket back to Little earlier.

'There are times when it is almost possible to believe Lady Anastasia is back with us again…' the other man murmured admiringly as he looked down the hallway at Stazy's retreating and stiffly determined back.

Jaxon nodded. 'Perhaps you had better bring a decanter of brandy and a couple of glasses through to Sir Geoffrey's study in about five minutes…?'

'Certainly, sir.' Little nodded smoothly.

Jaxon strolled down the hallway to where he had seen Stazy enter what had to be Geoffrey Bromley's study, sure that the next few minutes were going to be far from pleasant…

'You heard your grandfather's, Stazy,' Jaxon reminded her gently. 'He said there's absolutely no reason for you to rush up to London just now.'

Stazy was well aware of what her grandfather had said on the telephone, once she had managed to wrest the receiver out of Jaxon's hand and talked to her grandfather herself. Just as she was aware that she had no intention of taking any notice of her grandfather's instruction for her to wait to hear from him again before taking any further action.

Mainly because her grandfather's telephone call had revealed that he had rushed up to London two days ago, and security here had been increased, because he and some members of one of his previous security teams had been receiving threats. That threat had somehow escalated in the past twenty-four hours, and now her grandfather expected—instructed—that she just calmly sit here at Bromley House and await further news!

No way. Absolutely no way was Stazy going to just sit here waiting to see if someone succeeded in attacking her grandfather.

She turned to look at Little as he quietly entered the study with a silver tray containing a decanter of brandy and two glasses. 'I suppose *you* already knew what was going on before we spoke to my grandfather?'

'Stazy,' Jaxon reproved softly from where he sat in the chair facing her grandfather's desk.

'I'm sorry, Little.' Stazy sighed. 'Did you happen to know about these threats to my grandfather?' she asked, less challengingly but just as determinedly, as she watched the butler carefully and precisely place the decanter and glasses on the desktop.

Again Jaxon was sure that he hadn't imagined the butler's reaction—a slight but nevertheless revealing tic in his cheek—before the other man covered his emotion with his usual noncommittal expression as he answered Stazy. 'I believe the increased security measures here are only a precaution, Miss Stazy.'

'I'm not concerned about myself—'

'That will be all, thank you, Little.' Jaxon gave the older man a reassuring smile as he stood up to cross the room and usher the butler out into the hallway before closing the door firmly behind him. 'Taking out your worry concerning your grandfather on one of the people who works for him isn't going to make you feel any better, Stazy.' He spoke mildly as he moved to the front of the desk to pour brandy into the two glasses.

'Is it too much to expect you to understand how worried I feel?' A nerve pulsed in her tightly clenched jaw, and her cheeks were once again pale, her eyes suspiciously over-bright.

With anger or tears, Jaxon wasn't sure…

He straightened slowly to hand her one of the glasses of deep amber liquid. 'No, of course it isn't. I just don't believe insulting Little or me is going to help the situation.'

'Then what is?' She threw the contents of the glass to the back of her throat before moving to refill it.

Jaxon winced. 'Expensive brandies like this one are meant to be breathed in, sipped and then savoured—not thrown down like a pint of unimpressive warm beer!'

'I know that.' She picked up the second glass and took a healthy swallow of the contents of that one too, before slamming it back down on the desk to look up challengingly at Jaxon.

'Stazy, I really wouldn't advise you pushing this situation to a point where I have to use extreme measures in order to calm you down,' Jaxon said softly as he saw the reckless glint in her eyes had deepened.

'Such as what?' she prompted warily. 'Are you going to put me over your knee and spank me for being naughty? Or will just slapping me on the cheek suffice?'

He shrugged. 'I'm not about to slap you anywhere—but the first suggestion has a certain merit at this moment!' Ordinarily Jaxon wouldn't dream of using physical force of any kind on a woman. But this situation was far from ordinary. Stazy was way out of her normally controlled zone. Almost to the point of hysteria. Rightly so, of course, when her grandfather was all the family she had left in the world…

In these unusual circumstances Jaxon didn't at all mind being used as Stazy's verbal punchbag, but he knew her well enough to know that she would be mortified at her treatment of the obviously devoted Little once she had calmed down enough to recognise how she had spoken to him just now—out of love and worry for her grandfather or otherwise.

The uncharacteristic tears glistening in those eyes were his undoing. 'Oh, Stazy…!' he groaned, even as he took her gently into his arms. 'It's going to be okay—you'll see.'

'You don't really know that,' she murmured against his chest as she choked back those tears.

'No, I don't,' Jaxon answered honestly. 'But what I do know is that Geoffrey is a man who knows exactly what he's doing. If he says this problem is going to be handled, then I have no doubt that it will be. And, as you know him much better than I do, you shouldn't either,' he encouraged softly as he ran comforting hands up and down the length of her back.

'You're right. I know you are.' She nodded against him. 'I just—I can't help feeling worried.'

'I know that.' Jaxon's arms tightened about her as the softness of her body rested against the length of his. 'And so does Geoffrey. Which is why he asked me to take care of you.'

She raised her head to look at him, her smile still tearful. 'And this is you taking care of me…?'

'I could possibly do a better job of it if I thought you wouldn't object…?'

Stazy groaned low in her throat as Jaxon slowly lowered his head and slanted his mouth lightly against hers, her body instantly relaxing into his and her fingers becoming entangled in his hair as her lips parted to deepen that kiss.

It felt as if Stazy had been waiting for this to happen since the last time Jaxon had kissed her. Waiting and longing for it. Instantly she became lost to the pleasure of those exploring lips and the caress of Jaxon's hands as they roamed her back before cupping her bottom and pulling her into him.

She was achingly aware of every inch of the lean length of Jaxon's body against hers—his chest hard and unyielding against the fullness of her breasts, the hardness of his erection caught between her stomach and thighs, living evidence of his own rapidly escalating arousal.

Stazy gave another groan as Jaxon's hands tightened about her bottom and he lifted her up and placed her on the edge of the desk. His knees nudged her legs apart, pushing her dress up to her thighs as he stepped between them, and she felt the heat of his erection against the lace of her panties. That groan turned into a low moan of heated pleasure as he pressed into her, applying just the right amount of pressure.

Her neck arched and her fingers clung to the broad width of Jaxon's shoulders when his lips left hers to kiss across her cheek before travelling the length of her throat—kissing, gently biting, as he tasted her creamy skin before his tongue plundered and rasped the sensitive hollows at the base of her neck.

Her back arched as Jaxon's hand moved to cup beneath one of her breasts. The soft material of her dress was no barrier to the pleasure that coursed through her hotly as his thumb moved lightly across the roused and aching nipple, and she was only vaguely aware of it when his other hand slowly lowered the zip of her dress down the length of her spine before his hand touched the naked flesh beneath, revealing that she wasn't wearing a bra.

Jaxon heard the voice in his head telling him to stop this now. Offering Stazy comfort was one thing—what he wanted was something else entirely. He heard that voice and ignored it—had no choice but to ignore it when he could feel how Stazy's pleasure more than matched his own.

He reached up to ease the dress down her arms, baring her to the waist before he moved his hands to cup beneath the swell of her breasts. Such full and heavy breasts, when the rest of her body was so slender. Full and heavy breasts that Jaxon wanted in his mouth as he tasted and pleasured her.

His hands remained firmly on her waist and he moved back slightly to look down at her nakedness. The heat of his gaze on those uptilting breasts tipped by rosy pink and engorged nipples stayed for long, admiring seconds before he lowered his head to take one in his mouth.

Stazy moved her arms so that her hands were flat on the desk behind her, supporting her as the pleasure of having Jaxon's mouth and tongue on her coursed hotly from her breasts to between her thighs. She felt herself tingle there as he took her nipple fully into the heat of his mouth and began to suckle, gently at first, and then more greedily, as his hand cupped her other breast and began to caress her in that same sensuous rhythm.

She was on fire, the ache between her thighs almost unbearable now, building higher and higher, until she knew Jaxon held her poised on the edge of release. 'Please, Jaxon…!' she groaned weakly.

He ignored that plea and instead turned the attentions of his lips, tongue and teeth to her other breast. His lips clamped about the fullness of the nipple as his tongue and teeth licked and rasped against that sensitive bud, driving Stazy wild as she moved her thighs restlessly against his in an effort to ease her aching need for the release that was just a whisper of pleasure away.

She trembled all over with that need, her breath a pained rasp in her throat as she looked down at Jaxon with hot and heavy eyes. Just the sight of his lips clamped about her, drawing her nipple deeper and deeper into his mouth with each greedy suck, caused another rush of heat between her restless and throbbing thighs.

'Jaxon…!' Instead of deepening that pleasure, as she so wanted him to do, it seemed as if Jaxon began to ease away from her, gently kissing her breasts now, his hands once again a soft caress against her back. 'Stop playing with me, please, Jaxon!' she pleaded throatily.

'This isn't a sensible idea, Stazy,' he groaned achingly, even as his arms dropped from about her waist before he straightened away from her.

Stazy looked at him searchingly for several long seconds, easily seeing the regret in his eyes before a shutter came down over those twin mirrors into his emotions. 'Jaxon…?' she breathed softly.

He gave a shake of his head, his expression grim. 'We both know that you're going to end up hating me if I take this any further…'

'You're wrong, Jaxon.' She gave a disbelieving shake of her head, continuing to stare up at him dazedly as she pulled her dress back up her arms to hold it in front of the bareness of her breasts with one hand while she pulled the material down over her naked thighs with the other.

'I am?' he prompted huskily.

'Oh, yes,' Stazy breathed softly. 'Because I couldn't possibly hate you any more than I do at this moment!' Her eyes glittered with humiliated anger now, rather than tears.

Jaxon knew he fully deserved that anger—that he had allowed things to go much further between them just now than was wise when Stazy was already feeling so emotionally vulnerable. But he also knew that Stazy was wrong—she would definitely have hated him more if they had taken their lovemaking to its inevitable conclusion. And on the plus side—for Geoffrey and Little, that was!—Stazy was now far more angry with him than she had been earlier with either of them!

That, in retrospect, was probably the best outcome. He was scheduled to leave here at the end of the week, whereas Geoffrey and Little would both be around for much longer than that.

Jaxon kept his expression noncommittal as he stepped fully away from Stazy, his shaft throbbing in protest as he did so. No doubt another cold shower—a very *long* cold shower!—would be in order when he got back to his suite of rooms. 'There's the possibility you might even thank me for my restraint in the morning…' he murmured ruefully.

'I shouldn't hold your breath on that happening, if I were you!'

'Stazy—'

'I think you should leave now, Jaxon.' It was definitely anger that now sparkled in her eyes.

'Fine,' he accepted wearily. 'But you know where I am if you can't sleep and feel like—'

'Like what?' she cut in sharply. 'I thought we had both just agreed that this was a very bad idea?'

'I was going to say if you feel like company,' Jaxon completed firmly. 'And I don't remembering saying it was a bad idea—just not a very sensible one, given the circumstances.'

'Well, "given the circumstances", I would now like you to leave.' Her chin rose proudly as she held his gaze.

Jaxon gave her one last regretful glance before doing exactly that, knowing that to stay would only make the situation worse.

If that was actually possible…

CHAPTER EIGHT

'THAT really wasn't very clever, now, was it?' Jaxon looked at Stazy impatiently as he entered the drawing room almost two hours later, to see her pacing in front of the bay windows, now dressed in a thick green sweater and fitted black denims, with her red-gold hair neatly plaited down the length of her spine.

She shot him only a cursory glance as she continued to pace restlessly. 'Shouldn't you be fast asleep?'

He closed the door softly behind him. 'Little came and knocked on my bedroom door. He seemed to think I might like to know that you had tried to take my Harley in an attempt to go and see your grandfather tonight.'

'The traitor…'

Jaxon gave a rueful shake of his shaggy head, having quickly pulled on faded denims and a black tee shirt before coming downstairs. 'Exactly when did you take the keys to the Harley off my dressing table…?'

'When I heard the shower running in your bathroom.' She had the grace to look a little guilty. 'I am sorry I took them without your permission, but at the time I didn't feel I had any other choice.'

'Is that your idea of an apology?'

'No.' She sighed. 'It was very wrong of me, and I do

apologise, Jaxon. My grandfather would be horrified if he knew!'

'I'm horrified—but probably not for the same reason!' Jaxon gave her an exasperated glance as he too easily imagined what might have happened if she had managed to ride the Harley. 'How could you even have *thought* taking my motorbike was going to work, Stazy, when there are enough guards patrolling the grounds for them to hear a mouse squeak let alone the roar of an engine starting up?'

'I didn't even get the bike out of the garage,' Stazy acknowledged self-disgustedly.

There had been no excuse for what she had allowed to happen in her grandfather's study earlier that evening, and just thinking about those intimacies once Stazy reached the privacy of her bedroom had been enough to make her want to get as far away from Bromley House—and Jaxon—as possible!

Admittedly it had taken a little time on her part, but once it had occurred to her that she could 'borrow' the keys to Jaxon's Harley and then take the less used and hopefully less guarded back road out of the estate to leave, she hadn't been able to rid herself of the idea.

Unfortunately, as Jaxon had already pointed out, just starting up the engine had brought three of her grandfather's guards running to where the motorbike was parked at the back of the house. Quickly followed by the humiliation of having the keys to the motorbike taken from her before being escorted back inside.

With the added embarrassment that Jaxon now knew exactly what she had planned on doing too. 'Obviously I didn't really think beyond the idea of going to London to see my grandfather,' she accepted guiltily.

'Obviously!' Jaxon gave a disgusted shake of his head. 'You could have been killed, damn it!'

In retrospect Stazy accepted that her method of leaving Bromley House really hadn't been a good plan at all. Not only had starting the engine sounded like the roar of an angry lion in the stillness of the night, but there had still been no guarantee that she would have found it any easier to leave by the back road. She would never know now…

No, in retrospect, taking the Harley hadn't been a good plan at all. And, if Stazy was being honest, she now admitted it had also been an extremely childish one…

Why, oh, why did just being around Jaxon make her behave in this ridiculous way…?

She gave an impatient shake of her head. 'I just feel so—so useless, having to sit here and wait for news from my grandfather.'

Jaxon's expression softened. 'I'm sure Geoffrey is well aware of exactly how you feel, Stazy—'

'Are *you*?' she said warily.

'Yes.' He sighed. 'Look, it's almost one o'clock in the morning, and no doubt the kitchen staff all went to bed hours ago. So why don't the two of us go down to the kitchen and make a pot of tea or something?'

She smiled ruefully. 'Tea being the English panacea for whatever ails you?'

He shrugged. 'It would seem to work in most situations, yes.'

It certainly couldn't do any harm, and Stazy knew she was still too restless to be able to sleep even if she went up to bed now. 'Why not?' she said softly as she crossed the room to precede him out into the hallway.

The house was quiet as Jaxon and Stazy crossed the

cavernous entrance hall on their way to the more shadowy hallway that led down to the kitchen, with only the sound of the grandfather clock ticking to disturb that eerie silence.

A stark reminder, if Jaxon had needed one, that it was very late at night and he and Stazy were completely alone…

And if Stazy believed there had been no repercussions for him after having to walk away from her earlier this evening then she was completely mistaken!

A fifteen-minute cold shower had done absolutely nothing to dampen Jaxon's arousal. Nor had sitting at the desk in his bathrobe to read through the notes he had already accumulated for the screenplay. Or telephoning his agent in LA and chatting to him about it for ten minutes.

None of those things had done a damned thing to stop Jaxon's mind from wandering, time and time again, to thoughts of making love with Stazy in Geoffrey's study.

As he was thinking about it still…

Self-denial wasn't something Jaxon enjoyed. And walking away from Stazy—not once, but twice in the past two days!—was playing havoc with his self-control!

The cosy intimacy of the warm kitchen and working together to make tea—Jaxon finding the cups while Stazy filled the kettle with water and switched it on—did nothing to lessen his awareness of her. Not when his gaze wandered to her constantly as the slender elegance of her hands prepared and warmed the teapot and he all too easily imagined the places those hands might touch and caress. The smooth roundness of her bottom in those black fitted denims wasn't helping either!

'Feeling any better?' Jaxon prompted gruffly, once he was seated on the other side of the kitchen table from Stazy, two steaming cups of tea in front of them.

'Less hysterical, you mean?' She grimaced.

He shook his head. 'You weren't hysterical, Stazy, just understandably concerned about your grandfather.'

'Yes,' she acknowledged with a sigh. 'Still, I didn't have to be quite so bitchy about it.'

'You? Bitchy?' Jaxon gave an exaggerated gasp of disbelief. 'Never!' He placed a dramatic hand on his heart.

She smiled ruefully. 'You aren't going to win any awards with *that* performance!'

'No,' he acknowledged with a wry chuckle.

Stazy sobered. 'Do you think my grandfather is telling us the truth about this threat?' She looked across at him worriedly. 'It occurred to me earlier that he could be using it as a smokescreen,' she continued as Jaxon raised one dark brow. 'That maybe this screenplay and the making of the film might have brought on another heart attack…?'

'Why am I not surprised!' Jaxon grimaced ruefully. 'Do you seriously believe your grandfather would lie to you in that way?'

'If he thought I would worry less, yes,' she confirmed unhesitantly.

Unfortunately, so did Jaxon…

Although he honestly hoped in this instance that wouldn't turn out to be the case. 'Then it's one of those questions where I can't win, however I choose to answer it. If I say no, I can't see that happening, then you aren't going to believe me. And if I say it's a possibility, you'll ask me to consider dropping the whole idea.'

Stazy was rational enough now to be able to see the logic in Jaxon's reply. 'Maybe we should just change the subject…?'

'That might be a good idea,' he drawled ruefully.

She nodded. 'As you probably aren't going to be able to speak to my grandfather about it for several days yet, perhaps you would like to tell *me* what it is you found earlier and wanted to talk to him about…?'

Jaxon gave a wince. 'Another lose/lose question as far as I'm concerned, I'm afraid. And it seems a pity to spoil things when we have reached something of a truce in the last few minutes…'

'It's probably an armed truce, Jaxon,' Stazy said dryly. 'And liable to erupt into shots being exchanged again at any moment!'

'Okay.' He grimaced. 'Curiously, what I've found is something the reporter who wrote the biography seems to have missed altogether…'

'Hmm…'

Jaxon raised one dark brow at that sceptical murmur. 'You don't think he missed it?'

'What I think,' Stazy said slowly, 'is that, whatever you found, my grandfather will have ensured the reporter didn't find it.'

'You believe Geoffrey has that much power…?'

'Oh, yes.' She smiled affectionately.

Jaxon shook his head. 'You don't even know what this is about yet.'

She shrugged. 'I don't need to. If my grandfather left some incriminating papers in the library for you to look at then he meant for you to find them.'

That made Jaxon feel a little better, at least. 'There were two things, actually, but they're related.'

Stazy looked down at her fingertip, running it distractedly around the rim of her cup as she waited for him to continue.

He sighed. 'I found your grandparents' marriage certificate for February 1946.'

'Yes?'

'And your father's birth certificate for October 1944.'

'Yes?'

'Leaving a discrepancy of sixteen months.'

'Two years or more if you take into account the nine months of pregnancy,' she corrected ruefully.

'Yes…'

The tension eased out of Stazy's shoulders as she smiled across at him. 'I'm sure that there are always a lot of children born with questionable birth certificates during war years.'

'No doubt.' Jaxon was literally squirming with discomfort now. 'But—'

'But my father's place of birth is listed as Berlin, Germany,' she finished lightly.

'Yes.' Jaxon breathed his relief.

'With no name listed under the "Father" column.'

'No…'

'Meaning there's no way of knowing for certain that Geoffrey was actually his father.'

'I didn't say that—'

'You didn't have to.' Stazy chuckled. 'It would have looked a little odd, don't you think, to have the name of an Englishman listed as the father of a baby boy born in Berlin in 1944?'

'Well, yes…But—'

'More tea, Jaxon?' She stood up to put more hot

water into the teapot before coming back to stand with the pot poised over his cup.

'Thanks,' he accepted distractedly. He had been dreading having to talk to any of the Bromley family about his discovery earlier today, and especially the unpredictable Stazy. Now, instead of being her usual defensive self, she actually seemed to find the whole thing amusing. To the point that he could see laughter gleaming in those expressive green eyes as she refilled his cup before sitting down again. 'Like to share what's so amusing…?'

'You are.' She gave a rueful shake of her head as she resumed her seat. 'You're aged in your mid-thirties, Jaxon, a Hollywood A-list actor and director, and yet you seem scandalised that there might have been babies born out of wedlock seventy years ago!' She grinned across at him.

'I'm not in the least scandalised—'

'Um…protesting too much, much?' she teased, in the manner of one of her students.

Jaxon eyed her frustatedly. 'These are your grand-parents we're talking about. And your father.'

'Geoffrey and Anastasia never tried to hide from me that my father was actually present and sixteen months old at the time of their wedding,' she assured him gently. 'We have the photographs to prove it. Which I can show you tomorrow—later today,' she corrected, after a glance at the kitchen clock revealed it was now almost two o'clock in the morning. 'If you would like to see them?'

'I would, yes.'

She nodded. 'I'll look them out in the morning.'

'So what happened?' Jaxon said slowly. 'Why didn't

the two of them marry when Anastasia knew she was expecting Geoffrey's child?'

'They didn't marry earlier because Anastasia didn't know she was pregnant when she was dropped behind enemy lines in late February 1944. By the time she realised her condition she had already established her cover as a young Austrian woman, recently widowed and bitterly resentful of the English as a result, and it was too late for her to do anything but remain in Berlin and continue with the mission she had been sent there to complete. She always maintained her pregnancy actually helped to confirm that identity.'

'My God…' Jaxon fell back against his chair.

'Yes.' Stazy smiled affectionately. 'Of course my grandfather, once informed of Anastasia's condition, ensured that she was ordered out of Berlin immediately.'

'And she refused to leave until she had finished what she went there to do?' Jaxon guessed.

Stazy met his gaze unblinkingly. 'Yes, she did.'

'She went through her pregnancy, gave birth to her son, cared for him, all the while behind enemy lines under a false identity that could have been blown apart at any moment?'

Her chin tilted. 'Yes.'

He gave an incredulous shake of his head. 'God, that's so—so—'

'Irresponsible? Selfish?' There was a slight edge to Stazy's voice now.

'I was going to say romantic.' Jaxon grinned admiringly. 'And incredibly brave. What a woman she must have been!'

Stazy relaxed slightly as she answered huskily, 'I've always believed so, yes.'

Jaxon nodded. 'And so you should. You're very like her, you know,' he added softly.

'I don't think so, Jaxon.' Stazy gave a choked laugh. 'Even in her nineties Anastasia would have made sure she got on that Harley tonight and somehow managed to ride it out of here, despite all those guards trying to stop her!'

'Maybe,' he acknowledged dryly. 'But you definitely gave it your best shot.'

She shrugged. 'Not good enough, obviously.'

'Choosing the Harley for your first attempt was extremely gutsy.' In fact Stazy's behaviour tonight was so much more than Jaxon would ever have believed possible of that stiffly formal and tightly buttoned down Dr Anastasia Bromley he had been introduced to six weeks ago. 'So you think Geoffrey meant for me to find the marriage and birth certificates…?'

She nodded. 'I'm sure of it.'

'Why?'

Stazy gave a rueful smile. 'For some reason he seems to trust you to do the right thing…' she said slowly, knowing there was no way her grandfather would ever have put the reputation of his darling Anastasia in the hands of a man he didn't trust implicitly.

Something she should probably have appreciated more while resenting Jaxon these past six weeks…

He leant across the table now, to take one of her hands gently in both of his. 'And do *you* trust me to do that too, Stazy?'

She did trust him, Stazy realised as she looked across the table at him. That silver-grey gaze was unmistakably sincere as it met hers unwaveringly.

Yes, she trusted Jaxon—it was herself she didn't trust whenever she was around him!

Even now, worried about her grandfather, frustrated at not being able to leave the estate, Stazy was totally aware of Jaxon as he held her hand in both of his. Of the roughness of his palm, the gentleness of his fingers as they played lightly across the back of her hand, sending a quiver of awareness through her arm and down into the fullness of her breasts and between her thighs. Warming her. Once again arousing her…

'I trust my grandfather's judgement in all things,' she finally said huskily.

'But not mine?' Jaxon said shrewdly.

Stazy pulled her trembling hand out of his grasp before pushing it out of sight beneath the table, very aware of the heat of awareness singing through her veins. 'It's late, Jaxon.' She stood up abruptly. 'And tomorrow looks as if it's going to be something of a long and anxious day. We should at least try to get some sleep tonight.' She picked up their empty cups and carried them over to the sink to rinse them out before placing them on the rack to dry.

All the time she was aware of Jaxon's piercing gaze on her. Heating her blood to boiling point. Her legs trembled slightly, so that she was forced to resort to leaning against the sink unit for support.

'Stazy…?'

She drew in a deep breath, desperately searching for some of the coolness and control that had stood her in such good stead these past ten years. Searching and failing.

'If something I've said or done has upset you, then I apologise…'

Stazy had been so deeply entrenched in fighting the heat of her emotions that she hadn't even been aware that Jaxon had moved to stand behind her. The warmth of his breath was now a gentle caress as it brushed against the tendrils of hair at her nape that had escaped the neatness of her plait. If he should so much as touch her—!

She slipped away from that temptation before turning to face him. 'You haven't done anything to upset me, Jaxon,' she assured him crisply. 'I think it's as you implied earlier—I'm just emotionally overwrought.'

Jaxon could see the evidence of exhaustion in the dark shadows beneath her eyes. Her cheeks were pale, those full and vulnerable lips trembling slightly as she obviously fought against giving in to that exhaustion. 'Time for bed,' he agreed firmly, before taking a tight grip of her hand and leading her gently across the room to the doorway, switching off the kitchen light on his way out.

He retained that firm grip on the delicacy of her hand as the two of them walked down the shadowed hallway and up the wide staircase together, allowing him to feel the way her fingers tightened about his and her steps seemed to slow as they approached the top of the stairs.

Jaxon turned to look at Stazy in the semi-darkness. Her eyes were deeply green and too huge in the paleness of her face. 'Stazy, would you rather have company tonight…?' Even though he spoke softly his voice still sounded over-loud in the stillness of the dark night surrounding them.

Stazy came to an abrupt halt at the top of the stairs, frowning as she turned to look at him searchingly, the contours of his face sharply hewn in the moonlight, the expression in his eyes totally unreadable with those grey eyes hooded by long dark lashes and lowered lids. 'Exactly what are you suggesting, Jaxon…?' she finally murmured warily.

'I'm asking if you would like me to come to your bedroom and spend the rest of the night with you,' he bit out succinctly.

Exactly what Stazy had thought he was offering! 'Why?'

Jaxon chuckled softly. 'How about because I know how the hours between two o'clock in the morning and five o'clock can sometimes be tough to get through if you have something on your mind.'

Stazy raised auburn brows. 'Are you talking from personal experience?'

He gave a hard grin. 'Difficult as you obviously find that to believe, yes, I am. Never anything as serious as your present concerns over your grandfather, but I've definitely had my fair share of worries over the years.'

'Things like looking in the mirror for the first grey hair and wrinkle?' she came back teasingly.

'Hair dye and botox injections,' Jaxon came back dismissively.

Her eyes widened. 'Have you ever—?'

'No, I can honestly say I've never resorted to using either one of those things!' he assured her irritably, seeing her obvious humour at his expense.

'Yet.'

'Ever,' Jaxon assured firmly. 'I'm going to live by the adage and grow old gracefully.'

Stazy knew he was teasing her—was very aware that these last few minutes they'd both been talking only for the sake of it. Delaying as they waited to see what her answer was going to be to Jaxon's offer to spend the night with her…

'Well?' Jaxon prompted huskily.

He claimed he was making the offer so that she didn't have to spend the hours before dawn alone; and God knew Stazy didn't want to *be* alone, knowing that once she was in her bedroom her imagination was going to run riot again in regard to her grandfather's safety. Did that mean she was actually thinking of *accepting* Jaxon's offer to spend the night with her…?

CHAPTER NINE

'I PREFER to sleep on the right side of the bed.'

'So do I.'

'It's my bedroom.'

'And, as your guest, don't you think I should be allowed first choice as to which side of the bed I would like to sleep on?'

'Not if my guest is a gentleman.'

As conversations before leaping into bed with a man went, this one was pretty pathetic, Stazy acknowledged self-derisively. No doubt due in part to the fact that now they were actually at the point of getting into bed she was awash with flustered embarrassment.

To a degree that she questioned which part of her brain had actually been functioning when she had accepted Jaxon's offer to spend the night in her bedroom with her. Certainly not the logical and ordered Dr Stazy Bromley part! And even the less logical, easily-aroused-by-Jaxon-Wilder, Stazy Bromley now questioned the sanity of that decision too!

It had been an impulsive decision at best, made out of a desire not to lie alone in the darkness for hours with her own worried thoughts.

Having just returned from the adjoining bathroom in a white vest top and the grey sweats she slept in, she saw the soft glow of the bedside lamp revealed that Jaxon wore only a pair of very brief black underpants that clearly outlined the enticing bulge beneath. His bare shoulders were wide and tanned, chest muscled and abdomen taut, his legs long and muscular and equally tanned, allowing Stazy to fully appreciate just how ridiculously naive that decision had been.

Especially when her clenched fingers actually itched with the need she felt to touch the fine dark hair that covered his chest before it arrowed down in an enticing vee to beneath those fitted black underpants…

'Perhaps you should go to your bedroom first and get some pyjamas…' she said doubtfully—as if Jaxon wearing pyjamas was *really* going to make her any less aware of his warmth in the bed beside her!

'That would probably be a good idea if I actually wore pyjamas.' Jaxon eyed her mockingly across the width of the double bed.

Right. Okay. Definitely time to regroup, Stazy. 'In that case you can have the right side of the bed—'

'I was just kidding about that, Stazy,' Jaxon drawled softly when she would have walked around to the side of the bed where he stood. 'The left side of the bed is fine.'

To say he had been surprised by her acceptance of his offer was putting it mildly. That only went to prove that Stazy was even more complex than he had thought she was. To the point that Jaxon had no idea what she was going to do or say next. That was very refreshing from a male point of view, but damned inconvenient when a man was only supposed to be acting as a concerned friend…

For some reason he had expected her to be wearing one of those unbecoming nightgowns that covered a woman from neck to toe when she came back from the bathroom. Instead she wore a thin white fitted top with narrow shoulder straps, clearly outlining her up-thrusting and obviously naked breasts, and in the process allowing Jaxon to see every curve and nuance of her engorged nipples, along with a pair of loose grey soft cotton trousers that rested low down on her hips and gave him the occasional glimpse of the flat curve of her stomach. The cherry on top of the cake—as if he needed one!—was that she had released the long length of her red-gold hair from its plait and it now lay in a soft and silky curtain across her shoulders and down her back.

All of them were things that were pure purgatory for any man who was expected to behave only as a friend…

He should be grateful Stazy had a double bed in her room, he supposed; just think how cosy the two of them would have been in a single bed! Even so, Jaxon was well aware of how much space he was going to take up, so it was perhaps as well that Stazy was so slender.

He quirked one dark brow as he looked across the bed at her. 'Are we going to get in and get warm, or just stand here looking at each other all night?'

Stazy drew in a slightly shaky breath. 'Perhaps your spending the night here wasn't such a good idea, after all—Oh!' She broke off as Jaxon lifted his side of the duvet before sliding in beneath it to look up at her expectantly.

'It's much warmer in here than it is out there…' he encouraged, and turned the duvet back invitingly.

Stazy wasn't sure any extra warmth was necessary. She already felt inwardly on fire, her cheeks flushed, the palms of her hands slightly damp.

Oh, for goodness' sake—

'Better,' Jaxon murmured as Stazy finally slid into the bed beside him.

She turned to look at him as she straightened the duvet over her. 'Is that a statement or a question?'

'Both,' he assured her softly, before reaching out to turn off the bedside lamp and plunge the room into darkness. His arms moved about her waist as he pulled her in to his side and gently pressed her head down onto the warmth of his shoulder.

Stazy didn't feel in the least relaxed. How could she possibly relax when she was snuggled against Jaxon's warm and almost naked body, her fingers finally able to touch the silkily soft hair on his chest as her hand lay against that hardness encased in velvet, her elbow brushing lightly against that telling bulge in his underpants?

This had *so* not been a good idea. She was never going to be able to relax, let alone—

'Just close your eyes and go to sleep, Stazy,' Jaxon instructed huskily in the darkness.

Her throat moved as she swallowed before answering him softly. 'I'm not sure that I can.'

'Close your eyes? Or go to sleep?'

'Either!'

'I could always sing you a lullaby, I suppose…'

'I didn't know you could sing…'

'I can't.' His chest vibrated against her cheek as he chuckled, then Jaxon's hand moved up to cradle the back of her head as it rested against his shoulder. He settled more comfortably into the pillows. 'This is nice.'

Nice? It was sheer heaven as far as Stazy was concerned! Decadent and illicit pleasure. A time out of time, when it felt as if only the two of them existed.

Those 'witching hours' between dusk and dawn when anything—everything!—seemed possible.

'Stop fidgeting, woman,' Jaxon instructed gruffly when she shifted restlessly beside him.

Or not, Stazy acknowledged ruefully. 'I was just getting comfortable.'

When a man wanted a woman as much as Jaxon wanted Stazy, her 'getting comfortable' could just be the last straw in the breaking of his self-control. Especially when that 'getting comfortable' involved her hair spilling silkily across his chest, the softness of her breasts pressing into his side, and the draping of one of her legs over the top of his.

Her hand rested lightly on his stomach as she snuggled closer to his warmth… 'What's that noise…?' she murmured sleepily minutes later.

'Probably my teeth grinding together.'

'Why—?'

'Will you please just go to sleep!' Jaxon's jaw was tightly clenched as he determinedly held his desire for her in check.

'I thought people were usually grouchy when they woke up in the morning, not before they've even gone to sleep…'

Jaxon had a feeling he was going to be grouchy in the morning too—probably more so than he was now, if he had been lying beside Stazy all night with a throbbing erection! Worst of all, he had brought all this on himself, damn it. 'I'll try not to disappoint,' he murmured self-derisively.

Stazy chuckled sleepily, and the evenness of her breathing a few minutes later told him that she had managed to fall asleep after all.

Leaving Jaxon awake and staring up at the ceiling

in the darkness, in the full knowledge that he wasn't going to be able to find the same release from his own self-imposed purgatory…

Arousal.

Instant.

Breathtaking.

Joyous!

'Are you awake…?' Jaxon prompted softly.

'Mmm…' Stazy kept her eyes closed as she relished the sensation of Jaxon's large and capable hands moving lightly, slowly over her and down her body, as if he intended to commit every curve and contour to memory.

Her back. The soft curve of her bottom. Skimming across her hips. The gentle slope of her waist. Her ribcage and up over her breasts. Until he cupped the side of her face, his fingertips moving lightly across the plumpness of her parted lips before running lightly down the length of her throat to dip into the hollows at its base. Those same fingers ran a light caress over her clavicle, before pushing the thin strap from her shoulder and down her arm, tugging gently on the material of her top until one plump, aroused breast popped free of its confinement.

Stazy gave a breathless gasp as she arched into that large and cupping hand, its thumb and index finger lightly rolling the engorged bud at its tip before tugging gently. Pleasure coursed through her hotly as Jaxon alternated those rhythmic caresses for several agonisingly pleasurable minutes before the hot and moist sweep of his tongue laved that throbbing nipple.

'Jaxon…!' Her eyes were wide open now, and she looked down at him in the early-morning sunlight, the darkness of his hair a tousled caress against her flesh, those grey eyes smoky with arousal as he glanced up at her. 'Please don't stop this time…!' she encouraged achingly.

One of her hands moved up to cradle the back of his head and her fingers became entangled in the overlong darkness of his hair as she held him to her.

Pleasure lit his eyes before he turned his attention back to her breast, alternately licking, biting and gently suckling, before moving across to bestow that same pleasure upon its twin.

His skin was so much darker than hers as he nudged her legs apart and moved to settle between her parted thighs, all hard muscle and sinew where her hands moved caressingly down the length of his spine. Stazy was totally aware of the long length of his arousal pressing into her as her hands dipped beneath his black underpants to cup the muscled contours of his bottom.

Jaxon's hands tightly gripped Stazy's hips as he raised his head to draw in a hissing breath. Those slender hands squeezed and caressed him, turning his body slightly, and he encouraged those hands to move to the front of his body, ceasing to breathe at all as long and slender fingers curved around his shaft and the soft pad of her thumb ran lightly over the moisture escaping its tip.

He had fallen asleep fitfully, only to wake mere hours later. Stazy had continued to sleep. His body had been hard and aching, and finally he hadn't been able to resist waking her. He had needed to touch her—just a light caress or two, he had promised himself. And so he had caressed her hips. Her stomach. Her throat.

That was when he had lost it, Jaxon acknowledged achingly. The arching of Stazy's body into that caress had been more than his control could withstand, and the pulse of his shaft grew harder as he'd suckled her greedily into his mouth.

And now, at the first touch of her fingers on him, Jaxon felt as if he was about to explode—

'Lie back, Jaxon, and let me take these off for you,' Stazy encouraged huskily, and she pushed him back against the pillows before moving up onto her knees beside him, pulling off the tangle of her top to ease her movements before sitting forward to slowly pull his black underpants down over his hips and thighs. His eyes were riveted on her naked breasts as they bobbed forward enticingly, and he groaned low in his throat as his throbbing shaft was at last allowed to jut free as she discarded his underpants completely before looking down at him with greedy eyes.

Jaxon groaned again as he saw her tongue appear between those pouting lips before moving over them moistly. If Stazy so much as touched him with those wet and pouting lips then he was going to—

'Oh, dear God…!' Jaxon's hips lifted up off the bed as Stazy lowered her head, one of her hands once again firmly grasping his shaft and the other cupping him beneath, and her lips parted widely as she took him completely into the heat of her mouth, licking, sucking, savouring…

He could smell Stazy's arousal now—a hot and musky scent that drove his own pleasure higher than ever as her tongue laved him, fingers lightly pumping, before she took him fully into her mouth and sucked him deep into the back of her throat.

It was too much—Stazy was too much!

'You have to stop. Now!' Jaxon gripped her shoulders as he pulled her up and away from him, allowing the full heaviness of his shaft to fall damply against the hardness of his stomach. 'It's my turn,' he assured her huskily as he saw the questioning disappointment in her eyes, and he laid her gently back against the pillows and moved to roll the last piece of clothing from her body, sitting back on his haunches to look down at the pearly perfection of her naked body: pale ivory skin, the fullness of her breasts tipped with those ruby-red nipples, a red-gold thatch of curls between her thighs.

His nudge was gentle as he parted her legs to kneel between her thighs and reveal her hidden beauty to him. He enjoyed Stazy's groan of pleasure as he ran the tips of his fingers over and around her sensitive bud before lowering his head to move his tongue against her, again and again, until she arched into him as he gently suckled her into his mouth.

Stazy gave a low and torturous moan as Jaxon's finger caressed and probed her moist and swollen opening before sliding gently inside her, quickly joined by a second. Those muscled walls clasped around him and he began to thrust into her with the same rhythm as his suckling mouth. Stazy arched into those thrusts, needing, wanting—

Pleasure coursed hotly, fiercely through her as she began to orgasm. There was a loud roaring sound in her ears and a kaleidoscope of coloured lights burst behind her eyelids as ecstatic release ripped through her for long, relentless minutes. Jaxon gave no quarter as he coaxed the last shuddering spasm of pleasure from her boneless and replete body before finally releasing her, to lay his head against her thigh.

That was when Stazy became aware she still had that loud roaring noise in her ears. Her eyes opened wide as she looked down at Jaxon dazedly. 'What…?'

He raised his head lazily, eyes dark, lips moist and

full. 'I'd really like to take credit for being the cause of that phenomena, but I'm afraid I can't,' he murmured ruefully.

Stazy looked about the bedroom dazedly, completely disorientated—both by the satiated weakness she felt following the fierceness of her first ever orgasm, and by that loud, inexplicable roaring in her ears.

Her gaze returned to Jaxon when she could find no possible reason for that noise in the neatness of her bedroom. 'What is it?' she breathed huskily.

Jaxon had a feeling he knew exactly what it was. *Who* it was. Just as he knew it was a presence guaranteed to wipe away that look of satiation from the relaxed beauty of Stazy's face!

He gave Stazy's naked and satisfied body one last regretful glance before levering up onto his elbows and knees and crawling off the end of the bed to stroll over to the window. He twitched aside one of the curtains to look down on to the manicured lawn below.

'Yep, I was afraid of that.' He grimaced, letting the curtain fall back into place as he turned back to where Stazy now sat on the side of the bed, looking across at him with wide, still slightly dazed eyes.

'Afraid of what?' She gave a puzzled shake of her head.

Jaxon drew in a heavy breath before answering her. 'It's your grandfather. He's just arrived by helicopter,' he added, as Stazy still looked completely dazed.

Her eyes widened in alarm. 'He— I— You— We—' She threw back the bedclothes to stand up abruptly, completely unconcerned by her nakedness—and Jaxon's, regrettably!—as she hurried across the room to pull one of the curtains aside for herself. 'Oh, dear Lord…!' she groaned, obviously in a complete panic as she quickly dropped the curtain back over the window and turned to grasp Jaxon's arm. 'We have to get dressed! No—first you need to go back to your own bedroom!' She released his arm to commence frantically gathering his discarded clothes up off the carpet, before screwing them up into a bundle and shoving them at his chest. 'You need to take these with you—'

'Will you just calm down, Stazy?' Jaxon took the clothes from her and placed them on the bedside chair, before reaching out to grasp both her arms and shake her gently. 'You're twenty-nine years old, for goodness' sake—'

'And that's my grandfather out there!' Her eyes had taken on a hunted look.

'We haven't done anything wrong,' he said soothingly.

'If this were my apartment, or a hotel, then I would be inclined to agree with you—but this is *Gramps'* home!' She was breathing hard in her agitation, her face white against the deep green of her eyes as she hurried through to the adjoining bathroom to return with her robe seconds later.

'Stazy, I very much doubt that the first thing Geoffrey is going to do when he enters the house is come up to your bedroom to see if by some chance we might have spent the night together in his absence—'

'Please don't argue any more—just go, Jaxon!' She looked up at him pleadingly after tying the belt to her robe.

'I have every intention of going back to my own bedroom, Stazy,' he assured gruffly. 'But I think I should dress first, don't you? Rather than risk bumping into your grandfather or one of the household staff in the hallway when I'm completely naked…?'

He had a point, Stazy accepted with a pained wince. She hadn't expected— It hadn't even occurred to her— She hadn't been thinking clearly at all last night when she had agreed to Jaxon's coming to her bedroom and spending the night with her!

And her explanation—her excuse for what had happened with Jaxon this morning…?

She didn't have one. At least not one that she wanted to think about right now. She couldn't think at all now—not with her grandfather about to enter Bromley House!

'Nor,' Jaxon continued grimly, 'do I find it in the least acceptable to sneak out of your bedroom like a naughty schoolboy caught in the act!'

Stazy winced at the obvious displeasure in his tone. 'I wasn't implying that—'

'No?' He turned away to sort impatiently through the pile of clothes on the bedroom chair, giving Stazy a breathtaking view of the bare length of his back and the tautness of his buttocks as he pulled on those fitted black underpants. 'It seems to me that's exactly what you're implying.' His expression was bleak as he unhurriedly pulled on the rest of his clothes before sitting down on the side of the bed to lace his shoes.

'Look, we can talk about this later, Jaxon—?'

'What is there to talk about?' He stood up, towering over Stazy as she stood barefoot in front of him. 'In my profession I've learnt that actions invariably speak louder than words, Stazy,' he bit out harshly. 'And your actions, your haste to get rid of me, tell me that you regret what just happened—'

'And *you're* behaving like that ridiculous schoolboy—' She broke off as she saw the thunderous darkness of Jaxon's frown. His eyes were a pale and glittering grey as he looked down the length of his nose at her, a nerve pulsed in his tightly clenched jaw.

'Just forget it, Stazy,' he bit out bleakly.

Forget it? Forget that amazing, wonderful lovemaking? Forget that she had wanted Jaxon enough, trusted him enough, to share her first ever orgasm with him...?

That alone was enough to tell Stazy how inconsequential her two sexual experiences had been. Just how much of herself she had held back from those other men...

Just now, with Jaxon, she had been completely open. The barriers that she had kept erected about her emotions for so many years had come crashing down around her ears as she gave herself up completely to the pleasure of Jaxon's lips and hands on her body.

Meaning what, exactly?

She couldn't actually have come to *care* for Jaxon over these past few days alone with him, could she?

And by care, did she mean—?

No!

She wasn't going there!

Not now.

Not ever!

Jaxon was an accomplished and experienced lover—a man used to making a conquest of any woman he went to bed with. Those were the reasons—the only reasons!—for her own loss of control just now.

Her chin rose proudly. 'Fine, then I guess we won't talk later,' she said dismissively.

Jaxon looked down at Stazy from between narrowed lids, wishing he knew what thoughts had been going through her head during those few minutes of silence, but as usual her closed expression revealed none of her inner emotions to him.

He probably shouldn't have been so annoyed with her just now. No—he *definitely* shouldn't have been annoyed with her just now! His only excuse was that it had been irritating, galling, to be made to feel like a guilty indiscretion as far as Stazy was concerned—especially when he could still feel the silkiness of her skin against his hands and taste her on his lips and tongue. When he was aware that he was starting to care for her in a way he had never imagined when they had met six weeks ago…

'I really think you should go now, Jaxon.' Stazy backed away from the hand he had raised with the intention of reaching out and caressing her cheek.

Jaxon's hand dropped back to his side and he looked down at her searchingly for several long seconds before nodding abruptly. 'But we will talk about this again before I leave here,' he promised softly, his gaze intent, before he turned on his heel and crossed to the door, letting himself quietly out of the room.

Stazy felt awash with regret as she watched Jaxon close the bedroom door behind him as he left, having to bite down painfully on her bottom lip to stop herself from calling out to prevent him from going.

What would be the point of stopping him? Their lovemaking, her pleasure, might have been life-altering for her, but as far as Jaxon was concerned she had merely been another sexual interlude in his life…

CHAPTER TEN

'AND that, I'm afraid, is my reason for not telling you both yesterday evening that I was actually in hospital, having stitches put in my arm, when I spoke to you on the telephone.' Geoffrey concluded his explanation ruefully as he turned from where Jaxon stood in front of one of the bay windows in the drawing room to look concernedly at his still and silent granddaughter as she sat in the armchair opposite near the unlit fireplace.

It was an explanation Jaxon thought worthy of one of the dozens of film scripts presented to him every year!

Death threats from an unknown assassin. Gunshots in the night. The apprehension and arrest of a gunman by the security men who had been guarding Geoffrey in London. A gunman, it transpired, who held an old and personal grudge against Geoffrey, but had been unaware of exactly how and where to find him until he had seen and read that appalling biography on Anastasia published the previous year.

'You were shot at…?' Stazy was the one to break the silence, deathly white as she sat unmoving in the armchair.

Her grandfather looked down at the sling on his right arm. 'It's only a flesh wound.'

Stazy stood up abruptly. 'Someone actually shot you

and you chose not to tell me about it?' She still found it unbelievable her grandfather could have done such a thing. Or, in this case, *not* done such a thing!

Absolutely unbelievable!

'Well...yes.' Geoffrey gave a regretful wince. 'I didn't want to alarm you—'

'You didn't want to alarm me...!' Stazy breathed hard as she looked down at her grandfather incredulously. 'I don't believe you, Gramps!' she finally snapped exasperatedly. 'Some unknown man has been stalking you—only you!—for days now, he finally succeeded in managing to shoot you, and you decided not to tell me about it because you didn't want to *alarm* me!'

The same night she had spent in Jaxon's arms...

'I did tell you of a threat—'

'But not to you personally.'

'No, but—'

'Admit it, Gramps, you lied to me!' she accused emotionally, her cheeks burning.

'Stazy—'

'Don't even attempt to offer excuses for his behaviour, Jaxon,' she warned hotly when he would have interceded. 'There are no excuses. I was worried to death about you, Gramps.' She rounded back on her grandfather.

'Telling you I had been shot would only have worried you even more—'

'I'm not sure that was even possible!' She gave an exasperated shake of her head. 'I'm sorry, but if I stay here any longer then I'm going to say something I'll really regret. If you will both excuse me?' She didn't wait for either man to answer before rushing from the room.

'Well, that didn't go too well, did it?' Geoffrey

murmured ruefully as the door slammed behind Stazy with barely controlled violence.

'Not too well, no,' Jaxon confirmed dryly as he turned back from admiring how beautiful Stazy had looked as she left the room. That red-gold hair had seemed to crackle with electricity, her eyes had glittered like emeralds, her creamy cheeks had been flushed. The cream silk blouse and close-fitting denims she was wearing today weren't too hard on the eye either!

'Why doesn't she understand that I was only trying to protect her by not telling her the truth until the whole thing was over and done with?' the older man asked in obvious frustration.

Jaxon grimaced as he stepped further into the room, having deemed it safer to stand a little removed while granddaughter and grandfather confronted each other. 'I may be wrong, but I believe Stazy considers herself to be a little old to still be in need of that sort of protection from you or anyone else.'

'And what do you think I could have done differently in the circumstances?' Geoffrey frowned up at him.

Jaxon gave a rueful smile. 'I'm the last person you should be asking about how best to deal with Stazy.'

'Indeed?' Geoffrey's gaze sharpened speculatively.

'Oh, yes!' he said with feeling.

'Does that mean the two of you are still at loggerheads?' the older man frowned again.

Jaxon wasn't sure how his relationship with Stazy stood at this precise moment. Last night she had allowed him to comfort her. This morning they had almost made love to each other. Before having the most god-awful row when Geoffrey had arrived so unexpectedly!

No, Jaxon had no idea how Stazy felt towards him now.

Any more than he knew what to make of his feelings for her…

It had been both heaven and hell to hold Stazy in his arms all night long, and sheer unadulterated pleasure to be with her this morning.

Knowing how Stazy liked to keep her life compartmentalised and Jaxon didn't, the argument that had followed had perhaps been predictable—but that didn't stop it from being frustrating as hell as far as Jaxon was concerned.

Where the two of them went from here—if they went anywhere—Jaxon had absolutely no idea.

'More or less, yes,' he answered the older man abruptly.

'Do I want to know how much more or how much less…?' Geoffrey prompted softly.

Jaxon gave the question some thought. 'Probably not,' he finally answered carefully.

The other man looked at him searchingly for several long seconds before giving a slow nod of his head. 'Okay. So, do you think Stazy will ever forgive me…?'

Probably a lot more quickly than she was going to forgive Jaxon—if she ever did forgive him! 'I think it might be a good idea if you give her some time to—well, to calm down before attempting to talk to her again,' he advised ruefully.

'And in the meantime…?'

'I have absolutely no idea *what* you do in the meantime.' Jaxon grimaced. 'But now that security here has been lifted I intend to change into my leathers and go out for a ride on the Harley,' he said decisively.

'I'd ask to join you, but I think that might push Stazy into disowning me completely!' Geoffrey chuckled wryly.

'There's no "might" about it!' Jaxon assured him.

The older man nodded slowly. 'Let's hope she decides to forgive me very soon.'

It was a hope Jaxon echoed…

Stazy stood with her forehead pressed against the coolness of her bedroom window, looking outside as the Harley roared off down the gravel driveway with a leather-clad Jaxon seated on the back of it, the black helmet once again covering his almost shoulder-length hair and the smoky visor lowered over his face. Although it wasn't too difficult for her to imagine the grimness of his expression!

Was Jaxon leaving for good? Or had he just gone out for a drive now that there was no longer a reason for them to be confined to Bromley House?

Not that Stazy could altogether blame Jaxon if he *had* decided to leave. A part of her knew she would have to leave too. And soon. She longed for the peace and solitude of her apartment in London, desperately needed to be alone for a while—if only so that she could lick her wounds in private. At the same time she knew she couldn't leave here until things were less strained between herself and her grandfather.

How could he have lied to her in that way? Oh, she could appreciate the reason her grandfather had thought he should skirt around the truth, but that didn't mean Stazy had to be in the least understanding about his having so blatantly lied to her at the end.

Especially when those lies had resulted in her spending the night with Jaxon…

Damn it, spending the night with Jaxon hadn't been the problem—it had been waking up in his arms this morning and the things that had followed that made her cringe with embarrassment every time she so much as thought about it! Which had been often during the half an hour or so she had spent in her bedroom.

Thankfully the maid had been up to Stazy's bedroom during her absence downstairs, so the bed had been neatly remade and the room tidied by the time she returned from talking with her grandfather. Unfortunately, as Stazy had crossed the bedroom to take her suitcase out of the wardrobe and place it on top of the bed, that neatness had done very little to stop her from remembering each and every detail of what had happened here between herself and Jaxon…

The joy of kissing and caressing him. The pleasure of being kissed and caressed *by* him. The unimagined ecstasy of the mind-blowing orgasm he had so easily taken her to…

Even now Stazy could feel the ultra-sensitivity between her legs in the aftermath of her orgasm. Her first ever orgasm…

And her last if it resulted in her not only feeling physically vulnerable but emotionally too!

Although Jaxon's abrupt departure—without that promised talk between the two of them—would seem to imply that he had no interest in furthering a relationship between the two of them, so—

'May I come in…?'

Stazy looked up sharply at the sound of her grandfather's cajoling voice. 'That depends on whether or not you're going to lie to me again.' She raised censorious brows.

He gave a self-conscious wince as he stood in the open doorway. 'I have explained the reason for that, darling.'

She nodded abruptly. 'And it was a completely

unacceptable explanation. I'm no longer a child you need to protect from the truth, Gramps!'

'So Jaxon has already pointed out to me,' Geoffrey acknowledged heavily.

Stazy stiffened defensively just at hearing Jaxon's name, let alone wondering in what context he might have made that remark. 'Was that before or after he left on his Harley?'

'Obviously before.' Her grandfather grimaced before glancing at the open suitcase sitting on top of her bed. 'What's going on, Stazy…?'

She drew in a deep breath even as she gave a dismissive shrug. 'I thought I might leave too, later this afternoon.'

His gaze sharpened. 'Leave? But—'

'You've said yourself that the danger is over now and your wound isn't serious,' Stazy interrupted firmly. 'And now that Jaxon has left there seems little point in my not joining the dig in Iraq as originally planned.'

The fact that she had taken out her suitcase before she even saw Jaxon leave wasn't something her grandfather needed to know! Even if Jaxon hadn't decided to leave, how could she possibly stay on at Bromley House after the events of earlier this morning? There was no way she could continue calmly working on the details for the screenplay with Jaxon as if nothing had happened between them.

Stazy was extremely reluctant to delve too deeply into her own emotions and find out exactly what that 'something' meant to her…

'Jaxon hasn't left completely, darling. He's just gone for a ride on his motorbike after being confined here for the past few days,' her grandfather told her gently.

'Oh.' Stazy felt the colour drain from her cheeks.

Geoffrey gave her a searching glance. 'Is there something you want to tell me, darling…?'

The very last thing Stazy wanted to do was to confide in her grandfather about making love with Jaxon this morning! There was no way she could tell another man of the intimacies she and Jaxon had shared, and there wasn't the remotest possibility of her ever talking to anyone about how those intimacies had resulted in her first ever earth-shattering orgasm!

Although she might not have any choice if, as her grandfather said, Jaxon had only gone for a ride on his motorbike and intended returning to Bromley House later this morning…

'No, nothing,' she answered her grandfather abruptly as she carefully avoided meeting his piercing blue gaze. 'As Jaxon isn't here at the moment I think I might follow his example and go out—go for a run along the beach,' she added lightly. 'We can discuss later whether or not there's any point in our bothering to continue with the research.'

Her grandfather looked puzzled. 'What do you mean?'

Stazy shrugged. 'You said the unauthorised biography on Granny was the reason this man from the past was able to track you down, so just think how much more exposed you will be if Jaxon goes ahead with the making of his film.'

'There is even more reason now for Jaxon to make his film, darling,' Geoffrey insisted firmly. 'Don't you see. It's the only way to dispel the myth and show Anastasia for the true heroine that she was,' he added when she still looked unconvinced.

Yes, Stazy did see the logic of that. Unfortunately. She had just been clinging to the hope—the slim hope, admittedly—that this recent scare might result in her grandfather rethinking his decision.

She gave an impatient shake of her head. 'As I said, we can all talk about this later—when Jaxon has returned from his ride and I've been for my run.'

Geoffrey nodded slowly. 'That would seem to be the best idea.' He turned to leave before turning back again. 'Are you and Jaxon still able to continue working together…?' he prompted shrewdly.

Stazy felt the colour warm her cheeks. Surely Jaxon hadn't—? No, of course he wouldn't. 'I can't see any reason why not, can you?' she dismissed lightly.

Her grandfather shrugged. 'You both seem more than a little edgy this morning…'

'Is that surprising when we've been cooped up here together for two days?'

And nights... Let's not forget the nights!

As if Stazy ever could…

'Geoffrey has gone to his bedroom to rest for a while.'

Stazy looked up from where she sat in the library, reading one of her grandmother's diaries. Well… 'reading' was something of a misnomer; even she knew she had only been giving the appearance of doing so. Because inwardly her thoughts and emotions were so churned up Stazy couldn't have concentrated on absorbing any of her grandmother's entries if her life had depended upon it!

Sitting down to eat lunch with her grandfather and Jaxon earlier had been something of an ordeal—so much so that Stazy had finally excused herself after eating none of the first course and proceeding only to pick at the main course for ten minutes or so, leaving the two men at the table to continue talking as she hurried from the room with the intention of escaping to the library.

She and Jaxon hadn't so much as exchanged a word during the whole of that excruciatingly awkward meal. That wasn't to say Stazy hadn't been completely aware of him as the three of them had sat at the small round table where she and Jaxon had eaten dinner together alone the past two evenings.

In the same room where Stazy had wrapped her legs around Jaxon's waist as he had pressed her up against the china cabinet and kissed her…

Her expression was guarded now as she looked across the room at him. 'Rest is probably the best thing for him.'

And what, Jaxon wondered as he came into the room and quietly closed the door behind him, did Stazy consider was the best thing for the two of *them*?

Logic said they should talk about what had happened between them this morning. Emotion told him that Stazy's feelings were so strung out at the moment that even to broach that conversation would only result in another meltdown—something she definitely wouldn't thank him for.

Because the two of them had spent the night in the same bed? Because of the intimacies they had shared with each other this morning? Stazy bitterly regretting the lapse?

Jaxon would like to think that wasn't the reason, but he still smarted at the way she had tried to push him out of the bedroom before anyone discovered him there. Admittedly, her grandfather had just flown in by helicopter, but even so…

Jaxon had had plenty of time to think things over during his long ride earlier. He had come to know Stazy much better these past three days, and knew without being told that with hindsight she would view her uninhibited response to him this morning as a weakness. A weakness she had no intention of repeating…

His mouth thinned and his lids narrowed as she seemed to recoil against the back of her chair when he crossed the room in long, silent strides. He looked down at her frustratedly. 'Do you want me to make my excuses to Geoffrey and tell him that I have to leave unexpectedly?'

Her face was expressionless as she returned his gaze. 'Why on earth would I want to you to do that?'

'Maybe because you obviously can't stand even being in the same room with me any longer?' he reasoned heavily.

'Don't be ridiculous, Jaxon,' Stazy dismissed scathingly, inwardly knowing he was being nothing of the kind; she *did* find being in the same room with him totally overwhelming. The intimacies the two of them had shared this morning made it difficult for her even to look at him without remembering exactly where and how his lips and tongue had pleasured her this morning…

'I don't understand you, Stazy,' he bit out bleakly. 'We're two consenting adults who chose to—'

'I know exactly what we did, Jaxon!' She stood up so suddenly that her chair tipped over backwards and crashed against one of the bookcases. 'Damn. Damn, damn, *damn*!' she muttered impatiently as she bent to set the chair back onto its four legs before glaring up at him. 'I don't want to talk about this now, Jaxon—'

'Will you ever want to talk about it?'

She gave a self-conscious shiver. 'Preferably not!'

Jaxon breathed hard. 'You're behaving like some outraged innocent that I robbed of her virginity!'

Maybe. Because in every way that mattered that was exactly how Stazy felt…

She had been completely in control of the situation when she had chosen her previous two lovers so carefully. And she had been physically in control too. The loss of her virginity to her university lecturer had been perfunctory at best, the second experience four years ago even more so.

The rawness, the sheer carnality of Jaxon's love-making this morning, hadn't allowed her to keep any of those barriers in place. He had stripped her down, emotionally as well as physically, and in doing so had sent all her barriers crashing to the floor, leaving her feeling vulnerable and exposed.

Oh, she didn't believe Jaxon had deliberately set out to do that to her. In fact she was sure that he had no idea of exactly what he had done. But, whether Jaxon knew it or not, that was exactly what had happened. And Stazy needed space and time in order to rebuild those emotional barriers.

She forced herself to relax, and her expression was coolly dismissive as she looked up at him. 'Is it being an actor that makes you so melodramatic, Jaxon?' she drawled derisively.

'It isn't a question of melodrama—'

'Of course it is,' she said easily. 'You're reading things into this situation that simply aren't there. Yes, our behaviour this morning makes it a little awkward for us to continue working together, but—as I assured my grandfather earlier—I'm more than willing to do my part so that we finish the research as quickly as possible. After which time we can both get back to our own totally different lives.' She looked up at him challengingly.

At this moment the only thing Jaxon felt more than willing to do was carry out his threat to put Stazy over his knee and spank some sense into her! Or at least spank her until there was a return of the warm and sensual Stazy he had been with this morning!

Not going to happen any time soon, he acknowledged as he recognised the same cool detachment in her expression that had been there when they'd first met just over six weeks ago.

'Shall we get on…?' She pulled her chair out and resumed her seat at the table before looking up at him expectantly.

Jaxon looked down at her exasperatedly. He felt the return of all his earlier frustrations with this situation, appreciating how it had all seemed so much simpler when he'd been riding the country roads on the back of the Harley.

Obviously, he had reasoned, Stazy had been understandably dismayed by the unexpected arrival of her grandfather. But once she got over her surprise Jaxon was sure the two of them would be able to sit down and talk about the situation like the two rational human beings that they were.

Somewhere in all that thinking Jaxon had forgotten to take into account that Stazy as a rational human being could also be extremely annoying!

To the point where he now felt more like wringing her delicate little neck than attempting to talk with her rationally!

Had he ever met a more frustrating woman?

Or a more sensually satisfying one…?

Jaxon had made love with dozens of women during

the past fifteen years, but he knew that none of them had aroused him to the fever pitch that Stazy had this morning. To the point where he had been teetering dangerously on the edge just from the touch of her lips and fingers—

That way lies madness, old chum, he told himself as he felt himself hardening again, just at thinking about having Stazy's lips and tongue on him there. *Total insanity!*

'Fine, if you're sure that's the way you want it,' he bit out tersely, and he moved to sit in the chair opposite hers.

It wasn't the way Stazy wanted it at all. It was the way she knew it had to be. For both their sakes…

CHAPTER ELEVEN

'SO. THE work's done, and we can both leave here later this morning…' Stazy kept her tone deliberately light as she looked across the breakfast table from beneath lowered lashes as Jaxon relaxed back in his chair, enjoying his second cup of coffee after eating what could only be described as a hearty breakfast. Unlike Stazy, who had only managed to pull a croissant apart as she drank her own cup of morning coffee.

No, that probably wasn't the best way to describe Jaxon this morning—after all, it was the condemned man who ate a hearty breakfast, and on the morning of his departure from Bromley House Jaxon appeared anything but that!

It had been a long and stressful week as far as Stazy was concerned, with the long hours she had spent alone with Jaxon in the library by far the biggest strain. But only for Stazy, it seemed. Jaxon, when he hadn't been secluded in the study with her grandfather, had been brisk and businesslike in her company, with not even a hint of a mention of the night they had spent together, let alone that conversation he had seemed so intent on the two of them having five days ago.

Her grandfather's return to London late yesterday

evening hadn't brought about any change in Jaxon's distant manner either.

Had she wanted it to make a difference?

Stazy had no idea what she wanted, except she knew she found this strained politeness extremely unsettling!

Jaxon shrugged the broadness of his shoulders in the dark grey tee shirt he wore with faded blue denims. The heavy biker boots were already on his feet in preparation for his departure. 'It's over for you, certainly, but the real work for me—the writing of the screenplay—is only just beginning.' He smiled ruefully.

Stazy's heart did a little lurch in her chest just at the sight of that smile after days of strained politeness. 'Can you do that while working on the pirate movie?'

He raised a dark brow. 'I appreciate it's a common belief amongst ladies that men can only concentrate on one thing at a time, but I assure you it's just a myth!'

Stazy felt warmth in her cheeks at the rebuke. 'I meant timewise, not mentally.'

'I'll cope,' Jaxon drawled as he studied her from between narrowed lids.

Was it his imagination, or did the fine delicacy of Stazy's features appear sharper than a week ago? Her cheekbones and the curve of her chin more defined, with dark shadows beneath those mesmerising green eyes?

Or was he just hoping that was the case? Hoping that Stazy had found the time the two of them had spent alone together these last five days as much of a strain as he had?

If he was, then he was surely only deluding himself—because there had certainly seemed to be no sign of that in her cool and impersonal manner towards him these past few days as the two of them had continued to work together on Anastasia's papers and diaries. *Frosty* had best described Stazy's attitude towards him. In fact this was the first even remotely personal conversation they'd had in days. At five days, to be exact…

'When do you expect to have finished writing the screenplay?'

'Why do you want to know?' Jaxon gave a derisive smile. 'So that you can make sure you're nowhere near if I should need to discuss it with Geoffrey?'

A frown appeared on her creamy brow. 'I was merely attempting to make polite conversation, Jaxon…'

Jaxon had had it up to here with Stazy's politeness! He stood up abruptly to move across the room and stare out of the window, the tightness of his jaw and the clenching of his hands evidence of his inner frustration. 'As we're both leaving here this morning, don't you think you should start saying what you really mean?' he ground out harshly.

Stazy watched him warily, sensing that the time for politeness between them was over. 'I thought, for my grandfather's sake at least, that the two of us should at least try to part as friends—'

'Friends!' Jaxon turned to look at her incredulously. 'You can't be so naive as to believe the two of us can ever be *friends*!' he bit out scornfully.

She knew that, of course. But nevertheless it was painful to actually hear Jaxon state it so dismissively.

'Friends are at ease in each other's company,' he continued remorselessly. 'They actually enjoy being together. And that certainly doesn't describe the two of us, now, does it?'

Stazy clasped her hands together beneath the table so that Jaxon wouldn't see how much they were trembling. 'I'm sorry you feel that way—'

'No, you're not,' he contradicted scathingly. 'You've wanted me to feel this way. Damn it, you've done everything in your power to push me away!'

She shook her head in denial. 'It was what you wanted too—'

'You have absolutely no idea what I want!' he rasped, grey eyes glacial.

'You're right. I don't.' She swallowed hard, her expression pained. 'Nor is there any point in the two of us discussing any of this when we will both be leaving in a few hours' time.'

'I'm not waiting a couple of hours, Stazy.' He gave a disgusted shake of his head. 'My bag is already packed, and I have every intention of leaving as soon as we've finished this conversation,' he assured her hardly.

He spoke as if he couldn't tolerate being in her company another moment longer than he had to, Stazy realised. It was a realisation that hurt her more than she would ever have believed possible…

Her chin rose proudly. 'Then consider it over.'

Jaxon stared at Stazy in frustration, knowing he wanted to shake her at the same time as he wanted to pull her up into his arms and kiss her senseless.

Where the hell was the vulnerable woman he had held in his arms all night long because she had been so worried about her grandfather? The same warm and sensuous woman who had responded so heatedly to his lovemaking the following morning?

Did that woman even exist or was she just a figment of his imagination…?

Jaxon had found himself wondering that same thing often when, time and time again, day after day, he had been presented with that brick wall Stazy had built so sturdily about her emotions.

And now, the morning of his departure, when he might never see Stazy again, really wasn't the time for him to try to breach those walls one last time…

He nodded abruptly. 'In that case…I hope you enjoy your trip to Iraq.'

Stazy no longer had any real interest in going on the dig she had once looked forward to with such professional excitement. No longer had any real interest in doing *anything* with the rest of her summer break now that the time had come to say goodbye to Jaxon… Which was ridiculous. He had no place in her life—had made it perfectly clear during these last few minutes that he didn't *want* a place in her life! So why should just the thought of Jaxon leaving, the possibility of never seeing him again, have opened up a void inside her she had no idea how to fill?

It shouldn't. Unless—

No…!

Stazy stopped breathing even as she felt the colour draining from her cheeks. She couldn't possibly have fallen in love with Jaxon this past week?

Could she…?

The threatening tears and the deep well of emptiness inside her just at the thought of never seeing him again after today told her that was exactly what she had done…

Had she ever done anything this stupid in her life before? Could there *be* anything more stupid than Dr Stazy Bromley, lecturer in Archaeology, falling in love with Jaxon Wilder, A-list Hollywood actor and director? If there was then Stazy couldn't think of what that something could possibly be!

The best Jaxon could think of her was that she had been a temporary and no doubt annoying distraction while he'd been stuck in the depths of Hampshire for a week doing research. She didn't even want to dwell on the worst Jaxon could think of her…!

She swallowed before speaking. 'I wish you an uneventful flight back to America.'

He gave a rueful shake of his head. 'It seems we've managed to achieve politeness this morning, after all!'

And if that politeness didn't soon cease Stazy very much feared she might make a complete fool of herself by giving in to the tears stinging the backs of her eyes. She stood up abruptly. 'If you'll excuse me? I have to go upstairs and finish packing.'

No, Jaxon *didn't* excuse her—either from the room, or from instigating the strained tension that had existed between the two of them these past five days. If it hadn't been for the buffer of Geoffrey's presence then Jaxon knew, research or not, he would have had no choice but to leave days ago.

Damn it, what did it take to get through—and stay through!—that wall of reserve Stazy kept about her emotions? Whatever it was, he obviously didn't have it…

He breathed his frustration. 'Will you attend the English premiere with your grandfather when the time comes?'

She blinked. 'Isn't it a little early to be discussing the premiere of a film that hasn't even been written, yet let alone made…?'

Probably—when the earliest it was likely to happen was the end of next year, more likely much later than that. Jaxon had arranged his work schedule so that he could begin filming *Butterfly* in the spring of next year, and after that there would be weeks of editing. No, the premiere wouldn't be for another eighteen months or so.

And there was no guarantee that Stazy would attend…

Did it really matter whether or not she went to the premiere? At best the two of them would meet as polite strangers, if only for her grandfather's sake. At worst they wouldn't acknowledge each other at all other than perhaps a terse nod of the head.

And that wasn't good enough, damn it!

'Stazy, I don't have to go back to the States for several more days yet if…'

'Yes?' she prompted sharply.

He shrugged. 'We could always go away somewhere together for a couple of days.'

Stazy eyed him warily. 'For what purpose?'

'For the purpose of just spending time alone together, perhaps?' he bit out impatiently. 'Something that's been impossible to do since your grandfather arrived back so unexpectedly.'

'Oh, I believe we've spent more than enough time alone together already, Jaxon!' she assured him ruefully.

He scowled darkly at her coolness. 'What have you done with that night we spent together, Stazy? Filed it away in the back of your mind under "miscellaneous", or just decided to forget it altogether?'

Stazy flinched at the scorn underlying Jaxon's tone. As if she could *ever* forget that night in Jaxon's arms! Or what had happened the following morning.

Or the fact that she had fallen in love with him…

A love Jaxon didn't return and never could. A love she wasn't sure she could hide if, as Jaxon suggested, they were to spend several more days—and nights!—alone together.

Even if she did feel tempted by the suggestion. More than tempted!

To spend time alone with Jaxon away from here, to make love with him again, would be—

Both heaven and hell when she knew full well that at the end of those few days he would return to his life and she to hers!

Stazy feigned irritation. 'Why do you persist in referring back to that night, Jaxon, when you've no doubt filed it away it your own head under "satisfactory, but could do better"?'

His eyes narrowed to glittering slits of silver. 'Are you talking about my performance or your own?'

Oh, her own—definitely. Twenty-nine years old, with two—no—three lovers now to her name. Two of which had definitely been less than satisfactory, and the third—Jaxon himself—who had shown her a sensuality within herself she had never dreamt existed. A sensuality that she knew she would drown in if she spent any time alone in Jaxon's company.

'Oh, don't worry, Jaxon. If anyone ever asks I'll assure them you performed beautifully!' she told him scornfully.

His nostrils flared. 'Stop twisting my words, damn it—'

'What do you want from me, Jaxon?' She gazed across at him exasperatedly. 'Yes, we spent a single night together, but we certainly don't have to compound the mistake by repeating it.'

He became very still. 'That's how you think of it—as a mistake?'

Her brows rose. 'Don't you?'

'I have no idea what the hell that night—and that

morning!—was all about,' he rasped impatiently. 'But no doubt you do…?' he prompted hardly.

Stazy shrugged. 'The result of a healthy man and woman having shared the same bed for the night. I'm sure I'm not the first woman you've spent the night with, Jaxon, nor will I be the last!'

He gave a humourless laugh. 'You really don't have a very high opinion of me, do you?'

She very much doubted that Jaxon wanted to know what she really thought of him. That he was not only the most heartbreakingly gorgeous man she had ever met—as well as the sexiest!—but also one of the kindest and gentlest. It had been that kindness and gentleness that had prompted him to spend the night in her bed so that she wouldn't be alone with her fears for her grandfather. The same kindness and gentleness that she now had every reason to believe would ensure he wrote Anastasia's story with the sensitivity with which it should be written.

'It's probably best if you don't answer that, if it's taking you this long to think of something polite to say,' Jaxon bit out impatiently, and he crossed forcefully to the door.

'Jaxon—!'

'Yes?' He was frowning darkly as he turned.

Stazy stared at him, not knowing what to say. Not knowing why she had called out to him—except she couldn't bear the thought of the two of them parting in this strained way. Couldn't bear the thought of the two of them parting at all! 'I never thanked you,' she finally murmured inadequately.

'For what?'

'For—for being there for me when I—when I needed you to be.' She gave a pained frown.

Jaxon stared across at her, having no idea what he should do or say next. Or if he should do or say anything when Stazy had made it so absolutely clear she wanted nothing more to do with him on a personal level.

He had thought of her, of the night the two of them spent together, far too often these past five days. And of what had happened between them the following morning. The woman Stazy had been that morning, the warm and sensual woman who had set fire to his self-control, had been nowhere in evidence in the days since. But Jaxon knew she was still in there somewhere. She had to be. That was why he had suggested the two of them go away together for a couple of days—away from Bromley House and the restraints her grandfather's presence had put on them. A suggestion Stazy had not only turned down, but in such a way she had succeeded in insulting him again into the bargain.

He straightened. 'Forget about it. I would have done the same for anyone.'

'Yes, you would.' She gave a tight, acknowledging smile.

Jaxon nodded abruptly. 'Your grandfather has my mobile and home telephone numbers if you should need to contact me.'

She frowned. 'Why would I ever need to do that…?'

No reason that Jaxon could think of! Nevertheless, it would have been nice to think there was the possibility of unexpectedly hearing the sound of Stazy's voice one day on the other end of the telephone…

This had to be the longest goodbye on record!

Probably because he wasn't ready to say goodbye to Stazy yet—still felt as if there was unfinished business between the two of them. A feeling she obviously didn't share…

Jaxon forced himself to relax the tension from his shoulders. 'No reason whatsoever,' he answered self-derisively. 'I'll go up and get my things now, and leave you to go and pack.'

'Yes.' The painful squeezing of Stazy's heart was threatening to overwhelm her. Not yet. Please, God, don't let her break down yet!

'I'll look forward to reading the screenplay.'

He raised mocking brows. 'Will you?'

'Yes,' she confirmed huskily.

He nodded briskly. ''Bye.'

Stazy had to literally drag the breath into her lungs in order to be able to answer him. ''Bye.'

Jaxon gave her one last, lingering glance before opening the door and letting himself out of the room, closing the door quietly behind him.

Stazy listened to the sound of his heavy boots crossing the hallway and going up the stairs before allowing the hot tears to cascade unchecked down her cheeks as she began to sob as if her heart was breaking.

Which it was…

CHAPTER TWELVE

Three months later.

'I HAD lunch with Jaxon today.'

Stazy was so startled by her grandfather's sudden announcement at a table in his favourite restaurant in London that the knife she had been using to eat the grilled sole she had ordered for her main course slipped unnoticed from her numbed fingers and fell noisily onto the tiled floor. Even then Stazy was only barely aware of a waiter rushing over to present her with a clean knife before he picked up the used one and left again.

Not only was Jaxon in London, but her grandfather had seen him earlier today…

After three months of thinking about Jaxon constantly—often dreaming about him too—it was incredible to learn that he was actually in London…

She moistened suddenly dry lips. 'I had no idea he was even in England…'

'He arrived yesterday,' her grandfather replied. He was now fully recovered from the gunshot wound and back to his normal robust self.

That was more than could be said for Stazy!

Oh, it had been a positive three months as far as her work was concerned. The dig in Iraq had been very successful. And when she'd returned to the university campus last month she had officially been offered the job as Head of Department when the present head retired next year. She hadn't given her answer yet but, having worked towards this very thing for the past eleven years, there seemed little doubt that she would accept the position.

No, on a professional level things couldn't have been better. It was on a personal level that Stazy knew she wasn't doing so well…

A part of her had hoped that time and distance would help to lessen the intensity of the feelings—the love—she felt for Jaxon, but instead the opposite had happened. Not a day, an hour went by, it seemed, when she didn't think of him at least once, wondering how he was, what he was doing. Which beautiful actress he was involved with now…

Since returning from Iraq she had even found herself buying and avidly looking through those glossy magazines that featured gossip about the rich and the famous.

If she had hoped to see any photographs of Jaxon then she might as well have saved herself the money—and the heartache!—because she hadn't succeeded in finding a single picture of him during the whole of that time. With a woman or otherwise.

The last thing she had been expecting, when her grandfather had invited her out to dinner with him this evening, was for him to calmly announce that Jaxon was in England at this very minute. Or at least Stazy presumed he was still here…

'Does he intend staying long?' she prompted lightly, aware that her hand was shaking slightly as she lifted her glass and took a much-needed sip of her white wine.

'He didn't say,' Geoffrey answered dismissively.

'Oh.' There were so many things Stazy wanted to ask—such as, how did Jaxon look? What had the two men talked about? Had Jaxon asked about her…? And yet she felt so tied up in knots inside just at the thought of Jaxon being in London at all that she couldn't ask any of them.

Although quite what her grandfather would have made of that interest if she had, after her previous attitude to Jaxon, was anybody's guess!

'He's finished writing the screenplay.'

Stazy's gaze sharpened. 'And…?'

Her grandfather smiled ruefully. 'And I recommend that you read it for yourself.'

She slowly licked the wine from her lips as she carefully placed her glass back down on the table. 'He gave you a copy…?'

'He gave me two copies. One for me and one for you.' Geoffrey reached down and lifted the briefcase he had carried into the restaurant with him earlier.

That second copy, meant for her, told Stazy more than anything else could have done that Jaxon had no intention of seeking her out while he was in England. And after the way the two of them had parted how could she have expected anything else!

Her grandfather opened the two locks on his briefcase before taking out the thickly bound bundle of the screenplay and handing it across the table to her. 'Read the front cover first, Stazy,' he advised huskily as she continued to stare at it, as if it were a bomb about to go off in his hand, rather than taking it from him.

Her throat moved convulsively as she swallowed hard. 'Have you had a chance to read it yet?'

Geoffrey smiled. 'Oh, yes.'

'And?'

'As I said, you need to read it for yourself.'

'If you liked it then I'm sure I will too,' she insisted firmly.

'Exactly how long do you intend to go on like this, Stazy?' her grandfather prompted impatiently as he placed the bound screenplay down on the tabletop, so that he could lock his briefcase before placing it back on the floor beside him.

Her hair moved silkily over her shoulders as she gave a shake of her head. 'I don't know what you mean…'

His steely-blue gaze became shrewdly piercing. 'Don't you?'

'No.'

'You have shadows under your eyes from not sleeping properly, you've lost weight you couldn't afford to lose—?'

'I think I picked up a bug in Iraq—'

'And I think you caught the bug before you even went to Iraq—and its name is Jaxon!'

Stazy's breath caught sharply in her throat at the baldness of her grandfather's statement, the colour draining from her cheeks. 'You're mistaken—'

'No, Stazy, you're the one that's making a mistake—by attempting to lie to someone who's had to lie as often as I have over the years,' he assured her impatiently.

She ran the tip of her tongue over her lips. There was a pained frown between her eyes. She knew from her grandfather's determined expression that he wasn't about to let her continue prevaricating. 'Is how I feel about Jaxon that obvious?'

'Only to me, darling.' He placed a hand gently over one of hers. 'And that's only because I know you so well and love you so much.'

She gave a shaky smile. 'It's probably as well that someone does!'

'Maybe Jaxon—'

'Let's not even go there,' she cut in firmly, her back tensing.

'I have no idea how long he'll be in England, but he did say he would be in London for several more days yet, so perhaps—'

'Gramps, I'm the last person Jaxon would want to see while he's here,' she assured him dully.

'You can't possibly know that—'

'Oh, but I can.' Stazy gave a self-derisive shake of her head. 'If you thought I was rude to him at our initial meeting then you should have seen me during those first few days we were alone together at Bromley House!' She sighed heavily. 'Believe me, Gramps, we parted in such a way as to ensure that Jaxon will never want to see me again!' Stiltedly. Distantly. Like strangers.

'Are you absolutely sure about that…?'

'Yes, of course I'm sure.' Her voice sharpened at her grandfather's persistence. Wasn't it enough for her to suffer the torment of knowing Jaxon was in England at all without having to explain all the reasons why he wouldn't want to see her while he was here? 'Feeling the way I do, I'm not sure it would be a good idea for me to see him again, either,' she said emotionally.

Her grandfather sat back in his chair. 'That's a pity…'

Her eyes had misted over with unshed tears. 'I don't see why.'

'Because when I saw him earlier today I invited him to join us this evening for dessert and coffee.' Geoffrey glanced across the restaurant. 'And it would appear he has arrived just in time to take up my invitation…'

* * *

Jaxon was totally unaware of the attention of the other diners in the restaurant as they recognised him. He walked slowly towards the table near the window where he could see Stazy sitting having dinner with her grandfather.

Even with her back towards him, Jaxon had spotted her the moment he had entered the crowded room; that gorgeous red-gold hair was like a vivid flame against the black dress she wore as it flowed loosely over her shoulders and down the slenderness of her back!

'Stazy,' he greeted her huskily as she looked up at him warily from beneath lowered lashes.

Her throat moved convulsively as she swallowed before answering him abruptly. 'Jaxon.'

Close to her like this, Jaxon could see that her face was even thinner than it had been three months ago—as if she had lost more weight. The looseness of the cream dress about her breasts and waist seemed to confirm that impression. 'I appreciate it's the done thing, when you meet up with someone again after a long absence, to say how well the other person is looking—but in your case, Stazy, I would be lying!' He almost growled in his disapproval of the fragility of her appearance. 'And I know how much you hate lies…'

Her cheeks were aflame. 'And what makes you think you're looking so perfect yourself?' she came back crisply.

'That's much better,' Jaxon murmured approvingly, before glancing across the table at the avidly attentive Geoffrey Bromley. 'When I asked about you earlier today your grandfather was at pains to tell me how happy and well you've been this past three months…' He raised mocking brows at the older man.

'Yes. Well. Family loyalty and all that.' Geoffrey had

the grace to look slightly embarrassed at the deception. 'I did invite you to join us for dessert and coffee so that you could see Stazy for yourself. Speaking of which… No, there's no need to bring another chair,' he told the waiter as the man arrived to stand enquiringly beside their table. 'I have another appointment to get to, so Mr Wilder can have my seat.' He bent to pick up the briefcase from beside his chair before standing up in readiness to leave.

'Gramps—'

'I believe you told me yourself weeks ago that you're a big girl now and no longer in need of my protection…?' he reminded her firmly, before bending to kiss her lightly on the cheek. 'If you'll both excuse me…?' He didn't wait for either of them to reply before turning and walking briskly across the restaurant.

Yes, Stazy *had* told her grandfather that—but it had been in a totally different situation and context from this one!

That her grandfather had invited Jaxon to join them this evening with the deliberate intention of leaving her alone with him she had no doubt. Quite why he should have decided to do so was far less clear to her…

Especially so when the first thing Jaxon had done was insult her. And she had then insulted him back. Some things never changed, it seemed…

Her own insulting remark had been knee-jerk rather than truthful—Jaxon had never looked more wonderful to her than he did this evening. His silky dark hair was still shoulder-length, brushed back from the chiselled perfection of his face, and the black evening suit and snowy white shirt were tailored to the muscled width of his shoulders and tapered waist.

He looked every inch the suave and sophisticated

actor Jaxon Wilder. Something Stazy had already noted the other female diners in the restaurant seemed to appreciate!

'So…' Jaxon had made himself comfortable in her grandfather's recently vacated chair while Stazy had been lost in her own jumbled thoughts.

'So,' Stazy echoed, her heart beating so loudly that she felt sure Jaxon must be able to hear it even over the low hum of the conversation of the other diners. 'You've obviously finished writing the screenplay.' She glanced down at the bound copy on the tabletop.

His gaze sharpened. 'Have you read it…?'

'My grandfather only just gave it to me, so no—' She broke off as she finally read the front page of the screenplay. 'Why is my name next to yours beneath the title…?' she asked slowly.

He shrugged those broad shoulders. 'You helped gather the research. You deserve to share in the credit for the writing of the screenplay.'

This explained why her grandfather had advised her to read the front cover when he gave it to her. 'I'm sure my less than helpful attitude was more of a hindrance than a help—'

'On the contrary—it kept me focused on what's important.' Jaxon sat forward, his expression intense. 'Look, do you really want dessert and coffee? Or can we get out of here and go somewhere we can talk privately…?' He absently waved away the waiter, who had been coming over to take their order.

Stazy raised startled lids to look across at Jaxon uncertainly, not in the least encouraged by the harshness of his expression. 'And why would we want to do that…?'

Jaxon cursed under his breath as he saw the look of uncertainty on Stazy's face. 'I've missed you this past three months, Stazy,' he told her gruffly. 'More than you can possibly know.'

She grimaced. 'Couldn't you find anyone else to argue with?'

He smiled ruefully. 'There's that too!'

She shook her head. 'I'm sure you've been far too busy to even give me a first thought, let alone a second one!'

'Try telling my female co-star that—we've had to do so many retakes because of my inattentiveness that I finally decided to give everyone the week off!' he muttered self-disgustedly.

Stazy blinked. 'The pirate movie isn't going well…?'

'Totally my own fault.' Jaxon sighed heavily. 'I haven't been feeling in a particularly swash or buckling mood.' He picked up one of her hands as it rested on the tabletop and lightly linked his fingers with hers. 'I *have* missed you, Stazy.'

She gave a puzzled shake of her head. 'How can you miss someone you didn't even want to be friends with the last time we were together?'

'Because friendship isn't what I want from you, damn it!' Jaxon scowled darkly. 'The fact that I asked you to go away with me for a few days should have told you that much!'

'You seemed to feel we had unfinished business—'

'I wanted to spend some time alone with you—'

'People are staring, Jaxon,' she warned softly, having glanced up and seen several of the other diners taking an interest in their obviously heated exchange.

'If we don't get out of here soon I'm going to give them something much more interesting than this to stare at!' he came back fiercely.

Stazy looked at him searchingly—at the angry glitter

in his eyes, the tautness of his cheek, his tightly clenched jaw and mouth. 'Such as…?' she prompted breathlessly.

'This, for a start!' He stood up abruptly, his hand tightening about hers as he pulled her to her feet seconds before he took her into his arms and his head swooped low as his mouth captured hers.

Stazy had always been reserved, never one for drawing attention to herself, but the absolute bliss of having Jaxon kiss her again—even in the middle of a crowded restaurant, with all the other diners looking on!—was far too wonderful for her to care where they were or who was watching.

She rose up on tiptoe to move her hands to his chest and up over his shoulders, her fingers becoming entangled in that gloriously overlong dark hair as she eagerly returned the heat of his kiss.

'God, I needed that…!' Jaxon breathed huskily long seconds later, as his mouth finally lifted from hers. He rested his forehead against hers. 'You have no idea—' He stopped speaking as the restaurant was suddenly filled with the sound of spontaneous applause from the other diners.

'Oh, dear Lord…!' Stazy groaned as she buried the heat of her face against his chest.

'Show's over, folks!' Jaxon chuckled huskily as he picked up the screenplay before putting his arm firmly about Stazy's waist to hold her anchored tightly against his side. The two of them crossed the restaurant.

'Sir Geoffrey has already taken care of the bill, Mr Wilder,' the *maître d'* assured him as they neared the front desk. He handed Stazy her black jacket. 'And may I wish the two of you every happiness together?' The man beamed across at them.

'Thank you,' Jaxon accepted lightly, and he continued

to cut a swathe through the arriving diners until just the two of them were standing outside in the cool of the autumn evening.

Stazy had never felt so embarrassed in her life before—at the same time she had never felt so euphorically happy. Jaxon had kissed her. In front of dozens of other people. Not only that, but he hadn't denied the *maître d'*s good wishes. Of course he had probably only done that as a means of lessening the embarrassment to them all, but even so…

Jaxon had kissed her! And she had kissed him right back.

'Do you think you could stop thinking at least until after we've reached that "somewhere more private"?' he prompted persuasively.

Stazy looked up at him uncertainly. 'Where do you want to go?'

He shook his head. 'Your apartment. My apartment. I don't give a damn where we go as long as it's somewhere we don't have an audience!'

Stazy gave a pained frown and looked up at Jaxon in the subdued light given off by the streetlamp overhead. 'I'm not sure I understand…' She was still too afraid to hope, to allow her imagination even to guess as to the reason why he had done something so outrageously wonderful…

'It's simple enough, Stazy. Your place or mine?' Jaxon pressured as the taxi he had hailed drew to a halt next to the pavement.

'I—yours,' she decided quickly; at least she would be able to walk out of Jaxon's apartment whenever this—whatever 'this' was!—was over. With the added bonus that when Jaxon had gone she wouldn't have to be surrounded by memories of his having been in her own apartment.

Jaxon opened the taxi door and saw Stazy safely seated inside, giving the driver his address as he climbed in to sit beside her. 'Come here—you're cold.' He drew her into the circle of his arms after he saw her give an involuntary shiver in the lightweight jacket she wore over the cream dress. 'Do you have to be anywhere in the morning?'

Her face was buried in the warmth of his chest. 'It's Saturday…'

'That doesn't answer my question,' he rebuked lightly.

Probably because Stazy didn't understand the question! Why did it matter to Jaxon whether or not she—? 'Oh!' she gasped breathlessly. She could think of only one reason why he might possibly want to know such a thing.

'Yes—*oh*,' he teased huskily. 'And before your imagination runs riot I have every intention of keeping you locked inside my apartment until you've listened to everything—and I do mean everything—that I should have said to you three months ago. That could take a few minutes or could take all night, depending on how receptive you are to what I have to say,' he acknowledged self-derisively.

Stazy moistened her lips with the tip of her tongue. 'Will there be any swashing or buckling involved in this…this locking me away in your apartment?' she prompted shyly.

Jaxon arms tightened about her as he gave an appreciative chuckle. 'I think there might be a lot of both those things, if it's agreeable to you, yes.'

Stazy thought she might be very agreeable…

CHAPTER THIRTEEN

'So.' Stazy stood uncomfortably in the middle of the spacious sitting room of what had turned out to be the penthouse apartment of a twenty-storey building set right in the middle of the most exclusive part of London. The views of the brightly lit city were absolutely amazing from the numerous windows in this room alone, and there appeared to be at least a dozen furnished rooms equally as beautiful in the apartment Jaxon had told her he only used on the rare occasions when he was in London.

'Let's not start that again, hmm?' Jaxon prompted huskily.

'No.' She smiled awkwardly. 'This is a very nice apartment. Does it have—?'

'Hush, Stazy.' Jaxon trod lightly across the cream carpet until he stood only inches in front of her. 'Tomorrow, if you really are interested, I'll give you the blurb that I received on this place before I bought it. But for now I believe we have other, more important things to talk about…'

'Do we?' She looked up at him searchingly. 'I have no real idea of what I'm even doing here!' She wrung agitated hands together. 'You had lunch with my grandfather today. Came to the restaurant this evening supposedly to join us for coffee and dessert—and then didn't even attempt to order either one of them. You then kissed me in front of dozens of other people after my grandfather left—'

Jaxon put an end to her obvious and rapidly increasing agitation by taking her in his arms and kissing her again.

More intensely. More thoroughly. More demandingly…

'You know,' he murmured several minutes later, as he ended the kiss and once again rested his forehead on hers, 'if I have to keep doing this in order to get a word in edgeways this is definitely going to take all night!'

Stazy gave a choked laugh. 'I don't mind if you don't…'

'Oh, I'm only too happy to go on kissing you all night long, my darling Stazy,' he assured her gruffly. 'Just not yet. First we need to talk. *I* need to talk,' he added ruefully. 'To make it completely, absolutely clear how I feel.'

She caught her bottom lip between pearly white teeth. 'How you feel about what…?'

'You, of course!' Jaxon lifted his head to look down at her exasperatedly. 'Stazy, you have to be the most difficult woman in the world for a man to tell how much he loves her!' he added irritably.

Stazy stilled, her eyes very wide as she stared up at him. 'Are you saying you love me…?'

'I've loved you for months, you impossible woman!'

'You've—loved—me—for—months…?' she repeated in slow disbelief.

'See? Totally impossible!' Jaxon snorted his impatience as he released her to step away and run a hand through the darkness of his hair. 'There are millions upon millions of women in the world, and I have to fall in love with the one woman who doesn't even believe I love her when I've just told her that I do!'

It was entirely inappropriate—had to be because she was verging on hysteria—but at that moment in time all Stazy could manage in response was a choked laugh.

Jaxon raised his eyes heavenwards. 'And now she's laughing at me…!'

Stazy continued laughing. In fact she laughed for so long that her sides actually ached and there were tears falling down her cheeks.

'Care to share the joke?' Jaxon finally prompted ruefully.

She leant weakly against the wall, her hands wrapped about her aching sides. 'No joke, Jaxon. At least not on you.'

'Who, then?'

'Me!' She smiled across at him tearfully. 'The joke's on *me*, Jaxon! I'm so inexperienced at these things that I— Jaxon, I fell in love with you when we were at Bromley House together. I didn't want to,' she added soberly. 'It just…happened.'

Jaxon began walking towards her like a man in a dream. 'You're in love with me…?'

'Oh, Jaxon…!' she groaned indulgently. 'There are millions and millions of men in the world, and I have to fall in love with the one man who doesn't even believe I love him when I've just told him that I do,' she misquoted back at him huskily.

His arms felt like steel bands about her waist as he pulled her effortlessly towards him, his gaze piercing as he looked down at her fiercely. 'Do you love me enough to marry me…?'

She gasped. 'You can't want to marry a doctor of archaeology?'

He nodded. 'I most certainly can! That is if you don't mind marrying an actor and film director?'

'Excuse me,' she chided huskily, 'but that would be a multi-award-winning Hollywood A-list actor and director!'

'Whatever,' Jaxon dismissed gruffly. 'Will you marry me, Stazy, and save me from the misery of merely existing without you?'

She swallowed. 'Being alone in a crowd…?'

'The hell of being alone in a crowd, yes,' he confirmed huskily.

Stazy knew exactly what that felt like. It was how she had felt for the past three months since she'd last seen Jaxon…

Tears welled up in her eyes. 'I've been so lonely without you, Jaxon. Since my parents died I've never wanted to need or love anyone, apart from my grandparents, and yet you've managed to capture my heart…' She gave a shake of her head. 'I love you so much, Jaxon, that these past three months of not seeing you, being with you, has been hell.'

'Hence the weight loss and lack of sleep?' He ran a caressing fingertip across the dark shadows under her eyes.

'Yes.' She nodded miserably.

'When you said a few minutes ago you were inexperienced in things, you meant falling in love, didn't you…?'

She gave a self-derisive laugh. 'I've never been in love. I've had two lovers, spent one night with each of them, and they were both utter disasters!' She grimaced.

'Forget about them.' Jaxon reached up and cradled

each side of her face, his love for her shining out of his liquid grey eyes. 'We're going to make love, Stazy. Real love. And it's going to be truly beautiful.'

'Yes, please…' she breathed softly.

'You haven't agreed to make an honest man of me yet,' he reminded her huskily.

'Is that a condition of the beautiful lovemaking?' she teased.

'I do have my reputation to think of, after all…'

Stazy laughed huskily at the dig as she threw herself into his waiting arms. 'In that case—yes, I'll marry you, Jaxon!'

'And have my babies?'

Babies. Not only Jaxon to love, but his babies to love and cherish… 'Oh, God, yes…!' she accepted emotionally.

'Then you may now take me to bed, Dr Bromley.'

She chuckled at his prim tone. 'If you think I'm going to sweep you up in my arms and carry you off to the bedroom before ravishing you then I'm afraid you're going to be disappointed!'

'I'll do the sweeping.' Jaxon did exactly that. 'You can do the ravishing.'

'With pleasure, Mr Wilder,' Stazy murmured throatily. 'With the greatest of pleasure.'

And it was.

Just over two years later…

'I'm truly impressed,' Jaxon murmured teasingly in her ear as the two of them stepped down off the stage to the rapturous applause of his peers, after going up together to receive yet another award for Best Screenplay for *Butterfly Wings*. 'I think you thanked everyone but the girl who made the coffee!'

'Very funny,' Stazy muttered as she continued to smile brightly for the watching audience as the two of them made their way back to their seats.

Jaxon chuckled. 'And after you were once so scathing about the length of the speeches made at these awards, too!'

'Just for that, you can be the one to get up to Anastasia Rose if she wakes in the night!' Stazy dropped thankfully back into her seat, her smile completely genuine now as she thought of their beautiful six-month-old daughter waiting for them at home. Geoffrey had opted to stay with his beloved great-granddaughter rather than accompany them to another award ceremony that he had declared would be 'far too exhausting at my age!'

'I'll have you know that Anastasia Rose and I have come to an arrangement—I don't wake her up if she doesn't wake me up!' Jaxon grinned smugly.

'Really?' Stazy turned in her seat to look at him. 'Does that mean we can have our own very private celebration later…?'

Jaxon chuckled. 'Insatiable woman!'

She arched teasing brows. 'Are you complaining…?'

'Certainly not!' He kissed her warmly—something he had done often during their two-year marriage, whenever and wherever they happened to be.

They both knew and happily appreciated that life, and love, didn't come any better than this…

* * * * *

KEEPING HER UP ALL NIGHT

ANNA CLEARY

As a child, **Anna Cleary** loved reading so much that during the midnight hours she was forced to read with a torch under the bedcovers, to lull the suspicions of her sleep-obsessed parents. From an early age she dreamed of writing her own books. She saw herself in a stone cottage by the sea, wearing a velvet smoking jacket and sipping sherry, like Somerset Maugham.

In real life she became a school teacher, where her greatest pleasure was teaching children to write beautiful stories.

A little while ago, she and one of her friends made a pact to each write the first chapter of a romance novel in their holidays. From writing her very first line Anna was hooked, and she gave up teaching to become a full-time writer. She now lives in Queensland, with a deeply sensitive and intelligent cat. She prefers champagne to sherry, and loves music, books, four-legged people, trees, movies and restaurants.

CHAPTER ONE

GUY WILDER wasn't on the hunt any more. He'd given up chicks with promises of forever on their honeyed tongues. These days he poured his emotions into songs. Often tear-jerkers in the key of tragedy, best wailed after midnight in haunts for the broken-hearted. But they were tuneful, sexy, and always with a deep and honest soul beat. Songs a man could believe in, with no bitter twists at the end.

Yep, he was still a single man, and it was all good. By day he built his company, by night he dreamed up songs, and the Blue Suede boys were keen to perform them.

However badly they murdered his lyrics, the Suede showed promise. So, on the night of his return from a work trip to the States, the boys' need for an emergency venue persuaded Guy to let them into his aunt's apartment above the Kirribilli Mansions Arcade. Auntie Jean wouldn't mind. Well, she was trusting *him* to hang there for a week or two.

The thing was, the Suede could pound out a pretty stirring beat. Guy did give *some* consideration to the noise. When the boys crowded through the door with their instruments he eyed the flowery fanlight above the neighbour's place, but the apartment was in darkness.

It wasn't late enough for sleeping. Who'd have guessed anyone was home?

He ordered pizza, but once he and the guys started on the song dinner floated from their minds. It wasn't until the tempo had hotted up and they were into laying down chords that the distant ding of the bell penetrated the boys' enthusiasm.

Calling a halt, Guy abandoned the keyboard of his aunt's fabulous old grand and headed for the door.

The pizza lad was out there, all right, but not at Guy's door. At the neighbour's.

'I assure you it wasn't me,' the woman was saying in a low, melodious voice. 'I never order pizza. It must have been whoever's in there, making that awful racket. Did you try knocking? Though you might need a sledgehammer to make any…'

Impact. Guy finished the sentence for her in his head.

She swivelled around to look at him, as did the boy, and impact happened.

Violet eyes, dark-fringed and serious, and cheekbones in a piquant face. A mouth as ripe and sweet as a plum. Gorgeous, was his first dazzled thought. A gorgeous, desirable, tantalising—trap. She was five feet six or thereabouts, unless his expert eye was dazzled out of whack, with long, dark, lustrous hair tied back. Gloriously *rich*, long, dark and lustrous. And legs… Oh, God, legs. And heaven in between.

He couldn't see much of the heaven through the sweatshirt, but all the signs were there. Hills. Valleys. Curves. Anyway, a man didn't stare obviously at a woman's breasts. Or any other parts they might choose to conceal.

But if she happened to be wearing a short flimsy-looking dress thing, frilling out from under the longish sweatshirt, naturally his eye was bound to be snagged here and there. Particularly if she also had satin slippers on her feet. Tied on ballerina fashion, with criss-crossing strings.

He drank her in to the full, and she gave him every reason to believe she was eyeing him right back—only hers was a sternish scrutiny that seemed not to be dwelling on his manly appeal.

He smiled. 'I think they're for me.' He produced money and accepted the pile of boxes. 'Thanks, mate. Keep this for your trouble.'

The lad disappeared via the lift, the stairs—or maybe he vanished through the wall.

'Sorry if you were disturbed, Miss…?'

'Amber O'Neill.' Her tone was earnest. 'I don't think you realise how much the sound reverberates in these apartments. It magnifies, actually, and the walls are very thin.'

He lifted his brows. 'Yeah? The sound magnifies. Now, that's interesting. A unique accoustic. Thanks for mentioning it.'

Amber, he was thinking, riveted on her irises, drowning in the violet. And her mouth—so soft and full. A dangerous yearning stirred the devil in his blood. Oh, man, it had been a long, long time.

Apparently she still hadn't noticed his charm, for her luscious lips tightened. 'Some people have to work, you know. Some even have businesses to run.'

'Do they?' He smiled, refusing to be chastised at eight-thirty in the evening. Practically daylight. Enjoying stretching out the tease. Listening to her voice. 'Tsk. Don't those people ever play?'

Maybe he should suggest she throw him over her lap and spank him. Now, there would be an inspiration. And right next door, too.

At the exact moment his brain generated the backsliding thought, he noticed her flick a glowing little glance over his chest and arms and down below his belt buckle. Despite her indignation, her eyes betrayed an infinitesimal spark.

An intensely feminine spark that opened a Pandora's box of frightening possibilities.

Whoa, there. The hot rush on its way to his loins faltered and screeched to a halt.

Like a madman he turned back into his flat and shut the door. Stood paralysed, breathing for a dozen thundering heartbeats, before he realised the craziness of the impulse and snatched it open again.

Too late, though. She'd gone.

Breathing hard, Amber stood under the skylight in her empty sitting room and tried to resuscitate the mood.

Once more the ethereal chords of 'Clair de Lune' drifted on the air. Usually every note was a drop of silver magic on her soul, but though she rose on her toes and held up her arms to the moon filtering through the skylight… *arabesque, arabesque, glissé...*

Hopeless. The magic was gone. Murdered.

She switched off the music. She couldn't remember the last time she'd felt so annoyed. No use attempting to dance her insomnia away now. She could still hear the appalling racket from next door, even though they'd toned down the volume a notch. The truth was she didn't want to be aware of them in the slightest. Of *him*.

And it had nothing to do with his mouth, or the way he'd looked in those jeans. She was used to well-built guys with chests. She was up to *here* with them, if the truth be known. And no way was it his eyes. She'd seen plenty of large grey, crinkling-at-the-corners eyes in her twenty-six years.

No, it had been the mockery in them. That amused, ironic assumption that since he was a man and she was a woman she'd be keen. He was so sure of himself he hadn't even bothered to finish the conversation.

How wrong could a man be? The last guy who'd persuaded her to take that plunge had reminded her of all a woman needed to learn about heartbreak.

She peeled off her slippers and crawled back into her bed. For a while she lay on her side, as tense as a wire. Tried the other side. Still no good. Tossed. Turned. And in no time at all her brain was back to its churning.

Money. The shop. The renovations. Aloneness. Men who mocked you with smiling eyes.

Usually by late afternoon, the Fleur Elise end of the Kirribilli Mansions Arcade was quiet. This day, surely onc of the longest in Amber's memory, not a shopper stirred. After three disturbed nights Amber welcomed the possibility of snatching a quick reflective snooze in the room where the bouquets were made up.

Unfortunately Ivy, the book-keeper she'd inherited along with the shop, had come in to help out.

'...you're going to have to make cuts. *Amber*? Are you listening?'

Amber winced. It wasn't the first time she'd noticed the penetrating quality of Ivy's voice. With only the mildest exclamation the woman could break windows.

Amber laid her aching head on the bunching table. Sleep deprivation had brought her nerves to a desperate state, thanks to that man. For two days now there'd been this throb in her temples. Maybe if she ignored Ivy she'd shut up.

As far as Amber was concerned this was not the moment to be raking over her failures with the accounts. She was tired. She needed to brood on what was happening in Jean's flat night after night. The noise. The ructions.

That—*guy*. She clenched her teeth. The sooner Jean and Stuart got back from their honeymoon the better.

She so resented the way he'd looked at her, with that scorching glance, that lazy smile playing on his cool, very, very sexy mouth.

Maybe he'd thought she'd be flattered. What men didn't realise was that women *knew* when they weren't looking their best. If a woman was wearing an old sloppy joe over her nightie and a man happened to show a certain kind of interest in her, it wasn't flattering in the least. It immediately raised the likelihood that he automatically looked at every woman like that. In other words, he was likely to be the sort of chronic womaniser her father had been.

Oh, yeah. He looked the type, with that lazy grin. Typical narcissistic heartbreaker. If he saw her today, though, even *he* wouldn't look twice. She was a train wreck.

She rested her head on her arms. One of the songs his band had been bashing out was grinding an unwelcome path through her brain. To add to her irritation, when she'd been bathing this morning she'd heard him in his shower, actually whistling the same tune in a slow, sexy, up-beat sort of way.

Why hadn't Jean warned her? They were friends, weren't they? She was the one who was supposed to be looking after Jean's fish and watering her plants.

It was so unfair. With all she had on her plate, she shouldn't have to be so distracted.

'…cut your overheads.' Ivy's voice hacked through the fog of Amber's musings like a saw-toothed laser. 'That Serena's a prime example.'

Shocked into responding, Amber said hoarsely, 'What? Did you say I should sack *Serena*?'

'Well, unless you cut your expenditure elsewhere.'

Amber was flummoxed. 'Oh, Ivy. Serena's our only genuine florist. Neither of us has her sort of talent. All right, I know she's needed a bit of time off since she had the baby. But when she sorts out childcare that'll get better. She really needs the work. She and the babe depend on her hours here.'

'I'm not running a blessed charity,' Ivy muttered. 'Next you'll be talking again about opening up the side door to the street and spending a fortune on redecorating.'

Amber felt her muscles clench all over. Ivy wasn't running anything. Fleur Elise was *her* shop. *Her* inheritance from *her* mother. The words burned on her tongue but with a supreme effort she held them back. That business course she was studying strongly advocated the need to stay calm in times of conflict. Maintain her cool professionalism.

She drew a long, cooling breath. Several long breaths. She needed to remind herself her mother had had a great deal of faith in Ivy. Ivy's legendary ability to avoid outlay was an asset, her mother had said. And it almost certainly was. Anywhere but a flower shop.

Amber's flower shop, at least. Her shop should be spilling over with blooms. Poppies and tulips, snapdragons and violets, jonquils, forget-me-nots. Masses of everything—and roses, roses, roses. She dreamed of her rich, heady fragrances drawing people in from the street and following them throughout the arcade.

All right, she was the first to admit she might not be quite up to scratch yet as a businessperson—she was still in the early stages of her course—but instinct told her Ivy's miserly cheese-paring approach wasn't the way to go.

What *would* attract the customers was a mass of colours, textures and tantalising smells. The sort that would appeal to any sensuous, voluptuous *femme* like herself.

The self she could be, that was. On a good day. When

she'd had *sleep.* When her brain hadn't been tormented by *noise.* Today her sensuous, voluptuous quotient was at rock-bottom.

It was never any use arguing with Ivy, anyway. Nothing would shift her from her fixed position on any subject. If Amber hadn't been so punch-drunk with fatigue she'd have remembered that and kept her mouth shut. As it was…

'I'm thinking of getting a bank loan.' She yawned.

Oh, wow. *Wrong thing to say.* She'd have been better throwing a grenade. Ivy's short neck could stretch right out and swivel when she was outraged, alarmed and aghast.

Like now.

The small woman's mouth gaped into an incredulous rectangle. 'Are you out of your *mind*, girl? How will you pay it back if something goes wrong with the trade?'

'Oh, what trade?' Amber growled, incensed at being called 'girl'. For God's sake, though she might dress like it, Ivy was hardly her grandmother. She was only thirty-eight.

Amber pressed a couple of cooling roses to her temples. 'Do we have to talk about it now, Ivy?' she moaned. 'I have a headache.'

And she needed to brood. About men and betrayal. Love and pain. Passion unrequited. She wasn't sure why these things had to occupy her mind right now, when she was so tired and noise-battered, but for some reason lately they'd been looming large.

For three nights, in fact. Ever since she'd laid eyes on that—*hoon* next door.

It wasn't that she found him so hot. Oh, all right, he was sexy—in a down-and-dirty, unshaven sort of way. Those jeans he wore should be dumped on the nearest bonfire. And as for that ragged old tee shirt she'd seen him in yesterday morning at the bakery… It looked to her as if someone had tried to claw it off him. Some desperate person.

No, *not* like her at all. She wasn't desperate. She simply had a distinctive personality type that could be deeply affected by the sight of sweat glistening on bronzed, masculine arms. She was a highly sensual woman, with a sensual woman's needs.

Very much the Eustacia Vye type, in fact.

She'd discovered Eustacia yesterday, during a few guilty moments of escapist reading in the shop. Well, there were never any customers at that time. If Ivy hadn't insisted on coming in to help out this afternoon Amber might have had a chance to learn more about her exotic heroine. As it was she'd had to hide the book in her secret cache behind the potted ferns.

Eustacia was a woman so sensuous, so voluptuous, that if ever a dangling bough happened to caress her hair whilst she was rambling under the trees in the Wessex woods, the bewitching creature would turn right back and ramble under them again.

Fine. Amber accepted that she wasn't all that beautiful or bewitching. Unless swathed in tulle and feathers, that was. On stage, illuminated in a pool of magic light. She could be pretty bewitching then. Just stick her in front of the footlights with an orchestra swelling to a crescendo and Amber O'Neill could bewitch the pants off a sphinx.

And her hair craved caresses. Ached for them. Though preferably administered via a lean, masculine hand rather than a twig.

She yawned again. Weren't musicians supposed to have skinny arms and hollow chests?

'Tsk, tsk, tsk, tsk, *tsk*.' Even a tongue click from Ivy could attack the cerebral cortex like an ice-pick. 'Have you been hiding these bills, Amber?'

Amber felt herself getting hot. 'Not *hiding*. I just…may

have…put them aside for a… Look, Ivy, I don't feel like doing this now.'

But Ivy would show no mercy. Once she had her sharp little teeth into something she held on like a terrier until she'd pulled out all the entrails.

She waved a bunch of invoices in front of Amber's face. 'You know what I think? You're going downhill. You'll just have to face it, girl. Your best option is to sell. Do you want to be declared bankrupt?'

The word scrambled Amber's insides like a butter churn.

She tried to breathe. 'Ivy, try to understand. This was Mum's shop. She *loved* this shop.'

But the humourless round eyes beneath Ivy's straight brown fringe were as understanding as two hypodermic syringes. 'Your *mother* managed to pay the bills. Your *mother* knew how to take advice.'

Amber flinched. For a small woman, Ivy could pack a lethal punch. Amber knew very well Lise hadn't always been able to pay the bills. But she wasn't about to argue over her mother's faults or otherwise.

Her mother was in the cold, cold ground. And it scraped Amber's heart every time Ivy dragged her name into the conversation. She couldn't handle it with her loss still so fresh and piercing.

Amber drew a long, simmering breath. Lucky for Ivy, she was ace at controlling her temper. That was one thing she could do well. If left in peace. That was all she really craved now. Peace, and hours and hours of deep, uninterrupted sleep.

Was that so much to ask? Ever since she'd relinquished twirling around on her toes to care for her poor mother, she couldn't seem to find those essential things anywhere.

'Have you seen the price of those long-stemmed roses?'

Ivy carped. 'Why can't you just go for the cheaper produce? Why can't you *ever...*?'

The words prodded Amber's insides like red-hot needles. She held her breath.

'Just look at this item here. Why order freesias out of season? You can't afford them.'

Amber gritted her teeth and said steadily, 'You know Mum loves—*loved* freesias, Ivy. They're—they were her favourites.' Inevitably a lump rose in her throat and her eyes swam. Her voice went all murky. 'It's important to have flowers with fragrance.'

'Fragrance, crap. Fragrance is a luxury we can't afford.'

There were still ten minutes to go before closing. Amber knew Ivy was only trying to teach her the ropes, was doing her best according to her own weird lights, but Amber felt an overpowering need to escape. And quickly. Before she let loose and annihilated the little terrier with a few well-chosen words.

She staggered to her feet. 'I'm sorry, Ivy, I can't deal with all this now. I have a killer migraine. I'm going upstairs. Do you mind locking up?'

Ivy's jaw dropped, then she snapped her sharp little teeth together. Even so, her unspoken words fractured the fragile air like a clarion horn. *Your mother never left early.*

This was hardly true, but why should it matter? Amber wondered drearily. There'd barely been any customers then and there wouldn't be any now.

She shoved her way through the potted ferns and the sparse display of bouquets and made her escape into the arcade before the book-keeper had time to lash her with any more advice. As she stumbled down the arcade to the lifts, past all the other glossy shops, she felt her migraine escalate.

In truth, she was starting to feel slightly sick every time she thought of Fleur Elise.

The ninth floor was blessedly silent. Amber unlocked the door to her flat and was met by a wave of hot, musty air. Resisting the temptation of the air-conditioner, she lurched around opening the windows and balcony doors. Then she tore the pins from her hair and let it fall to her waist. Dragging off her clothes, she collapsed at last onto the bed, her nerves stretched taut as bowstrings.

She closed her eyes. If she'd still been in the ballet company she'd be on the tram now, heading home after a beautiful day of music and extreme exercise, humming Tchaikovsky, her muscles aching, her spirit singing with endorphins.

Would she ever feel like that again in her life?

A frightening thought gripped her by the throat. What if Centre Management acted on their rules? What if next she *lost the shop*?

Fatigued though she was, it seemed like an age before her panic wore itself out. Eventually, though, exhaustion started its work. Her anxiety released its grip, and the pain in her temples lightened a little. A merciful cooling breeze from Sydney Harbour rustled the filmy curtains either side of the balcony doors and whispered over her skin like balm, and she felt herself start to drift down that peaceful river, dozing towards sleep.

She was nearly there, soothed at long last into blissful oblivion, wrapped in sleep's healing mantle, when a heavy crash jarred through the floorboards and straight through her spinal cord. Her eyes sprang open and her jagged nerves wrenched themselves back into red alert.

The sound came from the other side of the wall.

'Oh, for goodness' *sake*.'

Amber leaped up and tore open her wardrobe to drag

out a skirt and the first top she could lay her hands on. There was no time for shoes. In a fury she flew out of her flat to hammer on her neighbour's door.

Her fist halted in mid-crash as the door opened abruptly.

It was him, of course. All six foot two of him. His stubble had progressed, and somehow his lashes seemed blacker too, though his grey eyes still held the same silvery glint. Leaning a powerful shoulder against the frame, he cast another of those long, slow, considering looks over her—like the king of the pride contemplating a plump little wildebeest.

'Well, well. Amber,' he said, in his deep growl of a voice. 'Nice of you to drop by.'

Was he trying to be *funny*? No doubt in his black tee shirt and the artfully scruffy jeans clinging to his bronzed, muscled frame he was exactly the sort of testosterone machine certain women might have enjoyed bouncing a bit of stimulating repartee back and forth with…

She wasn't one of them.

'That noise you're making,' she rasped. 'I'm trying to sleep and it's disturbing me.'

He lifted his black brows. 'At six in the evening? You should get a life, sweetheart.'

He started to close the door, but Amber was quick. She shoved her foot into the space. 'Now, wait a minute. I *have* a life. A busy life. And it's because you've been assaulting Jean's piano…' She shook her head, outraged at the scandal of it. Jean's beautiful Steinway… 'You and your friends with those stupid drums… That's *why* I need to sleep at six in the evening.'

He looked at her for a long, considering moment, his strong brows still raised in disbelief. 'You don't like music?'

Her? Whose first steps had been a dance? She clenched

her teeth. 'I like music, mister. When I hear it. I've already asked you politely. Now, if you don't keep your noise down…'

'Ah. Here it comes. The threat.' He tilted his head to one side and made a thorough appraisal of her from head to toe.

The full scorching force of bold masculine interest lasered through the thin fabric of her clothes. She grew conscious that in her rush she'd chosen a close-fitting top with a deep neckline, she wasn't wearing a bra, and her feet were bare. Only with difficulty did she prevent herself from crossing her arms over her breasts.

'I love women who talk tough,' he said, with a lascivious twitch of a black brow. 'What will you do to me?'

Wild words rocketed to her tongue. The frustrations and anxieties she'd been repressing over days seethed inside their cage. She wanted to rip open his arrogant jugular with her teeth and nails, claw at his lean face, draw his insolent blood.

He broke into a laugh and flash of white, even teeth lit his face. 'Don't do it. Why don't you come in and we'll see if we can work something out?'

She drew herself up. 'Look, Mr…' she hissed.

'Guy. Guy Wilder.' His sexy mouth broke into a smile, but she didn't care that it illuminated his rather harsh face like a sunburst and made him handsome.

'Whatever.' Her breath came in short bursts, as if Vesuvius was seething inside her, alive and molten. 'I came here to ask if your band can practise somewhere else. If you can't be more considerate I'll report you to the Residents' Committee.'

Amusement crept into his voice. 'We seem to be getting a bit heated.'

'Does Jean even know you're here?'

At her escalating pitch his black brows made an eloquent upward twitch. 'Not only does my dear aunt know I'm here, she *wants* me to be here. I'll give you her address, all right? You can check up. Set your mind at rest.'

'I know Jean well, and I know she would strongly object to your upsetting her neighbours. She would never have agreed to your setting up your band in here night and day.'

'It isn't here *night and day*.' His quiet, measured tone made a mockery of her emotion. 'I write songs. The band you've been privileged to hear the last couple of nights—in the *early* part of the evening, let me remind you—were unable to use their usual venue. They have a gig coming up so they needed a run-through. That means…'

'I know what it means,' she snapped. 'And it was no privilege. You might as well know now—your band sucks.'

His black eyebrows flew up and his eyes drifted over her in sardonic appreciation. 'I'll make sure I pass your critique on to the guys.'

She could hardly believe she'd said such a rude thing, but it gave her a reckless satisfaction. Even if he was Jean's nephew, he'd made her suffer.

If he was. She had some vague recollection of Jean's stories about various family members. There was the brilliant one who wanted to direct movies, the scientist who'd fallen in love on a voyage to Antarctica, the boy whose girlfriend—the love of his life, Jean had said—had stood him up at the altar and run away with a soldier. She couldn't remember any mention of a musician.

The guy moved slightly. Enough for Amber's critical eye to catch a glimpse of the indoor garden Jean kept in her foyer. Shocked by what she saw, she couldn't restrain herself. 'Just *look* at those anthuriums. Jean would be furious if she knew you were letting her precious plants die. Surely she explained her watering system to you?'

He gave a careless shrug. 'She may have said something.'

'And what about her fish?'

'Fish?'

'Don't tell me you haven't been feeding them? That aquarium is Jean's pride and joy.' She glared at him—at the grey eyes alight in his dark unshaven face, his black eyebrows tilted in quizzical amusement. She'd never in all of her twenty-six years wanted so much to do violence to someone.

'I'm not sure how the fish are doing,' he said smoothly. 'Why don't you come inside and check them out? You can take inventory while you're here, in case I've damaged something.'

She caught the sarcasm but didn't allow it to deter her. She pushed past him into Jean's beautiful, immaculate flat and halted in the middle of the sitting room.

Twilight had invaded. Only one lamp was lit, casting a soft apricot glow, but with the skylight in the foyer and the glow from the aquarium it was enough for her to see the damage. Newspapers were thrown carelessly on the coffee table beside a functioning laptop, more scattered on the rug. A sheet of Jean's expensive piano music had been tossed on the floor as well, near to where a couple of her Swedish crystal wine glasses rested against the rumpled sofa.

'Better, don't you think?' The guy's smug, complacent gaze shifted from the disaster scene to connect with hers. 'Some rooms are like some people. Just cry out for a little messing up.'

Words failed Amber. Too late to try resolving this conflict without the use of aggression. This man deserved aggression—he begged for it—and she was in too deep now to pull out.

She snatched up Jean's precious sonata from the floor, then marched over to the aquarium. It was almost annoying to see the tank as tranquil as ever. No bloated bodies floated on its placid surface.

She glanced back and saw him watching her with his thumbs hooked into his belt, a quirk to his mouth. 'You *have* been feeding them, haven't you?' In her aggravation she rolled Jean's sonata—rolled it and rolled it into a tighter and tighter cylinder. 'This was just a ploy to get me in here, wasn't it?'

He spread his hands. 'Aha. You've guessed my master plan.'

She made a sharp, repudiating gesture with the sonata. 'Don't you mock me. I have every right to complain about your noise.'

'Sure you do.'

He moved a couple of steps, so his big, lean body was close. Close enough for her to feel the heat of him. She couldn't step backwards without crashing into the fish tank, so she stood her ground, her heart rate escalating.

His growly voice was deep and smooth as butter. 'All right, I'm sorry to have stirred you up, Amber. I can see you're a woman of strong passions. I think maybe you *are* a bit tired. People get overwrought.' He drew his brows together and looked narrowly at her. *'Amber?* Are you sure that's your name?'

'What?'

'I think it should be Indigo. Or Lavender. Your oldies must have been drunk.' Missing her unamused glare, he shrugged. 'Never mind. I accept your apology. How about a drink?'

'I'm not apologising.' Her voice trembled as she lost the final vestiges of control and reasonable behaviour. 'And I don't want a drink. Just *look* what you've done to Jean's lovely home. You have no right to touch her precious piano. You're a—a vandal. I don't want to know you, or see you, or hear any more of your awful, awful *noise*.'

He studied her with a solemn, meditative gaze. But she knew, damn him, it was an act. Underneath he was dying to laugh. At her.

'You're a bit wired up.'

He advanced further, so that his chest was a mere five centimetres from her breasts. She inhaled the clean, male scent of him and sensed something else in him besides laughter. A high-voltage buzz of electricity that charged her own nerves with adrenaline.

'You should calm down.'

His sensual gaze touched her everywhere, caressed her hair, her throat, lingered on her mouth.

'I think I know a way I can help you to relax.'

'Oh.' Fury must have overheated her brain, because she lifted Jean's sonata and whacked him across the face with it.

Danger flashed in his eyes like a lightning strike. She watched, aghast, as a thin red line appeared where the rolled up edge of the paper had struck his cheekbone.

How could she have?

The universe shuddered to a stop. There was a moment when they both stood paralysed. Then in a quick, shocking movement he caught hold of her arms.

'You need to learn some control,' he said softly, steel in his voice, his eyes.

Her heart took a violent plunge as his hands burned her upper arms. The breath constricted in her throat.

'Let go of me,' she said, trying to sound calm while her thunderous heartbeat slammed into her ribs. She blustered the first thing that came into her head. 'Don't…don't you even *think* of trying to kiss me.'

His brows swept up in surprise, then his rainwater eyes sparkled like diamonds. As if she'd said something funny.

His lashes flickered half the way down. 'Are you sure you really mean that, Amber?'

Knowing her Freudian slip was flashing a bright neon, while her traitorous lips still tingled with… Well, for goodness' sake his lips were the most ravishing pair she'd encountered at close range for months. Her chaste, unkissed mouth was making a purely kneejerk and understandable chemical response.

Then, in an avalanche of bodily betrayal, her nipples joined in. She could feel a definite weakening arousal in them of a warming kind and wouldn't you know it? More arousal, all the way south.

At the exact instant those sensations registered with her a high-voltage, purely sexual flare lit Guy Wilder's eyes.

'Take your hands off me.' His grip slackened at once and she twisted away. 'Thank you.' Rubbing an arm, she hissed, 'There may be women who buckle at the knees when they meet you, Guy Wilder, but I can assure you I'm not one of them.'

The heat intensified in his gleaming gaze. He gave a knowing, sexy laugh. 'If you say so.' He crossed to the foyer in a couple of long strides and held the door wide. 'You'd better run home, little girl, and cool down. The wicked, wicked man might tempt you into doing something you enjoy.'

She brushed past him, racking her brains for a parting gibe. Then, with an insolent smile, she pointed to the angry patch on his cheek. 'Better put something on that.'

He touched the wound with his fingers. A smile curled the edges of his mouth as he retorted softly, 'Be seeing you, sweetheart.'

The door clicked to behind her.

Guy stood like a man who'd just been slammed somewhere strange by a tornado. It took some time for his aggravated pulse to ease. The fiery little exchange had stirred him in more ways than one.

He whistled. *Whew.* What a spitfire.

Nothing like a tempestuous woman to whip up a man's blood. His creative spirit was zinging. The way she held herself with that straight, proud back. If only he could get her in front of a camera.

He groaned, thinking of the way she'd glided across the room with that lithe, graceful walk. He felt aroused and at the same time amazingly energised, his whole being like an electric rod.

His blood quickened. How long since he'd felt this way? God, it felt great.

Safe inside her flat, Amber buried her face in her pillow, her mind churning with images of his handsome, taunting face. The things he'd said. The things *she'd* said.

Run home, little girl. The sheer arrogance of that. She clenched her teeth and tried to think of a hands-off way to murder the beast. Though with what she'd done so far, maybe hands-*on* would be more fitting. Why had she done such a terrible thing?

She should be wrung with shame, but to be honest she couldn't even feel very sorry. What was wrong with her? To have actually used violence like some wild virago was completely out of character for her. No one who knew her would believe Amber O'Neill, meek and mild as honeydew, could be capable of behaving with such a lack of restraint.

Well, no one *now.*

She'd once disgraced herself by pouring a glass of beer over Miguel da Vargas's handsome, lying head, but that was ancient history. Blood under the bridge. And he'd deserved it. *This* was all about sleep. If she didn't get some soon she'd have to be locked up to keep the public safe.

She punched her pillow, tossed and turned, but all to no avail. It was no use. She'd acted like a fool and she knew it. What had happened to her resolve to stay calm in a conflict situation? He'd been the one who'd stayed cool, while she…

She writhed to think of how easily he'd wiped the floor with her. *Run home, little girl.*

There had to be a way of salvaging her feminine honour.

Suddenly she froze on her bed of nails. She could hear him. He was in there, singing to himself like a man without a care in the world. *Or…* The thought stung through her agony. A man gloating.

Where was her feminine spirit? Was she just to lie down and take this?

She scrambled off the bed and took a minute or two to whip on a sexy push-up bra and some shoes with heels. She considered changing the rather deep-cut top, then discarded that idea. She didn't want him to think she'd gone to any trouble.

She smoothed down her skirt, ran a brush through her long hair. A little strategic eyeliner, a spray of perfume. Flicked the puff from her compact over her nose. Then, more presentable this time, more together, more *herself*—she took a fortifying swig of Vee juice from the fridge, and sashayed to his door for a second time.

Striding up to the bell, she gave it one imperative ring.

CHAPTER TWO

GUY WILDER took his leisurely time. When he finally stood framed in the entrance he seemed even more physical than she remembered. More hard-muscled and athletic. He didn't speak, just raised one arrogant black brow.

'Er…' Her mouth dried. She'd underestimated the sheer, overwhelming force of his presence. Bathed in that cool, merciless gaze, she felt her confidence nearly waver.

'Look,' she said, moistening her lips, 'I think we can be adult about this.'

In a long, searing scrutiny his eyes rested on her mouth, then flickered over her, leaving a scorching imprint on her flesh that wasn't altogether unpleasant, to her intense chagrin. He kept her pride toasting on the spit for torturous seconds, then opened the door just wide enough to admit her.

In the sitting room he leaned negligently against Jean's mantel, his bold gaze surveying her with amusement. 'What did you have in mind?'

It was the moment to apologise. She was a gentle person—*too* gentle, some said. Far too willing to accommodate the male beast. *Be more assertive, Amber. Don't be a doormat, Amber.* Those were the sorts of things girlfriends had said to her in the past.

Normally she'd have begged his pardon, flattered him

with a few waves of her lashes and been charmingly apologetic. But not this time. At the sight of him looking so insolently self-assured, his cool, intensely sensuous mouth beginning to curve in a smile, as though enjoying, *relishing* her discomfort, she felt her feminine pride challenged.

'I merely wish to reiterate the point,' she said coldly, 'that the walls in this building are thin. Now your singing is keeping me awake.'

He smiled, eyes lighting and creasing at the corners. 'You know, it concerns me that such a healthy woman—a woman so lithe, so supple and apparently fit…' He put his head on one side, his mouth edging up just the tiniest sensual bit as he wallowed in his contemplation of her body. 'In such *excellent* condition as yourself, should want to spend so much time sleeping. Do you ever do anything active, Amber? Go to the gym? Go clubbing? Dance till dawn?'

The irony of that. When she knocked herself out three mornings a week at dance class, ran a shop, studied, seized on any gigs going to keep the wolf from the door. 'That's none of your concern.'

He lowered his lashes, smiling a little. 'Well, I'm glad you've come to beg forgiveness.'

'In your dreams. O'Neills never beg.'

There was a glint in his eyes. 'No? Do thcy sing?'

He moved swiftly, and before she could protest grabbed her and pulled her down with him onto the piano seat. She gasped, braced to pull free, until his deep, quiet voice pinned her to the spot with a direct hit.

'Is it music you're allergic to, Amber, or men?'

She gave a dismissive laugh. 'Oh, *what?* Don't be silly. I like—*love* music.' He slid a bronzed arm around her waist and pulled her close against him. She made a token attempt to break away, but his body was all long, lean bone and muscle, iron-hard and impervious to her resistance.

The clean male scent of him, his vibrant masculine warmth, the touch of his hand on her ribs, sent her dizzy senses into spinning confusion. She should have pushed him away, should have got up and walked out, but something held her there. Something about his touch, her excited pulse and wobbly knees. Her pride. Her need to win this game if it killed her.

'What sort do you like?' Up close, his growly voice had an appealing resonance that stroked her inner ear.

'All sorts. Chopin. Tchaikovsky, of course.'

'Oh, of course.' He smiled.

'Don't mock,' she said quickly. 'Everyone's entitled to their own taste.'

'Sure they are. If you prefer to listen to the *dead*.' His breath tickled her ear. His lips were nearly close enough to brush the sensitive organ.

'They might be dead, but their music will live for eternity.' She flicked him a challenging glance. 'Can you say that about yours?'

He looked amused. 'Now you're really going for the jugular.'

A random thought struck her. She *could*, actually. His jugular wasn't so far away. With just a slight lean she could lick his strong bronzed neck and taste his salt. Relish him with her tongue.

Adrenaline must be screwing her brain.

'*Chopin*, of all people.' He continued to scoff, mischief in his eyes. 'Isn't his stuff a bit wishy-washy for you, Amber? A bit…' He made a levelling gesture. 'Flat?'

Of course he would think that. But there was no use pretending she wasn't a total nerd. Even before a firing squad her conscience wouldn't let her deny her true colours. Not with all the ways Chopin's piano works spoke to her. How subtle they were, and poignant. How they wound their way into the warp and weft of her most tender emotions.

'No. Those pieces just—seep into my soul.' She turned to look at him.

Guy met her clear gaze and felt the kind of lurch he should avoid at all costs. He *should.* But there were her eyes…

He heard himself say dreamily, 'You know, you're soft. Such curly lashes. And those sensational eyes…'

Amber felt a giant blush coming on. Unless a new heat-wave was sweeping Sydney.

Perhaps the man needed glasses or was a raving lunatic. She started to say something to that effect, and stopped. His mouth was gravely beautiful, and so close she had to hold her breath. His lips were wide and curled up at the corners, the upper one thin, the lower one fuller, more sensual. Lips made for kissing a woman into a swoon. Some poor hungry woman. Lips that could draw the very soul from that poor hungry, famished woman's…

For goodness' sake, Amber. Fatigue must be distorting her perceptions. Just because he had a lean, chiselled jaw and a stunning profile it didn't mean she should forget the male/female reality.

She gave herself a mental slap. Feet on the ground and an eye to the door. That was a woman's survival kit. That was what her mother had always told her, and Lise O'Neill had known better than most. When the going got tough, men disappeared.

Just because Amber had failed chronically to apply her mother's wisdom on certain other crucial occasions it didn't mean she had to fail now. Here was a prime opportunity to start inoculating herself against the cunning wiles of the wolfhound.

She didn't have to be susceptible. She *could* resist.

'Now, let's see, Amber.' At this distance she could almost feel the rumble of his deep voice in his chest. 'Your lips are like cherries, roses and berries.' He studied them appreciatively. 'Although maybe softer, redder and juicier. I guess I'll have to taste them to get that line exactly right…'

She tensed, waiting, pulse racing, but instead of delivering the anticipated kiss, he continued examining her.

'And your eyes…' He paused to inspect them. 'What rhymes with amethyst?'

He rippled a few tunes, then settling on 'Eleanor Rigby', sang softly. *"'Amber O'Neill, mouth sweet as wine. And her eyes are like clear am—e—thyst. Never been ki—issed. Amber O'Neill. She's twenty-nine and she goes to bed early to pine opp—or—tun—i—ties mi—issed..."'*

He didn't sing the next line, just played it. He didn't have to. She remembered how it went. *'All the...'*

Her heart panged. 'Very funny. It's not even true.'

'Which part?'

'Any of it.' Her breasts quickly rose and fell inside their confining bra. Anyone would be lonely in her situation. Of course she missed her mother every minute of every day. It was only natural. They'd only had each other. After she'd left the ballet company and all her friends there she hadn't had much opportunity to make new ones, apart from people who worked in the mall.

And she knew why he thought she looked twenty-nine. It had to be her clothes. If it had been any of his concern, she might have explained about her work costumes. The only thing wrong with them, apart from being relentlessly floral, was that they weren't all that shiny new.

Oh, this chronic lack of funds was approaching crisis point. There wasn't much more she could do about it—

unless the vintage shop around the corner had a sudden influx of barely worn clothes with flowery patterns.

She was signed up for Saturday night gigs at a Spanish club in Newtown for the next few weeks, though she'd planned to use those earnings for her stock explosion. She hadn't planned on it—the shop must always come first—but maybe she could use some of her show earnings to buy something modern. Some new jeans, maybe? A little jacket?

Then she remembered Serena. She'd promised to give her an advance on her salary in return for an extra Thursday evening. And Serena deserved all the help she could get.

Amber noticed he was examining her with a serious expression while those dismal musings were flashing through her head faster than the speed of light. Then his face broke into a slow, sexy, teasing smile. It lengthened his eyes, made them do that crinkling thing at the corners.

She risked a glimpse into the silvery depths. 'I'm sorry I swiped you with that sonata.'

He nodded gravely. 'Okay. It's a long time since I was smacked by a beautiful woman. Exciting, though.' His voice was a velvet caress. 'Do you often…?'

'No.'

'Pity. You've got quite a good wrist action there. I'd have thought you'd had a bit of experience.' He saw her quick flush and, though his mouth grew grave, the smile still lurked in his eyes. Rueful, not unkind. Anything but unkind. 'Never mind. Apology accepted.'

Her heart quickened and she dragged her gaze away. She shouldn't have looked. She was, after all, Amber O'Neill, notorious push-over for charming heartbreakers. Next thing you knew she'd be starting to flirt, indulging in a little verbal sparring, giving him the husky laugh, luring him in, laying sultry glances on his mouth…

'Tsk, now look. You have dark smudges here…and here.' He lightly ran his thumb-tip under each eye. 'You'll have to cut out all this partying, Amber. You need to get some sleep.'

She ignored the soft imprint his thumb left on her skin, though lightning flickered through her skin cells and her sexual sensors went into a swoon. She hoped they didn't lose their giddy little heads.

She tried to distract him with conversation. If she didn't mention anything sexual, said nothing at all to do with his lips… Hers dried, and though she fought the urge she couldn't resist running her tongue-tip around them. She noticed how the wolf gleamed at once from his knowing eyes. Oh, Lord. He was reading her like a traffic light.

'What are you doing here, anyway?' She kept her tone polite. Not too interested, just neighbourly. 'Jean never mentioned you'd be staying.'

He nodded. 'It was pretty last-minute. A builder's knocking walls out of my house and it's currently unlivable. Jean's honeymoon has come at the right time.'

She frowned, thinking. 'I don't remember seeing you at the wedding.'

His face smoothed to become expressionless. 'I wasn't there.'

'Oh. What a shame you missed it. It was fantastic. What a party. Jean must be sorry you couldn't make it.'

He shrugged and gave a brief harsh laugh. 'She'd have been surprised if I had.'

His knee brushed hers and she momentarily closed her eyes. At least he sounded fond of Jean, she thought, savouring the sparks shooting up and down her leg. That was one thing about him. Another was his voice. It was so deep and dark, and in its way musical, as soothing to the ear as a lute.

She noticed with some surprise her headache had just about departed. That might have been down to the lute effect. Or even the knee factor. The truth was, sound was not her only sensitivity. Like the beguiling Eustacia Vye, she'd always had this intense vulnerability to certain masculine knees.

Face it, there were times she felt like a sensory theme park. Right now the lights were on, the music was playing and she was glowing from the inside out.

'It could be fantastic being here with you, Amber, or it could be…fantastic. What do you think?' His lean, smooth hands rippling the keys made the notes sound like velvet water. She could imagine those hands playing along her spine like that. Gentling her, caressing her. Stroking her languid limbs, her hair. Better than a dangling twig any day.

She gave a throaty laugh—not her day-to-day one. 'I wouldn't say you're *with* me, exactly.'

'Getting closer, though. Don't you think?' His arm curved around her and he patted her hip.

'You wish.' She shifted away a little—though not as far as all that. 'I don't think you've demonstrated your desirability as a neighbour yet, Guy.'

He responded with a low, sexy laugh that demonstrated confidence in his abilities, if nothing else. 'I'm working on it. Let's see. Can I tempt you to some wine?'

She rarely drank alcohol. Fruit and veggie juices were her preferred drinks. Wine was not the ballerina's friend. But, having assaulted him, she could hardly afford to be churlish. Besides, he smelled so deliciously male.

She lifted her shoulders. 'Wine would be—fine.'

He was gone a few minutes. After a short while she

heard him in Jean's kitchen, opening drawers and cupboards.

She drew some hard, deep breaths to fill her lungs. Her exhilarated blood felt all bubbly. She felt pleasantly high and in control, as she sometimes did on stage. It gave her the same sort of out-of-body freedom—as if she wasn't so much Amber as Amber's avatar.

Looking more devastating by the minute, Guy returned with two glasses of red, along with the bottle. Amber recognised the glasses as Jean's special wedding crystal. She accepted hers with a twinge of guilt. But, hey. She wasn't the police. And she wasn't in charge here, was she? Sometimes it was best to go with the flow.

They clinked glasses, Guy watching as she held her wine to her lips, his eyes shimmering with a warmth she knew only too well. Her blood quickened.

Desire was in the air.

'Tell me about yourself, Amber,' he said. 'What do you do besides worship the dead?'

'I'm a— I have the flower shop down in the arcade.'

He wrinkled his brow. 'Don't think I recall a florist's. Where is that? It must be tucked down an alleyway.'

'No, it's not.'

He set down his glass and started rippling the keys again.

She tried not to watch. The less chance she had to obsess on the lean hand finding a tune with such casual expertise the better. Or the other one. The one absently stroking so close to her breast.

'It's right at the end, near the street entrance. I—haven't had it long. There isn't much stock yet so it's not quite up and running. When I have more stock—more flowers, et cetera—you'll be likely to notice it then. I'll open up the street doors and put a lovely awning out in the street to catch the passing trade. Maybe in six months or so.' With loads of luck, time and dancing gigs.

He frowned and put his head on one side. 'Yeah? How does that work?'

She looked quickly at him. 'How do you mean?'

'Just that. When you start something *off* you need to start as you intend to…' He hesitated, his eyes calculating something she couldn't read, then all at once his gaze narrowed and he looked closely at her. 'Ah, now I can see why they called you Amber.' His voice deepened, as if he'd made a thrilling, almost arousing discovery. 'Look at that. They're not straight violet, after all. The irises have the most beautiful little amber flecks.'

Stirred, she felt herself flush, and gave an embarrassed laugh. 'Oh, honestly. Guys like you.'

Though he smiled, his eyes sharpened. 'What about guys like me?'

'You'd say anything. No one has violet eyes—except maybe Liz Taylor.'

'Hush. Where's the poetry in your soul? Anyway, that's only half true.' Absently, he took a lock of her hair, ran it through his fingers as if it were made of some rare, precious silk. Her hair follicles shivered with joy. 'There aren't any other guys like me. I'm the original one-off.'

Certainly better than a twig. With the wine warming her cockles, she was starting to feel quite languorous. Voluptuous, even. Gently she removed the tress from his fingers. 'They all say that.'

'Do they? I'm starting to wonder what sort of guys you know, Amber.' Then glancing at her, he gave a quick, rueful smile. 'Oh, sorry. I guess a woman like you… You'd be used to men wanting to impress you.' He flashed her a veiled look. 'Do you receive a lot of offers?'

She supposed there'd been a few. Though always from

people no one in their right mind would consider viable—apart from Miguel. *Especially* Miguel.

Not caring to boast, she made a non-committal, so-so sort of gesture. 'Oh, well…'

'I'm not surprised,' he said warmly. 'There are so many of these blokes about. Operators looking for a beautiful woman to hook up with.' He nodded, sighing. 'Yeah, I know the type. First they use the old sweet talk routine to soften you up. Then they manoeuvre you into a clinch.' He glanced at her, his eyes gleaming. 'Or is that where they start these days? With a kiss?'

As if he didn't know. Her heart bumped into double time.

This conversation was heading in a certain direction, but it was undeniably thrilling. It had been ages since she'd felt on the verge of something truly dangerous and fantastic. All right, so he was an operator of the worst kind. She could be too, if she had to be. She hadn't taken a celibacy vow yet, had she? Why else was she wearing a push-up bra?

Right on cue Amber's avatar sashayed into centre stage and met his gaze through Amber's lashes. 'I'm already pretty soft, Guy,' she breathed through Amber's lips. 'There are times I prefer to go direct to the kiss.'

His eyes lit with a piercingly sensual gleam. He studied her, eyelids half lowered, reminding her even more of that sleek, smiling wolf.

The summer evening tensed. A shivery excitement prickled along her veins.

With his grey eyes shimmering, in dreamy slow motion he raised a bronzed hand to push a loose strand of her hair behind her ear. In the spot where his fingers connected her skin sprang into tingling life. Softly he trailed one finger over her cheek, down her throat to the hollow at its base.

Sensation rippled through her every nerve cell. Her lips parted as he stroked the delicate skin of her throat. Her skin fell into an enchantment. She saw his eyes drop to her mouth and darken and her heart gave a great bound.

She tilted her head, for a moment teetering on a magical edge of anticipation, then swiftly she leaned forward and pressed her lips to his. His sexy mouth felt, firm and so electrically alive, and tasted of wine. She moved her lips against his and a delicious fire sprang to life and danced along them.

His smooth hands slid up to cradle her head, and she leaned into him to gain a more comfortable position. He seized the initiative from her, intensifying the kiss to a searing, sensual charge. She felt something like a deep gasp whoosh through her, and her body shot into electric response as the tip of his tongue slid through to tangle with hers and tantalise the delicate tissues just inside her mouth.

Then, just when she thought desire was a pleasant hunger, his mouth took her tongue captive and sucked.

Oh, baby. Desire was no gentle longing. It was a raging furnace. She gave herself up to the mindless sensation. His beard rasping her skin, his vibrant chest firm and solid under her restless palms.

Liquid quivers shuddered through the top of her head, roused her through her breasts and thighs, down the backs of her knees to the tips of her curled up toes. His hands travelled caressingly up her arms, slid to her swelling breasts, while hers flexed on his biceps. Fire flamed in her blood, stirred all her secret, private places with yearning.

His breath mingled with hers and the masculine flavour of him went to her head like wine. He pulled her closer and she felt the friction of his hard chest pressing her nipples.

The blood boomed in her ears and lust swept her like a flame—wild, searing and erotic.

In the grip of the inferno, she thirsted to be closer. Struggling not to in any way diminish the connection, she kept glued to his lips while she squirmed her way onto his thighs. Straddling that impressive lap, she felt her appreciation of the kiss escalate to a whole new dimension.

As though divining her hunger, he tightened his arms around her and rocked her on the hard ridge of his erection with electrifying results. Pleasure roiled through her in waves.

And her body gasped for more. Much, much more. Until in one impassioned, over-enthusiastic plunge she rocked him right off the piano seat and onto the floor.

Thwack. She landed on top of him in a graceless tangle of arms and legs. Half groaning in a laughing complaint about her roughness, he adjusted his position beneath her. She laughed as well, while every inch of her was aware of the raw, virile flesh separated from hers by a couple of thin layers of material.

There was a moment when their laughter faded and they both stilled. His arms tightened around her again. She could feel his heart thumping against her chest while his masculine scent invaded her head. Or maybe that was her heart pounding in her ears like a jungle drum.

Anything could happen—but just like that? With a stranger? In Jean's flat?

She scrambled up, her head whirling. Adjusted her top. Smoothed her skirt. She might be a little drunk with that kiss, but parts of her brain were still connected.

Her host pulled himself up and adjusted his jeans. They almost managed to avoid one another's glances. The air sizzled with incompletion. It tugged at her breasts and feminine loins. Made her feel like doing something dangerous.

Guy felt every part of his body tingle to the imprint of

her soft, firm flesh. Was she about to slip through his fingers? Instinct told him not. Not if he played it easy.

He let his glance fall to where glimpses of her breasts tantalised at the edge of her shirt. Arousal had him in its grip. His erection was protesting the confinement of his underwear. Surely she must feel it too? Desire crackled in the air like electricity—a promise propelling them to an inevitable conclusion.

She *must* feel it.

Amber's gaze collided accidentally with his and she felt singed. She smoothed her hair. Maybe she should go home before his eyes carried her away. Home to her dark flat, with the sitting room furniture all jammed into the hall. The single lamp she read by. No company.

'I know what you're thinking.' he said softly. 'But you shouldn't go. Not yet.'

That piqued her pride. 'You don't know what I'm thinking.'

His eyes shimmered. 'Then show me. Let me in.'

As if she wasn't already intoxicated, she picked up her glass and drank more of the wicked, wicked wine. Glass in hand, she leaned on the piano and smiled. 'All right, tempter. Go on, then. Play for me.'

He frowned a little at first. She guessed he was disappointed. He'd had other entertainment in view. But he gave in with a gracious shrug and sat down at the piano.

He rested his hands loosely on the keys, then started into a song—some rare, long-forgotten tune that sidled into her heart with a haunting familiarity. He played it against the beat, like a true jazz man, drawing out its sexy sound.

Suddenly a door opened in her memory and a scene came rushing back.

Her mother and father, laughing and dancing in each

other's arms in the kitchen of their old house. When they were still together. When they still loved each other.

Now she knew the song. It was 'Ruby', an old number from a Ray Charles album her mother had loved. Lise had continued to play it long after Amber's father had left her. Left *them*.

It didn't even matter now that the lyrics weren't being sung. From down the decades Ray's beautiful dark golden voice was still in Amber's head, recorded there forever in high fidelity, the bittersweet pain of his song as fresh as ever.

Blame the wine or the song, but the music plucked unbearably at her heartstrings. Twisted her most vulnerable emotions and swamped her with nostalgia and regret.

Guy looked up and touched her with his gleaming glance. Something arced between them. Some mutual understanding.

Quickly she lowered her lashes, though she knew he'd seen her tears. But still he continued to play, wringing every last poignant drop from the song as if her response was only natural. Maybe it was then she confused the music with the man.

Fighting tears, she gazed at his lean, strong hands dancing on the keys, on her heart, and her desire bloomed into an intense hunger.

Devouring him with her eyes, she was shaken by a fierce wanton need to bite his mouth, lick his strong neck, feel his warm skin under her fingertips. All at once being near him was both anguish and ecstasy. Yearning for him while at the mercy of the song, she pressed her fingers hard to the piano. Caressed the silky wood, stroked the elegant lines, urgent in her longing to be touched and held.

Guy could hardly keep his eyes from her. Attuned to the quickening sexual current, he switched into one of his own songs. Sexed up the tempo in time with his accelerating desire.

At the change of melody Amber felt both sorry and relieved. At least without the song's weakening associations her defences managed to firm themselves up again. Good grief, she'd come close to an emotional meltdown. She was conscious of having allowed Guy, a *stranger*, to see too much, and everything in her scurried to cover up.

For goodness' sake, this was hardly the time or place for tears. This was the bewitching hour.

Slipping off her shoes, she crawled up onto the piano lid.

Clunk. The music hit a bump. Cool, casual Guy Wilder must be startled. Amber giggled with delight when she saw his stunned face. He was staring at her, his eyes gleaming with an amused and intensely sensual light.

He gave a deep sexy laugh. 'You bad, bad girl,' he said softly. 'What are you up to?'

Encouraged, she slithered across the lid to him, making herself as sinuous as a serpent. A voluptuous serpent, with a longing to feel the contact of hard, muscled man against her skin.

Her ravenous, tingling skin.

He stared at her, eyes ablaze, his hands suspended over the keys.

She rested her chin on her hands and smiled. 'Did you know I can do the splits?'

The piercing hot gleam in his eyes could have set her aflame. 'I'd really like to see that.'

The challenge in his husky voice revealed such a depth of wolfish excitement a laugh of pure exhilaration bubbled out of her. Amber O'Neill was flying high, as energised as if she'd just pirouetted right across the stage on points.

Loving her power to galvanise such warm admiration—

very warm, judging by the bulge in Guy's jeans—she ordered him to keep playing.

Guy was happy to accommodate. Eager, one might say. He did his best to comply, continuing to thump the keys while staring, mesmerised. At first she sat up, straight-backed, and tucked up her skirt into her pants' elastic.

Then, before his hypnotised gaze, she folded her supple self into the lotus position. Each time his fingers faltered on the keys she nodded at him to play on. He started into something—though who knew what? His hands were on an erratic auto-pilot, since every other part of him, from his fascinated gaze to his painful, throbbing erection, was riveted on her.

His brows lifted in disbelief as she smoothly stretched first her right leg, way out to ninety degrees at one side, then her left to the other. All the impossible way. Until both gorgeous legs made a perfect one-eighty. His gaze was riveted to the tender, crucial little bridge touching the piano lid in the middle. His jeans tightened unbearably.

She gazed down upon him like some oriental goddess, her eyes shadowed and mysterious. 'We call this the straddle position.'

Inside his constricting jeans, the skin of his engorged penis felt ready to burst.

Then, before his lustful gaze, she stretched her right arm over her head and with graceful ease laid her head down on her leg while she touched her left foot with her fingers, the long switch of her hair falling away from her neck.

Then she straightened her taut back and did the reverse, her left arm over her head, fingers touching her right foot. The graceful line of her body, the agonising beauty of her lithe form, her vulnerable neck, dragged at his heart.

It was too much for a guy two years on the sexual wagon.

He sprang up and seized her. With fire thundering in his blood, he lifted her off the piano and set her down on the floor.

Like a wild man, he took her sweet mouth in possession while somehow stripping off his clothes and fumbling with hers.

'Hurry, hurry,' she was trying to say through his frenzied kisses, as though he wasn't rushing as fast as any painfully aroused guy was humanly able.

When she stood naked before him, the beauty of her nude body made his insides tremble. Her breasts small and so achingly perfect. The areolae around the rosy, pouting nipples flushed with arousal. Her waist so slender his hands could have spanned it. The smooth curve of her hips and the pretty triangle of curls sent what was left of his sanity flying out of the window.

Free at last, his rampant erection reached the zenith of rock-hard demand. He stooped gingerly for his jeans and dug for the condom in his wallet, grateful to have one on hand.

For a moment she stood facing him, her eyes as hot as he knew his must be. Then she moved forward and put her arms around his neck, kissing his mouth and jaw, touching him, pressing herself to his chest and nuzzling his neck in the sort of confiding, feminine way that could weaken a man.

'You're beautiful,' she whispered, huskiness in her sweet voice. 'Such a strong, beautiful man.'

It tore at him in some way to reject her sweetness, but he couldn't encourage the softer expressions. Gently but firmly he put her away from him. He didn't require any further stimulation. And satisfaction could best be obtained for all concerned without too much of the demanding intimate stuff.

He pushed her onto the sofa. Deliciously willing, she lay there panting, scrutinising him, her lovely eyes dark and stormy with arousal. When he joined her, she met his passion with equal fervour.

He tried not to be rough or too greedy. While his lust raged over her fragile beauty with hands, lips and tongue, he drew on all his experience to please her. And she reciprocated, stroking and caressing him, playful and languid as a cat, while at the same time hungry. So primitively, devastatingly female.

When her moment was ripe, her sex as plump and juicy as a peach, he thrust his straining shaft into her gloriously tight aperture, unable to hold back a groan. It had been so long for him. The silky grip of her hot inner sheath felt like the closest he'd ever come to heaven.

Fearful of splitting her in two with his straining bulk, he took care with her at first, moving gently inside her to give her time to accustom to his size, watching the play of shadows on her face, feasting on her beauty.

Their eyes met. Locked. Something in her expression sent a rush of silly things to his tongue. Affectionate words, passionate phrases to express his appreciation, the sheer trembling pleasure in his heart. But some divine prudence held him back.

Best to avoid the lyrics.

Anyway, she arched her supple body under him then, locking her gorgeous legs around him to take him further in. He required no urging, and any random moment of tenderness that might have happened passed.

With the fiercest imaginable pleasure he plunged, thrusting his aching penis deep into her sweet, yielding flesh with rhythmic, ferocious vigour.

And she strove with him, tendons straining in her neck just as in his. In some ways—maybe it was her awesome gymnastic ability—he thought of her as his equal and his opposite. The supple muscles working under the skin of her slim abdomen thrilled and delighted him. Catapulted him towards his climax.

But he was still a gentleman where it counted.

With his urgent need for release straining at the very leash, he used all the control at his command to hold himself back. Concentrated on other things. Her sighs. The little cries issuing from deep in her throat. Her swollen mouth. And at last he was rewarded. Her orgasm blossomed. He saw it written in the flush of her skin, in the sort of ecstatic absorption that came over her face. Tears…were they tears?…spilled on her cheeks.

Then, blessedly, he felt her inside walls grip his grateful length with that bliss-making, rhythmic pull.

Ohh. Oh, Amber O'Neill.

With a groan he allowed himself to spill, surrendering to his own ecstasy.

It was cramped on Jean's sofa. After a few thundering heartbeats Guy hauled himself up and off her. Amber grimaced at the ridiculous blur in her eyes and gave them a hasty wipe with the back of her hand.

Smiling, she reached to touch Guy. Dragging his fingers through his hair, without any further eye contact he stumbled away in the direction of the bedrooms.

She heard taps go on and turned on her side, relaxed now that her heart had slowed its pounding, her skin feeling pleasant against the sofa fabric. She closed her eyes and snuggled into the cushions, grinning to herself.

How the world could change in a few short hours. Amber O'Neill had snagged herself a gorgeous playmate with no trouble whatsoever. A lovely, lovely man. Sexy. Musical. *Hot.* She really should knock on people's doors more often.

She waited so long she must have drifted into a little doze. After a while she woke to the chill on her cooling skin. There was no sign of Guy. She started to feel naked, and not in a good way.

She got up and started to dress, intending to go and investigate.

With her clothes on and the man missing, her amazing mood deflated. Taking stock of the scene, she hastened to plump up the sofa cushions, shuddering to imagine what Jean would have thought of her shenanigans.

Her shoes were under the piano. *Jean's* piano. How would she ever look Jean in the face again? She crawled under it to retrieve her shoes, and was slipping them on when Guy strolled in.

'Oh, Amber,' he said. 'Okay?' He smiled, but his glance slid off her before it could gain any foothold. He strolled to the coffee table and bent to switch on his laptop.

He was in fresh clothes, his hair gleaming wet. It looked as if he'd showered.

Questions flashed through her mind like quicksilver. Could he have been standing in the shower all that time? Why? Had he forgotten about her? It seemed as if he was avoiding looking at her.

She felt all at sea. Miguel had been cool, especially when he'd had something to hide, but this was *über*-cool.

She smiled, searching his face. 'Where'd you get to?'

He blinked rapidly. 'Well, I just…er…had something I needed to do. Look here, that was…that was really something, Amber. You're a beautiful woman. A very lovely woman. So, so sexy.' He took her arms and planted a little kiss on the corner of her mouth. 'Thing is,' he said, moving away, eyes screened by his lashes, 'I have an early start in the morning. Sorry if this seems a bit—abrupt, but I have things I need to prepare for work tomorrow.'

'Oh, right. Well…'

She looked searchingly at him, but he'd absented himself to somewhere remote. Shock must have fogged her brain, because she couldn't think up a sassy comment with which to ease the moment forward with a laugh and a wiggle.

She lifted her shoulders. 'Well, then. I'll be seeing you.' Stunned, confused and stinging, she walked to the door.

She opened it before he could, and was about to step outside when he murmured her name. She glanced back, her heart lifting.

But there was no farewell clinch. Just a brusque touch of her cheek. When he spoke his voice sounded gruff. 'Goodnight. Sleep well.'

She tried to get some words to form. Some cool words. But even Amber's avatar let her down this time and none would come.

She reached her front door, confusion and anger swelling in her chest.

She felt like such a fool. Such a silly, worthless fool.

CHAPTER THREE

AMBER saw him in the arcade next morning, first thing, when she was hurrying home from her early dance class at the Wharf. Not many shops had yet opened their doors.

Guy appeared at the opposite end, loping up the near-deserted mall with a fluid, easy motion. He was in running shorts and a singlet, a sheen of perspiration on his neck and arms. The instant she spotted him her pulse revved up and her lungs forgot to breathe.

The gorgeous symmetry of all that muscle, bone and sinew working in symphony washed over her and left her feeling—raw. As any woman might feel after a long, anguished night curled up into a ball of shame and misery.

Thank goodness sheer exhaustion had mercifully blacked her out in the end.

She knew the exact moment he spotted her. There was a slight check in his gait, then he slowed to a walk. As he advanced towards her she tried to steady her face. She wasn't ready for this. She hadn't yet decided how to play it. How best to protect herself. If she had to share the lift with him she doubted she could trust herself to stay cool and unruffled for nine whole floors.

He drew level with her, his acute gaze taking in the shortish dress and the casual cardi she wore over her leotard, her sports carry-all.

'Er…hi.' He looked keenly at her with veiled eyes, then dropped his lashes. Perhaps she would detect something behind his casual greeting. Constraint. 'You're up early. Been to the gym?' He continued to gaze down at her, then turned with her towards the lift.

Amber pressed the button. 'Nope.'

'Yoga?'

'No.' She held her head high, not looking at him, but she could feel his quizzical gaze scrutinising her face. If he dared to make a joke about her flexibility…

The lift doors shuddered apart.

'Morning must make you brisk. I seem to recall you were much friendlier last night.' The mocking sensuality in his voice hit that raw spot in her vital organs, but she maintained her cool.

Stepping inside the narrow lift, she pressed for the ninth and turned deliberately to face him, arms extended to block his entrance. 'Must have been because you're such a warm guy, Guy.'

She smiled sweetly as the doors slid shut in his face.

With his coffee cooling, Guy clicked through his presentation to staff. Stared at it.

Hardly surprising, but he didn't take much in. What with last night constantly intruding, and now the encounter in the mall…

His fingers stilled on the mousepad. He hadn't been so aloof, had he? He'd tried to be gentle with her. Polite. He thought he'd expressed his sincere appreciation quite fulsomely.

He could admit to feeling a certain discomfort about the way things had gone down at the end of their sexy little interlude. Maybe she was right to some degree. He guessed he could have been smoother.

All right. *Kinder.* Thing was, he was out of practice.

The choking sensation rose in his chest and he squashed it down. He wasn't geared up for all the stuff with women.

Anyway, he rejected outright any blame for succumbing to sex. She'd been seductive, and so…so utterly…. For the whole of this morning's fifteen-kilometre run he'd been as preoccupied with recalling the highlights as a teenager after his first woman.

The *feel* of her. The sheer physical pleasure of holding her supple form in his arms. And at the same time her yielding softness. Her eyes, so gentle and giving and…

His heart quickened and he closed his eyelids. Even after the longest shower in history that softness had stayed on his skin the night through. Hell, what had come over him? He should have used more finesse.

But…

He couldn't risk getting into all that.

No doubt in this world, where men were the bad guys and women saints, his reserve at the end there could have come across as seeming casual. All right, cold.

Callous was far too harsh a term. Exploitative… Where had that sprung from?

Never.

He sprang up and paced. It was in no way true. If he wasn't the sucker he'd once been, he was still in every way a decent, caring and honourable guy. She couldn't deny she'd been equally enthusiastic. He hadn't promised her anything, had he?

This was just life. Amber O'Neill needed to toughen up. Sure, he'd noticed signs of emotion in her, but none of it had been down to *him*. He'd done nothing to bring that teary sparkle that had come and gone in her eyes. And for a woman to actually shed tears during sex…

What guy *would* cope?

He ignored the smart little voice piping, *The guy you used to be.* And he ignored the gnawing twinge that had been occupying his chest since he'd closed the door after her last night. Whatever had upset her was *not* his responsibility.

Men had to shield themselves or they could be swept along on a woman's emotions and end up a wreck before the eyes of the world.

He slammed the door on his old nightmare before it could properly materialise. Breathed carefully for a while. In. Out.

The wedding debacle had no more power to gut him. It was over now, the bad time long gone. He'd learned his lesson, and there'd be no more debacles for Guy Wilder.

If Amber O'Neill was too soft for the rough and tumble of casual sex she should look elsewhere for a playmate.

Regrettable, though, in some ways.

Amber chose one of her prettiest costumes: capri pants patterned in rose coloured daisies with a rose-pink top and heels. With a little make-up she looked cheery enough, and that was good. The customers didn't have to know she'd taken a few lacerations to the spirit.

Determined to swan through the day with a smile here and a sunbeam there, she made porridge—her favourite—then ended up washing it down the sink.

Food was impossible with her insides churning so fast. If only she hadn't encountered him in the mall.

There were so many things she could have said, but she was glad she'd restrained herself. Last night she might have felt like trash, but it was a sensation she'd experienced before. She just hadn't expected it. Not with him. He'd seemed so…lovely.

Anyway, no use brooding. Write him off as a mistake.

Wallowing in angst and recriminations wouldn't help. She'd found that out the hard way with Miguel, when her mother had needed her there every night. Some men were tone deaf to feelings.

Pity she could still make the same mistakes with that knowledge so deeply inscribed on her soul.

Anyway, forget Guy Wilder's smile and his crow's feet and his music. How charming he'd been until he'd achieved his… Oh. She flinched to think of it and her eyes were awash again.

She blotted them carefully with her fingers, but the tactic wasn't all that successful.

Great. Now she'd have to fix her mascara. What was wrong with her anyway? She was turning into an emotional wreck. She just mustn't *think* about it. It was too demoralising. It wasn't worth another second of her time.

She reminded herself of her resolutions. She wouldn't tolerate disrespect. Her next love, if she found one, would know how to value her. Gone were the days when she gave a man her all, while he took all he could.

She pressed her lips into a firm line. The old Amber was gone. The new Amber was sparing with her gifts. The *new* Amber took no prisoners.

Well, those were her resolves, at least, as she steeled herself to walk past Guy's door and into the lift.

Unlocking the shop door was a relief. At least here she had a safe haven from the perils of the ninth floor. And, since she was on her own for the day, she'd have no time to dwell on whether a man had deliberately conned her into believing he was a human being for the sake of an orgasm.

She'd barely received her daily flower delivery and commenced the task of sorting, before Roger, the smooth, bald CEO from Centre Management, strolled in.

He was doing the rounds, he said. Reminding everyone

of the next evening's residents' meeting. She noticed his shrewd, light eyes dart about, not missing a thing.

'Doesn't your lease come up for renewal soon?' he said blandly. 'Two months from tomorrow, isn't it?'

As if he didn't know. And as if she needed reminding.

He cast a measured glance at the shuttered glass wall. 'You know, Amber, some of our tenants consider this a very desirable location. That access to the street is valuable. Properly used, with a good display, the whole arcade would stand to benefit from that entrance being wide open and attractive.'

Amber was reminded of what one of her neighbours had recently said. Marc, the tenant of Homme, the menswear shop next door, had jokingly offered to swap premises with her. Homme could make a great splash at that entrance, Marc had enthused, making her and Serena laugh till they cried with his hilarious demonstrations of how he might arrange his favourite mannequins to attract attention.

Listening to Roger now, Amber wondered if Marc's suggestion had been more serious than she'd imagined.

After Roger drifted away, she sat disconsolately at the counter and stared around the shop. To make a worthwhile display out on the street as well as in the mall would require heaps more stock. Then there'd be the necessary awning, the stands, the cost of the sign…

Added to the cost of improving its interior, the shop's current takings weren't anywhere near sufficient to cover it.

She held her head in her hands. Even though she'd only had the shop a couple of months, she couldn't help feeling guilty. It was hers now, and like all the tenants there she had a responsibility in upholding the style of the arcade. With its wood panelling and leadlight framed windows, most of Kirribilli Mansions possessed an old-fashioned chic. *Most.*

Somehow her mother had always managed to wind the arcade management around her little finger. As far as Amber knew Fleur Elise had never been refurbished in the nine years since Lise had taken Ivy on. Amber often wondered if her mother would have had more success if she'd ignored Ivy's advice and taken another approach. Spent money to make money.

As so often these days, her thoughts crept to the possibility of a bank loan. Wasn't that how real business people commonly operated? Even without Roger's prompting, this felt like the moment to strike with the changes she wanted. And how else was she to do it?

Though what if Ivy was right? What if she purchased more stock and it all just withered and died? No return for the money, and no way to repay the loan?

What was it Guy had said about the need to begin as you intended to carry on?

She pushed thoughts of him away. Anyway, what would he—a songwriter—know about it? Sure, he seemed quite musical, but that was hardly a qualification for success in business.

At lunchtime she turned the 'Closed' sign to face outwards and strolled down to the deli for a sandwich. As she waited at the counter Marc, her mall neighbour, came up behind her with a cheery, 'Hi.'

He bent to look closely at her, his liquid dark eyes anxious. 'You're looking a bit peaky, darl. You haven't been listening to those poisonous rumours, have you?'

She lifted her brows. 'What rumours?'

'Oh, nothing to worry about. Just that silly old madam again. Take no notice of anything she says.'

Amber understood he was talking about Dianna

Delornay, the elegant proprietress of Madame, the shop across the mall from Fleur Elise.

'Come on, now. What did Di say?

He didn't take much coaxing. It seemed Di had requested a move to the other end of the mall. Apparently Di felt her glitzy little boutique was in danger of being embarrassed by the vibes from Fleur Elise.

'Goodness. *Embarrassed?*' Amber's amused little tinkling laugh was pure fraud to cover her indignation.

For heaven's sake. Surely Fleur Elise wasn't all that bad? She hadn't been aware of all this dissatisfaction with it when her mother was alive.

Despite Marc's sympathetic cooing, Amber walked back to her counter with doubt clouding her mind. Everyone knew Marc and Di were cronies. Maybe she should take up his offer of a swap.

Turning to examine the shutters that hadn't been opened for years, she tried to visualise the sort of display Marc would be likely to mount there. Underneath all his fooling, he seemed pretty much in love with his dreams of what he could do.

But what about *her* dreams? She couldn't suppress the thought that she'd given up her first big dream. She'd rushed home from Melbourne, left it all behind her, but for very good reasons. Her mother's need had been desperate. But would she truly give up on the shop's potential over a little bit of needed capital?

The trouble was she was *green*. Greener than one of her philodendrons. She was meant to be a dancer, not a businesswoman. With all the conflicting advice being flung at her from all directions she had no idea who to believe.

During the mid-afternoon lull she checked her Facebook page for news. Serena had posted her a funny comment.

Smiling, she typed a reply. Then, all by themselves, her fingers typed Guy's name into the search bar.

There were a few Guy Wilders in the world, but none of them appeared to be him. Probably a blessing. Who would want to know him better, anyway?

Her fingers, apparently. Because they went one further and Googled him.

Bingo.

She felt a small shock. There he was, looking impossibly crisp, clean-shaven and corporate. Involuntarily her blood started the same painful pounding she'd experienced this morning in the mall.

Breathing hard through her nostrils, she compressed her lips. He wasn't a genuine musician at all. He was in advertising. Wilder Solutions, his company was called. 'The most vibrant, up-and-coming ad co on the scene.' Right. She could imagine that.

She read through the whole site, stung by every glossy piece of spin. No doubt it was all true, and they were brilliant geniuses at selling things to people who didn't mind being cheated. Guy was certainly charming when he wanted to be. Persuasive. Seductive. He had all the gifts essential to a con man. She'd seen it with her own eyes. Felt the overwhelming effects. That was what professional liars were like.

He hadn't even bothered to tell her the truth about himself. What he *was*. In fact, he hadn't told her anything real about himself at all.

Guy stood outside Amber's door. He was in no way nervous. He was a guy, and he didn't have a nerve in his body. If something interpersonal needed fixing he'd do it, as he always did, with a few calm, succinct words.

Words were his forte. He shouldn't need to remind himself of that.

He braced himself, then knocked. No glow from inside illuminated the opaque glass of her fanlight, but although night had fallen he'd learned that didn't mean a thing. She could still be in there. In the dark. Doing who knew what.

He suddenly noticed his heart muscle thudding way too fast, and started as her low, musical voice issued through the door.

'Who is it?'

'It's me. Guy.' His words came out like a croak. What had gone wrong with his voice?

There was a long pause. As the silence stretched and stretched, Guy felt his tension tighten a couple of notches. Surely she wouldn't actually ignore him? Then a light went on and the door was snatched open.

'Well?'

He blinked. He couldn't see much of what she was wearing because she was only poking her head around the door. One thing, she seemed smaller all of a sudden. More petite. Vulnerable. Though the instant that emotive notion kindled in him he stamped it out before it could take hold.

He noticed behind her some sofa chairs and rolled-up rugs piled in the hall, while his ears picked up the gentle, plangent notes of some classical piece.

He squared his shoulders. 'Amber, could I—talk to you? I just wanted to—er…set something straight.'

Her brows arched. 'Oh, yes? What might that be?'

He pressed his lips together and scanned her unforgiving face. Whatever he'd done—*not* done—had offended deeply. 'Well, I don't really want to talk about it out here.'

She hesitated.

He read the wariness shadowing her eyes with a sudden rise in his blood pressure. For God's sake, did she think he was an axe murderer? 'I think it's a bit late to worry that I might try to steal your virtue.'

He may have sounded a bit terse, because she started to close the door. She'd have succeeded if hadn't moved swiftly to jam it open with his knee.

He should have remembered how startling the violet flash from her eyes could be. Miss Spitfire wasn't always all whipped cream and honey.

He held up his hands. 'All right. I'm sorry, I'm sorry. I shouldn't have said that. I only want to talk to you, I swear. Three minutes. Please?'

'I'm busy,' she said coolly. 'Write it down and slip it under the door.'

He was too stunned to resist her closing the door a second time. With a harsh, incredulous laugh, he shrugged and turned away.

Women. What did a man have to do?

CHAPTER FOUR

AMBER woke early. At least something woke her.

She was barely out of her dream. A wicked, forbidden dream, in which her senses felt drenched in the taste, the scent, the sheer sexual heat of Guy Wilder.

Before she'd even managed to winch her eyes open her ears picked up the sound of a piano. Was she still in the dream? Vaguely she understood she was hearing a piece of Frederick Chopin's. Played very softly. One of the nocturnes.

Oh. Her insides smiled and curled over in bliss. Her favourite. Her most beautiful, all-time most romantic…

At some point she realised it was no dream.

As the poignant tones thrilled through her, playing havoc with her susceptible heartstrings, *manipulating* her, she lay unwillingly mesmerised, careful not to move, angrily straining for every last note.

With her ravished bones melting, she fought against herself.

Oh, come *on.* What was he up to?

Guy's steps slowed when the shop loomed into view. He needed to get it straight in his head what he wanted to say. Obviously last night had been a mistake. She'd probably assumed he'd rung her bell at that time intending to angle for more sex.

He felt the prickle of heat under his collar. A little from shame. *Admit it.* Although there was pride involved as well. He'd sincerely wanted to make amends. If that had involved kissing her…

For God's sake, he was a *man*. He couldn't deny that the desire to feel her in his arms again was torturing him. But he was a civilised person. He could admit when he was in the wrong.

Was this where he was at now? So inept at dealing with women they wouldn't give him the time of day? Anger and indecision pinched his gut. Surely that was a reason to cut his losses? Move on. Forget about her.

Despite his warring impulses, the nearer he approached the stronger his anticipation grew. Dammit it, he was curious to see her at work in her shop.

Like the others in the arcade, her window was framed in leadlight, though the pattern here was of flowers, with 'Fleur Elise' romantically inscribed at the top in flowing gold. No doubt the gold had gleamed brightly at one time. Now it looked faded, with curls of paint peeling from a couple edges.

A small array of blooms raised their heads in a brave little front display.

He had to look hard before he spotted Amber. She was inside among the flowerpots, standing with her back to him. Her blue floral dress was perfectly moulded to her pert little behind, and as she reached up for something on a shelf the movement pulled the hem high on her thighs.

High enough to reveal the long flowing muscles and slim shapely legs he remembered so well.

His blood quickened, but he controlled the response. He hadn't come here to be engulfed in another maelstrom of lust. Merely to apologise, if that was what it took. To recover some of his—whatever.

He could hardly believe he had to stop and consider his approach. A guy like him. With all his experience of women. In the past he'd have eased his way in with an irresistible line guaranteed to melt a glacier, if there'd been any of those left. These days he seemed to have lost the poetic touch.

Inside, Amber was just considering a redistribution of the shelves, with a view to somehow masking the tired paintwork, when a movement from the window caught the periphery of her eye.

Aha. A suit.

The man straightened up, and Amber's heart fishtailed like a trailer on an oil slick. Surely not. Not him. Not *here.*

She went hot and cold all over. With her heart racing like a fool's, she patted the coil of her hair and pinned the hydrangea more firmly behind her ear. After that Chopin this morning she couldn't say she was all that surprised he hadn't given up yet—but here of all places? Surely her workplace should be sacrosanct?

Why on earth had she told him where she worked?

She darted an anxious glance about. Oh, man. Chaos was threatening from every direction. For one thing Georgio, their supplier, hadn't turned up yet with the fresh blooms, so the display was even thinner than usual. For another Ivy could arrive at any minute. If she was here at the same time as Georgio her sharp, forensic eye would spot the extras Amber had sneaked into the stock order.

To make matters worse, Serena was coming in late. Which wouldn't be very comfortable, what with Ivy's antipathy towards her.

Taking his time to select a bouquet, Guy could feel his adrenaline pumping. He could tell she'd already spotted him by the way she was avoiding looking his way. Unless she slammed the shop doors in his face, this time she'd have to talk to him.

He checked. The doors were still open.

Positioning herself behind her counter, Amber composed her face. Cool. Not hostile. Indifferent. Unaffected. Though as he strolled in her muscles tensed. He was holding a bunch of pale pink and cream roses extended to avoid the drips. As he halted before her counter, his big masculine form somehow managed to control the entire space and soak up all the air.

She prayed her body didn't exhibit her awareness. Even after everything, seeing him looking so lean and sexy evoked that breathless, reckless feeling.

Today he was the straight, clean-shaven Guy from his other dimension. Her treacherous senses, apparently still steeped in the memory of passion, drooled at his crisp, freshly-washed scent. Sharply garbed in a charcoal suit, with pale blue shirt and darker blue silk tie, it was hard to reconcile him with the lazy, casual musician she'd thought he was. He looked sophisticated. Handsome.

His gaze captured hers. Their mutual intimacy blazed again in the air between them, as if his chiselled lips had only just that moment left hers tingling. Wanting.

He lowered his briefcase to the floor and handed over the flowers. He didn't smile, though his deep voice caressed her ear. 'Hi.'

With an effort of will she steeled herself to resist the force field. 'You don't have to do this.'

'Do what?'

'Come here. Buy flowers.'

'Why?' His sensuous lips made a wry curl. 'Were you intending to invite me for coffee?'

She felt the flame in her cheeks. 'There's no chance of that.'

'You're angry.'

Her heart thudded, but somehow she held her nerve. 'Not angry. Just—realistic.'

He hesitated. 'Look, Amber, I'm sorry if I—did anything to make you feel upset.'

She couldn't speak for a second. Then all the emotions she'd thought she had under control came bubbling to the surface like geysers.

'You need to know I am a human *being*, Guy.' Though her voice wobbled and her heart was whirring fit to burst, adrenaline lent her the necessary nerve to keep going. 'Not a—a *thing* a man can just *use*.' Her voice scraped at the last, but she fought back the ready tears with all her might.

Shock registered in his eyes, then a flush darkened his tan. 'Amber? *What?* I had no *intention*— That *wasn't* my…' His voice was hoarse. 'Believe me, I'm not that sort of guy. I—I really like you. I *respect* you. I'd never dream of treating you or—or any woman like…'

The glittering intensity in his storm cloud eyes might have been convincing if she hadn't been down here before. Seen a beautiful man's ability to lie like an angel.

She supplied his missing word for him. 'Trash.'

He flinched. Held very still. His lashes screened his gaze. She noticed his lean hands clench to fists, then saw him make the deliberate effort to relax them.

Though his shoulders retained their rigidity, he fired back, his gaze cool and level. 'That's quite a misinterpretation. I think you're reading too much into a small thing. Hell, it was never meant to be…' Shaking his head, he swung about, reefed his hand through his hair as if gathering more words. Then he turned back to her again. 'Look, as far as I'm concerned it was just a pleasant, casual evening between two consenting—people.' He added with a small sardonic laugh, 'We're not exactly *engaged*.'

Curiously, her flush was outflanked by his. Before her eyes he turned a dark, distressed red.

Clearly a champion at recovering his poise, though, after he'd blinked once or twice his voice was as steady as a rock. 'We need to sort this out rationally. Without all this emotive language. Somewhere more…' He glanced about as if his location was uncomfortable. 'Anyway, if you could just listen.' He spread his hands. Hesitated. 'You're a gorgeous woman. But I'm not looking for any sort of—ties. I guess the other night I may have thought…'

His flush was back in evidence. As no doubt was hers, though indignation was her excuse.

'What? That I was a slut? Easily disposable?'

He waved his hands in shocked denial and was protesting in some non-emotive, rational language when Georgio poked his head in the door.

'Helloo—helloo.'

Amber started, dragged from the conversation. There was Georgio, grinning and as bright and breezy as if his delivery was right on time.

'Oh.' Torn between conflicting urgencies, she gave Guy a cold look, then turned away. Why did even framing those words herself have to hurt her so much? Grabbing her apron, she slipped it over her head and dashed outside to the street, where Georgio had parked his van.

Guy hung there in limbo, his brain still reeling from the damning things she'd said. Oh, he got it all right. In shock and utter shame he understood that as far as Amber O'Neill was concerned he was a barbarian. The lowest of the low. While full and total comprehension seeped through his brain and into his gut like a toxin, he tried to stem the flow with some upbeat self-protective guy talk.

Since when did sex have to be so complicated? He hadn't signed any contract. He didn't *do* all this stuff any more.

His *heart*, if that was what people wanted to call that particular bunch of chemicals, had been cauterised for all time. And rightly so. The sucker had caused him enough grief. For goodness' sake, near enough despair.

From outside, Amber's light and lovely voice floated back to him. 'Georgio, I've been trying to call you for ages. What…?'

A minute later she reappeared, assisting an old guy to manoeuvre a trolley-load of boxes into a room at the rear. The old guy was puffing and rattling on about a hold-up in the tunnel.

While Guy continued to grapple with his devastated ego a short woman with an uncompromising brown fringe walked in and, without any greeting, straight past him through to the back room where the stock was being unloaded.

Her sharp voice penetrated to the front of the shop. 'What's this, Amber? Are they just getting here now? What the hell do you think this is, Georgio? Do you know what time it is? And, here. We don't want these. Or these. Take them back.'

Guy pricked up his ears. For a second he ignored his blistered pride and eavesdropped on the conversation in the back room.

'Wait, Georgio. No, don't take them back.' It was Amber's voice. 'I ordered them, Ivy. I want them.'

There was a rapid murmured exchange, finishing with, 'I thought I'd explained this yesterday, Amber. Here—give me that invoice. Where's Serena, anyway? *She* should have sorted this lot.'

'Serena's had a problem with her…'

Guy saw a harassed-looking Amber pass by the open doorway. She halted when she caught sight of him still standing there.

'Oh.' She came flying across the room, flushed, hair dishevelled, wiping her hands on her apron. 'Look,' she said urgently, 'I can't talk now. Our delivery's arrived late and everything's in a bit of a shemozzle.' Catching sight of the roses, she said impatiently, 'Do you really want these?'

Unwilling to be ejected so summarily after he'd been downgraded to the level of brute, with no right of appeal, he insisted. 'Sure I do. Of course.'

Flustered, perhaps distracted by the voices issuing from the back room, she wrapped them in silver paper, tied a ribbon around them, then sped through the transaction. It was clear to Guy by the way her fingers flew over the keys that she was eager to be rid of him ASAP.

She thrust his card and the receipt towards him. He accepted them, then snaked his hand out to grab hers. 'Meet me in the city after work.'

Her hand quivered in his, cool and burning hot at the same time, but she yanked it away fast. There was a momentary spark in her violet eyes that he could almost have sworn teetered on capitulation, then they chilled pretty convincingly.

'No. There's no point.'

Hope died hard. He might have deserved punishment, but the rejection hit the old nerve. A man should have at least *half* a right to defend himself before execution.

He was about to intensify his attempt to retrieve some of his honour when the small woman reappeared from the back room, muttering, 'That Serena's useless.'

Amber turned her gaze to the woman. 'She really couldn't help it, Ivy,' she said quietly. 'Her babysitter was sick. She rang in to warn me.'

'You're too soft, Amber,' the woman snapped. 'You'd swallow anything. Yes?' This to Guy. 'You still here? Can we help you?'

Guy saw the quick flush flare in Amber's cheeks.

'It's all right, Ivy. I'm helping the customer.'

'He's had time to help himself to the whole shop by now.'

'Ivy.'

The small woman threw up her hands and stomped into the back room, where her sharp voice could be heard harrying the old man.

Conscious of more tension in the room than just his own, Guy picked up his briefcase and the roses. Refusing to accept defeat, he gazed down at Amber. 'We'll finish this later. Do you know the Shangri-la Hotel?'

Her eyes darkened, her lashes fluttering down to hide them. She shook her head. 'No. Look, I have to attend a meeting tonight at six. Anyway, I told you. There's no point.' She hardened her expression. 'No *point.*'

He felt his gut tighten. There was a point for him. He couldn't leave it like this. Not like this.

Luckily, when the chips were down, inspiration could strike him. Right at that moment he had an image of his aunt's face, and along with it the calendar she kept pinned to her fridge with all her social commitments.

Something about a meeting of the Kirribilli Mansions Residents' Committee. At six p.m. on the thirtieth. Wasn't this the thirtieth?

CHAPTER FIVE

AT THE end of a difficult day, Amber wished, rather than pressing for the lift to take her to the residents' meeting, she could be far away. On a Pacific cruise, like Jean, or better still the planet Saturn.

Somewhere free from the threat of hungry wolves with sexy mouths. The sooner the honeymooners were home, the happier she would be. The safer. The sheer energy cost of having met Guy Wilder was exhausting. *Twice* while he'd been in the shop this morning she'd been tempted to soften. Twice. She'd actually, for a fleeting instant, considered his demand to meet him. Visions of exotic temptations at the Shangri-la had floated in her imagination for a teensy, tantalising second. Before her brain had cut in.

Give in to that and where would her self respect be?

After he'd gone, though, she hadn't been able to stop thinking of his expression when he'd turned to leave. The lines of his face had tautened to make him look so—grim.

Oh, Amber. Please. What was wrong with her? Had she forgotten everything she'd learned? She stiffened her spine and shoulders in resistance for a second or so, then let them slump.

Who was she kidding? She knew what was amiss, all right. Having once tasted the wine, the Eustacia Vye in her was craving another sip. A stroll under the gum trees.

Perhaps even a swipe of her head from the palm fronds at the Shangri-la.

She had to fight it—*had* to. Hadn't she learned only too well how powerfully that addiction could take hold? It was so insidious. The effects of even that single sexual encounter had sunk so deep. Everything about him seemed to have crept into her senses. His hands, his eyebrows. That way he had of considering her every light word as if it had been carved in concrete.

And it was becoming blindingly clear that, regardless of the things she *said* to him, every moment she spent in his dangerous company only fuelled the flames.

To add to her quandary, this afternoon she'd received an e-card in her junk mail from Jean.

> Having a sensational time!!! Everything fantastic. The food, the wine, the ports, the people. Look out for Guy, won't you? Mind you give him some TLC. Lots of love x

Amber had puzzled over it for minutes. TLC for *Guy*? Was Jean kidding? Did she realise what TLC meant? Maybe she had her acronyms mixed up.

The residents' meetings were usually lacklustre affairs, though the oldies got a kick from the gossip. Amber had been to a few of the smaller ones, but tonight's was the big annual affair, where the residents and arcade tenants combined.

Though everyone she'd talked to in the mall seemed to be planning to attend, Amber felt tempted to bypass the entire event. Go straight home and soak in a long, soothing, chamomile-scented bath. Wash her hair and paint her toenails. Chill and stop thinking of wine and—that man.

If only tonight's gathering hadn't been slated as especially important. Roger had told her that once the tower residents' issues were dealt with the business owners would be discussing future directions in the arcade.

A worrying thought occurred to her. What if they discussed her shop and she wasn't there to defend herself? Though surely they wouldn't do anything so unprofessional? The shopkeepers were all friends, in a low-key sort of way. Regardless of Roger's quiet hints to her, everyone was always treated with consideration at the meetings.

With a sigh, she braced herself to be bored, pasted on a smile, and walked into the assembly room.

What? She nearly choked. Shock speared through her from head to toe.

Guy was there.

Not only was he there, he was occupying Jean's place at the official desk. But why? As secretary of the committee, it was Jean's usual role to take the minutes. In her absence anyone else could do it. But there *he* was, laptop open before him, conversing with people, as relaxed and confident as if he belonged there.

On the other side of the room, some instinct or vibration on the air made Guy glance up. Despite what had happened between them this morning, his heart-rate bumped up a notch. Spring had walked into the room. She was hesitating just inside the rear entrance, as slender and fragile in her flowery dress as an iris.

He noticed her stiffen and the set of her delicate jaw firm slightly.

She'd spotted him, then. As a spontaneous response, it was hardly flattering. More like a skewer through the guts. One way or another, he really needed to fix things with her.

Amber's heart thumped with the stress. What was

he doing here? Invading her professional life? This was wrong. All wrong.

An elderly major from the eighth floor was bending his ear while Guy lounged in his chair nodding, occasionally smiling. She could see him charming the old digger's socks off. Smiling. Convincing the old boy there was nothing in the world as interesting as his reminiscences about the war.

Guy looked around at her then and their eyes clashed. She saw his face stiffen for an instant, but that might have only been a shadow because it was gone in a trice. He just nodded coolly and went back to the war story as if she was no one of importance.

Strangely, though, in spite of her cynicism, she had the strongest sensation his cool was a total sham. He was as aware of her as if there was no one else in the room.

She knew it with absolute certainty. Because although the room was filling up, buzzing with people, groups chatting here and there, the usual throng gossiping by the desk, she felt gripped by exactly the same obsessive awareness herself.

Heaven forgive her, but right at this moment no one else in the room existed. In fact, it wouldn't have come as a surprise to her to learn that he'd engineered his way into the meeting specifically to pursue her. But why?

Her tension increased. Had he thought she was playing some game with him this morning? Didn't he understand she wanted nothing of him?

She waited until a couple of people blocked his line of sight before sidling up to the table and reaching through a chink between bodies for a copy of the agenda.

Before she could snatch one Guy's hand was there first. His fingertips brushed hers, and it was like a couple of electric wires crossing. As his intense darkened eyes clashed with hers the breath was knocked from her lungs.

She had a wild fleeting impression of showering sparks, sizzling air, walls shaking.

He handed her the sheet. 'Hello, Amber.' His voice had that darker, quarry pit quality from the other night.

'Oh. Hi…er…thanks.'

She backed away, then scouted about for a chair, choosing an inconspicuous place near the exit, from where she could keep her eye on the desk without seeming to.

She wasn't shaking, was she? No. She just felt…a little…shaken up.

She felt pretty sure the thudding going on in her chest was from adrenaline. But if he was hoping to succeed in seducing her again by intruding into every area of her life he was wasting his time. Nothing he said could make the way he'd treated her acceptable. *Nothing.*

That was exactly the trap she'd fallen into with Miguel. Time and time again. He'd make her feel sorry for him, she'd forgive him, then he'd act like an even bigger jerk than before.

Across the room she caught sight of Roger in a huddle with some of her arcade neighbours, including Marc and Di Delornay.

Amber glanced again. Was there was something strange about them? They looked quite secretive. Conspiratorial, almost. Were they plotting something?

Di looked over at that moment and crossed gazes with her, then muttered something out of the side of her mouth. Worryingly, the others all stopped talking. Some cast Amber covert glances, then the group broke up.

Had they been talking about *her*? What about? Something to do with the shop?

She tightened her hold on the agenda. Too bad. They could talk all they liked. She had nothing to apologise for, and right now more pressing issues to deal with. Despite her edgy pulse, she threw them all a breezy wave and pretended to read.

If he had to be here, it was a good thing Guy was taking the minutes, actually. Because it meant she could slip away before the meeting ended. Before he had a chance to waylay her. He'd be stuck here, noting down every last word.

The moment arrived when the hum of conversation eased. The chairperson, large in cyclamen, gathered her majestic bulk and called the meeting to order.

'Most of you will have met Jean's nephew, Guy,' the chair announced, twiddling her pearls and beaming through the diamanté frames of her specs. 'Guy's kindly offered to fill in for Jean in her absence. I think you'll agree it's wonderful of this busy, busy man to give us a slice of his precious time.'

'Hear, hear.'

There was a small round of applause, then the meeting got underway, with sundry minor items being thoroughly dissected by the residents while the business owners sighed and stared at the ceiling. Guy seemed to take his secretarial role seriously, typing occasional bursts on his keyboard and listening intently.

Every so often the chair turned to him and asked for his opinion, just as she usually did with Jean, and he answered with such calm, intelligent reason Amber gritted her teeth. All right, she could admit he appeared to have a certain authority.

She could see people warming to him. And why wouldn't they? He was charming. *She'd* warmed to him. And he had that sophisticated aura of the city hanging about him. Honestly, every time she saw him he looked less and less like the musician she'd made love with. Though how her mind could even *think* those words in reference to him without *choking*...

No, now he looked quite the slick, corporate advertising man he appeared on his website. A purely objective scan of his face revealed his five o'clock shadow, advanced since this morning. And it so suited his lean face. Drew aching attention to the sensuousness of his chiselled mouth. A mouth she'd kissed.

Had kissed her.

That trick he had of smiling with his eyes as he listened to someone…

Involuntarily, her insides curled over. She fixed her gaze firmly on her agenda. Looking at him was painful.

If everyone here knew how deeply cold and ruthless he was in his private life, they wouldn't all be queuing up to agree with his opinion. As if he was now the final authority on how to deal with everything from the City Council to the janitor. Considering his casual way of treating Jean's flat, there was such irony in that.

Amber's eye fell on the last item on the agenda. 'Tenancy Relocations'. What was that about? Marc was probably hoping it referred to Fleur Elise.

Guy gave half his brain to the proceedings, sifting out the crucial points with the expertise of experience. The other half was focused on framing some words. Lyrics had never been so tricky. How had he ever made such a complete hash as he had this morning?

Still, was there a woman in the world who was straightforward? This morning he'd finally comprehended something about Amber. It had rocked him. Made his heart clench at odd moments all day. It was no wonder his conscience was burning like hell.

He'd seen it in her before without understanding. But now…

He hated this feeling of having bruised something delicate. It had hit him with blinding force that Amber O'Neill was as tender as one of her own rose petals.

Roger, the CEO, rose from his chair, still blathering, and walked around to plant himself before the assembly.

Foiled by good manners from making an early escape, Amber shifted restlessly in her chair. How much longer did she have to stay here, avoiding Guy Wilder's piercing gaze?

Roger cleared his throat and she gave him her unwilling attention.

'As you know, in a centre like this it's the management's job to guarantee that every business maintains a professional standard. I've been in discussion with some of you about your particular issues, and most tenants—' here he cast an approving look around the room '—in fact I think I can report that nearly *all* have either complied already or have signed the agreement to meet our renovation deadline.' He frowned down at his notes, then scanned the assembled faces. 'There are still a couple of people who haven't settled their plans with us yet.'

Amber's insides lurched as his probing gaze scanned the faces, then settled on her.

'Just wondering how you're travelling with this, Amber? I have at least one applicant willing to lease your location if you don't want to keep it on. Let's see—your lease expires two months from now. Have you made any arrangements to move out of the arcade?'

Amber blenched with shock. To *move*?

Her brain seemed to slow down to a sort of paralysis. Was he being serious? Could he really be saying what it sounded like?

Hot with confusion, she grew aware of all eyes turning in her direction. With a pang she realised Guy was witnessing this. Her public humiliation.

With all her being she wished he was a hundred miles away.

Unable to help herself, she shot a covert glance in his direction. Not focusing directly, of course, but she could feel his gaze torching her face. She felt herself turning a slow, agonised red.

If there truly was a heavenly host, now was the time for them to sink her through the carpet. She could sense everyone waiting. What did they expect her to say? They knew she didn't want to move. She couldn't afford to. Roger knew it. They all knew it.

Guy sat very still, a pulse ticking in his temples, uncomfortably conscious of her embarrassment. He willed her to speak.

At last.

Her voice when it came was low and sweet. Proud. Scared.

'I wasn't planning any such thing. My mother bought this lease and I'm hoping to extend it. I'm intending to stay right here.'

'Ah.' Roger smiled again smoothly. 'Well, good…good.' He flicked a glance towards one of the groups. 'Then, in that case, I have some copies of the agreement here with me now, Amber. For everyone's peace of mind I think it best we settle this for good and all. Right here, right now. Everyone okay with that?'

Guy noted the chorus of mixed responses. It seemed not everyone thought the matter should be handled in a public forum. Thank God there were a few good people who murmured dissent. He studied the guy handling the discussion. What was going on here, really? Why publicly embarrass one of his tenants? There had to be a hidden agenda.

Conscious of feeling under attack, Amber noticed to

her eternal gratitude that some people sprang to her defence. Even the fruiterer spoke up.

'Mate, give the girl a break. She's only had the reins a few weeks. Let her find her feet. We can all wait a little longer.'

Though not all her friends acted like friends.

'No, people. *No.* That is *so* not the point.' Marc sprang to his feet and clutched his sideburns in agitation, his huge dark eyes showing their whites. 'This is the moment to strike. We all need certainty that this issue is being dealt with. I for one need *closure*.'

In shock, Amber gasped, *'What?* Closure of my shop?'

'I'm afraid I agree with some of what Marc says,' Roger said. 'With all due respect to your recent situation, Amber, people here have a legitimate right to expect certainty. Are you prepared to meet your obligations to us all and have your premises renovated within two months?'

Amber stared at him. She tried to swallow, but her saliva evaporated. It was mortifying, hearing the pleading note in her own voice. 'Oh. Does it *have* to be within two months?'

'I'm afraid it does. With respect, we tried for several years to negotiate with your mother to do the same thing. I'm afraid our patience has run out. Other owners are expressing their concern about the lack of an appealing entrance at that end of the mall.'

Guy almost felt the flinch in Amber's face as a small vociferous group swarmed with offers to take over her location.

'It's so dreary down there I'm ashamed to be seen coming in that way,' one woman declared.

'Oh, I know,' one heavily made-up harpy drawled, with posh, plummy vowels. 'If *I* had the location Madame would have a stunning, very chic display. I'd want it to be *vibrant.*' She flung out her bejewelled hands. 'Eye-catching enough to attract the traffic trade and pull customers in from the street.'

The approving smirk the manager turned on the woman opened Guy's eyes as to what might be going on.

He flicked a glance at Amber. Sure, none of this had anything to do with him. He was here purely to smooth things over with her, not to get involved in the politics of the place. Still, the eye messages he caught passing between some of the stakeholders made him realise he was witnessing an ambush.

Did these jackals have any idea of the damage they were doing?

The old Guy must still be in him somewhere, because he burned to spring up, stride across the room and punch the disgraceful manager in the face for encouraging this free-for-all. If he could have knocked a few of the scavengers flat on their faces at the same time he'd have relished it.

Then he wanted to grab Amber O'Neill and remove her from the brutality.

Take her somewhere quiet and green, by a flowing stream. Soothe her, stroke her beautiful proud face and neck. Hold her to him. Ease her down on the soft grass.

Kiss her.

Rock her in his arms.

Amber heard the insults flying thick and fast in horrified disbelief. Surely she was in a nightmare? People she'd thought were her mother's friends were scrabbling now for her location before she was cold in her grave.

'Of course it's up to you who you decide to give it to, Rog.' That was Di Delornay, beaming at Roger. 'It's pretty clear Amber isn't capable of doing it justice.'

Incensed, Amber sat upright, straightened her shoulders. 'Now, wait just a minute there, Di. While I hold the lease it's up to me. I *can* do justice to it. I fully intend to open Fleur Elise's doors to the street.'

Marc rolled his eyes. 'We'll believe that when we see it, sweetikins.'

The heat rose in Amber's cheeks, along with her blood pressure. 'You *will* see it. You would have before, except… Well, Mum always intended to do that too, but Ivy said… And Mum… Well, she had difficulties…' Her throat thickened and her voice wobbled. 'It wasn't—easy for her, with everything she had to… And then when she got sick…' Predictably, her eyes swam, and she had and stop to struggle for control.

There was an embarrassed pause, then people started shuffling and coughing. Some of the same people who'd been standing beside her at her mother's graveside only eleven short weeks before. Some of them had been weeping too. Some of them had had their arms around her, while others had patted Ivy and tried to soothe her hoarse, inconsolable sobs.

Roger cleared his throat. 'I'm sure we all sympathise, Amber, but I have to be fair to *all* tenants. Before we can approve an extension to your lease I need to know what you have in place to improve your shop's performance. If anything,' he added grimly.

'Well…' Blinking fast, she twisted her hands in her lap.

There was an excruciating pause. People were avoiding meeting her eyes.

Guy held his breath. He saw the red tide of shame rise to Amber's hairline. With a sharp twist in his chest he recognised exactly how Amber O'Neill felt at this moment. Her brave, straight back, her dignified, distressed face transported him with painful immediacy right back to a moment in time he'd never wanted to revisit.

With grim finality he closed his keyboard and opened his briefcase, the clicks of the catches loud in the expectant silence.

Terrified her tenancy was slipping away from her, Amber knew she had to say something. *Anything.* She drew a shaky breath.

'I intend to expand the range of our stock and to make a stronger impression. I've only been here a few weeks, and I just need time. To paint it and everything. I know it needs brightening up, and you all have a right to feel… But—I *am*—I'm doing everything I can to—to…'

The honest truth was she had a million ideas a day. But right at this moment, when she had to produce them under intense pressure from a gang, in a life-or-death situation with the heat on, her brain completely dried up. As did her words.

'I—I really am doing *everything…*'

Her tortured croak hung on the air, substanceless, unconvincing. Her bread and butter, her commitment to Serena and Ivy, teetered on the edge of a cliff.

Then from out of the haze Guy Wilder's deep voice cut through the strained vibrations with sure, casual clarity. 'Don't forget the advertising campaign we've planned, Amber. That kicks off after you've done the interior. And you're starting that next week. Isn't that what you told me you'd decided?'

She stared at him, dumbfounded. Heads swivelled around to him in surprise. With measured calm he got up from his desk and strolled around to join Roger, his tall, lean frame stealing Roger's space.

He held out his hand with cool authority. 'Did you say you have a copy of that agreement, Roger? Mind if I take a look?'

'It's all absolutely above-board,' Roger said huffily as

Guy neatly whipped it from Roger's open folder and perused it. 'If you have any legal training—as *I* have—you'll see it's a standard agreement used by all mall managements. Everyone else has seen fit to sign. I'm prepared to witness Amber's signature now, if she really *is* taking steps…'

The owners broke into a murmured hubbub while Guy took his time, examining the document thoroughly with a meditative frown.

After a minute or so he gave an easy shrug and strolled with the document to where Amber sat hypnotised on her chair. 'Might as well, Amber,' he said. 'Now's as good a time as any. Have you read this? All this stuff is totally in line with your plan.'

She looked hard at him, fascinated. 'Is it? My…?'

He smiled. 'Your plan to hire *me*. Of course.'

CHAPTER SIX

THE Kirribilli Mansions lifts were far too cramped. Especially when shared with six feet or so of unscrupulous, scheming man.

Guy Wilder leaned against one wall, nonchalant, hands shoved in pockets, while Amber leaned against the opposing one. Contradictions wrestled for supremacy in her bamboozled brain. He didn't want any ties, yet he seemed to be pursuing her. *Seemed* to be. Even after she'd rejected him. She'd never forgive him—*couldn't* if she had any pride—but he'd rescued her from a nightmare.

Was it some ploy? Some devious opportunistic trick to get her back on Jean's sofa?

Arousing though that image might be, she must not allow herself to forget. Essentially he was a cold, cold man.

Though hot.

Smoking hot.

The lean solidity of his hard-muscled person was hard to ignore. Up this close, and seemingly accessible, naturally he exerted a strong magnetic pull.

A treacherous flame licked through her insides and warmed her intimate parts. Well, she was only human. With his pleasantly clean, masculine scent taunting her senses, the crispness of his hair and eyebrows making her fingertips itch, Ms E. Vye was hovering over her shoulder.

She met his grey gaze. 'Why did you do it?'

His brows lifted. 'Do what?'

'Make up that story? About me hiring you?'

He gave a lazy shrug. 'I didn't like that Roger's face. People who smirk always worry me.'

The lift stopped at the ninth floor and the doors cranked open. It took a second for their arrival to register with her, so caught up was she in the moment.

Once she'd extracted herself from the confined space, she turned to him in the hall. 'No, really. Why did you?'

He flickered a considering glance over her, then dropped his eyes. 'Maybe I don't like to see someone being bullied by a gang.'

Her heart clenched in acknowledgement. There was truth to his words. That was exactly how she had perceived the event herself. Violent. Uncivilised. People she'd liked and trusted leaping onto the bandwagon to attack. But could she bear sympathy from him?

'But it wasn't everyone,' she said quickly. 'Only a few.'

'An influential few.'

She flushed as though the shame was hers, and Guy was reminded of how he'd felt after his public evisceration. There was nothing more humiliating than that look of pity in a would-be comforter's eyes. Pity could feel so dangerously close to contempt.

'Maybe.' Amber lifted a shoulder. 'I certainly wasn't expecting any of that. But I hope you weren't thinking I was some kind of victim?'

'Hell, no.'

Each of their apartment doors was close at hand. She hunted around in her bag for her keys, her skin prickling with awareness of him. At least the ice had been broken. She supposed they could be on normal speaking terms now.

Normal for neighbours, that was. Not for sleeping partners. Though sleeping, *per se,* had never happened between them. Only sex. And the sex could certainly never be repeated. Even if he had saved her life from a horde of butchers waving knives. Not unless he came up with a corker of a satisfactory explanation for his poor performance in the afterglow department.

In fact it would be best not to think about him in that way at all. Forget the sex and how it had felt skin to skin with him. Chest to chest. Eliminate all that. All thoughts of kissing.

She paused to level a firm glance at him. 'We O'Neills can defend ourselves.'

'Oh, I know that.' He made a wry face. 'Actually, I was impressed by the way you stood up to them. Reminded me of a warrior princess.'

'Oh, right.' She rolled her eyes. Might even have laughed except that right then, despite her warrior tendencies, she seemed to be seized with a fit of the shudders.

'Are you all right?' He moved a little closer to her.

He looked serious, concerned, even, as if he thought she might be about to keel over. His hands twitched towards her, then changed their minds and curled into fists.

'Of course.' She rubbed her arms to warm them, and his frown deepened.

'You're probably in shock. You should have a hot drink.'

'Shock? *No.* I'm fine. Just a bit empty. Haven't eaten much today.' Oh, God, why tell him that? Why not just tell him outright that since he'd inflicted the wound on her soul she couldn't eat, think or concentrate properly on anything but him? And on passion, pain, and what it meant about her that she was attracted to people like him? 'I'm just getting over how vicious some people were.'

'Mmm.' He was still looking her over with concern.

Well, it looked like concern. Unless she was reading too much into things again. 'Greedy is the word that springs to mind.'

Again, his words struck a chord. That was exactly how she'd viewed it herself. 'Really? Did you think so?'

'Of course,' he said warmly. 'They were just trying to get their grubby hands on your location. How long since you've had the shop?'

'Ten weeks.'

He curled his lip in disgust. 'So they decided this was their chance? Before you had time to settle in?'

'Seems that way. Though they probably thought they had right on their side. The shop could certainly do with a make-over. Somehow I'll have to organise that now.' She heaved a worried sigh. Now all she had to do was find a way to fulfil the contract she'd signed.

'Can I have those?'

She was too surprised to react. He just casually slipped the keys from her grasp and unlocked her door.

'Do you have any tea in here?' He was already half inside, holding the door wide.

'I do. But, look, don't *you* worry. I'll be…'

He didn't appear to hear her protest. He urged her in, clearly intending to come along. Her trouble was her mother had instilled manners into her. Even if a rattlesnake had insisted on hustling her into her flat five minutes after it had seen off her enemies, she would probably have complied gracefully.

While in *his* case…

Well, it was impossible to be deliberately rude to a man who'd just saved her bacon—even him. Before she knew it she was politely pointing out the easiest route around and over the furniture in the hall. Lucky he couldn't see her face. Her mouth and jaw were locked into a grimace of discomfort.

She absolutely *prickled* with the strange and disturbing sensation of seeing Guy Wilder opening her cupboard doors, wresting the kettle from her nerveless grip and taking charge of her kitchen.

Her very small kitchen. Smaller than it had ever been before.

She sat tensely at the table. While boiling water was poured, milk and sugar located, strange and disturbing notions of what he might be up to assailed her brain.

On the surface he was all cool efficiency. He gave no clue as to whether he was intending to throw her onto the nearest sofa or not. Just as well, because hers was in the hall, buried under a pile of stuff. He'd have to resort to her bed, unless he was considering this very table.

'Do you have any sweet biscuits?'

'On the third shelf. There, under the yoghurt.'

Was he trying to reclaim some credit with her? No way could she sit at a table and drink tea with him as if everything was suddenly hunky-dory. Perhaps he felt the same, because while he sat down too he only half shared the table, his chair partly turned away as if he might need a quick escape. He bypassed the tea and biscuits altogether.

She warmed her ice-cold fingers on her cup. 'You don't drink tea?'

'Not just now. I'm not the one with the shakes.' His glance drifted to her mouth and his brows edged together.

She frowned too, wishing her lips wouldn't turn dry at the merest hint of—anything. 'Oh, that. It was nothing. Just a low blood sugar thing.'

Though, really, the tea was very welcome. She only gave the biscuit a token couple of nibbles. It was hard to eat with an interested protagonist seated directly opposite her. What if chocolate adhered to her lips?

Even though his eyes were veiled, her body was alert to his powerful masculine pull. Seemed as if all her nerves were crackling in awareness and it affected everything. Her breasts, her insides, her general steadiness.

It was the age-old problem. Intense physical attraction seemed designed to be unbearable. Surely that was a flaw in the blueprint?

It even occurred to her, watching his body language, that he was feeling the discomfort as keenly as she was. Good. Great. Let him suffer.

'That's better,' she said after a couple of gulps. 'Thanks. Anyway… It was really—good of you to intervene at the chopping block. You've bought me some breathing space, at least. I appreciate it. Thanks very much.'

He shrugged. 'My pleasure.' The edges of his sexy mouth curled up a little, and she tried not to think of how those lips had tasted. So firm, so warmly arousing and addictive. If things had been different…

No. Exile the thought. There'd be no biting of lips—gently or otherwise. No sexy little lip-tugs between lovers. This guy didn't do loving.

'Right,' he said authoritatively. Straightening his chair, he faced her directly, clasping his hands on the table before him. His dark brows edged together, his eyes taking on a serious focus. 'We need to start at once. Those jackals haven't given you much of a timeframe.'

'Sorry?'

He gestured. 'Planning. The campaign. Your ads for Fleur Elise.'

A dim understanding began to penetrate her fog. She widened her eyes in surprise. 'You mean you were serious about that?'

He blinked. 'Well, sure I was. What did you think? You've signed their agreement now. You have to do *something*. And fast. And, from my own point of view, my professional reputation is at stake here. Just think. More than thirty people are now witness to the fact that you and I have struck a deal. Luckily I've a little leeway with my schedule this month. We can get things underway right now or…' He appraised her with a glance, then looked at his watch. 'It might be best done over dinner. You can outline your operation for me, and the goals you've set.'

'Goals?' She lifted her brows. Heck. Goals. It wasn't that she was especially slow. Well, she probably was in a business sense. No, it was more that he was *fast*. Rushing her into things before she'd had time even to get used to the idea she was actually talking to him.

How the world had changed in a short time. Here he was, *in her kitchen*, when she'd resolved never even to think about him again.

'What are you saying? Heavens, I can't possibly accept *charity*. From y—anyone.' She went hot just thinking about it.

His eyes glinted. 'No. Course not. You are an O'Neill, after all.' His tone was gently mocking. 'But no need to panic the rugged old ancestors. I'm not offering charity. We'll do it strictly low-budget, using resources we already have. Then, once you start to turn a decent profit, you can pay me for any small costs that accrue along the way. It's my version of working *pro bono*.' He gave a ghost of a smile. 'Works for me. Okay?'

It sounded good. Maybe that was why her alarm bells were clanging. *Good* was too good to be true. What was in it for him? He had to have a motive. Everyone had a motive, it seemed. And his offer might not be one of charity, altogether, but whichever way she looked at it she'd owe him.

She couldn't help noticing he was looking far more relaxed now he'd switched into his ad man mode. Crisp. Bristling with confidence and know-how. Well, naturally. He had all the answers.

Whereas she… Did she want to be under an obligation to him?

He was studying her, reading her wariness, a wry twist to his mouth. 'You have two months, Amber. *Two months.* It isn't very long to mount a campaign. Most of ours take double or triple that in the planning, what with the research and the artistic work. This one will have to be realised in a matter of days. I'll have to snatch a few hours here, a few there—whatever I can fit in with my current schedule. If it's to work you'll have to open your mind to the possibilities and go with the flow.' He added softly, 'That's if you're serious about wanting to improve your shop's performance.'

'I am, of course. But…' It was no use. A massive elephant was towering between them and she couldn't continue to pretend it wasn't there. 'Are you *using* this situation? Does this have something to do with the other night?'

She met his eyes full-on. Though only for an instant. Because after that one charged instant he slid his away from her and screened them with his lashes.

His brow creased. A muscle shifted in his jaw then he said, so gruff his voice was a growl, 'Look…' He made a constrained gesture. 'About that. I understand I hurt your feelings. I regret it intensely. I'm honestly sorry if I made you feel…'

He appeared to be gazing through the glass at her mother's precious china teapot collection, but from the rigidity of his posture, the taut tendons in his bronzed neck, she doubted he was thinking about china.

'I'm ashamed to have bruised your feelings. I'm hoping we can put it behind us and forget it ever happened.'

A savage pang sliced through her. What with the pricking at the back of her eyes it took her a second to bring out an answer. Without the liberating fuel of anger, openly referring to the distressful matter wasn't easy. But at least there was some relief in recognising the ring of sincerity in his apology.

'Yes, well…' Her own voice was gruff. 'I suppose we can all be wrong. All right. We'll put it behind us.'

He glanced at her. 'Accept it was a mistake. All of it.'

She nodded, eyes lowered.

His voice was smoother. A little warmer. 'Maybe we both got carried away with excitement. Out of our comfort zones.'

She shrugged acquiescence. Of a sort. There had been some moments there when she'd been right within hers. Best not to revisit that. 'Let's just forget the whole thing.'

'Fine.' He frowned, serious and meditative, as sober as a bank manager. 'We'll write it off to experience, then. Deal?' He held out his hand.

Despite the managerial sobriety she noticed his eyes shimmer.

Manners warred with her instinct for self-preservation, and as usual self-preservation was the big-time loser.

'Deal, then.' She let him clasp her hand in his warm, firm grip.

Oh, Amber. Mistake. Fireworks sizzled up her arm and for a second or two her giddy brain couldn't quite remember what the deal was. Or the day. Or her name.

Though his mouth remained firm and cool, there was no concealing the silvery gleam in his irises. 'Great,' he said, straightening his shoulders, a new buoyancy in his tone. 'Right. We need to start planning ASAP. I'm thinking dinner—somewhere local to save time. I'll leave that with you, since you have the local knowledge. It'll be on me. Half an hour enough time?'

She hadn't been thinking about dinner—not with him at any rate. But, carried along on the flow of this sudden burst of crisp, authoritative energy, she nodded. Well, a girl had to eat. Whether or not she'd be able to swallow in his presence would be another story.

She supposed she could telescope her need to bathe, dress, work on her face and reflect deeply into half an hour.

He sprang to his feet and headed out with a brisk step, pausing to glance around at her as he fought his way through the obstacle path in the hall. 'Have you only just moved in here?'

'No, no. This stuff is only temporarily here. I needed to clear some space.'

'Ah.' He nodded, peering into the shadows of the sitting room. There wasn't enough moon yet for the skylight to make much difference. 'Space for what?'

'Well, it helps me to sleep sometimes if I dance.'

He turned to gaze at her, his brows elevated. *'Dance?'*

'That's correct.' She ignored the way his eyes lit up, as if she'd confessed to being a closet trapeze artist. She dampened her tone to keep it as flat and uninteresting as possible. 'I used to be a dancer. The exercise helps to relax me. Before I sleep.'

'Right. I see.' He moved to the door. Stood there with his back to her. 'That explains so much. Every time I've seen you I've thought… Er…' He cleared his throat and turned to her. In the short silence one of those moments of intense suspense gathered.

She waited—expectant, hardly breathing—then he lifted his eyes to hers. They were glittering, quite intense and sincere.

'About the other night. Well, I hope you *know* that at no time did I think you were anything but beautiful, gorgeous and exciting.'

The words swirled meaningless around in her head. All she *knew* was that her heart was bumping like crazy.

But she gave him a cool, repressive glance. 'Half an hour, then?'

She closed the door firmly after him.

CHAPTER SEVEN

'I CAN'T believe I didn't guess.' Guy adapted his stride to fit Amber's. 'That first night we met. Remember? The pizza guy? You were wearing your ballet slippers then. You must have been dancing that night.'

She was leading him on a winding, undulating trek through residential streets down towards the harbour. Summery fragrances wafting from behind garden walls mingled with hers. She had on a violet dress in some soft fabric. Narrow straps pressed into the smooth, satin flesh of her shoulders.

He was careful not to brush her bare arm. Each time they passed under a streetlamp a different angle of her face was illuminated. His eye kept being magnetically drawn to look again. Her mouth. Her neck. Her mouth.

It felt good to be out with a woman. Chatting, even if it was a little strained. Seeing the world through feminine eyes. Not that this was anything like a date. Hell, no.

Banter was strictly off the menu. No flirting allowed. Looking was the most he could aspire to now. Unless there was a way to reassure her she could trust him to…what? Be more the sort of guy she could cuddle up to? Could he even trust himself?

'It wasn't the pizza guy who disturbed me.' She threw him a smiling look.

Aha, a smile. His blood quickened with pleasure and relief. A smile was the beginning of many a fantastic evening. He could do great things on the inspiration of a smile.

Sex, of course, was a no-go zone. He would have to stay well clear of the topic. Which was hard, what with sex and the art of the dance being so closely related. Interwined. Like lovers, one might say.

In response to her gentle gibe he covered his heart with mock humility. 'In my defence, Your Honour, I didn't think anyone was home.' He glanced at her, invigorated to a bit of over-recklessness on the strength of that smile. 'Do you always do it in the dark?'

Her lashes flickered down to make soft concealing arcs. He could have bitten his tongue off. Was he insane? Where was his control? He held his breath for fear he'd damaged the delicate accord.

But she ignored his witty *double entendre*. Maybe she hadn't even noticed.

'It isn't usually all that dark,' she said evenly. 'If there's a moon, the skylight makes the room bright enough. There isn't anywhere near enough space in there, of course, but it's my biggest room.'

He glanced at her once, then again. Her delicious lips were tightly pressed. She was wearing that expression. The one that froze him out. The snowball's chance in hell one. She'd noticed, all right.

He felt chagrin. No doubt he was a blundering fool, but eggshells had never been so precarious for walking on. If she didn't want him to continue desiring her, she shouldn't have told him she danced in the dark. What was *that* all about, anyway? And why tell a helpless visionary like him about it unless to enchant and seduce him?

'What I meant to *say* was…' He scrambled to right himself. 'What if there isn't a moon? Is there anything wrong with dancing in the light?'

Her voice was a little gruff. 'No. It's…' She hesitated, gave a shrug. 'Oh, well. I'm probably conscious of needing to save on the electricity bill. I try to go without using it wherever I can.' A flush suffused her cheek.

It slayed him. Call him a bleeding heart, but that small simple truth devastated him. It was so obvious. Why hadn't he realised? What an idiot he was. What a spoiled, complacent, *rich* idiot.

She glanced at him and added earnestly, 'Though there can be something really atmospheric about dancing in the dark. If the music is right. If you could imagine that.'

He could imagine it so vividly he could barely meet her eyes. He said constrainedly, 'I think I can. What sort of dancing do you do?'

'Well, I was with the Oz Ballet. Now I do a bit of everything. Whatever I get the chance to do.'

Didn't he just know it?

'Wow,' he said. 'The Australian Ballet. That's really impressive. That's like being an Olympic champion.'

She gave him an ironic look meant to convey his crassness in not understanding the difference between sport and art.

And it was just, to some degree. His imagination was hooked on her gymnastic ability. On a piano. Her lithe and lovely form folding into a flower. Then unfolding. Into a woman. Driving him wild.

Wicked, witty lines he might have used to remind her of that moment rose to his tongue, but regretfully he had to restrain them. All forbidden, alas. He must behave as though he'd never touched her. Never tasted her mouth or sunk himself into her silken flesh.

'Oh.' She lifted her head. 'Looks like it's pretty busy. I hope they kept our table.'

Following the direction of her gaze, he entered a surreal moment. Of all things, his bemused gaze assured him, she was leading him to a church. Set on a grassy knoll overlooking the harbour, with its pretty spire and stained glass lit invitingly from within, it looked charming enough to attract a swarm of unbelievers.

But not Guy Wilder. Never him.

His heart went stone-cold.

'You mean we're eating *here*?' He halted abruptly, hardly knowing what he said. 'This is it?'

She nodded, beaming up at him. 'I know. Isn't it gorgeous? I've always wanted to try it. They say the cuisine is quite authentic.'

Guy barely heard. Must have been the shock. Before he could stop it the last fateful time he'd stood in a church rolled right back to sandbag him in full vivid Technicolor.

Flowers. Everywhere flowers. All of their friends, even his parents. The priest, gorgeous in her celebratory robes. Violet edged with gold. He'd concentrated on them while he waited. Colours for festivity. Joy. Her encouraging smiles beginning to wear a bit thin. More waiting. An eternity of waiting.

Relentless minutes ticking by. Murmurings. The bride was late, someone said. Ridiculously late, surely? He'd begun to wonder himself.

The suspense. In his nerves. In the air. And the restlessness he'd suddenly started to sense. Little rustlings amongst the congregation. Murmurs.

His hands had suddenly been damp, his beautifully laundered collar uncomfortably tight. His man's finery wilting. But he'd stood upright, sure and confident, trusting to the end. Though others around him were giving in, twisting to scan the long, empty aisle.

The anguished look he'd caught between a couple of his mates… It had confused him, while at the same time cutting him to the quick. What were they thinking? And then the moment. That gut-wrenching moment when he'd understood.

All at once he felt the weight of Amber O'Neill's clear gaze. He realised his hands were clenched. With an effort he dragged himself back to the here and now.

Hell, it was nothing to do with her. Amber wasn't to know what a fool he'd been made. Made of himself. He wasn't a madman, for goodness' sake. Just the common or garden variety of lunatic who'd entrusted a piece of himself to a woman.

The church had come as a surprise, that was all. But it was a restaurant. Only a restaurant.

'Guy?' She looked concerned. 'Are you all right? You look so grim all of a sudden.'

'Yeah?' Deliberately he made his muscles and everything inside him unclench. He breathed normally and flashed her a grin. 'Must be hunger. You know that low blood sugar thing?'

Amber smiled, though uncertainly. Grim had been too mild a word for what she'd imagined. For a second there she'd imagined something almost stark in his expression, though there was no sign of it now. Still, she'd heard the note of surprise in his voice when he'd spotted the restaurant.

A dismaying thought struck her. What if he couldn't afford it? Since this was only meant to be a discussion about the shop, maybe he'd intended a café or somewhere more simple.

Had she blundered with her choice?

Though he seemed too well dressed for a café, looking so groomed and sleek. Not that she was looking. Or smelling. All the way here she'd made a point of *not*. She'd deliberately kept her hand from brushing his sleeve and kept her eyes fixed on the path ahead. Though it was impossible not to notice the smoothness of his lean cheek. Clearly he'd shaved for the occasion, because she remembered how he'd looked beforehand. Vividly. And he smelled quite—woodsy.

Probably not like the Wessex woods, of course, where Eustacia Vye was wont to roam. When she wasn't stalking Kirribilli like a cat on a hot tin roof.

'Look, Guy,' she said. 'This place looks a lot more expensive than I realised. It's probably a bit up-market for a business discussion. But I'm pretty sure we can still cancel.' She dug for her mobile. 'There are plenty of other places.'

His expression lightened. 'Hey—no, no. Put that away.' His strange mood, if it had ever been there, vanished without a trace. 'Here will be fine. Honestly. You're my client, and the client must be properly wooed.' His grin was reassuring. 'Up-market is how we do biz at Wilder Solutions.'

'Is it really?' Amber wasn't altogether convinced. But, however Wilder Solutions chose to operate, she felt honour-bound to pay her share.

She resolved not to eat much. If she ordered the cheapest dish on the menu it would keep costs down. This wasn't an occasion for the letting down of hair, anyway. She'd be keeping hers tightly bound up.

In fact it would certainly be unwise to accept wine, should Guy suggest it. She wondered if a French restaurant would be likely to serve vee juice. It was important to remember how reckless she'd been on the night of the wine. Not that the wine had been totally to blame. Other things had been in play then.

The music. His hands. His mouth.

As though to mock her, as soon as she stepped inside the gothic portal the ripple of a piano slunk into her ears. An old lovesong with a haunting refrain. The old black magic slithered wickedly along Amber's veins, inevitably bringing to mind her late erotic adventures.

She could have groaned. Why did she have to be so susceptible? That 'adventure' had had serious consequences to her peace of mind. Ignoring the liquid tones tugging at her heartstrings, she steadfastly resisted looking at Guy. The last thing she wanted to do was remind him. Something told her any references to that night would be dangerous in the extreme.

The trouble was it was reminding *her.* This tight rein of control she was attempting to exert on her primitive instincts needed to be yanked tighter and tighter. Why did the senses have to overrule everything? The more she saw of Guy, even with what she'd learned, the more alive she was to his appeal.

It seemed their sexual exchange was branded on her body's memory. A barrier had been removed and, though a different one was in place, the lack of the first was having a weakening effect.

If she wasn't careful, before she knew it she'd be crawling up on that piano lid.

He was glancing around him, taking in the fittings. 'Well, it doesn't *feel* like a church. Doesn't sound like one either.'

He smiled, but she pretended not to understand his meaning. Before he could make any other sly references to recent history she said, 'Not with all those delicious aromas coming from the kitchen. Mmm... Smell the garlic.'

The place was abuzz, with waiters swishing adroitly between tables and bearing steaming dishes. The tantalising fragrances made Amber's stomach juices yearn. Lucky her years of ballet training hadn't been for nothing. In the food department, at least, she could do abstinence standing on her head.

As she approached their table, conscious of Guy behind her, she felt his light touch in the small of her back. Just the standard polite, masculine touch. Instantly a tiny electric tingle shimmied up her spine and infected her blood.

She settled into her place, lashes lowered. That quickening in her blood and the warm tidal surge to her breasts was too pleasant a sensation to quell all at once. But, tempting though it might have been to meet Guy's eyes, it was important not to. She had to keep her focus on the shop. The meeting. Not on his hands. Not on his mouth.

He slipped off his jacket and hung it on his chair. Impossible not to glance at least once. His linen shirt, white against his tan, was cut with a casual elegance that suited his lean build. Perfect for the warm evening. His sinewy forearms, those hands, would have tempted a nun's eyes to linger, but she made herself look away while the image burned in her retina.

She needed to remember. Though grateful for his apology, and respectful of it, it couldn't essentially change what she'd learned about him. About how much he was prepared to offer another soul. During the midnight hours, when the need for human comfort was at its most searing.

When the sommelier arrived and Guy suggested champagne or a cocktail she politely declined and enquired about juice.

'Very wise,' Guy said as the waiter took her modest order. 'We need to keep our wits about us.'

But she noticed that for himself he ordered a glass of

champagne. Watching it foam into his glass, so zingy and alive, she couldn't help thinking how refreshing it looked. Guy savoured his first sip like a connoisseur, closing his eyes in a sort of ecstasy.

She couldn't restrain herself from commenting. 'Anyone would think it was nectar.'

'That's what it reminds me of.' He held the flute high, the better to appreciate the wine's pallid sparkle. 'The divine nectar of the lotus. Would you like a taste?' His eyes shimmered into hers, enticement in their depths.

'No, thanks.'

What did he mean by bringing up the lotus, anyway? Was it some sort of sly jab about the other night? She retreated to her carrot juice. Tried not to notice how flat it was. How thick and pointless. But tonight abstinence was her middle name. So when it came time to order the food she remained wedded to her resolve.

'I'll just have a green salad, thank you.'

The waiter, a small dramatic man with a not-very-convincing French accent, seemed mortally wounded by her restraint.

Guy was even harder to convince. He stared at her above the top of his menu and his black brows shot up. 'Truly? Is that all?'

She reached for her juice. 'That's all I require, thanks.'

He studied her, his head a little to one side. A gleam crept into his eyes. He glanced at the waiter, then back at his menu, his brow wrinkling. 'Hmm…I'm tempted by the *potage*, myself, but I'm not entirely sure how substantial onion soup is likely to be. So for my entrée, along with my soup, I'll order the duck parfait with balsamic onion jam and cornichons, and the cheese and walnut soufflé with frisée and pear salad.'

'All for *monsieur*?' The waiter could scarcely keep the shock from his voice. 'While *mademoiselle* goes hungry?'

Guy nodded gravely, though his eyes danced with amusement. '*Mademoiselle* prefers to dine lightly, while I find myself ravenous. For my main course I'll have the Châteaubriand with the mushroom ragout, witlof salad, Dutch carrots and Pommes Lyonnaise.'

A look of sly triumph occupied the waiter's face. 'Aha. It *desolates* me to inform *monsieur* that the Châteaubriand is only permitted for two diners. If you read on further, you will see there is a single-serve dish of *filet* with Brussels sprouts and a lentil *jus*. *Very* substantial—even for such a hungry man as yourself.'

Guy shook his head. 'I don't think so. I'm not much of a Brussels sprouts man. I'm afraid I have my heart set on the Châteaubriand.'

Amber nearly gasped. Was the man a glutton?

The waiter shared her concern. 'But, *monsieur*. This Châteaubriand is a very *large dish*.' He demonstrated excitedly with both hands. 'There are two platters and side dishes to accompany. The Pommes Lyonnaise alone...' He threw up histrionic hands as though words failed him.

'I find I have a very large appetite,' Guy said. 'In fact, I see here in your *dégustation* menu you suggest a wine to accompany each individual dish.'

The waiter's brows shot high on his forehead. He said incredulously, '*Monsieur* is wishing to order different wines with *each individual dish*?'

Guy frowned. 'Oh, hang on there. Not *every* wine. Just this *sauv blanc*. And yes. I think the Bordeaux. The Châteaubriand deserves the finest available red, don't you think? And bring the rest of this bottle, will you?'

He indicated the champagne. Rolling his eyes, the

waiter departed, but soon the bottle was produced and placed in a *très* elegant ice bucket.

Amber eyed Guy bemusedly. Surely he wouldn't drink all that, and then *more*? The man would be sloshed. How much planning would get done?

She watched him pour himself more champagne from the bottle and raise it to his lips. As he savoured the sip, a strange expression crept over his face. 'I'm not sure this is the same wine.' He examined the label, sniffed it thoughtfully, then sipped again. 'Nope. If it *is* the same it's from a different bottle. This stuff's off.'

'*Off*? Are you sure?' She glanced about at the austere gloss of the exclusive place. Every surface gleamed with class and honour. 'What do you mean? Surely they wouldn't—? Not *here*.'

He gave a solemn nod. 'I'm afraid it can happen anywhere. If you don't believe me…here, look. Give me that glass. Tell me if this tastes sour and vinegary to you.'

She handed over her empty water glass and he poured her a substantial drop of champagne. 'Now, try that. Tell me if you think the quality has been compromised.'

Conscious of his grey gaze sparkling with alertness, she took a cautious sip. After the carrot juice, the wine tasted pleasantly tart on her tongue. Swallowing was like drinking a delicious mouthful of ocean wave. Almost as soon as the zesty bubbles hit her stomach streams of sensuous warmth irradiated her middle.

'What do you think?' There was a veiled gleam in Guy's eyes, his crow's feet charmingly apparent.

She glanced at him from under her lashes. 'I can't really tell yet.'

Well, it was essential to conduct a test rigorously. These French champagnes didn't come cheap.

If Ivy could see her now…

If Ivy had read the prices on this menu…

She smiled. 'I think perhaps the carrot juice could still be affecting my palate. I could probably give you a more accurate reading next time.' She held out her glass. 'A little more, please.'

This time she closed her eyes and swirled the blessed drop on her tongue before swallowing. 'Mmm. Oh yes, *yes*. A little tangy to start with. Creamy. And then you get the full surge effect. And what a fantastic climax. *Bliss*.'

Heavens. Her eyes flew open. Had she actually *said* that, or just thought it?

He was scrutinising her, and with that silvery shimmer in his eyes, and the almost-smile curling up the corners of his mouth, she had the impression she might have actually said it.

'So?' he said, as smoothly as a wolf emerging from the trees of the Wessex woods. 'What's the verdict?'

She smiled. Gave a small bewitching laugh. 'Don't think I don't know your game. You did that deliberately. You're devious, Guy Wilder.' She shoved her glass across the table at him. 'Go on, then. Fill it up.'

It would have been unreasonable to drink his wine and then refuse to participate in any of the feast when it was delivered. Whether by art or coincidence, Guy found he didn't really care for soufflé after all, or onion soup. He finagled a swap with her green salad, yet somehow she ended up eating as much of it as he did. As for the Châteaubriand, her half was sublime, especially washed down with a drop of Bordeaux.

And it was only a tiny drop. She wasn't entirely seduced by the wine. But by the man…?

She was grappling with that. Desire seemed to burn more fiercely when emerging from under a cloud. Her memories of his lips and hands on her body were powerful enough. The glow in his eyes seared her to the marrow.

As if by mutual accord neither she nor Guy made any reference to past wounds inflicted. Somehow, over dessert, he managed to listen to her dreams about the shop without laughing. And on the way home, after she'd tucked a copy of the menu into her purse to show Ivy, she must have forgotten for the moment who she was talking to—because she told him all about her mother.

He kept nodding and looking very grave, asking her things about Lise when she'd been well and strong, as if she was still a person worth discussing. Strange as it might seem, it was a relief to talk about her mother as a woman who'd lived and loved and achieved things. It was as though Guy understood about losing someone.

Strolling along moonlit streets after an evening replete with fine food, wine and more than a few laughs made conversation the safest option. And strangely, even after her ordeal earlier in the evening—or maybe because of it—it didn't feel so weird to share things with him.

One good thing a fling achieved was to break the ice, she reflected. Especially a failed fling. There was no point holding back on the family skeletons when people already knew the worst about each other.

'Coming home to nurse your mother was a great thing to do,' he said. 'But what about your career? When will you take that up again?'

She dropped her gaze. 'Well… That's pretty well over now. My place in the company has been given away long since.' She made a rueful grimace. 'Lucky I've got the shop. Now I'm a businesswoman. At least being so bright green I fit in with the stock.'

She laughed, and he smiled along with her, though soon she noticed him frowning to himself.

'What about you?' she said, eager to shrug off the subject of the shop for once. 'Where are your parents?'

He made a laconic face. 'Around. Last I heard they were in Antarctica.'

She glanced at him in surprise. 'Don't you keep in touch?'

'Not very often.' He shrugged. 'They're scientists. They do *vaguely* know they've got a son somewhere, I think.'

She chuckled. 'So they do remember?'

'Mostly. But their focus is saving the planet.' He flashed her an ironic grin. 'You can hardly blame them. There are far more fascinating specimens than this.' He spread his arms to indicate himself.

She wasn't so sure of that. He had her full attention.

She gazed at him in disbelief. 'How long has this gone on?'

'Always. I guess you'd say my grandfather had the pleasure of raising me while they gadded about the globe.'

'Oh, no!' she exclaimed, not sure whether or not his amused description concealed resentment. 'Aren't you angry with them?'

He shook his head. 'Not really. It probably seemed sensible not to keep dragging me out of school. My grandfather was a great old guy.' He smiled in recollection. 'Always had something to laugh about.'

'Oh.' She lifted her brows. 'So…your grandfather… is he…?'

He nodded. 'Yep. Couple of years ago, now. That's partly why I find myself holed up in Jean's flat. Not solely to annoy Amber O'Neill and keep her awake.' The moonlight picked up the silvery gleam in his eyes. 'My grandfather left me his house and I've been renovating it. I've done a lot of it myself, but now it's at that tricky stage where you have to call in the professionals.'

Maybe *she* was at a tricky stage.

The evening air felt unusually warm, almost languorous on her skin. Other couples might have been tempted to take advantage of the occasional shadowy niches between garden walls to indulge in a sexy clinch.

But not her and Guy. She sensed his desire, though. Every lingering glance from his darkened eyes burncd. And every longing nerve cell told her he was as alive to the conditions as she was herself. If he once touched her…

She walked carefully, so as not to brush his sleeve with her hand. 'I'm sorry about your grandfather. Do you miss him?'

He nodded. 'I guess. I think of him often. Things he said.' He smiled at her. 'What about you?' His brows edged together. 'I can't get over what a sacrifice you've made, leaving your career like that.'

She wanted to cover her ears. He shouldn't be sympathising with her, tugging at her old desires like that. Heaven knew, she was weak enough to give in to self-pity over the way her life had turned out without being given more encouragement.

'Look,' she said firmly, 'it's not as noble as it sounds. I never intended to totally abandon it. That was just how it turned out. Gradually, over time. I took leave from the company in pieccs—whenever there was a crisis. A few weeks here, a few there. I always expected Mum to get well. In the end I realised I was causing the company problems, so I resigned.'

'But surely they'd take you back? Surely?'

She looked hesitantly at him. All her doubts and anxieties crowded into her mind. Would she even be up to it now? Eighteen months was a long time to go without full daily rehearsal. 'But I have the shop now. I'm fine.'

He didn't look convinced. Kept searching her face, frowning. 'Where's your old man in all this?'

'Nowhere.' She grimaced. 'He left us when I was a kid. Flew to LA for a business conference, never to be seen or heard from again.'

He glanced sharply at her. 'Is that right? Never again? Didn't he ever contact your mother?'

'I suppose he must have, because they did divorce finally. I guess I didn't really know all that went on between them. Just the days Mum looked weepy and upset.'

'Life's hard, isn't it?' He walked in silence for a while, frowning. Then said quietly, 'She must have been devastated.'

'Oh, she was. After a while, though, she kept saying it was for the best. He was never going to grow up.'

That silence lasted for minutes. She couldn't help thinking how amazing it was to be talking to Guy like this. Maybe she should give herself a good pinch. Her feelings about him over the last couple of days had been so negative.

While tonight he seemed so accessible. Gorgeous. Though initially the other night he'd been warm, too. And gorgeous before the sex. Was she being a fool? Being sucked in again by easy charm and that pulse that kept drawing her to him like an electromagnet?

They were in the street that led to the arcade when he asked, 'Do you think if he'd asked to come back she'd have given him another chance?'

She looked quickly at him. Where had that come from? But she couldn't read his eyes. 'I doubt it. I saw how hurt she was. How—shattered. Humiliated in every sense. Once your illusions have been destroyed...'

'Yeah.' There was heartfelt agreement in that single low syllable.

He didn't speak again until they were in the lift, where vibrations between them seemed to intensify.

'How about you, Amber?' Though his voice sounded casual, the darkened eyes on her face were intent. 'Would you have given him a second chance?'

Her heart skidded. The subtext was clear now. He was talking about her and him. Would she give him another chance? Another chance to make love to her.

She knew what her body yearned for her to say. The temptation to touch him was extreme. But pride, self-esteem or whatever else forced her to hold her nerve.

'I'd have needed to be convinced, Guy.'

A muscle twitched in his cheek. 'What would you expect? A preview?'

'A reasonable explanation would be a start.'

Frowning, he dragged a hand through his hair. The air tautened with suspense, with an almost tangible sense of his reluctance. Each time his darkened gaze clashed with hers the intensity in his glance dragged at her breasts and turned her insides to liquid.

When they reached her door she paused, hoping against hope he would say something. *Anything* to revive her illusions.

'Well…' Her voice was husky with night fever. 'That was a lovely dinner. Thank you. It was good to—talk.'

He remained silent, his mouth compressed to a firm straight line.

She added, 'I feel as if we understand each other a bit better.'

His jaw set hard.

'Which is good, if we're to work together.'

There was nothing more to say, so she turned to unlock her door.

'Amber.'

His deep voice interrupted her as she inserted her key. She faced him again.

'I…' He lifted his arms from his sides and let them fall again. 'I haven't taken a woman out in a while.' Unwilling at the start, the words finished in a rush.

Her ears pricked up, her heart tensing with thrilled anticipation. 'Really?'

'No.'

She waited for more, but he didn't add anything. Just stood looking like a rock that had reluctantly squeezed out a precious drop of its lifeblood.

She lifted her brows. 'Is that *it*?'

He drew an exasperated breath. 'Look, I don't *talk* about all that relationship palaver. It's just that you might as well know I had a—' He swung away to evade her eyes. 'A break-up, I suppose you'd call it, with a woman a while back, and I've probably been avoiding all the—stuff.'

'The stuff?' she mused aloud, though inside her spirit was doing cartwheels at having commanded such a grand achievement. 'And what would that be, I wonder? The *stuff*?'

His eyes glinted and he took her arms in a firm grip. 'You're just loving this, aren't you? You think you've got the power.'

She gave one of those tinkling little laughs. But it was filled with excitement, fuelled by the thrilling sensation of electricity tingling where his skin collided with hers. 'Don't be silly. As if women ever think about power.'

He gave a brief sardonic laugh. Then his expression lightened. 'I don't suppose you'll be dancing tonight?'

A sliver of excitement shot down her spine. 'Probably. After everything today, I might have to.'

'Ah. Do you know…' the gleam in his eyes intensified '…I'd really love to see that?'

CHAPTER EIGHT

AMBER had changed into a simple white dress with a hem that floated around her knees. Guy could see through the flimsy fabric to something white she had on underneath.

What he was about to witness was the real thing, he realised, taking in her preparations with a weird thrill down his spine. A sense of how lucky he was, how *privileged* to be allowed into something so essentially private, gave him a pang of misgiving. What if he blew it again? What if he said the wrong thing and somehow bruised her feelings?

She was right, though, about the atmosphere without electric light. The moon filled the room with a ghostly glow, reflected in the wall mirrors she'd placed at either end. Along the third wall she had an empty bookcase turned on its side to serve as her *barre*.

When she moved across the room to the stereo his anticipation sharpened into suspense. She touched something, then the opening chords of 'Clair de Lune' shimmered on the air.

He held his breath.

Gliding to stand under the skylight, she extended her arms upwards. Then, after casting him a long, mysterious glance, she started. She rose on her toes and reached up to the moon and danced—a spirit of the night in thrall to the music. She seemed possessed by some elemental magic. It was spellbinding, every movement perfection, every line of her graceful form lovely.

As she swooped down, then reached up to glide and twirl gently on her toes, the moonlight turned her skin translucent and caught a faint lustre in her dress. Once or twice she sent him another of those long, galvanising glances. It was so—intimate. Almost confiding. He felt as if she was inviting him in to share her experience.

His heart hammered like a schoolboy's.

He sat motionless on top of the pile on the sofa in the hall, mesmerised, hardly daring to breathe for fear of breaking the spell. Never in his life had he expected to be affected by *ballet*.

But the purity and simplicity of her movements, so expressive of the music, enslaved him.

As the last note faded he sat frozen, moved to his soul.

She turned to look at him. He could see the rise and fall of her breasts from her exertion, then he realised with shame his initial fascination in the whole business had been sensual. Still was, of course, on some level. Face it, *every* level. But the reality had been so much more than that.

'Amber…' His voice sounded as if it had issued from the centre of the earth.

Smiling at the crack in his voice, she strolled across to the stereo in her ballet slippers and switched it off. Half turning to deliver him an apologetic shrug, she said, 'It'd be better if I had more space.'

He clambered down from his perch. 'Oh, no,' he said, striding across to her, feeling like a great, hulking clumsy brute. 'No, it couldn't be better. It was…'

He was breathing so hard his insides might have been shaking. Faced with her gorgeous eager face, her eyes shining with comprehension of his appreciation, he felt his best words desert him.

He took her in his arms. 'Amber, I… Really, I…'

He couldn't help it. He risked everything and kissed her. Thank the gods or angels or whatever, she melted her soft, yielding curves against his hungry, burning bones and kissed him right back, her wine-sweet mouth so luscious, so arousing, he was instantly harder than a log.

He drew her lips into his mouth, glorying in their soft, addictive resilience. Her honeyed breath mingled with his, tongue tips touching. When the intoxicating event finally ended, to his extreme relief she took his hand and led him into her bedroom.

Exhilarated after her dance, and drunk with the kiss, Amber turned to face him, her veins ablaze with fever. Excitement made her tremble.

He dropped his jacket on the floor, then opened both hands before him. 'I'm crazy for you. But are you sure that you want this?'

Even if she hadn't read the faint sheen on his forehead, the tension apparent in his muscles, there was an intensity in his voice that spoke of his desire.

She moved close and placed her hand flat over his heart. She could feel the big muscle under her palm. Thumping like crazy, all right. Like her own.

'Oh, I want it,' she said, breathless in her heartfelt sincerity. 'Want you.'

He kissed her again fiercely, possessively, pushing her up against a wall, his big hot hands seeking the fastenings of her dress while he pinned her with his pelvis and ground his hips against her.

She could feel the hard bulk of his erection against her abdomen. The friction was great, but it only made her sex burn with more need. She parted her thighs and hooked a leg around him, the better to rub her maddened flesh against that seductive ridge.

'Rock me, rock me,' she rasped, her body yearning for contact of the sexy, masculine kind.

'Steady now,' he warned. 'Not so fast.'

Though he seemed unable to take his own advice. He devoured her with kisses and caresses, including obligingly stroking that delicate spot with his fingers through the thin covering of her body stocking. She clung to him, moaning as waves of liquid pleasure thrilled through her aroused flesh.

The incredible friction was fantastic, but only served to increase the burning demand inside her.

Thirsting for total skin contact, she helped him find the fastenings to her dress. She could feel the heat in his urgent hands as he lowered the zip, interspersing every small act with more hot, greedy kisses. Her face, her throat, her breasts.

'I could eat you alive,' he breathed with husky fervour. 'You're gorgeous. So beautiful. So—so everything.'

The dress fell to the floor and the body stocking soon followed. Amber bent to untie her slippers.

'No, leave them a minute,' he commanded. 'I want to—look at you.'

Breathing hard, he reached a hand to stroke her, tracing a gentle line from shoulder to hip, as if she were made of some rare and precious material.

The dark flame in his eyes burned. 'You know, I never expected to be with you again.' His voice had that deep, gravelly quality.

Her heart lurched. Was he mocking her for her turnaround?

'You didn't want to be?' She searched his face.

He took a moment to answer. 'I was a fool. I thought I'd ruined my chances with you.'

She saw the seriousness in his eyes and realised there was no mockery.

'Well…' Her voice sank to a whisper. 'Things can change.'

He was silent, shadows she couldn't read coming and going in his expression.

She stepped forward and put her lips to his throat. At the same time her nimble fingers released his shirt buttons. Hungry for more of his salty, alluring *man* taste, she pushed his shirt aside and explored his muscled chest with her hands and lips.

He put his arms around her and kissed her lips, his chest hair grazing her breasts. Then, seized by a mutual urgency, each of them went for his belt buckle, excited hands colliding.

When at last he stood naked Amber's eyes widened in awe. 'Heavens.'

His penis was so thick and engorged, pulsing with the urgent life, she was nearly overcome. In rapturous worship she went down on her knees, held the marvellous creature in both hands and licked the salty tip.

He shuddered and let out a wild groan. Amazingly, his length thickened and grew harder in her hands.

'I suppose this must be quite tender here?' With a grin she closed her lips over the end and gave a mischievous little suck.

Guy tensed, making a quick move to quell the delicious procedure before it catapulted him too far, too soon. 'Hey—no way,' he bit out. 'Amber.' He pushed her away from his too-willing shaft, shaking his head with mock sternness. 'You could live to regret that.' Without ceremony he hauled her to her feet and thrust her onto the bed.

With a giggle at his expression, Amber lolled in luxurious anticipation of his next move. 'You're being very bossy.'

'That's because, sweetheart, right here and right now I *am* the boss.'

'Promise?' She fluttered her lashes. 'I admit I'm finding you really quite—dictatorial. I shudder to think what you might do to me.'

'Here,' he said, smiling, 'give me that foot.'

She lifted the foot and playfully wiggled it at him. He caught it, and with eyes gleaming untied the strings and peeled off her slipper.

'Aha,' he said, taking her foot in his big, warm hands.

It felt so pleasant, having her foot held. Comforting, even.

'There's magic in this pretty foot.'

He undressed the other foot, then kissed her toes and kneaded her soles with his thumbs. Guy's touch was far more exciting than the physio's at the ballet company. Her very soles felt aroused.

But what he did with the backs of her knees was pure devilry.

'Oh, yes,' she cried at the sensations tingling up her leg. 'There. *There.*'

Breaking from her, he bent down to where his clothes lay on the floor and searched. Then he sat on the side of the bed and sheathed himself.

Leaning up on an elbow to watch the operation, she observed with a smile. 'Well, well. I see you came prepared. In *spite* of your misgivings.'

He cast her a gleaming glance. 'And aren't you glad I'm an ever hopeful, upbeat kinda guy, even against all odds?'

'Oh, I'm glad, all right. I'm celebrating.' She giggled and kicked her legs high.

She was feeling so deliciously high and aroused, it occurred to her that what she was experiencing right here and now was happiness. Guy Wilder was *sorry*, still gorgeous, and here they both were. Against all the odds.

He stretched out beside her and took her in his arms. Then he kissed her lips. When he drew back, his eyes were warm and tender. 'You're making me feel so good I want to do something for you.'

'Oh, yeah?' She was suddenly breathless. 'What sort of thing?' Though she might be studying him cagily, the truth was she was eager. Wildly eager.

His eyes brimmed with amused comprehension and desire. 'Roll over,' he instructed, and when she complied he groaned with a conviction that was truly flattering, 'Oh, this gorgeous peach of a behind. I've dreamed of this.'

She was happy for him to enjoy her behind, or any other part that took his fancy. So when he started kissing the insides of her knees, and continued a fiery journey to the silky skin inside her thighs, divining where he might be headed, she co-operated with every move in a mounting ecstasy of hope and suspense.

And she wasn't disappointed. Soon his clever fingers were lighting tingling little fires as he stroked the highly aroused and sensitive skin of her bottom.

And *then*, thank the Lord, they slipped between her legs to softly massage the burning folds of her feminine mound.

'Ohh...' She sighed in helpless bliss, lifting her hips a little to accommodate the fabulous friction.

Time slowed. The temperature in the room skyrocketed. There was no sound but the rasp of their breathing, her moans, and her heart booming in her ears. Then softly, tenderly, Guy Wilder put his mouth between her legs and sucked. Creating the most intense and trembling rapture she could ever remember experiencing, he licked her sweetest, most intimate spot with his tongue.

Streams of intense delight irradiated her flesh. Blissful sensations swelled inside her like the sun on a spring morn, building and building to an irresistible, ever-beckoning pinnacle, and then when they were too much to endure, bursting into a thousand glorious rays of pleasure.

And that was only the beginning.

Amber O'Neill was floating. It felt so fantastic to be made love to. To share passion with a lover who laughed one minute, then in the next moved her heart unutterably.

'You're the real thing, aren't you?' he said at one point.

Bemused, she gazed at him. 'The real…*woman*?'

He laughed. 'Oh, no worries there. No, I mean…' His grin faded. 'You're a genuine ballerina. Do you do all the stuff? Swans and everything?'

She nodded, trying not to grin at his enthusiasm. 'Sugar plum fairies, princesses, firebirds—I do them all. Though swans are my specialty.'

His voice thickened. 'I'd love to see that.'

She smiled, though she didn't say what she thought. *I doubt you ever will.* Instead she said casually, 'You can come to see me at the Spanish club doing flamenco some Saturday evening, if you like.'

There were few long heartbeats. Then he said, 'I *would* like.'

And then there was that amazing moment when he entered her with one searing, virile thrust. He gazed down at her, his eyes fierce and at the same time so tender her heart shook.

'I never thought I could have this again with another woman.'

Questions sprang up in her mind, but were soon discarded as he took her higher than high, making love to her in every which way, bringing her to multiple orgasms, holding back on his own pleasure until at last, hot, hard and convincing, he reached his own shuddering climax.

After that, she slept in his arms.

CHAPTER NINE

'WE'LL need a few flowers. All right?'

Guy swept in mid-morning, smiling and charged with plans, his eyes still warm from the night before. The several nights before. Up to thirteen now, by Amber's counting. Nights of sampling the local eating houses, cooking in Amber's kitchen, making out in the cinema, enjoying long and voluptuous lovemaking in Amber's bed.

Not that any evening ever started out that way. No definite plans were ever made. It always seemed just to happen that, whenever Amber was wondering if she would see Guy that night, by accident, and often in the most casual way, she'd bump into him somewhere. Then, before she knew it, things escalated and passion was the outcome.

It was fun to speculate how 'accidental' those heavenly meetings were. The ones she didn't engineer herself, that was. Though the L word hadn't been used, some beautiful things had been said, and her fingers were perpetually crossed.

This particular Tuesday morning she felt especially chirpy. Guy had phoned her soon after nine from his office. Something in his schedule had been delayed, he'd told her, so the crew had a timeslot to spare for Fleur Elise.

At last. Amber had been beginning to wonder if it would ever happen.

But today was all go, and she was bubbling with excitement. He was taking her to meet his team, and if they could come up with some satisfactory props, and the weather held, they might even start actual shooting. Outdoors, he told her they'd decided, as a cost-cutting measure. And, as another way to reduce costs, Guy seemed to think *she* could be the model for her own ad.

She kept grinning, imagining herself on camera. It wouldn't be the same as being on stage, of course, but shooting with Guy would be better than going over the accounts. Doing *anything* with Guy was better than anything else she could think of.

Amber had begged Ivy to come in and help the customers while Serena worked on the bouquets. She'd guessed Ivy would be eager, and Ivy was. Any opportunity to be running the show without Amber getting in the way was her bonus.

For once Amber didn't care. Oh, joyous day. She could *escape*.

Not that she didn't love her shop. She was absolutely grateful to have it. Especially when Guy breezed in, exuding energy and purpose. Everything glowed then.

Including her heart when he strolled up to her at her counter.

'How are you feeling?' He held her in his gaze as if she was the only woman in the world.

It was only a few hours since they'd been in each other's arms.

Amber had realised both Serena and Ivy had guessed about their connection. Ivy had accused her of being besotted. Amber didn't care if the whole world knew. She was happy, though she felt relieved that Guy understood that here in the shop there could be no touching. He was such an intuitive, professional, reliable, sensitive, gorgeous guy.

'Ready to be a star?' he added, his eyes gleaming.

'You'd better believe it.' It would have been churlish to mention she'd already tasted stardom for a couple of glorious years. 'And I feel—fantastic.' She used her husky voice. 'How about you?'

'Fan—tastic.'

And he looked it. Even with Ivy hovering nearby over a potential customer, and Serena poking her head out from the bunching room, flashing Amber grins and thumbs up, it was impossible *not* to eat him with her eyes.

He was in jeans today, though not the scruffy ones. These were more the sleek type preferred by movie directors and Italian racing car drivers. A crisp white shirt with the sleeves rolled back exposed the tanned desirability of his arms. Arms that had held her through the night. Arms she'd have stepped into right then and there if they'd been alone.

His gleaming grey gaze travelled over her outfit, reinforcing her pleasant inner blaze. 'Look at you. You're inspiring my vision. You look gorgeous.'

She smiled. 'And you look—edible.'

For some reason he wanted her in one of her work outfits to meet his team, so she hadn't changed from her satiny floral sheath. In shades of blue and lavender, with a hint of turquoise, it was shortish, and looked good with her one and only pair of four-inch heels. As well, she'd swirled her hair into a chignon and stuck in an iris.

Considering the last time he'd seen her she'd been naked apart from a sheet, she was glad she'd flowered up. Flowery had its advantages. It was hard not to look pretty when smothered in blooms.

Ivy bustled over, to elbow Amber out of the way so she could ring up a transaction, and Guy sharpened up his conversation for Ivy's benefit.

'It'll be good for the team to see you in your workwear,' he said gravely. 'It'll help them understand the theme.'

'Humph,' Ivy grunted, rolling her eyes. '*Theme*. Unless you're purchasing something, would you mind moving away from the counter, sir?'

As Amber turned an incredulous look on Ivy, Guy said smoothly, 'But I am purchasing something, Ivy. I'm buying all your stock.'

Ivy's jaw dropped. '*What?* You can't. I'll have nothing for my customers.'

'Yes, he can, Ivy,' Amber cut in firmly. She smiled at Guy. 'Maybe you could just leave us a few blooms in case we get a wild rush?'

'Aha! Do you get those too?' he said. 'I think I had one this morning, in fact.'

It was hard not to laugh with Ivy looking so dour, but Amber managed to hold it in, though she had to avoid Guy's eyes, knowing they were brimming with amusement.

Keeping his mouth grave, he pointed to the iris in her hair. 'Can you spare some of those? And we might take some of these, these, and those over there. And more of the roses. My vision of you involves lots of roses.'

Amber retrieved a delivery box from the back room, and with Serena's help started to layer in the blooms while Ivy glowered, totting up the cost like a distrustful hawk.

By the time Guy had finished selecting the flowers he wanted for his scenario they'd filled a second large box.

'What do you plan to do with them all?' Amber said when they were in the car. Divine fragrances issued from the boxes in the rear.

Guy leaned over and, cupping her face, kissed her. Along with his own exciting personal flavour, at this time of day he tasted of coffee. Although her lips still felt tender from the ravages of the night, it seemed impossible to satisfy their insatiable desire for more of him. Somehow they would never listen to reason. Nor would her breasts and her other erotic parts.

But, to her grateful pleasure, his exploring hands found all her secret places through her clothes and aroused her all over again.

Guy was similarly afflicted. 'I shouldn't have done that,' he groaned, drawing away from her. 'You taste too good. If the team wasn't waiting…'

Marvelling at how her eyes actually did resemble jewels, and at how he might even be tempted to say such a mushy thing aloud if he didn't keep a strict check on his tongue, Guy felt an unnerving thought flash into his head.

Not for the first time, in fact. Only now it was about to *happen* he was seeing more clearly than ever before how difficult it might be to keep this romance—or fling, or whatever he was engaged in—under wraps.

If the crew cottoned on to it…

He could imagine it only too well. The trouble was they knew too much. Most of them were aware of his ancient history. Some had *witnessed* the event, for God's sake. He didn't care about that any more. He was over it. He just couldn't stand for them all to get excited. To be watching from the sidelines, avidly appraising every move he made. Hoping he'd be lucky this time. Whispering among themselves about whether or not he could pull it off.

Guts clenching in sudden distaste, he started the car and reversed out of the park with an unexpected screech of tyres. Nosing the car into the traffic stream, he said grimly, 'I'll just have to keep my hands off you today, that's all.'

Clutching her seat belt, Amber stared at him in surprise. The lines of his face seemed suddenly tense. But as though he sensed her curiosity he relaxed his expression and flashed her a warm glance.

She glanced at the long muscled thighs appealingly encased in denim on the other side of the console. 'But I don't have to keep my hands off *you* just yet, do I?'

By the time he drove them into the basement of the steel and glass tower in Castlereagh Street, where his office was located, she'd covered a lot of territory.

After he pulled on the handbrake they each straightened their clothes. Amber checked her face in the sun visor mirror and patted her hair in place.

'What do you think? Lipstick?'

Smiling, he softly drew his forefinger across her mouth. 'No need.'

The light, sensual touch made the blood swell helplessly in her veins.

'You may be right. It'd be a crime to cover up that last kiss.'

Desire flared in his eyes and he kissed her again—another long, breathless, sexy clinch—causing them to have to go through the tidying-up procedure all over again.

He sat back then and frowned a little, squaring his shoulders. 'There is just one small point I should probably mention.'

'Yeah?' She gazed expectantly at him.

'It's about the team.' Beneath his dark brows his grey eyes were glittering with some intent calculation. 'They're a great team, but you might find—especially at first—they can seem pretty businesslike.'

She nodded. 'Well, that's good, isn't it?'

'Yeah, it's good,' he said warmly. 'It's the way it has to be. But they…er…' He gestured, evading her eyes. 'Well, they don't know about us knowing each other personally, of course.'

She studied him through her lashes. 'Well, of course. How would they?'

He flicked her a glance of amused appreciation. Then he said carefully, 'It's better they don't know.'

'Fine.' She reached and drew a finger from his cheekbone to his jaw. 'I'll try not to lust. And I promise I won't blab about what you were doing at three o'clock this morning.'

He gave a small laugh. 'I know you won't do that. But because they won't understand the real situation, I just don't want you to feel as if anyone's trying to—push you around.'

'Why would I feel like that?'

He waggled his hand. 'Well, they can be a little abrupt. I know how sensitive you are, and I'd hate you to take it personally. They're used to dealing with professional models. So if anyone gives you instructions, or comments on your appearance, you need to understand it will be strictly for professional purposes.'

'I see.' She nodded.

'The thing is…' He hesitated. 'I would hate your tender feelings to be hurt.'

She thought of some of the savage insults the director of the ballet company had been likely to shriek at the dancers when rehearsal wasn't going well. It was tempting to laugh, but his concern was so genuine, so kind, she was filled with a fierce tenderness for him. She just squeezed his knee and gave him a reassuring grin.

'Relax. I'm used to showbiz. Don't you know I'm an O'Neill?'

'Oh, I know.' His eyes gleamed.

Still, she wondered if she was imagining he looked a bit stressed.

Up on the forty-eighth floor a small group was waiting

to meet her. There was an older guy, one young executive type in his late twenties, a youngish red-haired boy, and two capable-looking women—one with flaming hair who introduced herself as Maggie.

As Guy had predicted, they all shook hands with Amber in a friendly and professional manner, then promptly forgot she was human.

A wall screen glowed with a picture of a beautiful fifteenth century painting of people in a garden wearing long floaty dresses. Amber wasn't sure which one of the characters was supposed to represent her, because no one bothered to explain. She tilted her head to read the label printed along the side of the reproduction. *La Primavera* it was called. Spring.

They strolled around her, discussing her attributes as a model so frankly Amber was glad she'd been warned. Still, it was all quite clinical. She might as well have been a blow-up doll.

Guy stood by while they inspected her from top to toe, not commenting much, but clearly in command. Since the car park he'd morphed into 'The Boss'. She had to keep looking at him to believe he was the same person who'd borrowed her toothbrush, then actually confessed.

His demeanour made it clear to any interested parties that though he might have seen her flower shop in the distance *once*, by pure chance only, she remained a total stranger to him. Lucky she was no stranger to the way professionals worked behind the scenes, or she might have been offended.

The team directed comments to Guy from time to time, but his replies were minimal, as if he didn't want to join the party. Amber noticed they kept sending him faintly surprised looks.

His eyes were inscrutable, but alert, and there was a

certain tension in his posture as they pulled her apart. Nothing about her was sacred, it seemed. Her face, her figure, her hands, legs and ankles. Even her knees. All came under discussion and, though most bits seemed to pass the photobility test, she flinched at some of the comments.

'If she was even an inch taller…'

Ha. They had to be *kidding*. She'd been one of the tallest in the company. What did they want? A giraffe?

Guy seemed to feel the same way. 'How tall do you want her, André?' he said pleasantly. 'That height looks excellent to me.'

'Oh sure, sure. I was only thinking of, you know, screen presence.'

'Doesn't beauty count for anything?' Guy said mildly. 'Grace?'

He flushed a little after he'd said that, and Amber felt herself pinken. There was a small silence. People were exchanging astounded glances with each other, then someone hastened to say, 'Oh, yeah—sure, boss.'

Amber made a face at Guy but he pretended not to catch it. After a fraught second the torture started again.

'Turn this way, dear. No, the other way. The right is her best.'

'Look up there, sweetheart. Now walk over to the desk. Now back.'

'Oh, yes, yes. Lovely walk. Look at those calves. And the arms. Nice muscle tone.'

They didn't mention her behind, though she felt pretty certain Guy was holding his breath waiting for it.

One of the women's jobs was to write instructions onto a notepad as fast as they fell from the experts' lips.

'That's it, that's it!' someone exclaimed. 'If we can catch her like *that*. Watch for that angle, André.'

'What about her hair?' the older guy asked. 'Do you want it up or—?'

'Down,' Guy cut in. 'Definitely.'

'Shouldn't we turn her into a blonde?'

'Why?' Guy said sharply. 'Her hair's a rainbow. Catch her in the sun and you'll see it's filled with light. It's rich in chestnut, reds, golds, violets.'

He checked himself, blinking a couple of times. Amber thought she could detect another faint stain to his cheek.

'Anyway, there's no time,' he added curtly, deflecting more startled glances from his team.

'Yeah, course. Fine,' the older man hastened to reply. 'Works for me.' He shrugged and sent Amber a wink.

'What about that costume? I could have put something really good together if I'd had more advance notice,' Maggie grumbled in an aside. 'What's the big rush, anyway?'

There was a small silence while people held their breaths.

'Are you saying you can't do it, Maggie?' When he spoke Guy's tone was level. Pleasant, even. But it left an edge that had Maggie scrambling to backtrack.

'Oh, heavens—course not. I have one or two things we can use. I'll just have to do a few tweaks here and there.' The sudden tension in the room relaxed as Maggie got herself off the hook.

'Which one is it?' Amber enquired.

'Here.' Guy directed her gaze to a lady in the picture wearing a delicate floral gown, her hair decked in flowers. She was scattering roses from some she carried in the apron of her skirt.

'We need to put you in a floaty number like one of these.'

Amber stared at the screen. With the lighting behind it

the picture looked almost transparent. 'Floaty?' she murmured doubtfully. 'It's not see-through, is it?'

'Yeah, see-through.' The young red-haired guy guffawed, nudging his neighbour and grinning. 'Exactly.'

Guy turned a stern glance on the boy, then coolly beckoned him aside. The lad's grin was wiped. Whatever Guy had murmured to him was inaudible to everyone else, but the boy visibly wilted. When he slunk back to rejoin the team he didn't look nearly so chipper.

Amber felt so sorry for him. It was soul-destroying to be shamed in front of a group. Honestly, Guy needed to get a grip. To make matters worse, he intercepted the sympathetic glance she gave the boy and sent her a warning frown.

What the…! He wasn't deluded into thinking he was *her* boss now, was he?

Amber noticed Maggie shooting glances between her and Guy, and had the sinking feeling the game was up.

'All right—er—Amber,' Guy said briskly, suddenly seeming to pull himself together. 'Maggie'll take you down now for some make-up.' He turned his gaze in Amber's direction. But only in her direction, not right *to* her. He didn't meet her eyes, as a friend would. Or an acquaintance from the local flower shop. Even a perfect stranger who'd just happened in off the street.

Only lovers covering up tried not to gaze at each other. She knew it, Maggie knew it, and she wouldn't have been surprised if the whole crew knew it.

She'd have laughed if Guy hadn't been so concerned about his team knowing. At the same time she felt her insides melting with love for him for not being able to conceal his passion.

Maggie's manner as she beckoned Amber to follow her made Amber wonder if the woman was peeved about something. She hustled her along to a suite of wardrobe rooms not unlike the rooms backstage at a theatre, though on a much smaller scale. Then after measuring her, without much ceremony Maggie pushed, prodded and pinned her into a variety of dresses.

Usually Amber adored the whole costume business, and entered into the spirit of the thing with gusto. This time the experience was bit too brusque to enjoy.

'This feels quite tight,' she suggested to Maggie as she was being pinned into a long dress.

'Hmm.' Standing with pins in her mouth, a stapler in her hand and a tape around her neck, Maggie was the picture of the long-suffering seamstress. 'Hang on while I clamp this bodice.'

'*Oof.* I do have to breathe, you know.'

'Think how it enhances your shape. He'll love it.' Maggie glanced at her then, a challenge in her eyes.

Amber didn't waste time pretending not to know who Maggie meant. She just lifted her brows haughtily. 'So long as it works for his scenario, Maggie. That's all Guy will be interested in.'

Maggie glowered, focused on her pinning. After a while she said fiercely, 'Guy's a *nice man*. He's not the sort who plays around with people.'

It was Amber's turn to frown. Did this Maggie assume *she* was the sort to play around with people? She was strongly tempted to inform Maggie that she actually found Guy really very playful, but decided against it. She and Guy were none of the woman's business.

Besides, she didn't want to risk being stuck with pins.

Once she was back in her own clothes again, a young woman introduced as Kate sat her in front of a fluoro lit mirror and started smoothing stuff onto her face.

Maggie's phone buzzed and she turned away to deal

with it. 'Thanks, boss.' Slipping the phone away, she turned to Amber and Kate. 'Guy's given us an hour. Where's that picture?'

There was a massive amount of hustle, with Maggie darting about collecting things in between madly machining darts into the dress to make it fit. Meanwhile, Kate worked magic on Amber's face and powdered her throat

When her make-up was done to their satisfaction, Maggie helped her back into the dress. It was ivory, with a deep-scooped neckline, long lacy sleeves and a softly billowing skirt.

'I'm not sure,' Amber said doubtfully, trying to suck in her tummy while Maggie fastened at least a hundred buttons. 'The fabric's good, but I don't know how spring-like it is. It feels a bit as if I should be walking up the aisle of Westminster Abbey.' She surveyed Maggie's copy of the picture again. 'Do you really think this dress will cut it?'

'It'll just have to do,' Maggie said grimly, piling flowers onto her workbench. 'It's long, isn't it? If people don't give you any notice to work miracles they have to be satisfied with what they get. Italian paintings, for pity's sake. What next? Did the boys bring up that other box of flowers, Kate?' She started rooting through shelves of plastic packing boxes. 'Don't you worry, my love. We'll tart you up with so many flowers old Botticelli himself wouldn't know the difference.'

Guy stood staring through his precious viewfinder at the Chinese Garden of Friendship. His camera team—André and the red-haired boy—lounged on the grass. As an informal make-up station for Kate, they'd set up a folding table and a couple of chairs.

The location looked tranquil enough, with its waterfalls, willow lawns and charming little bridges. At least this time early on a Tuesday afternoon every man and his dog were partying somewhere else. Apart from the risk of accidentally including a pagoda in the shot, there had to be at least one good angle here where a goddess could scatter roses.

Guy decided on the most likely spot and galvanised the red-haired boy to help him distribute a few of Amber's flowers about. 'Try to make it look natural,' he said, stapling a rose to a twig. 'Remember she's a flower goddess.'

The boy started to speak, then checked himself, casting Guy an anxious look to see if he'd heard. Guy made a wry grimace to himself. He'd seen their knowing glances. He knew they were surmising over his relationship with Amber.

He gritted his teeth. Why couldn't they all get over it and let him get on with his life? It seemed that everyone he knew was constantly on the lookout for a happy ending for him. Of the *marriage* variety. As if that was the only kind of ending that counted.

If only people understood how humiliating that was.

Normally he loved a shoot. This was what he enjoyed most: seeing his vision come to life and capturing it on camera. It was a beautiful day, the city traffic was barely audible here, and he was about to see Amber looking even more impossibly desirable than ever.

He had to admit, though, he was having second thoughts. Not about Amber. Hell, no. Just thinking of her made his heart beat faster. *And* the sex. How had he survived so long in the wilderness without a warm, lovely body to curl up to?

No, it was *this* that was wrong. Involving his team in his personal affairs. Risking dragging it all up again. How could he have forgotten that some of them were friends with Jo? The other day Maggie had even casually dropped in to the conversation that Jo was back in Sydney. As if *he* might be interested.

For pity's sake.

But what if one of them hinted something to Amber? She'd be racing for the nearest set of hills like a horrified gazelle. Embarrassed.

Even worse, she'd be embarrassed for *him*. Imagining her reaction, he felt himself start to sweat. He ran a finger around the inside of his shirt collar. If only there was some way he could insulate her from people who knew him.

It had definitely been a mistake, rushing to her rescue like that. Who did he think he was? Sir Galahad?

But was it too late to call a halt today? He was nearly as good with a camera as André. If he could come up with a reasonable excuse he could send them all off home and do the whole shoot himself.

He was just racking his brains for one when the sound of voices echoing down the path alerted him to the approach of the women.

His pulse quickened. His vision was about to crystallise. Enter Spring.

Kate appeared first, carrying a box with her make-up case balanced on top, while Maggie walked alongside Amber, holding her bunched up skirt off the ground. At first glance the three were all clumped together. It took Guy's bedazzled brain a moment to separate them into their individual components.

The same instant he did, Maggie allowed the dress she was holding to fall around Amber, and stepped away from her. Guy's lungs seized as something like a twelve bore shotgun blasted a hole through him.

What were they thinking? They'd done her up as a bride.

The women fluttered around her, tweaking her dress

and the little flower sprays pinned all over her—at her bosom, her waist, on her skirt. A wreath of pink, red and white flowers adorned her head, while more were plaited through her long hair.

André and the lad hauled themselves up off the grass and clustered around her, goggling as if they'd never seen a woman with a pretty cleavage before in their lives.

The boy kept saying, 'You look hot, Amber. Hot.'

'Nice one, Maggie.' That was André, circling Amber like a grinning shark.

'Thanks, boys,' Maggie said. 'Scrubbed up all right, didn't she?'

Guy saw Amber give them a quick modest smile, then look straight to him for his reaction. Thing was, he couldn't say anything right then. A cold wind was whistling through the space in his guts.

He read puzzlement in her blue eyes, and had to turn away before he disgraced himself with some blistering comment.

André swanned into the foreground, salivating like Mr Fox. 'Stand over here, Amber, and let me see you with the trees behind you.' Smooth as butter, kneeling down with the camera on his shoulder, pretending he was interested in the shot when it was plain to anyone with half a brain he just wanted an excuse to ogle her.

The boy just continued gaping with his mouth open.

With superhuman resolve Guy snapped himself together. This was his disaster. He was in charge and he'd set the course.

Blinking, he said, 'Let's not waste time oohing and aahing. Thanks, Maggie, that'll have to do, though I'm not sure a wedding was quite what I had in mind. Did you bring some roses for her to scatter?'

They were all looking strangely at him. Maggie's hand

flew to her mouth in a betraying little gesture of dismayed comprehension that jabbed his raw spot like a knife.

And Amber…

What had he done? The hurt in her face, the confusion. How harsh had he sounded? What had he actually *said*? He closed his eyes, trying to recall his exact words, his blood pressure pounding in his temples.

What was wrong with him? She wasn't a bride. This was another time, another place, and he was two years older. Amber O'Neill *was not a bride.*

'Amber,' he said hoarsely, shielding his eyes against the sun so as not to see his vision too clearly, 'show us how you can walk like the springtime.'

CHAPTER TEN

THE shoot took longer than Amber had anticipated. She was asked to float like a goddess and scatter roses so many times their store ran out. Then people had to scramble about picking them up again.

Guy seemed a little worried about how she was standing up to the repetition, but after a while he relaxed. If she'd wanted to she could have reminded him she was used to far more strenuous exertion at a highly concentrated level. But she didn't care to bring up her past glories. Not in front of the crew.

Eventually the strained atmosphere mellowed slightly, thank goodness, and there were even some fun moments when the whole company collapsed in laughter, though it was an edgy sort of laughter. Guy joined in, but something in him felt different. Not so much a coolness, as a quietness.

A reserve.

When he and André were finally satisfied with their footage, and they'd wrapped up, the crew congratulated Amber and told her she'd been excellent. Professional, André said. Maggie especially seemed to be making an effort to be kind, actually suggesting she might drop by the shop the next time she was in Kirribilli. Amber was scratching her head. Had Maggie forgotten her dastardly plan to run off with her beloved boss and screw his brains out?

She noticed Guy look too hard at Maggie when she made that astounding suggestion. The lines around his mouth were rather grim.

The trip home had a vastly different mood from the morning's. Guy didn't have much to say, while Amber felt anxious and confused. Awash with misgivings, in truth. Considering how frankly passionate he'd been towards her a few hours ago, this constraint was depressing. The big question was *why*? What had she done to make him go off her so dramatically?

'Do you think the shoot went well?' she ventured at last, her heart thumping like an idiot's.

He nodded. 'Oh, yeah. I'm pretty sure we'll be able to do something with it.'

She made her tone bright and upbeat. 'What a relief. What happens next?'

'Well, we'll edit it. Play around with it to get the tones and colours right. Layer on some music, of course. Something to suit the motion of the piece. A voiceover, some graphics…' He smiled to himself. Or maybe it was a grimace of nauseated derision.

'Plenty of airbrushing, I hope?'

He shrugged. 'Maybe a bit of enhancement. To the dress,' he finished, with a rather sibilant hiss.

She was silent for a while, wondering if she'd imagined that he was burning with resentment over something. 'Sounds like a lot of work.'

'Yep. The next part will have to be filmed in your shop.'

'Oh?' She glanced at him in surprise. 'You mean there's more?'

'Only a couple of seconds' worth. But that couple of seconds will have to show the shop in the best light possible. I'm thinking we may as well send the people who do our set designs around to start your makeover.'

She felt a flutter of excitement followed by anxiety about how much it must all be costing.

She glanced at him, hesitating. 'Look, I'm so grateful to you for all this, Guy. Honestly. Offering all your resources, your—your people. It's so very generous. Truly kind. But I can't help worrying about the money. I know it must be costing you heaps.'

He frowned, embarrassed, and shook his head. 'No need to feel like that. This is business. If we can make Fleur Elise attractive, the glow will reflect on Wilder Solutions. When you're rich we'll add it to the bill.'

'No,' she said firmly, a decision she'd been mulling over for weeks suddenly crystallising in her mind. 'That's good of you, but—I want to pay for my own renovations. It'll be great if you recommend your designer. But I'll pay for all the work and the materials myself.'

He looked sharply at her, but didn't question her ability to pay. Just as well. She had no intention of asking anyone's permission to seek a small business loan from her bank. It was her shop, and it was her decision. She'd borrow the bare minimum and use some of the money for stock.

He glanced at her, his grey eyes appraising. 'Would you object if I suggested a couple of guys that could do the actual work?'

'No, of course not. So long as they're excellent.' Amber smiled, pleased with her decision. She glanced at him. 'Will I be wearing the same costume for the shop part of the ad?'

He drew in a sharp breath through his nostrils. *'No.'*

Amber started. The harsh syllable echoed in her ears as the air crackled with tension.

What was wrong with him? So he hated that dress. Or was it her? Questions kept popping into her head, only for her to dismiss them just as quickly. Whatever was eating him had to do with her *in* the dress, obviously. She herself hadn't thought it a great representation of the gown in the painting. Was he still mad because Maggie had failed to realise his divine vision?

Something had happened today. And she had the feeling the crew—or at least some of them—were in on it. She'd noticed the hurried exchange of glances and Maggie's unhappy face.

As they approached the Harbour Bridge, against all her prudent instincts she asked tentatively, 'Have you worked with Maggie a long time?'

'Yep.'

'She seems to think a lot of you.'

He glanced searchingly at her, eyes narrowed, a sudden tension in his manner. 'Yeah? What did she tell you?'

'Nothing—except that you're a wonderful guy.'

'Now, why would Maggie feel compelled to say that?' The words sounded casual. But there was an edge she didn't miss.

She shrugged guiltily. Maggie had talked about him, and now *she* had foolishly blabbed. She tried to get out of it by being flippant. 'How do I know? She could just be a compulsive liar. Or maybe she has a secret crush on you.'

The man was not amused. She could tell. Partly by his heavy beetling brows. Partly by the hardening of his jaw for the several blocks between the bridge and home.

Maybe she should just shut up if everything she said was wrong. But she couldn't bear it when people were mad at her and she didn't even know what she'd done. Maybe he was regretting his generous impulse and getting stuck with having to make this ad for her. Or perhaps he resented her invading his workplace, getting to know his team.

Or maybe… Her heart turned to ice. The taboo thought that had been lurking all day suddenly materialised.

Just *maybe* it was over.

The signs were all there. Call her a spineless coward, but while this was the ideal opportunity to clear it up, she dreaded knowing.

For the remainder of the trip she vacillated between asking and not asking. If she did, it would be a terrible risk. It might make him feel pressured. In her experience, put a man under pressure and you'd most likely face a rejection. But Guy seemed to be on the brink of rejecting her anyway. If she had any self-respect she should at least toughen up and find out why. She owed herself that much, didn't she?

By the time they drew up into his parking spot in the arcade basement her insides were quaking and she had that strangulated feeling in her chest.

There was a tense moment when neither of them spoke.

She was the one who broke the silence, gazing straight ahead to keep her voice steady. 'I was just wondering why you weren't very pleased with me in the scene? Why you looked at me as if you wanted to throw up? As if you—couldn't stand the sight of me.' She tried to sound supercool and in control, but towards the end her chin insisted on wobbling, and that came through in her voice.

His hands flexed on the wheel. 'No, Amber.' He ground out the words. 'That's *not*—true. Not—how it was.'

There was a remorseful intensity in his voice that might have meant he was being truthful, or might have meant he was riddled with guilt. Guilty as sin for wanting to dump her on the nearest rubbish tip.

He turned to her, his eyes ablaze with some unreadable emotion. 'I know I may have seemed a bit taken aback when I first— But that had nothing to do with you. Honestly.'

'Didn't it?' After all she'd endured today, this was just too much. Her veins swelled with indignation. 'Well, I've got news for you, Guy Wilder. It feels pretty personal when someone glares at you as if you look like a slug.'

He made a jerky gesture. 'I'm sorry, sweetheart. Honestly. It wasn't *you*.'

At least he wasn't trying to deny the ghastly moment had happened.

'Who was it, then?'

He grew silent, his face hardening to a cool, unreadable mask. Then he lifted his shoulders. 'Look, we all have *things* in our lives we don't want to talk about. When I saw you at that moment just for an instant I was reminded of something that happened once. A long time ago…' He waved his hands. '*Ages* ago now. It was just one of those stupid flashbacks from out of the blue. It was nothing, I swear. It's all ancient history, but just for a minute there it hit me. All right?'

She stared down at her hands, mulling over all the denials, all the minimalising, then flicked him a glance. 'Was it her? That woman you were with before? The one you had a break-up with?'

He closed his eyes and sighed. 'Look, Amber, let's just leave it now. Shall we?'

'Fine.' Shrugging, she released the seat belt and got out of the car.

It was blindingly apparent now why he was over her. Today she'd reminded him of someone else. The woman he wished he was still with.

When they each stood outside their respective doors, he drew in a breath and glanced at her, as if he was bracing himself to say something difficult. Something like, *Well, it's been fun. But I think you understand it can't ever be anything more than that. I've just realised I still have this deep-seated passion for my old love. So...sorry Amber. No more hanging out. See ya round.*

But Amber got in first.

She glanced in his direction and yawned. 'Well, it's been a big day. I hope I can stay awake long enough to finish my management assignment tonight.'

His brow creased. 'Oh? So you'll be staying in for dinner?'

She avoided his eyes. 'I'm not that hungry. I'll probably just make a sandwich.'

He flicked a glance at her, then frowned at the floor. 'Right.'

'So…' She unlocked her door, hesitated. 'See you, then.'

She could feel his grey gaze sear her face like a torch. But then he just gave up. Just like that. The guy who was worried he'd ruined all his chances with her.

'Okay,' he said. 'Good luck with it. See you.'

Inside, she bumped her shin on the edge of the coffee table in the hall. Cursing in extreme agony, it occurred to her that she'd rather have this pain than the one she knew was about to slice up her heart once the full ramifications sank through.

Whatever Guy *said*, however much he declared that woman was in his past, he was still in love with her. Why else would he have been so affected today?

In fact, now she'd been shown a glimpse of the bigger picture, a few thousand little clues began to add up.

She limped into the kitchen and opened the fridge, smarting all over. He hadn't been concerned about not having dinner with her. There hadn't been the least sign of disappointment. Since when had a management assignment taken precedence over a night of excitement and romance?

Simple. Since the romance had hit a rock.

As she stared gloomily into the freezer, an even more lowering thought struck.

It was clear she must resemble that woman pretty closely. That must be why he'd been attracted to her. It had never been anything to do with her personally at all.

Tears swam into her eyes. All the time he'd been making love to Amber O'Neill, cuddling her, saying all those passionate things, he'd really been thinking of his true love. He was probably thinking of her right now.

Searching for a silver lining while she was choking down her toasted cheese sandwich, it did occur to her that he hadn't actually said goodbye yet. Maybe she should have tried to seduce him good and proper to drive that woman from his mind? But not in the car. Not in a car park. There could be nothing 'grand passion' about that sort of venue.

Anyway, he'd looked too remote. If only he'd said something warm. Something to give her hope.

It was all too distressing. Instinct told her there'd be no accidental meeting tonight. How was she to kill time? She supposed she could shift all the furniture back into the sitting room and watch TV. Though that would require energy and motivation, when she urgently needed distraction. If she was to get through the next few hours she *had* to have something to paralyse her brain. Even her assignment was starting to look like an option.

With a groan of surrender she got up and switched on her notebook. Sighing, she clicked open the file. The prereading she'd already done had been about as exciting as the arcade on a Sunday afternoon. *'Supervision of staff'*, she read. Yeah, fat chance anyone had ever had of supervising *her* staff.

She read on and, surprisingly, started to become quite absorbed. At some point she must have stopped listening for sounds from next door, for clues of Guy's activities, because before she knew it she was in the zone, writing some pretty hard-hitting stuff about Ivy. Not mentioning her by name, of course. But if ever there was a bona fide case study requiring a management plan Ivy was the candidate.

Maybe because she was miserable and confused, she found the plan was a great outlet. In a way it was like choreography, and she'd always found that satisfying. She'd just finished designing some seriously rugged hoops for Ivy to hop through when she noticed the time was close on eleven.

She rubbed her eyes, then gave the great work one last read through before hitting the 'save' button. Rising and stretching, she headed for her bedroom. At least she'd achieved something today.

Like a lorryload of boulders, her memory and the day's events crashed into her heart. There'd be nothing else for Amber O'Neill tonight but an empty bed and a good night's sleep.

Grabbing a fresh nightie, she headed for the bathroom.

Guy frowned over his text. How to encourage customers to think Fleur Elise first when they desired their little piece of spring? It was tempting to write a whole bunch of poetic lyrics, but the film-maker in him knew that in this case less was better. Nothing could be as powerful as the image of Amber floating through that garden.

His heart quickened. She was as lovely as the roses they'd decked her in.

Oh, for God's sake, why couldn't he have controlled

himself? He leapt up and started to pace his aunt's sitting room. What a fool he'd been. The very thing he needed to bury, once and for all, was now back in the headlines with his film crew. The whole office was probably abuzz by now. Speculating about his 'new relationship'.

He shuddered. How he hated those words. Useless to hope Amber never found out about his laughable history. If Maggie didn't tell her, someone else would.

With cold misgiving he contemplated the future. He could see it clearly now. The longer Amber stayed with him, the more likely it was she'd be meeting his friends. Already he'd planned to talk a couple of the Blue Suede boys into giving her a hand with her shop.

And wasn't the Suede's big night coming up? He slapped his forehead. He'd been so obsessed with her he'd neglected to think ahead. She'd be meeting the guys *and* their girlfriends. Not to mention everyone at The Owl who'd remember him and Jo from the old days.

Someone would be eager to fill her in. He could just imagine how the sordid tale might be presented. No doubt with a whole lot of schmaltzy spin about how he'd been destroyed forever—shattered, et cetera.

As if he was some sort of lily-livered comedian. He punched his fist into his palm. It flashed through his head that he might just have to grit his teeth and tell her himself first. Some of it, anyway.

If he could just work out what to say in advance. Maybe there was a way to keep it low-key. If he could think of it as a script. A technical challenge…

Amber lay back in the chamomile-scented water and closed her eyes. In the grim reality of not having heard from Guy for hours the chopped-up feeling in her chest had intensified. There'd been nothing. Not even a text. It was crushing to think of how empty her life would be if he dropped her. There'd be nothing to look forward to.

But what if they continued to see each other? Being besotted was one thing. It was all about having fun with someone. But where was the fun now? Somewhere along the way she'd gone much further than that.

She had to face it. She was madly in love with him. Oh, she'd known it for ages, but never so strikingly as in the car this evening. Even if he still wanted to play with her, could she go on with him knowing she was a mere substitute?

She was roused from her dismal reflections by a sharp ring of her doorbell. *Hah!*

She sat upright. It could only be him at this hour. With a surge of fearful excitement she heaved herself out of the tub, gave herself a hasty towelling, then dragged on her silk wrap.

At the front door she stood hesitating, momentarily paralysed with fear about what he might be going to say. She switched on the hall light. 'Who is it?'

There was a loaded pause. Then Guy's voice came, deep and subdued. 'It's me.'

She opened the door. He was standing with head lowered, though he glanced up at once. His eyes sparked when he saw her state of undress, but his expression was serious.

Her heart started to thump. Was this *it*? He'd come to make the cut? He had on the black tee shirt that so enhanced his gorgeous arms and made him look dangerously handsome. As well, her eagle eye noticed he'd shaved. Had he been out? Or was there some other reason he needed a smooth jaw at eleven-thirty at night?

'Hi,' he said, his deep voice sonorous. 'I was thinking it might be good to talk.'

'Oh? Well, I—I was just bathing.'

His eyes assessed her with that piercing gleam. 'You smell fresh. Sorry if I interrupted. Tub or shower?'

'Tub.' He was no stranger to her tub. She pulled the edges of her wrap closer, moistened her lips. 'Come through.'

She led the way to the kitchen. Quite a few of their most exciting evenings had started in her kitchen. She could tell by the light in his eyes he was aware of that too. Even so, there was a purpose in his demeanour that didn't suggest seduction.

They faced each other standing, like adversaries, and she noticed his brows edge together as he considered his words. He drew in a breath. 'Er…about what we talked about…'

'The ad?'

His eyes narrowed in rebuke of her little tease. 'No, not the *ad*. The…the thing I—I remembered today. The…er…the flashback.'

'Oh, the woman, you mean?'

He lifted an impatient shoulder, then opened his hands. 'Look, you knew I wasn't a virgin. It's pretty hard to reach thirty-three without having a few re— *lovers* along the way.'

'Of course. Not that it's any of my business. We aren't exactly a couple.' She gave a silvery little laugh at the very absurdity of the idea.

His face smoothed. Some of the tension leaked from his posture. 'Exactly. So, if I went out with a woman a few times, naturally certain circumstances could bring her to mind. Or any other woman I might have dated. I don't know why you thought it was such a big thing.' He lowered his lashes. 'No doubt you've kissed a guy before.'

She delivered her sweetest smile. 'Though rarely ever so well. What's her name?'

He blinked and turned his eyes away. 'Look, what difference—?' He threw out his hands in exasperation. 'All right. It's Jo. All right?'

Amber couldn't speak for a second. She could easily loathe, despise and ridicule a woman from the past if a mere fleeting memory of her was capable of paralysing her lover for hours. But once that woman had a *name...*

And a nice name. The sort of name one of her girlfriends might have had.

'She must have been quite special to you?'

He looked non-committal. Shrugged. 'For a while. Yeah, she was. But these things end, don't they? It's no big deal.'

She gazed steadily at him. He must have quickly reviewed his last words, because he hastened to correct any poor impression they might have left.

'Look, I liked her for a while. Okay? But I'm glad I'm not with her any more.'

She nodded, relieved he'd said that even if she wasn't sure how true it was. 'I see.'

'Do you, though?' He looked keenly at her. 'I like *you*, Amber. I *really* like you.' His eyes were intent on her face, ablaze with sincerity.

'Oh.' She flushed, her ridiculous heart rushing and fluttering like a trapped insect. 'Well, I like you too, Guy.'

His expression lightened. Smiling, he pulled her towards him. 'Even after I was so prickly with you today?' He started to nuzzle her hair, face and throat with his lips.

'Yeah. And you *were*, you know. It made me think I must look just like her.'

'No.' He took her shoulders and gazed into her eyes, denial in every line of his face. 'You don't,' he said with conviction. 'Not at all. Not in the slightest. You look like your own unique and beautiful self.'

He pulled her close to him again, holding her and stroking her as though she genuinely was someone rare and precious. She could feel his big heart thudding against her own.

Call her an obsessive, but curiosity needed to be appeased. 'What does she look like?'

He gave a sigh of exasperation. 'It doesn't *matter* what she looks like. I never want to lay eyes on her again.'

'I'm glad.' She kissed his Adam's apple. 'What colour's her hair?'

'Amber.' He grabbed her shoulders and gazed sternly at her. 'What difference does it make? I'm telling you… Look, the last time I saw her she had short reddish hair. Okay?'

'Fine. It makes no earthly difference to *me*. Not a bit. I just like to have a mental picture, that's all. You're the vision man. You must know what that's like.'

He sighed. 'What else can I say to you?' His lips moved against her ear. 'She's short and stocky with freckles. And you know what I'm thinking now?'

'What?' She held her breath in sudden hopeful anticipation.

'It's high time I took a bath.' Desire deepened his voice.

'Oh.' She smiled, partly in self-mockery at her weakness. 'You poor man. You're too late. Sadly the water will now be cold.'

He grinned, his usual cocksure confidence reasserting itself. 'I think you know I can heat it up.'

In truth, the bath was one of his better inspirations. It eased away the doubts and pains of the day. There was much playful loving, and even more serious, panting loving. One thing about being in a bath was the total nakedness it imposed. There was no possibility of lying or deceiving someone when you were both stripped bare and washed by the same water.

In the new, though still careful spirit of sharing, she confessed a little about the Miguel fiasco, and the swathe he'd cut through her friends in the ballet company. She only related the barest minimum, of course, sensing it wouldn't be wise for Guy to focus on her former relationship, however scant it had been.

She sighed. 'I think the worst thing…this probably sounds vain and pathetic…but I honestly think the worst thing was how much of a fool I felt. How absolutely *diminished* in the eyes of my friends. Can you understand that?'

He pulled her closer to him. 'Oh, I can.' There was heartfelt conviction in his tone. Then he said fiercely, 'What was *wrong* with the guy? What the hell else would he want in a woman?'

At that she broke into laughter. 'Variety?'

And he was so understanding, so warmly comforting, at the same time as making her laugh at some of the things that had so mortified her, she felt her intimate confession draw her closer to him. As if by sharing that tiny snippet of her historical truth they'd passed through a door.

His arms were still around her, hers around him, their hearts beating as one, when she said, 'What happened with Jo that made you end it?'

She felt him go quite still. Then he said matter-of-factly, 'Oh, she ended it.'

She stayed still herself, listening to her heart thundering in the gathering silence. Then she said, 'What did she say?'

'Nothing. She stood me up. '

'On a date?'

He made a sardonic face. 'Yes. A date.'

'So you just…?' She stared at him in surprise. 'What? No second chances?'

It took him a while to reply, and when he did it was brief. 'Nope.'

CHAPTER ELEVEN

Ivy didn't take kindly to jumping through hoops.

She refused to say cheery things to customers, either to compliment them on their choices or wish them a beautiful day. And when the interior designer dropped in to discuss with Amber and the staff the kind of renovations they dreamed, of Ivy wanted no part of the wasteful business. Instead she hovered, glowering, among the ferns.

Even so, their discussions were fruitful. Serena, with her artistic flair, came up with some fantastic ideas that were in tune with Amber's. The designer took on board everything they said and made several of her own suggestions about fittings, wallpapers and shelving, showing Amber online site after online site where she could view the amazing array of choices.

Inspired by Guy's theme for the advertising campaign, after much mulling and discussion, Amber had come to a decision. She understood some of her management difficulties stemmed from her need to break with the past and stamp her own personality on the business.

Since Fleur Elise had been her mother's name for the shop, Amber decided to rename it with something more significant to herself. When she told the designer her idea of calling the shop La Primavera, after the old painting Guy had used for her ad, the designer's eyes lit up. She went away to work on a 'spring' design, then e-mailed Amber some sketches.

Amber was thrilled with them. Suddenly everything seemed possible.

In the shop, that was. On the ninth floor, nothing could be taken for granted. For one thing, Jean and Stuart would be back home in a few days, and Guy would be moving back into his house in Woollahra. It wasn't so far from Kirribilli, as the crow flew, but since it was on the other side of the harbour Amber knew it would feel like a million miles.

How long would he keep seeing her? It would hardly be every night. Their accidental meetings would have to end. If they were to continue with any sort of meaning, some more binding form of acknowledgement of their relationship would be required. She didn't even have the status of girlfriend. So what was she? A fling?

And since the night of the bath, though Guy had treated her with more tenderness than ever, something was on his mind. He was forever frowning to himself, failing to hear things she said to him. Sometimes he studied her when he thought she wasn't looking, searching her face as if answers to the mysteries of the pyramids might be encoded there.

It made her anxious and unsettled and prone to gloomy imaginings—most of them starting with J.

'Is something on your mind?' She made this tentative enquiry when Guy was driving her to The Owl for a pub night.

Imagine *her*, Amber O'Neill, en route to a *pub night*. Strangely, though, she was keen to go and had dressed accordingly, applying loads of smudgy eyeliner and shadow that gave her a sultry siren ambience. She had the feeling

Guy wasn't exactly comfortable with it. There was an aura of tension percolating around him.

'Are you worrying about how your band will do?'

She could understand if he was. The Owl was a popular venue for bands starting up, he'd explained. He'd been so enthusiastic at first when his friends, the Blue Suede, had been offered a performance slot. Since then, though, he seemed to have cooled off.

Having heard the Suede in rehearsal, Amber could appreciate his doubts.

Feeling the weight of her clear blue gaze, Guy hastened to allay her suspicions.

'More the song,' he lied, giving himself a mental slap for betraying his—whatever. Edginess? Cool was what was needed tonight. If he was to be on display to a bunch of old acquaintances whose most recent memory of him was…

He started to sweat. No. He wouldn't think of it. He'd stare them all down and act as if it had never happened.

If he could just get through this one night, the next time and the times after should be a cinch. With grim amusement he reflected that if he survived long enough he might eventually live the whole sorry saga down.

So long as he could trust old friends to act like friends. Trouble was, it was such an entertaining story. There was bound to be some mischievous soul who felt compelled to fill Amber in.

Amber noticed his knuckles whiten on the wheel. Her trouble sensors pricked up their ears. Something was up.

She said carefully, 'You know, I've had the feeling you aren't all that keen for me to come.'

She heard him draw breath, the tiny beat as he sought the right words, and with a pang her misgivings deepened. Was *she* the problem?

'Not at all,' he said smoothly. 'I'm just wondering how much you'll enjoy it.' He cast her a teasing look. 'You know there'll be an awful noise?'

'Huh! The cheek of that.'

He flashed her a smile. 'You think you're up to it?'

She narrowed her eyes at him in disbelief. She'd only made Serena transfer a whole flock of butterflies up her arm, starting from the inside of her wrist. 'Let me get this straight. Are you saying I'm a nerd?'

He laughed. 'Hell, no.'

'I have *been* to a pub, you know. I have drunk beer.'

'You don't say?'

But though he grinned her doubts deepened. She felt mystified. He couldn't *really* be worried about how she'd react to a few bands? If it was about her, it wasn't *that*. Anyway, now the challenge had been issued. Even if a night of boy bands was worse than a week in prison, she'd enjoy it if it killed her.

Stepping up onto the wooden verandah of the old public house, she felt the very floorboards vibrate. Inside, some group was doing its best to break the sound barrier. And when she strolled through the entrance, with the handsomest guy in Sydney holding her hand, she could see why the building was being rocked off its foundations. There was a frenetic crowd of dancers.

So far, so—great.

In her skintight jeans, heels and clingy top she felt she fitted just fine. Her hair was flowing free. No camellias tucked behind her ear. Nary even a daisy. If she did forget and hum something classical no one would hear. Her nerdiness could go undetected.

She noticed Guy glancing about, scanning the room. As she waited with him in the bar queue, to place their order for pizza, every so often she felt him absently bunch some of her hair in his hand, then release it. Normally she'd have given herself over to basking in the sensual chills and doing her best to surreptitiously bump him with her behind. Just to give him a thrill. This wasn't that sort of occasion, though. A different kind of tension was communicating itself to her.

When it was their turn to order, the lad behind the bar was momentarily interrupted by an older barman who poked his head around and called to Guy.

'Hey, *mate*. Long time, no see.'

Though Guy grinned and lifted his hand in a friendly gesture, Amber noticed he didn't linger to chat. As soon as their order was complete he drew her away from the bar area to find a table in one of the adjoining rooms.

As they scanned for a spot someone else called to him from across the room, then a couple seated there rose and made a beeline for Guy.

Guy coolly shook hands with them and introduced Amber.

Apparently well acquainted with Guy, Jane and Tony were keen to know everything about how long he and Amber had been together and how they'd met. Though Guy was calm, deflecting their questions with smooth courtesy, the lines of his lean, chiselled face revealed nothing of what he was thinking. An expression Amber recognised with some misgiving.

From the tone of Jane's and Tony's conversation Amber gathered Guy hadn't been at The Owl for some time. She could feel the couple's interested gazes switch back and forth between her and Guy, as if eager to divine every nuance between them.

'And are wedding bells on the agenda here, Guy?' Jane was at last driven to ask, coyly arching her brows.

Amber felt a bolt of shock at the woman's naked curiosity. Guy's face remained impervious. His only betraying response was the tiny flicker that registered in his grey eyes.

He pulled Amber closer to him, smiled down at her. 'Are you wanting to know every last detail of our relationship, Jane?' he said.

Apparently sensing at last that his partner's curiosity had taken her too far, the husband nudged his wife in the ribs. 'Shh. Don't put them on the spot,' he said, with an uneasy laugh.

After that the couple talked very fast about the beauties of marriage with children, then implored Amber and Guy to join them at their table. Thankfully Guy declined.

As the couple walked away, Amber was still reeling. 'What ghastly people,' she said fervently. 'I'll tell you something, lover, if you ever marry a woman like her I'll never talk to you again.'

Guy glanced sharply at her, then his face relaxed in an amused smile. 'No need to worry about that. I never, ever will.'

After that it seemed every time she and Guy looked around someone would be there, overflowing with friendliness or curiosity or both, and there'd be more handshaking, back slapping. Introductions. Catch-up conversation.

'What are you doing now?'

'Whatever happened to old…?'

'Did you hear I had a new…?'

'Mate, did you catch the Grand Final?'

At one point a bunch of young blokes, some with girlfriends in tow, cornered Guy like a long-lost friend.

'Hey, man, what's goin' down?'

'Man, you wanna hang tomorrow?'

Amber was given the pleasure of meeting the Blue

Suede boys. They welcomed her with wide grins and appreciative glances.

'You do know Amber's my next-door neighbour,' Guy said, his arm around her waist

'Oh, *that* Amber,' one of them said. They grinned at each other, looking a little sheepish.

Laughing, Amber pointed to the beamed roof. 'I hope they've got that screwed down well.'

The Suede pressed her and Guy to join their party, but Guy waved vaguely towards another section of the capacious pub. 'Thanks, but I think we're over there.'

Amber turned to gaze enquiringly at him, but he squeezed her waist.

'Come on,' he murmured in to her ear. 'I'm hungry enough to eat your ear.'

She joined Guy in wishing luck to the boys, then allowed him to hustle her to a table closer to the performance dais. She looked curiously at him. On this side of the room the noise from the band made conversation a struggle. She had to practically shout to be heard. 'Don't you want to sit with your friends?'

'I am. I'm sitting with my girlfriend.'

'Oh, really? Where's she?' She glanced around, as if that mythical creature might be somewhere in the crowd. Secretly, though, she was so madly chuffed she felt herself going pink. She turned back to beam at him, then leaned over and kissed his lips. 'There. That's what girlfriends do. A little something in advance.' She widened her eyes meaningfully and he smiled.

Somehow the food waiter found them. With their feast before them, Guy exhaled a relieved breath.

He began to feel he could maybe relax. Even at the hairy meeting with Jo's cousin, Jane, no one had actually used Jo's name, though he could read the knowledge of his past in some people's eyes. There'd been plenty of assessing glances at Amber, but he'd even noticed people he didn't know checking her out. Who could blame them? What red-blooded guy wouldn't?

All he had to do was make it through the Suede's gig, then he could honourably escort his woman home.

The current band finally finished their last number and vacated the space.

Amber's ears had barely grown accustomed to the blessed respite before a smattering of applause and a few catcalls alerted her to more punishment about to strike.

She glanced up to see the Suede swagger on and start setting up.

One of them stepped forward and introduced the first song, nervously mumbling a few words into the mike she didn't quite catch. Then some heavy opening chords from an electric guitar zithered up her spine with a blood-curdling familiarity she couldn't mistake.

She whipped excitedly around to Guy. 'That's *it*. Your song.'

'Yep.' His eyes gleamed. He listened intently, a small smile curling up his lips, nodding very slightly in time to the beat.

As the song got underway a couple of dancers started gyrating and throwing themselves about. Then several more joined them. Then a whole crowd swarmed onto the floor.

Relieved at last to see the light of pleasure in Guy's eyes, Amber reached to squeeze his hand. 'Look. They love it.'

He returned the squeeze, then urged her to her feet. 'Come on, then. Dance with me.'

To the seriously dedicated dancer a few billion decibels of amplification could actually sound fantastic in the cavernous old Owl, with its high beams and dark-varnished wainscoting. Especially when it came to Guy's song.

Amber could hardly believe she'd scoffed at it. Now, while its emotional, passionate lyrics tore at her very heartstrings, that sexy beat infected her feet with fever. She joined the mass of bodies on the floor and threw herself into the dance with abandon.

When the song finished the crowd roared their appreciation so compellingly the boys in the band played it over.

A little self-conscious to be dancing with a professional, Guy made the minimum moves required by a male—shaking, shuddering, and shifting about from one foot to another. After all his tension, he felt uplifted as much by the thrill of the communal response to his song as by the sheer, joyful, physical exuberance of Amber. Soon they could leave. A few congratulatory drinks with the boys, then he could hardly wait to get her home.

Swinging about to wave to his friends in the band, he received a massive shock.

His heart and lungs froze within him.

At the bar entrance the sight of a familiar red head struck him like a blow. Jo. She must have spotted him at the same time, because he saw her stand still, shock registering on her own face.

Fear.

She turned sharply on her heel to backtrack. Ferocious blood roared to Guy's head. A wild, visceral fury blazed to life inside him, obliterating all other considerations. Oblivious to other people, he fought a path through the crowd. Vengeful words pounded his brain.

He'd make her explain.

He had to make her explain.

Still dancing, Amber was singing, swaying, floating on endorphins when she noticed she and Guy had become separated. Searching for his familiar form among the nearby dancers, she realised he wasn't actually there. Gazing about, her astonished eyes finally located him. He was making for the bar entrance with a grim purposeful stride, seemingly in hard pursuit of someone.

Taken aback, Amber hesitated for a moment or two, wondering whether or not to follow him. Whoever he wanted to talk to, if he'd wanted her along he'd have signalled her, wouldn't he? But, beginning to be jostled by the people whirling and stamping around her, she threaded her way through the crowd and followed in the direction Guy had taken. Through the front of the pub and out onto the verandah.

And stopped.

Her jaw dropped. Guy was in the car park with a woman. In the bright glare of the security lights Amber could see the woman quite well. With a thumping heart, Amber saw she wasn't all that short. She was at least her own height, in fact—maybe even taller—and very sexily dressed in a silky dress, with smooth reddish hair cut in a fabulous sleek bob.

It had to be Jo. Who else?

After her initial shock, Amber could see some bitter words were being exchanged. There was an almost electric fury in Guy's body language. He was doing most of the talking, gesticulating in a style most women would have found intimidating.

Then, to Amber's agonised disbelief, the woman suddenly waved her hands in front of his face, seized Guy's shoulders and kissed him on the mouth.

Hot knives of pain and jealousy sliced Amber's heart to shreds. Clinging to the balustrade for fear of collapsing or imploding, she had no option but to witness the clinch. It wasn't so much that the woman was kissing Guy. It was that Guy wasn't pushing her away. Not at once.

The kiss ended, but Amber saw him hold her fast in his arms as if she was someone rare and precious.

Then he pushed her away. Only then.

Seething with hurt and shock, Amber called out hoarsely to him. But he didn't hear. He was far too fascinated by his old love. The woman was talking now, and Guy was questioning her, apparently riveted by her every word.

They turned back towards the pub, still talking. Amber waited for a break when she might attract his attention, but their conversation continued in the same intense, urgent vein.

Totally engrossed. As if they were besotted.

She tried calling out again, though her voice was pretty croaky now. Anyway, if Guy heard her he preferred to ignore distractions like mere girlfriends. With confusion and despair mounting in her heart, Amber couldn't hide from herself the damning evidence of how good they looked together. How right.

The last she saw they were heading into the deserted beer garden at the side of the pub, where tables had been left out under an awning for patrons who preferred a little night-time privacy.

Amber stumbled back inside, her body numb, her heart a crippling ache. Nothing could explain away what she'd witnessed. In pursuit of that woman, Guy had looked as if he was ablaze. If ever passion had existed in him, it was in him then.

She stared unseeing at the scene around her. The noise, the activity left her untouched.

She'd seen him looking pretty incandescent. What about that night she'd danced? And last night there'd been passion in him, all right. *And* this morning. And all those other times.

What a monstrous cheek that woman had, anyway, thinking she could just sashay back into his life and snatch him away from his official girlfriend.

The Suede were still belting out songs, but Amber didn't feel like dancing. Not right then.

Instead, operating on instinct, she sashayed up to the bar and asked for a vee juice. The bartender, not a very bright-looking lad, seemed bemused. 'Vodka?'

'Vee,' she rasped, thumping her fist on the bar. 'You know? *Vegetable* juice.'

'Oh. Er…er… Yeah. Hang on…' The guy dashed away and came back with a can of it and a tall glass. 'Any ice in that?'

'No, thanks,' she said shortly, handing over a note. 'I need it fast.'

She didn't bother with the nicety of a straw, just swigged the stuff straight down, lip to rim. Then she checked her reflection in the bar mirror.

Her eyes still had that sultry, sulky look conferred by the shadow. Her neckline still plunged. Good. She whipped out a lipstick and plumped up her pout, good and red to match her toenails, and then, bracing herself, she strode out of the bar entrance and down the steps to the beer garden.

CHAPTER TWELVE

THE beer garden was enchantingly lit with Chinese lanterns.

At first glance Amber didn't see Guy. Only the woman she felt certain must be Jo. She was seated at a table with her head down. A second glance gave Amber the impression the woman was quietly weeping. Then she saw Guy leaning against the wall by the pub entrance.

Frowning, he had his hands in his pockets and was looking distinctly uncomfortable. Amber wasn't sure what she'd expected to find. Another clinch? Passion in the beer garden?

What she did feel was that she was intruding on something that didn't concern her.

'Oh,' she said uncertainly, preparing to back away.

Guy and the woman both looked up. 'Oh, here she is,' Guy said, suggesting Amber had been the topic of conversation.

Amber nearly goggled. Even with a streaky face the woman was quite stunningly beautiful, with deep, wide-set eyes, fabulous cheekbones and a gorgeous chin. The kind of timeless beauty that cast mere mortal prettiness into the shade. The sort of beauty possessed by the Eustacia Vyes of this world.

Guy detached himself from the wall and strolled over

to slip his arm around Amber. His eagerness to claim her made Amber suspect he viewed her entrance as something of a relief. She had to repress a grin. Weeping women never had been his forte.

'Amber, sweetheart, meet Jo.'

Amber's antennae for emotional disturbance were registering extreme turbulence. Jo's tearwashed gaze did nothing to dispel that impression, although she still managed to give Amber a thorough rival-check.

'Hi, Jo.' Amber took Jo's beautifully manicured hand, noting it felt a little clammy. As well, she had a soggy tissue balled into it, which she tried to palm away, restricting the area available for shaking to a few cold fingers.

'Hi.' Jo looked her over, then applied the tissue to her perfect schnoz, mopped up around the mascara area, and glanced at Guy. 'Trust you, darling,' she said in a wobbly voice. 'You've always had a good eye.'

'Not always,' Guy said at once.

Amber thought she saw Jo flinch.

Guy smiled at Amber then. 'But it might be improving.'

Jo's smile twisted, but she half-lowered her extraordinarily long lashes and said charmingly, 'So. You're a ballerina, I hear?'

'Used to be. Now I'm a florist.'

Guy looked keenly at Amber, narrowing his gaze. Then he said, 'I think it's time we said goodnight, Jo. Amber and I have a big day ahead of us tomorrow.' Then he murmured to Amber, 'We mustn't forget to congratulate the boys.'

Jo had been looking from one to the other of them, a barely perceptible sardonic tug to one side of her voluptuous mouth, but at that she pulled herself gracefully to her feet.

She scattered a few careless farewell words over them, as if walking away from her old love was as much a cinch as strolling down any catwalk. Then, lifting her hand in a backward wave, she undulated on her fabulously long legs out into the car park.

After a few steps, though, she halted. Turned. Undulated back.

As she approached Amber noticed Guy's brows edge closer together. His face hardened and grew stern.

Standing before him once more, Jo made a helpless gesture, all at once sadness and resignation in her lovely eyes. 'You're probably right, darling. I never deserved you. At least now we can give our past a decent burial.'

It was a great exit line. Amber might have felt sorry for her if she hadn't been throwing about the darlings with a frequency that could only be considered indecent. It was such poor taste—especially in front of a man's girlfriend.

Certainly Jo's sadness might be sincere. If it wasn't an act. But there was no doubt in Amber's mind Jo was deliberately and knowingly signalling that she was the woman with the prior claim.

Was she hoping to ease Amber out with her wiles and dramatic exit lines? She needed bringing down to earth.

Amber moved forward a little. 'Is there anything we can do for you, Jo?' she said sympathetically. 'Buy you a pizza? Give you a lift home?'

Jo's eyes clashed with Amber's for a glinting second, then she lifted her brows. 'That won't be possible for you, dear. My home is in Tuscany.'

Then, with a semi-wave, the bewitching woman straightened her shoulders and walked quickly across the car park.

Amber turned to look wonderingly at Guy. '*Does* she live in Tuscany?'

He grimaced and shook his head. 'She might. Who knows?'

'What was that all about?'

'Buy me a drink and I'll tell you. Everything.'

Amber looked closely at him. His eyes gleamed into hers.

'Now, everything, mind,' she said, when they were finally seated in a private little corner Guy happened to know of. *How*, she dreaded to imagine.

At least they were far from the Suede, who were still belting out encores. Drinks were before them. Scotch for Guy, juice for Amber, since she was the one driving home.

She waited for him to start, then urged him into it with a little prompt. 'The last I saw you were racing to catch her like a man possessed.'

'Mmm.' He nodded. 'I know. I'm still reeling. I just can't believe that after all this time I've actually seen her again.'

Amber's heart, still a little rocky after its earlier battering, gave an ominous lurch. 'She clearly means a lot to you.'

'*Meant* a lot,' he said quickly. He lowered his lashes. 'The last I saw of her… Well, I didn't. She didn't show up.'

Amber felt as tense as a wire, questions she didn't care to face forming in the back of her mind. 'Yes, I know. You said she stood you up.'

'That's right.' He met her gaze briefly, a twist of a smile on his mouth. 'In a church. St Andrew's Cathedral, actually.'

The shock rendered her speechless for seconds. Then, as comprehension finally illuminated her brain, she was overwhelmed by the enormity of it.

'You mean you were getting married?'

He shrugged. 'Yep.'

'You asked her to marry you?'

He gave her a resigned look.

'And she stood you up in the church?'

'Yes, she did.'

'But why? Why'd she do it?'

'She told me just now she changed her mind.'

'What?' Her voice squeaked in indignation. 'She changed her mind so she just left you *standing there at the altar*?'

'Shh...shh. Don't get excited.' He glanced about. 'You'll have Jane and Tony over to find out what we're up to. But, yeah, that's about the size of it.'

'But—didn't she let you *know*? Why didn't she phone?'

'She couldn't. She was on a plane heading for the Riviera with her old boyfriend.'

'Oh.' The sheer disgrace of the agony and public humiliation that had been inflicted on him brought tears to Amber's eyes. 'I can't believe it. How can anyone be so *selfish*...so *cruel*? No wonder you were... Oh, I see—I see it all...' And she did. Suddenly so much was falling into place. 'Oh, Guy...Guy, you poor, poor man. I...'

She was stroking his shoulder, his back, patting him, touching his face, his hand.

He turned his face away and something dawned on her. He was embarrassed by her emotion on his account. She bit her lip and held off with the words. No one wanted to be reminded of the fool they were once made to feel.

At least when she'd found out the awful truth she'd had that heaven-sent opportunity to pour a pot of beer over Miguel's head.

'Yeah. I think I get it now.' She nodded. 'She probably found out about your weakness for other people's toothbrushes.'

He turned to look at her, then a smile lit his eyes and he broke into a laugh. 'Come here.' Grabbing her, he kissed her lips with a convincing, malt-flavoured fervour that did him credit, considering he'd just bumped into his beautiful ex-bride. Then he said thickly, 'Come on, Amber O'Neill. I want to take you home.'

CHAPTER THIRTEEN

'MARRIED life's wonderful,' Jean said, beaming at Amber over her champagne and raising her voice a little to be heard above the throng of people crammed into Amber's bunching room. 'I'd never have imagined it could be so much fun. I've known Stuart for years, but the things I've learned since I married him—*well*.'

Amber smiled. Jean certainly did look happy. Her face was so radiant she looked twenty years younger.

It was the Saturday of Amber's grand re-opening as La Primavera. Every inch of the shop not covered in flowers was thronging with people.

'I think it comes of knowing that you don't have to face the big horrors of life alone,' Jean went on. 'And of course *that's* all about finding the right partner. Someone who sincerely cares about you and is on your side.'

'Heavens,' Amber said. 'You're making me all weepy.'

'Oh.' Jean's eyes widened in dismay. 'I'm sorry, dear girl. I don't mean to imply you must be married to be happy. Far from it. I was happy for years as a single woman. I'm just glad I've had this chance to be happy in a new and different way.'

Amber leaned over and kissed her. '*Be* happy, Jean. I'm thrilled for both of you.'

And she *was* thrilled to have Jean back, but it meant

that Guy had collected his belongings and moved over to his own residence at Woollahra.

It had cost Amber more than a small pang to see him move, but he'd said he was keen to be back under his own roof. Amber hadn't seen his house since the renovation stage, but Guy had promised to show her the finished product soon.

'Won't you miss me over there?' she'd said when he was packing his stuff, only half joking.

'I'll make sure I don't,' he said, eyes twinkling. Whatever that meant.

She hated to sound needy. Anyway, she was far too busy to be concerned about it this weekend.

'No need to ask how you got on with my favourite nephew,' Jean continued, giving Amber a guilty start.

For a wild second Amber wondered if she'd left behind some trace of her disgraceful tomfoolery on the piano. She doubted she'd ever be able to drink a cup of tea on Jean's sofa without choking.

But Jean's gentle face was as serene as ever. She smiled warmly at Amber over her glass. 'I doubt if he'd have put so much into your advertising campaign if he didn't think the world of you.'

Amber nodded, smiling. 'We do get on quite well, actually.'

When they had the chance. When he wasn't on the other side of Sydney Harbour.

But she shouldn't complain. The shop's grand re-opening weekend had got off to a splendid start, coinciding with the advertising campaign. Guy had managed to turn the Chinese Garden of Friendship into an Italian painting, and there Amber was, scattering roses on television screens and billboards all over the city.

Best of all was her song—a lyrical little jingle with a

catchy tune the boys in the band belted out with all their might. Now everyone seemed to be singing it. 'Springtime at La Primavera'. What was even more fantastic was that Blue Suede's popularity meant her ad had gone viral.

Amber saw La Primavera below her shamelessly inviting smile everywhere she looked. It had taken some getting used to, not cringing when she saw it. Not to mention being instantly recognisable to large numbers of strangers.

And her Facebook list had exploded.

Friends from the ballet had texted, or written on her wall—including Miguel, of all people. Even others she hadn't been in touch with for ages. Some merely to remind her they were alive, though one of her old instructors had actually begged her to come back to Melbourne and take up the life she was meant for.

That had cost her a pang. As if she really had a choice.

Anyway, her new shop was a delight to the eye.

With the doors open to the street and an abundance of flowers massed inside and out, including an alluring array under her pretty green- and blue-striped awning, the shop was charming. Inside it was like a spring jungle, filled with fascinating little nooks. The boys in the band had painted all the shelves and freshly papered the walls for her, and Serena had painted a beautiful flowery mural of riotous pastels.

Trade had picked up from the very day Serena had started the mural. Since she was working more often than her regular babysitter could accommodate, Amber had suggested Serena bring her baby in to work. Amber wasn't sure if it was the rosebud sleeping in her pram that drew the crowds, or the sight of Serena painting with her newborn cuddling up to her like a koala in her sling, but every day it was becoming necessary to order more and more blooms to keep up with the vigorous demand.

It was only temporary, though. Serena's mother was moving into a flat not far from the arcade tower so she could help Serena more with her babysitting. Soon Serena would be able to work five days.

Ivy hadn't been very comfortable with the changes. She'd felt the open street doors would allow in germs, and for her the baby had been the final straw. Amber had written her a glowing reference and, to everyone's surprise, Ivy had landed a position with Di Delornay.

Amber suspected it suited Ivy to work at Madame because it allowed her to keep an eye on La Primavera without having to put up with Amber's dangerous ideas.

Everyone came to Amber's opening, drank her champagne and bought the charming little bouquets she'd risen at dawn to bunch. Jean and Serena helped to distribute food and help members of the public with their purchases.

Of course Roger from Centre Management dropped by, exuding warm approval of Amber's improvements. Salacious rumours, always doing the rounds in the mall, now had it that at the time of the residents' meeting Roger had been Madame's plaything. Since then, the eager gossips reported, Madame had given Roger his marching orders.

Amber wasn't sure who had started these particular rumours, but she had her suspicions.

Anyway, without an apparent axe to grind *vis-à-vis* tenancy relocations, when Roger met Amber these days he smiled like a congenial uncle. All was forgotten.

Though Guy still didn't like him.

Some of Guy's crew had dropped into Amber's celebrations for a toast, including Kate and Maggie. And naturally the Suede were an item. Besides never missing any sort of party, the boys were on the up and up in the local music scene, and were receiving excellent exposure from Amber's ad.

They rocked in early, skinny in leather and denim, with their hair flopping over their foreheads, and performed Amber's song and several others in the mall before an admiring crowd.

Afterwards they hung around the shop, tossing roses to any attractive young women who happened to stroll by, signing autographs, and eating and drinking anything they could get their hands on.

Most of the arcade tenants found time to come, bringing wine and nibbles and warm congratulations. Some of them were a little sheepish about their part in the pressure applied to Amber to achieve her renovations, especially Marc. He apologised profusely, claiming none of it had been his idea. His excuse was that his strings had been ruthlessly pulled by Madame across the way.

Amber and Serena laughed heartily at this explanation, noting how Marc's dark eyes darted about at all the new fixtures, checking for cracks in the wallpaper. A couple of times Amber caught him staring disconsolately at her gorgeous street entrance.

At the end of the day Ivy accompanied Madame herself for a state visit. Amber was intrigued to notice Ivy had dyed her hair the same coppery colour as Di's, and was wearing one of Di's burnt sienna off-the-rack suits with heels. She'd even had her nails done.

'You look lovely, Ivy,' Amber told her sincerely.

'Oh, well. You have to make an effort to fit in,' Ivy said. 'It never mattered over here. But over *there*...'

Amber lifted her brows and smiled. Poor Ivy couldn't hurt her. No one could.

Everything in her life was rosy. Her shop, her friends, her man.

Although of course he wasn't her man *officially*. And maybe he never would be. A man who'd suffered the trauma Guy had would be unlikely to want to make the sort of commitment most women dreamed about.

It didn't matter to Amber. She could be happy with the way things were. She felt pretty sure they'd still see each other regularly, although it would be a wrench not to wake up beside him every morning.

With the pressures of work for both of them, it wasn't realistic to think she'd see him every day. Though she had been hoping he'd spend a little more time at her party. He had come for an hour this morning, but then he'd had other things to do.

She wasn't worried any more about the Jo situation, of course. Guy had explained a little about Jo's motivations in backing out of the wedding, and he didn't seem to bear any rancour.

'It's a funny thing,' he'd said, leaning up on the pillow beside her one afternoon. 'You know how you read about the scales falling from people's eyes?'

Amber nodded.

'Well, that's how I felt when I talked to her at The Owl. I don't blame her for changing her mind. Anyone should be allowed to draw back—right up until the moment of saying *I do*. It was her explanation for not letting me know that stunned me. She said she was too busy with the preparations for her flight. It was all so sudden, she just didn't think until it was too late.'

Amber was still unable to imagine being in such a hurry as not to remember a waiting bridegroom.

But she was pleased she and Guy had finally talked through the painful experience. Guy had really opened up about the whole thing. Sometimes she had the feeling he'd kept it locked inside for fear she'd in some way hold it against him.

As *if.*

By late on Saturday Amber's energy for the celebrations had begun to flag a little. There were only so many hours of socialising and retailing a woman could do in one day, and she'd been working since before dawn.

'Why don't you go up and have a rest?' Jean had come down again for another bout. 'I'll mind the store for the last hour if you trust me.'

Amber turned to her. 'Oh, Jean, that's a lovely offer. But I couldn't…'

'Yes, you could. Sure you could. Come on. Accept it.' That was Guy's deep voice.

Amber spun around. He'd strolled in, looking dangerously gorgeous and athletic in jeans and leather jacket, his grey eyes gleaming with some barely concealed excitement.

Amber's sharp eye instantly zeroed in on his jaw.

Aha. He'd recently shaved.

She narrowed her eyes. 'So, what brings you back here?'

Heedless of his interested aunt and the party crowd, he bent to kiss her lips. 'There's something I want to show you.'

Amber hardly needed persuading. There were infinite ways of relaxing, and she was always open to suggestion.

Once in the car, Guy seized her in a steamy, breath-stealing, wide-ranging clinch that convinced her of his genuine pleasure in seeing her. Then he drove her across the bridge and through the city to nearby Woollahra.

Amber loved the area, with its pretty tree-lined streets and elegant villas. The house Guy had inherited from his grandfather was on the crescent of a hill, with harbour views from its upper storey.

Pulling on the handbrake in the garage, Guy said, 'Come on upstairs.'

The house was built on several levels. Some walls on the garden side had been replaced with glass, to increase the spacious feel of the old residence. There was a faint scent of freshly hewn timber and sawdust.

Amber slipped off her heels so as not to mark the wooden floors.

She felt his eyes on her naked feet and knew at once that their ever-simmering desire was at risk of escalating at any moment. He took her through the sparsely furnished rooms, showing her all his home's beauties of harmony and style. Then on the upper floor he opened a door and stood aside for her to enter first.

She stepped inside and her heart seized. This room was long and wide. As long as the entire house. There was no furniture, apart from a piano at one end, but three of the walls were mirrored and one of them had a *barre* rail. The fourth had wide windows with views of the bay.

'Oh,' she gasped. 'Oh, Guy.'

She walked into the middle of the room, this room that wrenched her heart, hardly knowing what to say. Questions clamoured in her mind. *How come?* she wanted to ask. *Who's it all for?*

What's the point?

She turned to look at him, speechless.

He moved towards her, his grey eyes uncertain, even a little anxious. 'You see, I can't believe you're ready to give it up.'

A huge sea of buried emotion somewhere deep inside her welled up and sprang a leak. Tears swam into her eyes. 'Oh, Guy.'

'I thought…correct me if I'm wrong…I thought you

might like to…once the shop is on its feet and thriving… let someone else run it and take up your career again.'

Why *then* she would never understand, but hearing her most secret fantasy spoken aloud was too much for the dam inside her, and whatever had been walling it up so tightly for so long burst. She covered her face with her hands and cried.

Guy held her while sobs racked her body and tears rained on his leather jacket, stroking and soothing her, patting her and murmuring things like, 'My darling…' 'My beautiful girl…' 'My sweetheart…'

If the poor man was as frightfully embarrassed as she supposed, he didn't even show it. And when at last she'd slowed enough to make a hoarse cry of, 'Tissues!' with urgent pointing motions towards her bag, he rummaged in its depths and brought out a whole bunch, which she gladly accepted.

'You do know,' she said, dabbing tissues in all the wet areas, 'I might not be able to get back into the company? And my life is here in Sydney now. You. The shop. You.'

'But there are dance companies in Sydney, aren't there?'

She nodded. 'But places here are fiercely contested. I've been out of it so long I'd have to work like mad even to reach scratch for an audition.'

'Then that's what you'll do.'

He was so confident for her it gave her such a boost.

Maybe she could do it. She could. If she didn't have to run the shop full time.

'I've been thinking about your shop. How about letting Serena run it? She seems to like the business. She could hire a couple of people to work weekends for her. And you could let her stay in your flat.'

'But where will I stay?'

He smiled. 'Here.'

Eventually he led her downstairs where, thankfully for her wobbly legs, he had a sitting room with a proper sofa and chairs. Even a thick Persian rug. The plastic covers were still on the sofas, so instead she let her feet sink into the sumptuous pile of the rug.

'The whole place needs furnishing properly,' he said, looking around. 'I thought you might like to have a say in that.'

She lifted her brows. 'Me?'

'Yeah. You see, I was hoping…'

She noted a sudden tension in his stance.

Her pulse made an excited leap and her heart began to bump against the wall of her chest. A throbbing, vibrant tension inhabited the space between them, as if something momentous was about to happen.

He dropped his gaze. 'You know, I never thought I'd trust a woman to love me after what happened.'

'I know.' Her heart ached for him so fiercely she had to apply another tissue to her eyes. 'I'm not surprised. It was a horrible tragedy. No one would get over it easily.'

He shrugged. 'Oh, well… Worse things have happened to people. But when I met *you*… When I saw you for who you are…'

It was hard not to cry when someone was saying such beautiful sincere things. But she willed back the tears, pressed her lips together and held her breath.

His eyes were so warm and tender it was worth the struggle. 'I fell in love with you right away.'

She smiled. 'Did you?'

'Yeah. That day you told me off in the shop. I'm still madly in love with you, if you want to know.'

'I do want to know.' She felt her smile bubbling up inside and pouring through every pore.

'Yeah?' He grinned and kissed her.

She kissed him in return. 'I want to know every single thing.'

He laughed, and she laughed too, though it was pretty shaky, what with her feeling so excited and emotional and her eyes being constantly washed with salt water.

'You know,' she said breathlessly, 'I've been wanting to tell you for so long. About how I love you.'

His eyes glowed. 'Honestly?'

She beamed. 'Honestly and sincerely. With all my heart.'

He took her in his arms and kissed her. It was a deep, fervent and intensely satisfying affirmation. Afterwards they were both breathless, and not a little aroused. He was such a passionate, emotional guy. He always brought out the best in her.

'You know, you're the most beautiful, unique and special woman I ever knew in my life.'

'Truly?' she breathed, hardly able to believe what she was hearing.

'Absolutely,' he said firmly. 'So now I want you to tell me the honest truth about something.' He held her a little away from him and studied her face. 'Honestly, now. Do you want to actually get married?'

He crinkled his brow a little. His crow's feet were charmingly in evidence, somewhere between a frown and a wince.

She hesitated, trying to read his eyes. What if she said the wrong thing here? She could absolutely ruin the moment. But…it was their moment of truth. Would any moment so tender ever come again?

And she knew she just *had* to be true to her inner nerd.

'Well, actually, Guy…' she said, her heart bursting with love and hope. Crossing her fingers, she took a deep breath. 'In actual fact…yes.'

He smiled. Then he laughed. 'Yeah, I thought you'd say that.' He grinned again. 'Great. We'll get married.'

Her heart nearly exploded, her joy was so rapturous. But other sensations were fast asserting themselves—some of them due to that rug and its marvellous feel under her feet.

There was something truly sensuous and voluptuous about a Persian rug.

As her lover kissed her to the floor, thrilling her with the intensity of his desire, she couldn't help sparing a thought for that silly, empty woman who'd thrown away the most gorgeous man on the planet. The most honourable. And the most loving. And very possibly the most virile.

Inspired by the impressive manifestations of his affection, she said huskily, 'Would you like me to show you Straddle Position Number Seven?'

A piercing hot flame lit his eyes. When he spoke his voice was deeper than a subterranean seam of the purest dark chocolate. 'Oh, Amber.' The heartfelt growl in his voice was utterly convincing. 'Sweetheart, you truly are the most bewitching woman alive.'

* * * * *

BUTTONED-UP SECRETARY, BRITISH BOSS

SUSANNE JAMES

Susanne James has enjoyed creative writing since childhood, completing her first – sadly unpublished – novel by the age of twelve. She has three grown-up children who were, and are, her pride and joy, and who all live happily in Oxfordshire with their families. She was always happy to put the needs of her family before her ambition to write seriously, although along the way some published articles for magazines and newspapers helped to keep the dream alive!

Susanne's big regret is that her beloved husband is no longer here to share the pleasure of her recent success. She now shares her life with Toffee, her young Cavalier King Charles spaniel, who decides when it's time to get up (early) and when a walk in the park is overdue!

CHAPTER ONE

SABRINA'S heartrate quickened slightly as she walked along the unfamiliar street. If it wasn't for the money that was being offered for this post, no way would she have considered applying for it, she assured herself. But the straitened circumstances they were in at the moment left her little option. She would have to bite the bullet and hope that her face fitted.

Most of the houses in this part of north London were rather grand, Sabrina noted, yet now and again a distinct shabbiness was apparent. But when she arrived at the one she was looking for—number thirteen—she saw at once that it stood out from the others. And why wouldn't it, when you considered who lived there? The imposing, deep-blue front door had been freshly painted, its brass knocker and bell-push gleaming brightly in the mid-morning September sunshine.

She pressed the bell once—its discreet tone reminding her of the one at the dentist's—and waited, trying to imagine what her interviewer, the world-renowned author, might look like in the flesh. Of course, she'd seen him featured in the newspapers from time to time, but press photographs were never accurate or flattering.

Suddenly, the door was opened by the man himself—and Sabrina recognized him straight away. He must be nearing forty by now, she thought instinctively. His dark, tousled hair had begun to grey slightly at the temples, and there were discernible frown lines on the handsome, rugged face. But the penetrating, inky blue-black eyes were clear and discerning as he looked down at her. His expression was somewhat implacable, though not unfriendly, as he opened the door wider.

'Ah, good—Sabrina Gold?' When Sabrina smiled up at him in acknowledgement, he said, 'I'm Alexander McDonald. Come in. You found us all right…clearly,' he added.

His voice was businesslike, strong and authoritatively resonant, and Sabrina couldn't help feeling just slightly in awe of him as he led her up the thickly carpeted stairs to the first floor of his house. Treading carefully behind, Sabrina was more than aware of his athletic, vigorous body. He obviously worked out daily, she thought, no doubt with a personal trainer. Well, he and his equally famous brother Bruno—the well-known impresario with so many successful musicals to his credit—seemed to hold a permanent position in the Times Rich List. They could have whatever they wanted of this world's goods.

Realizing that she'd barely spoken since her arrival, Sabrina cleared her throat. 'Actually, I don't know this part of the city,' she said. 'But I had no problem finding you. And the walk from the tube was quite pleasant, especially in this sunshine.'

He glanced back at her casually as she spoke, feeling reasonably cheered at his first impression of her. She was simply dressed in jeans and a cream shirt, her long, fair hair pulled well back from a somewhat nondescript face which was devoid of any make-up, he noted. But she had expressive, large, grey-green eyes which he found interesting; they had a most unusual, feline shape.

They reached the first floor and he pushed open a door at the top, ushering Sabrina in before him, and as she brushed past he caught the drift of the perfume she was wearing, only just enough for him to be aware of it. Good; women who soaked themselves in heavy scents unnerved him. It was something he'd always hated. Since of necessity the successful applicant for the vacant post of his personal assistant would be sharing his space for a good part of every day over the next few months, it was essential that he found her presence acceptable. If ever she was going to materialize, he thought ruefully. Was Miss Gold number six or number seven so far? he thought wearily. He'd lost count.

Sabrina took in her surroundings at a glance. It was a large, high-ceilinged room, its full-length windows permitting daylight to reach every corner. A huge Persian rug covered much of the well-worn dark-oak flooring, and generously stocked bookshelves lined the walls. The whole room was dominated by an untidy, massive mahogany desk holding a computer and telephone and littered with random sheets of paper and other writing materials. Slightly apart from it was another, smaller desk with another computer—obviously awaiting Alexander McDonald's new assistant, Sabrina thought. There were also a couple of easy chairs and at the back, away from the light, was a *chaise longue* covered in brown velvet with a few cushions scattered on it haphazardly.

Alexander pushed one of the easy chairs forward. 'Have a seat, um, Miss Gold,' he said, as if he'd already forgotten her name, before moving behind the desk and seating himself in his large leather-upholstered swivel chair.

Doing as she was asked, Sabrina looked across at him steadily, trying to remind herself that she was here for one reason only—to secure the very highly paid employment he was offering, which could be hers if luck was on her side.

He came straight to the point. 'I see you have a degree in psychology,' he said, glancing down at some papers on his desk. 'Are you sure that this job, working for me, is what you want? What you think you can…tolerate, shall we say?' he added, the uncompromising mouth twisting slightly at one corner. The remark surprised Sabrina. She hadn't anticipated any degree of diffidence from Alexander McDonald. She decided she wasn't going to tip-toe around—she'd tell him the truth and be done with it.

'I think what you really want to know, Mr McDonald, is why I am not using my qualification,' she said coolly. 'And the answer is that it is difficult, with all the cut-backs, to get suitable work in my own field at the moment. My department was halved last year, and I was one of the unlucky ones that had to be let go. I'm sure you've heard the term.' She paused. 'It means that I was sacked for being too highly qualified and they could no longer afford to pay me on that level—and I was not prepared to accept the rather demeaning position I was offered instead.'

She hesitated before adding, 'The salary which the agency told me you were prepared to pay the right person encouraged me to try and persuade you that I could be the one.' She swallowed, realizing how awful that must sound, avaricious and money-grabbing. She might as well explain now, she thought desperately. 'It isn't that I *want* the money,' she said quietly. 'I need the money. And I've decided that I have to aim high.' If only he knew, she thought. They had just acquired their first house—their first real home after always living in rented places—and with it a rather crippling mortgage.

He paused for a moment before speaking, his observant eyes noting the rosy flush which had swept her cheeks, and his heart warmed instinctively at her words. He liked honesty in a woman—in anyone—and she had just been childishly direct. She could have made any other excuse for wanting to try something different. He looked down at the papers again.

'I see that you have all the necessary business skills, and are more than computer literate,' he said. 'Which is an essential requirement, because computers and I are often not best friends.' He looked up at her again briefly. 'A note pad and pen are usually sufficient for my own needs but unfortunately my agent, and my editor, both require something more technical from me—and, I suppose, something more legible,' he added.

Sensing that the interview was going quite well, Sabrina said calmly, 'I am well acquainted with most office machinery, Mr McDonald, but of course I would like some idea of what else the job might entail.'

There was silence for a few moments while Sabrina studied the carpet beneath her feet as she waited for him to answer her.

'Are you married, Miss Gold?' he asked bluntly, looking across at her again. 'Have you family? Children?'

'I am not married,' Sabrina answered. 'I live with my sister.' She paused. 'It's just the two of us,' she added. 'And last year I decided—I mean, *we* decided—to buy our own house, which I am desperate not to lose.'

He nodded. 'Does your sister work?' he asked.

Sabrina looked away for a second. 'Um, well, not all the time,' she said carefully. 'She has always been somewhat fragile, and succumbs to minor things now and again which tend to set her back. When she's well enough, she runs aerobics classes, and teaches dance and keep-fit very successfully.' She swallowed. She was not going to tell him that Melly was a brilliant dancer, and fabulous singer, and that she'd auditioned twice for his brother but had never been successful, had never managed to hit the big time in the theatrical world.

Alexander had been watching her as she'd spoken, watching the fleeting expressions which mirrored her thoughts. He sat forward suddenly, picking up a pen and twirling it between his finger and thumb.

'What I'm actually looking for, Miss Gold, is a PA,' he said. 'And I have to say that the hours are not necessarily nine to five. If there's a deadline I'm having difficulty with, I'd expect you to stay late sometimes. You know what I do; I write books on all kinds of subjects.' He leaned back, running a hand through his hair. 'My last assistant, who'd been with me for many years, finally admitted defeat and retired.'

He looked up at the ceiling for a moment. 'She now spends all her time in her garden, where she keeps some chickens—a lifelong ambition of hers, apparently.' He shook his head slightly, as if marvelling at the vagaries of human nature. 'Anyway, my filing system is wrecked and I need a reader, an editor, someone strong enough to cope with me when I'm frustrated. I need someone to type up my work when I don't feel like doing it, someone to field almost all my telephone calls and to be able to find all the things I keep losing.' He paused. 'I'm afraid I'm somewhat a nightmare to be around at times. Do you—do you think you're capable of meeting all those requirements?'

Sabrina let his words float into the air for a few

moments before a slow smile spread across her features. In spite of herself, she was beginning to like Alexander McDonald.

'Mr McDonald,' she said in the gentle tone she had often used when dealing with disturbed clients, 'I think you could safely leave everything to me.'

Putting his pen down, he stood up immediately and came around the desk, holding out his hand. 'Then it's a done deal,' he said, looking down at her solemnly. 'Can you start next week?'

Sabrina automatically slowed her steps as she walked up the short path of their modest semi-detached house on the outskirts of the city, admitting to feeling both elated and disturbed by her encounter with Alexander McDonald. He was undeniably drop-dead gorgeous, she thought. Did she really want to be working so closely with someone like him? Did she dare risk it, dare risk her feelings being churned up all over again? Because she was honest enough to realize that it was a distinct possibility—something she could well do without.

As she went inside, her sister was just coming down the stairs, dressed to go out.

'Hi, Sabrina,' she said briefly. 'Any luck on the job front?'

'Um, well, yes, actually,' Sabrina said guardedly. 'But it may only be temporary, for a few weeks. I'll see how my new boss and I get on. He's a writer,' she added, not bothering to mention his name. She went into the kitchen to put the kettle on. 'Are you just off to your aerobics class?'

'Yes—and I had a phone call this morning asking me to take over two dance classes later on—the usual girl has gone down with something—so I won't be home until about eight o'clock.'

The two girls were not very much alike to look at; Melinda was tall, dark-haired and brown-eyed with strong facial features, while Sabrina was only five-foot-three with a more delicate bone-structure and widely spaced eyes.

'I'm making something hot for our dinner,' Sabrina said, pouring boiling water into her mug. 'Will lasagne and salad do?'

'Brilliant,' Melinda said, going out and slamming the front door behind her.

Staring thoughtfully out of the window as she sipped her tea, Sabrina cast her mind back to the morning's interview, and to her new employer. To her, he seemed the typically self-assured alpha male, exuding British masculinity with just a hint of ruthlessness somewhere. There was also a brooding, slightly mysterious air about him, as if behind those black, magnetic eyes there was a tantalizing secret he'd never share with another human being.

She realized that she knew nothing at all of his past, whether he was, or had ever been married. In the press or society magazines, she'd never seen him pictured with a female in tow. His brother seemed to be the Lothario of the piece, frequently seen surrounded by pretty women.

Sabrina narrowed her eyes as her thoughts ran on, her analytical mind informing her that Alexander McDonald undoubtedly had a many-layered personality which wasn't necessarily going to be easy to cope with. She shrugged inwardly. The money he was offering would be a powerful incentive to keep her head down and do as he demanded.

Later, as Sabrina was frying the steak for their lasagne, her mobile rang and, frowning, she went across to answer it. She hoped it wasn't Melly in some sort of fix.

The dark tones which reached her ears made her senses rush. 'Miss Gold? Alexander McDonald here…' As if she needed telling! 'I was just thinking, there are still two working days left in the week—could you start earlier than we agreed? Like tomorrow?'

Without stopping to think, Sabrina said, 'Yes—I think so. Yes, all right, Mr McDonald.' He didn't need to know that she'd actually intended to go in to town to buy one or two things to add to her wardrobe. She hadn't been shopping for a while but, tough, he'd have to accept her as she was with not much of this year's fashion on show.

'Good—about nine, or earlier if you like,' he said. Then the phone went dead and Sabrina stared at the instrument for a second. Well, that was brief and to the point, she thought.

Back at number thirteen, Alexander leaned against his desk, a glass of whisky in his hands. He couldn't explain it, but he definitely had a good feeling about this new employee. There was something no-nonsense about her that appealed to him, besides a few other things, he acknowledged, remembering her candid green eyes, her neat hairstyle, her short, unpolished fingernails… And the soft, rather pleasing tone of her voice—a voice that wouldn't get on his nerves.

Still, all that mattered was whether her work proved to come up to his exacting standards, he thought, and that she'd be prepared to work a very long day when necessary.

Mulling over his interview with Sabrina Gold again, he realized that she was going to be very different from Janet. For one thing, Janet was a grandmother obsessed with her family and their new babies, while Sabrina was young and, from what he'd gathered from their conversation, lived with a sister, free of any emotional ties. That had to be a good thing, he thought—no commitments which might stand in the way of her work and their business association.

Feeling restless, as he often did when beginning to reach the end of a novel, he decided to go for a stroll before settling back down to do some more work later.

It was a delightfully soft, still, warm evening as he wandered along the pavement towards the local park at the end of the road, and he suddenly thought nostalgically of his wonderful home in France. With some luck he could arrange to be there by the end of October. He'd only managed two quick visits so far this year, he reminded himself ruefully, so he might even try and stay on over Christmas this time. That thought definitely appealed, because it would mean avoiding family and all the tedious *joie de vivre* that always took over the festive season. He could make the excuse that he was already committed to his next book and needed space and solitude.

His luxurious place abroad filled his mind. It was a large converted barn, standing almost alone amongst vines and olive groves, and in his absence safely watched over by his near-neighbours Marcel and Simone. Its large swimming pool, always warm and soothing, was surrounded by an expansive patio where on placid evenings he and some local friends would share freshly baked baguettes, sip wine from local vineyards, savour home-grown olives steeped in garlic-flavoured oil and just talk and let time slip by.

It was nearly dark as he wandered, lost in thought, through the almost-deserted park. He nearly fell over a courting couple lying on the grass. He stepped away quickly, muttering an awkward apology. But he needn't have bothered. They were oblivious to anything but themselves, their intertwined bodies and audible cries demonstrating the erotic pleasure of their coupling.

For some reason which he couldn't explain, a peculiar sadness came over Alexander for a few seconds. Those two were so young, so in love. He looked back to his own youth and the women he'd known. It seemed such a long time ago, another time, another country. Why had he indulged in no-strings-attached affairs for so long? Why had he never wanted true commitment? Was he that selfish? Had his disastrous relationship with Angelica put him off for ever? For heaven's sake, that was nearly ten years ago.

When he got back home he poured a fresh glass of whisky, then flung himself down on his bed. Ten minutes' sleep would do him good, he thought, before he returned to the study and perhaps the conclusion of that penultimate chapter which was worrying him.

Almost immediately, he fell into a deep sleep. A sleep filled with unbelievably colourful dreams which made his head move restlessly from side to side, his lips forming incomprehensible murmurings.

He was lying naked beside the beautiful, unclothed body of a woman. To his amazed delight, she was responding to his passionate advances with uninhibited ardour as she encouraged him to caress her body, her slender limbs, her cool, smooth breasts… When he knelt over her and possessed her completely, she parted her moist lips to receive the warmth of his mouth, the urgent thrust of his tongue…

Suddenly, he awoke and sprang up into a sitting position, his brow beaded with sweat. What the hell was that all about? What had set those particular bells ringing? This wasn't like him! He couldn't begin to remember the last time his emotions had been stirred with such an erotic, white-hot passion, either consciously or subconsciously.

Swinging his legs over the side of the bed, he stripped off his clothes and went into the bathroom. What he needed now was a long, very cold shower, he told himself.

Because in that so-immediate dream, the woman he had been making such intense love to had been unmistakable. She had been small with long, fair hair, unpolished fingernails and green, green eyes like those of an enchanting cat.

CHAPTER TWO

JUST after eight o'clock the following morning, wearing black trousers and a grey-and-white pin-striped shirt, Sabrina found herself standing once again outside number thirteen. Just as she was about to ring the bell, the door was thrust open and she came face to face with a short, grey-haired, middle-aged woman who was just coming out of the house, a couple of carrier bags in her hands.

'Oh, hi…' Sabrina began uncertainly, and the woman moved back for the girl to enter.

'Miss Gold? Ah. Mr McDonald left a note saying I might see you. I'm Maria, his daily—or his three-times-a-week, I should say.' She smiled. 'I haven't seen him this morning. He isn't up yet—probably getting over a heavy night!'

'Oh, I see,' Sabrina said, slightly taken aback. From yesterday's phone call, she'd imagined him to be an early riser. Shouldn't he already be hard at work and ready to spell out his instructions for the day?

'Anyway, go on up to the study—he said you knew where it was,' Maria said. 'I don't expect he'll be too long. By the way, the kitchen's just along there in the hall, first door on the right. Have some coffee, why don't you?' She paused, smiling again. 'Make yourself at home—and good luck!'

With that, Maria departed, leaving Sabrina feeling like some sort of intruder.

She decided against making herself acquainted with Alexander McDonald's kitchen just yet. Anyway, she'd had her usual light breakfast of cereal, yoghurt and honey and wouldn't need any coffee for a while. There was no sound at all in the house and for some reason Sabrina felt distinctly embarrassed to think of her employer tucked up in bed. As she trod lightly up the stairs, she wondered which room he was still sleeping in, whether it was one of those on the next floor. Trying to contain her thoughts, she reached his study and went inside.

The place was a total shambles. The rug on the floor had been pushed at a slightly drunken angle, and numerous books on the desk were scattered everywhere haphazardly, only just making room for three empty, stained coffee-mugs. Two baskets on the floor alongside were full of crumpled, screwed-up paper, and there seemed to be dust everywhere; Sabrina could see its lazy motes moving and shifting in the shafts of strong sunlight streaming in from the windows. She made a face to herself. This room was obviously out of bounds to Maria, she thought. It also felt over-warm and stuffy; impulsively she went over and unlatched one of the windows, throwing it wide open to let in some fresh air. She didn't know how long she would survive in this atmosphere.

Glancing down, she saw that the long, narrow garden was laid out in a strip of lawn, and here and there were clusters of stone pots filled with bright-red geraniums.

'Good morning.'

Alexander's voice made her turn quickly—she hadn't heard him come in—and immediately her pulse quickened as she looked up at him. He was wearing chinos and a black shirt, his hair roughly brushed and still damp from his shower. His face was unshaven, the line of dark stubble along his chin drawing Sabrina's helpless gaze to the seductive black hair just visible beneath his open-necked shirt. He came over to stand next to her and stared down, his dark, sensuous eyes trapping her enquiring green ones for a second.

'Sorry I wasn't here to greet you on your first morning,' he said, swallowing. The memory of last night's fantasy was still vivid, and uppermost in his mind. How was he going to rid himself of it and act normally? he thought briefly. He straightened his shoulders.

'I didn't get to bed until very late last night—well, it was early this morning, actually,' he added. 'But I have to keep going until I'm satisfied that I've got things right, whatever the hour. Not that it worked this time, I'm afraid,' he added.

Sabrina frowned briefly, not knowing how to respond to that remark. She moved away from him and went towards her own desk.

'Well, sometimes a new day can bring fresh ideas?' she suggested, cross at the way her cheeks had flushed at being alone with Alexander McDonald. She hadn't felt this way yesterday at the interview. But that was different. Then she had employed all her clinical instincts to get what she wanted—this job. It had kept her cool, calm and rational, deflecting her thoughts from any other feelings she might experience at being in close proximity to one of the most lusted-after—and apparently elusive—men on the London scene.

But this morning realization set in. She was going

to be closeted in this room with him for many hours for the foreseeable future, and once again Sabrina felt threatened and in danger of becoming emotionally affected by a member of the opposite sex. She didn't need her professional qualifications to work that one out, yet she was quietly horrified. Hadn't fate's cruel hand made her decide to stick to work and to the needs of her sister from now on, for all time? She was not going to allow life ever again to bring her to the dizzy heights of supreme happiness, only to dash her to the ground and break her heart into pieces.

She should have been married to Stephen by now, but in a tragic, mad moment destiny had taken over. Stephen had lost his life in a friendly rugby-game, never regaining consciousness from a one-in-a-million chance accident on the pitch.

Sabrina had considered herself the luckiest woman in the world when he'd asked her to marry him. Not just because he was so good-looking, with the most amazing deep-gold hair with eyes to match, but because he was funny, loyal and kind. He had promised Sabrina that Melly would always have a home with them, for as long as she needed it. Life had been so good—too good to be true. How many other men would have understood the sense of responsibility towards her sister made so acute by the family background? Their father had walked out a long time ago, and their mother, Philippa, had remarried when the girls were in their teens and at their most vulnerable. She was now living in Sydney with her husband, and rarely came back to the UK, confining her interest in her daughters to somewhat irregular phone-calls. So everything that had happened had made Sabrina feel as if she really was left holding the baby—and knowing with absolute certainty that now she'd never hold one of her own. Because she'd never trust love again, never risk losing again, and she'd managed to convince herself that her need for a man, any man to share her existence, had died for ever.

Yet the burgeoning rush to her senses now told its own story. It was undeniable that Alexander McDonald was seducing her—in thought, if not in deed! It was hardly his fault, but it was the worst possible scenario for a successful business-arrangement, so she'd better get a grip and keep any wayward thoughts well under wraps, she told herself.

Alexander pushed back the chair by his desk and sat down heavily, glancing down with some distaste at the disorderly mess in front of him.

'I should at least have washed up these mugs before I eventually went to bed,' he said. He glanced across at Sabrina. 'Do sit, Miss Gold.'

Sabrina didn't sit down, returning his glance squarely. 'I hope you'll call me Sabrina,' she said, thinking almost immediately that maybe Alexander McDonald preferred to be more formal with his staff.

But straight away he said, 'Good. And I'm usually known as Alex. So at least we've cleared something up this morning.'

He smiled across at her briefly, his full lips parting to expose white, immaculate teeth. Desperately trying to rein in her imagination—and failing once again—Sabrina fleetingly wondered what it would feel like to have that sensuous mouth close in on hers. He was impossibly handsome, she thought, as his blue-black eyes searched her face. Yet Sabrina was aware that there was a hint of something more behind Alexander's overtly masculine features, his obviously desirable appearance. There was something about him that both excited and intrigued her. She tried to stem the annoying tingling at the back of her neck, and as he continued scrutinizing her Sabrina had the uncomfortable feeling that he was reading her mind. She certainly hoped not. She tore her eyes from his penetrating gaze, clearing her throat.

'Do you have any sort of set plan for me…to make a beginning?' she said tentatively, glancing around and wondering where on earth they were going to start. She hoped she wasn't expected to come up with any brilliant ideas for the current project he seemed to be having difficulty with. She'd never tried her hand at creative writing, though she'd always been an avid reader from as far back as she could remember. Alexander McDonald's books were known to be serious and highly literary tomes, and from what she'd read in the book reviews his plots were strong, often dark and with no happy endings guaranteed. They were not really her own choice of reading matter at the end of a working day spent trying to unravel troubled lives and situations for her patients. She wondered briefly when she'd be able to return to her own profession.

'Have you ever read any of my books?' Alexander asked bluntly, desperately trying not to keep looking at her. Sabrina coloured up again; he *was* reading her mind! She paused for only a fraction of a second.

'No—I haven't,' she said simply. 'I have read *about* your books in all the reviews, and they seem…somewhat heavier material than I can cope with.' She hesitated. 'My normal reading time is an hour or so before I go to sleep,' she explained. 'And what I need then is total relaxation, a distraction. I mean, I wouldn't want to be thinking, dreaming, worrying about all your characters, to have them on my mind all night.'

There was a moment's silence after that and Sabrina

hoped she hadn't put a nail in her own coffin. If she wasn't careful this could turn out to be a very short-term employment. She didn't think Alexander McDonald appreciated criticism—or, worse, a lack of interest—especially from someone like her.

But she couldn't have been more wrong, because she was treated once more to a brief, heart-wrenching smile as he looked at her, his eyes narrowing. The woman might have said she'd read everything he'd ever written and that she considered it all wonderful, he thought. But she'd been honest enough to say she'd never even read the first page of any of his books.

He got up and came around to stand in front of his desk, leaning casually against it and staring down at her.

'Good. That means you've got no preconceived ideas. Your opinion on something that may be a sticking point for me is going to be invaluable.' He paused. 'Janet—my faithful secretary for the last fifteen years—was a useful contributor in this way now and again, but lately it had become a matter of her trying to please me, to tell me what she thought I wanted to hear. That's no good.' He thrust his hands into his pockets. 'It was something of a relief when she decided to retire.'

Sabrina swallowed, biting her lip. By the sound of it, this job was certainly not going to be stereotypical, as he'd made clear from the start. But she'd not envisaged it including her having to offer her opinion on the esteemed writing of one of the most successful authors in the world. But then, she thought, she'd read most of the classics—read and re-read them—and was a regular visitor to the library and bookshops, keeping up with all the modern output. Maybe she'd be some use after all, in a small way. She wanted to be useful to Alexander

McDonald. And it might prove to be an interesting diversion for her.

He turned around now, picking up a large diary and handing it over to Sabrina

'This is an essential part of my life,' he said. 'And from now on, you're in charge of it, Sabrina. I need you to remind me at frequent intervals what's coming up and where I'm meant to be, and who with. I tend to be forgetful most of the time.' He moved beside her, flicking the pages over. 'Oh, and I would rather you always answer the telephone—just tell the caller to hold while I decide whether I want to talk or not. If I do, I'll pick up my extension; if not, I'll give you the thumbs down and you can think up some excuse.'

For the next hour, Sabrina listened as he explained how he liked everything done, and learned that he didn't like things moved about unnecessarily. 'If you tidy up too much, we'll never remember where anything is,' he said flatly, and Sabrina smiled inwardly. She'd been right in thinking that Maria wasn't welcome here. She threw discretion to the winds; she did have some requests of her own.

'Am I at least allowed to clean some dust from my desk—and from yours?' she said. She feigned a dainty sneeze. 'It would be advantageous for both of us,' she added.

He shrugged, as if the matter of dust had never entered his head. 'Feel free,' he said casually.

Finally, she was handed an A4 note pad with pages full of scribbled writing.

'Type this up and print it out, will you? See if you can make sense of my scrawl.'

Sabrina took a long, deep breath, feeling upbeat for a moment. She knew she could handle this job, because she wanted to, desperately. Twenty-four hours ago she hadn't even met Alexander McDonald, but she owned up again to a feeling of warmth towards him. He seemed quite nice, as new bosses went, though it was obvious to her that he might be touchy at times. Well, she could handle touchy, she thought.

They were standing close together now, their heads bent over the script they were looking at. His tall frame made Sabrina feel tiny, insignificant and distinctly shivery as he towered above her, the titillating musk of his bronzed skin reaching her nostrils. As he turned another page, their hands touched briefly and Sabrina was painfully aware of his long, sensitive fingers.

She moved away from him slightly, trying to keep her mind from intrusive thoughts, and went across to boot up her computer, thinking that all that writing didn't look too impossible to interpret, but it was full of alterations and crossings-out which would take time to sort. She bit her lip, feeling that the worst part of the job was the fact that she and her employer were going to be here in this room together all the time. She'd much rather have an office of her own—a decent cupboard would do—where she wouldn't feel those eyes judging her, assessing her every move. Surely he'd go out sometimes and leave her in peace?

Reading her thoughts, as usual, he said, 'I'm due at the gym for a couple of hours this morning. But first I'm going to make us some coffee.'

Sabrina stood up. Surely making the coffee was one of the duties of his personal assistant? 'I'll do it,' she said quickly. 'Maria showed me where the kitchen is.'

He nodded, walking towards the door and glancing back at her. 'OK,' he said, relieved that he was feeling more in charge of himself by this time. 'And I might as well show you the domestic side of things straight away. We may need to make ourselves something to eat at the end of a long day.'

He led the way down the stairs and along the hall to the kitchen, Sabrina following in his wake. She remembered him saying yesterday that he would expect her to stay on after normal working hours when necessary, and she shrugged inwardly. She'd do whatever it took to keep this highly lucrative position. Her expression clouded briefly as she remembered how low Melly had been this morning when she'd looked in on her in her bedroom.

The kitchen was large, immaculate and welcoming. There was a spotless Aga, a large refectory table and chairs. Holding prime position in the centre of the room was a double oven with overhead lighting and shining granite surfaces. *Goodness me*, Sabrina thought, *what does he need all these facilities for when he is the only occupant of the house?* Perhaps he was always entertaining, she thought, though somehow that didn't seem likely. She sighed inwardly, thinking of her own small kitchen that was badly in need of a refit.

Alexander threw open the door of one of the cupboards. 'Everything you may need is here, or in the fridge,' he said, looking back at her. 'Maria does all my shopping, makes sure I don't run out of essentials—though I do eat out rather a lot.' He paused. 'I've become adept at scrambling eggs, and that's just about it.'

Sabrina smiled up at him briefly and went over to the sink to fill the kettle.

'I'll go and get changed and come back in a minute for my coffee—which I like black,' Alexander said. 'And feel free to help yourself to anything you want, whether I'm here or not,' he added.

Sabrina set out the things she needed, putting coffee granules into the cafetière, and was just reaching for two mugs when the telephone rang. She frowned. It wasn't the land line, it was a mobile, and it certainly wasn't hers. Then she saw that Alexander had left his on one of the surfaces, and she went over to answer it. Before she could open her mouth, a woman's rather strident tones filled her ears.

'Alexander? You have not been returning my calls. That is extremely naughty of you!'

'Excuse me,' Sabrina said hastily. 'Um, I'll see if Mr McDonald is in.'

There was a second's pause. 'Is that Janet?' the voice demanded.

'No, I'm Mr McDonald's new secretary,' Sabrina said. 'Janet does not work for him now.'

'*Really?* He didn't tell me anything about getting a new secretary,' the voice said in a rather complaining tone. 'Oh, well. I want to speak to him, please.'

'I'll see if he's in,' Sabrina repeated. 'May I ask who's calling?'

'This is *Lydia*,' the voice said, as if that should have been obvious to anyone with half a brain cell.

'One moment,' Sabrina said, putting the phone down carefully and leaving the room, running up the stairs two at a time. Alexander was just coming out of one of the rooms dressed in a white T-shirt and shorts, his brown, muscular thighs and calves shadowed with dark hair. He was looking so unutterably seductive that Sabrina almost forgot what she was supposed to be doing.

'There's a call on your mobile—which you left in the kitchen,' she faltered.

'Oh, I'm always mislaying the wretched thing,' he said. 'Who wants to speak to me?'

'Someone called Lydia,' Sabrina replied, turning to go back down the stairs.

He didn't reply to that, but followed Sabrina into the kitchen and picked up the phone.

'Good morning, Lydia,' he said casually. Before he could utter another word, Sabrina could hear those distinctive tones sailing on uninterrupted.

'Why haven't you been returning my calls?' the woman said petulantly. 'It really is most annoying, Alexander.'

'Yes, I know. Sorry, Lydia.' He paused. 'It's just that I've been extremely busy, and rather distracted, because Janet has left and I've had to find someone else suitable.'

'Yes, I've just been told about Janet,' the woman went on. 'Your problem is you work too hard, Alexander. Anyway, enough about all that. I hope you're still free for Sunday week?'

As Sabrina poured the boiling water onto the coffee, she couldn't help being riveted to the conversation going on beside her. Alexander made no effort to exclude her from listening in. Who was Lydia? Clearly an over-familiar lady friend who didn't seem very important to Alexander, if the expression on his face was anything to go by.

'Sunday week?' he repeated, frowning.

'Yes, Sunday week,' the woman said. 'Look, I'm not taking no for an answer this time, Alexander.' She paused. 'There are going to be lots of party people there you'll know.'

'I don't do parties. You know that, Lydia,' he said.

'You always used to! Your…social reputation was very well-known at one time.'

'That was a *very* long while ago, Lydia,' Alexander

replied. 'I have, shall we say, outgrown parties.' *Especially your parties*, he thought. 'I really do not find them entertaining any more.'

'Well, I can promise you that you'll find this one entertaining,' Lydia persisted. 'Do say you'll come?'

Alexander glanced at Sabrina, raising his eyebrows in mild exasperation.

'Oh, well, OK. If you insist, Lydia,' he said at last. 'I'll do my best.'

'Wonderful! And, by the way, Lucinda is back in England and she'll be at the party.' There was a long pause. 'She particularly asked whether you were going to be there when we spoke on the phone. Mentioned something about an old score to settle.'

Alexander's mouth turned down at the corners. 'I wonder whether Lucinda and I will recognize each other,' he said. 'After all this time.'

There was a girlish giggle at the other end. 'I doubt that there will be *any* difficulty with that. You were *very close* once, weren't you?'

'That also was a very long time ago, Lydia,' Alexander said, clearly irritated by now. 'Um, look, I have to go. But thanks for the call.'

'Don't forget—Sunday the sixteenth. And don't be late!' was the parting shot.

He ended the call and Alexander turned to pick up his coffee, glancing down at Sabrina, his eyes narrowing slightly.

After a moment he said thoughtfully, 'Could you possibly arrange to be available on the evening of the sixteenth to come to this function it seems I can't get out of?' He paused. 'It might be useful to have you there.' He cleared his throat. 'I'm sorry it's a Sunday, when

I wouldn't normally ask you to work, but it would be helpful if you could.'

Sabrina frowned thoughtfully. She hadn't realized how demanding this job was going to be, but if needs must she'd better do as her employer wanted. She made a mental note to bring a note pad and pen with her.

'When I get home I'll double check I'm free,' she said. 'But I think I can do as you ask.'

'Great. Thanks.' He finished his coffee and turned to go. 'I very rarely see my mother these days, and sometimes I just have to fall in with her wishes.'

'Your mother?'

'Yes—Lydia. My mother,' Alexander said as he left the room.

CHAPTER THREE

BY THE middle of the following week, Sabrina felt she was beginning to get to grips with her secretarial duties, starting with the countless pieces of mail which arrived in the post each morning, and fielding all the telephone calls—most of which Alexander refused to follow up.

'They're always about being asked to go places, attend functions,' he grumbled once, as she showed him the list. 'Can't be bothered.'

After Alexander had left to go to the gym the previous Thursday, Sabrina had concentrated on trying to decipher his terrible handwriting. Bit by bit she had managed to unravel the meaning of the subtle and sophisticated prose, all of it, naturally, in perfect English—even if his spelling didn't quite match up. She even felt privileged to have sight of it, to be the first to read this particular new piece, to share the inner workings of his illustrious mind.

But more of those warning bells began to ring for her when, after a particularly poignant page or two, Sabrina had found herself stopping to trace the script gently with her forefinger, as if by touching the words he'd written she was touching him. Getting close. How dreadful was that? Alexander McDonald was arousing dangerous feelings in her which she thought she'd ruled out for ever.

By Friday afternoon she was able to hand him the countless pages, everything he'd asked her to type up, and he seemed genuinely pleased with the result.

'Thanks very much,' he said later, after scrutinizing each page carefully. 'That even makes some sense to me now.' He shot Sabrina a quick glance, thinking his new secretary had cottoned on to his requirements quicker than he'd dared to hope.

One thing which Sabrina was grateful for was that Alexander went to the gym on Tuesday and Thursday mornings, so she did have some time when he wasn't sitting a few feet away from her. He'd also been away on two occasions for meetings with his agent. It was so much easier to concentrate when she was by herself—especially as several times when they'd been together she'd looked across briefly to see him watching her, one finely arched eyebrow raised thoughtfully, his perfect, sensuous lips parted slightly. Sabrina had coloured immediately, a surging tide of feeling seeping down to her groin.

Sensing her discomfiture, Alexander had said hurriedly, 'I was admiring the speed at which you type, Sabrina. I can never manage more than one finger at a time.'

'Well, what I do is the easy bit. I mean, where does all this come from, or start from, Alexander? I mean, *Alex*?' she'd asked, feeling uncomfortable at using his Christian name. 'How on earth do you compose such intricate and beautiful work?'

'With the utmost difficulty, most of the time,' he'd replied. 'Someone once said that writing was the same as hacking lumps out of granite—and it often feels like that.'

'Well, you'd never know it from this,' Sabrina had said, meaning it. 'All these words which I've typed seem to just spill off the paper, like oil running from a spoon.'

He had seemed pleasantly surprised at that. 'Does that mean you might even read one of my books one day?' he'd said, only half-teasing. She'd looked up at him, hoping she hadn't said the wrong thing or been over-familiar with her boss.

But Sabrina readily admitted that in the short time she'd known him he'd appeared far less demanding than she might have expected. There'd certainly been no evidence of the moodiness he'd hinted at during the interview. But it was early days. Perhaps this was the calm before the storm.

The thing which she was dreading was Sunday evening being spent with Lydia, and it seemed a host of other people as well, none of whom Sabrina would know. To hang around for hours with a load of complete strangers, not to mention her very new boss, wasn't exactly an enticing thought. Why had Alexander asked her to go with him, anyway? Surely he'd find her a hindrance? What would be expected of her? Thinking about it again, she shrugged inwardly. However boring she found it, it could only last a few hours, and the almost outrageous rate which Alexander was paying her to do his every bidding should be compensation enough.

Now, with the end of her first full week in sight, Sabrina looked across at Alexander as he sat bent over the desk with his head in one hand and scribbling furiously with the other. Her heart missed a beat or two as she watched him silently, unable to resist her body's reaction to the powerful sexuality he exuded. It wasn't just his achingly seductive appearance, it was something far deeper and totally indefinable.

Alexander McDonald should wear a warning notice around his neck, Sabrina thought: *to all females everywhere: danger. Keep away.* Clearly, he had no wish to be tied down to any female, otherwise he should surely be committed to someone by now. But his single status was a well-known phenomenon, and was an occasional topic in the gossip magazines. As she continued studying him thoughtfully, Sabrina felt she was beginning to understand him a bit. He was obviously married to his work, she thought, and living his life through his characters. That was what steered him through. And it was enough.

'Are you going to make some tea?' he asked suddenly without looking up. With a rush of self-consciousness, Sabrina wondered if he'd known she'd been gazing across at him.

'Yes. I was just going to do that,' she said, getting up and leaving the room.

In the kitchen, she was just filling the kettle when her mobile rang and she took it from her jeans pocket, frowning briefly. It could only be Melly.

It was, and the girl's excitable voice almost deafened Sabrina as she listened.

'Sabrina? You'll never guess! You know those dancing classes I took over at short notice because the girl was ill? Well, they've asked me to step in again, only this time it's something much more exciting!'

'Go on, tell me,' Sabrina said patiently.

'I've been asked to go to Spain! To teach at a summer school—well, an autumn school, really. And it's a two-week contract to include musical theatre, aerobics and dance, and I think some singing as well. People have enrolled from all over the place to take part, and participants, as well as those of us who'll be running the classes, will all be put up at various houses. Everything's taken care of, Sabrina. All I need is to take my clothes and passport—oh, and some money, of course—and turn up on Sunday morning when the minibus will be taking us to Heathrow!'

Melly hardly paused for breath, not giving Sabrina a chance to interrupt. 'It's a wonderful opportunity, Sabrina—and I know two of the teachers who are going. They've done this sort of thing before and they say it's fantastic fun, and a holiday as well—all expenses paid—and we get a respectable cheque for our services at the end! What do you think?'

Well, what *could* Sabrina think or say other than to join in her sister's enthusiasm? 'Bring home all the necessary literature for us to check out, Melly,' she said reasonably. 'But I should think it will be perfectly OK. Though I'm sure you'll have to work pretty hard for your holiday!' She bit her lip, hoping that Melly wouldn't suffer from any depression during the proposed assignment. Her attacks were so unpredictable, and she'd be too far away for Sabrina to help her.

'Oh, I know that. There will be several sessions each day, but time for breaks as well.' There was a pause at the other end. 'The only thing is, I don't have much money at the moment—as you know, Sabrina—so could you lend me a bit? I'll be able to repay you when I get home.'

'Oh, don't worry about the money, I'll sort that out,' Sabrina said, suddenly elated at her sister's news. This could be stimulating for Melly, she thought, a complete change—and a much-needed boost to her confidence.

* * *

Early on Sunday morning, Sabrina waved the minibus out of sight. She was thinking that, if nothing else came from this experience for her sister, it was going to be the first break away from her, Sabrina, and from home, for a very long time.

She sighed briefly, biting her lip as she watched the bus disappear around the corner, before walking back the short distance to where she'd parked the car. Melly was twenty-six years old, after all. Yet she was the kid sister, vulnerable and easily hurt, her fragile emotional state often rocked by outside influences. Sabrina fervently hoped that this trip would turn out to be everything Melly thought it would be, with no complications.

Sabrina did feel relieved to have met the leader of the excursion this morning—a youngish man called Sam—who'd reassured her that everyone would be in safe hands and that these events were always well organized.

Driving slowly back home, Sabrina tried to think about this evening and how she was going to get through it. She had not liked the sound of Lydia one little bit. And how strange that Alexander called his mother by her Christian name—what was that all about? Perhaps that was what elevated people did, she thought idly. Then something else struck her: what should she wear to this do? Alexander hadn't given her a clue about any of it; his only directive as they'd parted company on Friday was that she must be ready when he arrived to pick her up at seven o'clock.

Still, she thought now as she parked outside their modest front gate, her black dress would have to be her salvation again, her suitable-for-anywhere item. It was well-cut, of good-quality material and wearing it always made her feel sure of herself, confident. If she kept it plain and didn't deck it out with any jewellery, it could be classed as a perfect number for her role as secretary to Alexander McDonald. Not that he would bother about what she was wearing, or even notice what she had on, Sabrina thought.

The traffic that evening was abnormally heavy, and it had gone eight by the time Alexander drove his sleek, bronze Aston Martin slowly up the wide approach to his parents' mansion, set in the Surrey countryside.

As Sabrina peered ahead at the imposing building, she saw lights from every open window shining out like beacons. As reverberating waves of high-pitched chatting and loud laughter could easily be heard, she felt like jumping out of the car and running away. But that thought lasted for less than a second as she remembered who she was with, who her employer was, and she hardened her resolve to be the perfect personal assistant to Alexander McDonald. To be ready for anything he might need her for, and to remain professional and businesslike.

The huge oak door was thrown open by a uniformed maid, who ushered them straight away into a brightly lit room, which to Sabrina seemed to stretch almost out of sight. There must be more than a hundred people present, she thought, realizing in those first few seconds that everyone seemed extravagantly dressed.

Alexander, his dark eyes sweeping the scene at a glance, knew he'd been right in not wanting to be here. It was one of his mother's usual parties, he thought with distaste, where she invited just about everyone she knew—many of them young women, some not so young, who laughed too loudly and drank too much. His perceptive gaze had already spotted two whom he knew to be immensely rich, thanks to the well-known escort agencies they owned and ran in town.

Putting his hand lightly on Sabrina's arm, he guided her across the room towards the long, white-clothed table laden with alcohol of every description. Before he could pour either of them a drink, the easily recognizable voice of Lydia reached Sabrina's ears as the woman bore down on them.

She was wearing a three-quarter-length sheath dress in a brilliant purple colour, and its smooth, satiny material perfectly accentuated her hour-glass figure. Her silver hair was an elegant, shining knot on her head, her sculpted lips painted a bright glossy red. Alexander's mother was certainly a very handsome woman who had clearly passed on her looks to her son. Her arms outstretched in welcome, she embraced Alexander carefully, offering him her cheek and making sure her make-up was not disturbed.

'Alexander! Darling! I was afraid you weren't going to turn up!'

Yes, mother dearest, I know exactly how that feels, he thought cynically, remembering the countless times his mother had not bothered to turn up at the regular boarding-school events to which parents were always invited. Remembering how he'd kept on hoping, until the very last minute, that she'd arrive. But she'd clearly felt that her maternal obligations ended the moment her sons left home at the tender age of seven; she had never left them in any doubt about that.

Alexander could recall her exact words as she'd waved him off on that first day.

'Remember, Alexander,' she'd said, 'that you are no longer a child—and you must accept responsibility for yourself.' She'd paused only briefly. 'And from now on

I want to be known as Lydia, not Mummy—do you understand? Mummy is a silly, childish word.'

'But when I write to you can't I put "dear Mummy"?' Alexander had asked earnestly.

'Certainly not,' his mother had replied. 'Someone might see it. Just put "dear Lydia". That is my name, after all.'

Staring down at his mother now, Alexander realized that he and Bruno, who was two years his senior, had never discussed the matter but had accepted their mother's directive without question. At least their father, Angus, had made no such demands and was always affectionately known as Dad. The older man didn't seem to be here tonight, Alexander noticed, but that was nothing new. Their parents had lived separate lives for years.

'Yes—a lot of traffic, I'm afraid,' Alexander said, in answer to his mother's remark.

'Never mind, you're here now. Though, of course, Bruno is otherwise engaged this evening—what's new?' Lydia sighed with a little pout. 'A heavy meeting with some influential new backers, apparently. Still, there are *masses* of your friends here tonight, all desperate to see you again. It's been too long since you've been circulating; someone said it's as if you've disappeared off the face of the planet!'

'Well, I hope this evening will lay that supposition to rest,' Alexander said flatly. He paused, flickering a glance at Sabrina. 'As I'm aware that your guest list is always flexible, Lydia,' he went on, 'I've brought someone along with me tonight—my personal assistant, Sabrina. Janet's replacement,' he added.

Sabrina was only too aware that Alexander's mother had barely noticed she was there at all—or, if she had, she'd chosen to ignore it.

The woman turned now to look briefly at Sabrina. 'Oh yes, I remember speaking to you on the telephone,' she said dismissively. 'How do you do?' she added as an afterthought. Then she took hold of Alexander's arm firmly. 'Now, come along,' she said. 'Dinner is going to be served in half an hour, so you've a little time to catch up with everyone first.'

Alexander's lips set in a hard line as he deliberately prised his mother's hand away from him. 'All in good time,' he said. 'Sabrina and I would like a drink first.'

'Well, don't be long,' Lydia said, waving to someone at the other end of the room. 'Look, there's Danielle, I must go and talk to her…' she said, moving away.

Waving briefly to several people who were calling out and wanting to gain his attention, Alexander poured out two glasses of white wine, handing one to Sabrina, and their eyes met for a second. He looked down at her thoughtfully, noticing for the first time that evening what she was wearing. The black dress she had on suited her dainty, curvaceous figure perfectly, he thought, and he liked her hair coiled up like that. It gave her a cool, elfin, distinctive look, and tonight those eyes which he found so fascinating seemed brighter and greener than ever. She wasn't wearing a scrap of jewellery or make-up, as far as he could tell, but why should she bother? She didn't need anything, her natural attributes were entirely sufficient.

Irritated at his own thoughts, and still looking at her, he took a drink from his glass. He didn't look at women any more, he reminded himself. Not in the way he always had. The youthful, carefree days of enjoying the pleasures of the opposite sex had long gone and the experience had taught him many things—uppermost of which was in future to steer clear of the sort of women he'd so often come in contact with. Vain and self-seeking, many of them were overtly promiscuous, leading little, brittle lives.

It had all made him realize, believe, that he didn't actually *like* women very much at all. He admired them, some of them; well, that was the male instinct and not his fault, he thought. But there had not been one in his past, apart from Angelica, whom he could imagine might have been prepared to settle down and be a faithful wife to someone like him, forced to spend so many hours in isolation as he worked. Nor to understand his moods when he became quiet and withdrawn sometimes, or that he didn't particularly like the heady London life and all that went with it.

He took another swig from his glass. One thing he was damned sure about—he would never find himself in the same wretched position as his father, providing untold wealth to a fickle and demanding partner who lived solely for her own gratification. His brow knitted briefly. His solitary state—though not always entirely fulfilling, he admitted—was at least comfortable. Sorting out the lives of the characters in his books was difficult enough, heaven only knew. To have a real life woman to deal with and to try to satisfy was never going to be one of his problems. He'd come to that decision a long time ago, and it was final.

Sabrina, realizing that he had been scrutinizing her for several moments, felt her cheeks begin to burn and she glanced up quickly. 'Are you expecting your agent to be here tonight?' she asked innocently. 'Or someone from your publisher's?' she added, wondering why she was there at all, what her role was to be.

'Good grief, no, I hope not!' Alexander said at once.

'No, this is just one of my mother's pointless parties, and I didn't particularly want to come to it alone, that's all.'

And that was the truth, he thought. It had been a somewhat impetuous act on his part to ask Sabrina to accompany him, but for some strange reason the thought that she would be there had made the prospect of the event slightly more acceptable. He shrugged inwardly. She was his personal assistant, after all, ready to do as he asked when the need arose, and she hadn't seemed to mind coming along. His brow furrowed again as he remembered Lydia's reaction when he'd introduced Sabrina just now. His mother had been totally uninterested to meet his new secretary—and was that such a surprise? Sabrina did not fit the mould of the women his mother had always liked being with.

Suddenly, like a minor earthquake approaching, three women rushed up and gathered around Alexander, all talking at once, and each embracing him effusively, almost making him spill his drink.

'Alex!' they chorused together. 'Long time, no see. Where have you been hiding?'

Alexander put his drink down on the table and looked at the women. 'Not hiding, just working,' he said blandly. 'How's everyone doing? I must say, you're all looking as lovely as ever.'

They all gushed their pleasure at that remark, and as they all began to babble on, each vying to make herself heard above the others, Sabrina stood back, fascinated to witness their over-exuberant behaviour—and to see Alexander's casually charming manner as he responded to everything they were saying. It was clear that they were absolutely besotted by the famous, handsome, reputedly unavailable Alexander McDonald. She looked away for a moment, feeling as if she was a voyeur witnessing a mating game. But what was also clear was that she herself hadn't even been noticed, nor the fact that Alexander had someone with him. Well, secretaries were supposed to make themselves invisible when the occasion demanded, she thought. It was as if she wasn't there at all as she was faced with the backs of the three extravagantly dressed women clustered around Alexander, still chattering non-stop.

After a few moments of this, he eased himself away and reached over to take Sabrina's arm.

'Sally, Debbie, Samantha—let me introduce you to my secretary, Sabrina,' he began, and for the first time the women turned, deigning to look at Sabrina, their faces blank.

Just as they were murmuring their polite greeting, another woman arrived and draped her arms around Alexander's neck. 'Alex,' she breathed. 'At last…'

'Hello, Lucinda,' he said, disentangling himself gently. 'You're looking wonderful, as usual.' He drew Sabrina into the gathering. 'Meet my new assistant, Sabrina.'

Lucinda was tall, raven-haired and swathed in a tight-fitting, low-cut red dress which left nothing to the imagination. She stared at Sabrina, a curious expression on her hard features.

'Oh. So what happened to funny, little, old dowdy Janet?' she said, turning to Alexander again. 'Did she die quietly at her desk?'

'Funny, little, old dowdy Janet, as you put it, decided that she'd had enough and is now spending much-deserved time with her family,' Alexander said, and Sabrina could see that the woman's remarks had angered him.

'Oh, so you're the new typist, then, are you?' Lucinda

said, looking down at Sabrina, her eyes taking in her appearance at a glance. 'I wonder how you'll put up with Alexander the Great?'

'I've had no difficulty so far,' Sabrina said neatly, suddenly rattled at the company she was in, and realizing that she herself had hardly uttered a word to anyone yet.

Lucinda shrugged. 'Efficient typists are difficult to find; I know *that* to my cost,' she said. 'Though I'm afraid secretarial work would drive me absolutely bonkers, *whoever* I was working for,' she added. 'I mean, any office work is deadly boring—surely only a stop-gap before finding other more intellectually fulfilling occupations for the more intelligent among us?' She blinked, her false eyelashes sweeping her cheek. 'I run my own marketing company,' she drawled importantly. 'Which regularly keeps me out of the country. But I'm afraid my secretary in the London office comes under the heading of "brain dead". Lazy and utterly useless!'

The others all tittered at that, and Alexander cut in calmly, 'You've obviously lost your powers of discernment, Lucinda,' he said. 'I have no such problems. Janet was a loyal, hard-working, good-natured professional and was seldom away. She was with me for fifteen years.' He paused, glancing at Sabrina. 'And I very much hope that Sabrina will beat that,' he added, though thinking that that wasn't likely. Sabrina would want to return to her own line when the time was right.

Lucinda slipped her arm through Alexander's and held him to her. 'Oh, we don't want to waste time talking about boring work. Now, Alex, you do remember our little arrangement…?' she said eagerly.

The expression on Alexander's face told its own story

as he stared at the woman. He answered coolly, 'What arrangement was that?'

'Oh, you *must* remember, surely?' Lucinda cried.

'Bad luck, Lucinda,' the others laughed. 'We told you he wouldn't have given it another thought!'

'Then I'll remind you, Alex,' Lucinda persisted. 'We agreed that when I came back to the UK, if neither of us had, shall we say, settled down, we'd see what fate had in store for us. Remember now?'

'It was all a very long time ago, Lucinda,' Alexander said calmly, thinking, *and I only said that to keep you out of my face.*

'Well, *Lydia* has certainly not forgotten,' Lucinda said. She paused. 'Your mother has prepared the west wing for anyone who might need it tonight, Alex—who may prefer not to go home until tomorrow, I mean.' She looked up into Alexander's eyes. 'We'll be able to discuss things, Alex, be alone. It'll be like getting to know each other all over again.'

Sabrina felt herself go hot and cold with embarrassment at the unbridled talk going on over her head. Not embarrassed on her own behalf, but on Alexander's. But he merely shrugged his shoulders as if Lucinda had just given out the weather forecast.

'No can do, I'm afraid.' he said casually. 'It's always an early start on Mondays, and deadlines are deadlines.'

At that moment, Lydia came up to them, her face wreathed in smiles as she saw her son surrounded by adoring females. Totally ignoring Sabrina, she said, 'There, isn't this wonderful? There's nothing like a get-together with old friends!' She glanced at the expensive gold watch on her wrist. 'Dinner's being served, so come along, everyone—the night is young!'

Sabrina suddenly felt angry at the situation she was in, because it was being made absolutely clear that she was not really a guest. After all, Alexander hadn't even told his mother he was bringing her. Nothing so far had managed to put Sabrina at her ease. She was like a fish out of water. How *could* he have put her in this position, and not give a thought to her sensitivities?

By now the noise and forced gaiety in the over-crowded room was deafening, making Sabrina's head thump uncomfortably. Then she was aware that Lydia had moved next to her son, not bothering to keep her voice down.

'What on earth made you decide to bring some-one—that woman—with you tonight, Alexander?' she complained.

'Why—is there a problem?' he asked mildly.

'Yes, there is. I've naturally seated you at dinner with everyone you know,' she said firmly. 'I mean, I had no idea you were bringing anyone with you tonight, so your secretary Sabrina will have to take her place at the other end of the table. Will that do?'

Alexander waited a moment before replying, then said, 'No, I'm afraid it will not do, Lydia. For all sorts of reasons,' he added.

'Oh, *please* don't be difficult, Alexander,' Lydia said crossly. She didn't bother to lower her voice. 'The wom-an's your secretary—or your personal whatever-she-is; describe it as you will. She's not…she's not one of our crowd, is she? Surely she won't expect to be included among our inner circle?'

Not if she's got any sense, Alexander thought. He moved closer to Sabrina who, amongst this highly coloured crowd, looked to him like a desirable goddess.

Suddenly, energized into action, Sabrina spoke up, her voice clear and authoritative. She looked at Lydia squarely.

'There is no need for you to concern yourself about me,' she said. 'In fact, I don't feel like anything to eat.' She paused. 'But allow me to apologize—on Alexander's behalf—that I'm here at all, and that you were not informed that I was coming to your home tonight. Uninvited guests are seldom welcome.'

She chose not to look at Alexander, but if she had he'd have been in no doubt what her feelings were. He'd had no right to bring her with him; she hadn't wanted to come, and she wasn't wanted. He'd have the benefit of her opinion later, she thought grimly, angry colour flooding her cheeks once more.

Despite Lydia's earlier protestations, a seat next to Alexander was found for Sabrina, and in a few minutes everyone was seated at the impressive table waiting to be served. Lydia was three seats away from Sabrina, and her voice carried clearly to everyone nearby as she gossiped with the women around her.

'I cannot imagine why he brought *her* along with him,' she said, picking up her glass and drinking freely. 'I mean, that dress! You'd think she was going to a business meeting, not a *party*!'

'She obviously hasn't got a clue, Lydia,' Lucinda said loudly enough for everyone to hear. 'I mean, she doesn't look that young to me. You'd think she'd have learned *something* about what's expected.' She giggled. 'She's like a little dormouse, isn't she? I hope you've got plenty of cheese for her later!'

All those around her giggled loudly at that. Sabrina felt so totally overwhelmed at the position she was in now, she had difficulty not bursting into tears. She should never have come, never, never, never. And she'd never forgive Alexander for asking her.

Suddenly, unable to tolerate this for another moment, Alexander stood to his feet, pulling Sabrina up beside him. She glanced up quickly, her eyes moist with unshed tears.

He cleared his throat, looking around him. 'I think this is as good a moment as any to let everyone into our little secret—don't you, Sabrina?' he added, looking down at her.

'What secret? What are you on about, Alexander?' Lydia said shrilly.

'Well, for one thing, we can't stay for dinner with you after all,' he said.

'Not staying for dinner? Why ever not?' Lydia demanded.

Alexander waited a second, his eyes sending a dramatic signal to Sabrina as he squeezed her hand tightly.

'I'm afraid your…Sunday spectacular has coincided with a rather more important date in my life, *Lydia*,' he said. 'In fact, it's high time we were off.' He drew Sabrina closely to him. 'We have a rather *special* celebration of our own to attend, don't we, Sabrina?' he said.

Wide-eyed at this totally unexpected change of plan, but realizing that Alexander was looking for an excuse to leave, Sabrina returned his gaze calmly. She would respond in which ever way suited her boss, she thought.

'Of course,' she said. 'And I don't want to hurry you away, but I did make the booking for nine-thirty, and it's almost that now.' She paused. 'We mustn't be late,' she added.

Lydia was almost ready to explode with annoyance.

'What on earth is so important that you have to dash off?' she demanded.

Alexander hesitated just long enough to give his words full impact.

He glanced at his mother, and at the other women, a faint smile on the uncompromising mouth. 'Tonight, Sabrina and I are about to celebrate the fact that I have asked her not only to be my personal assistant, but to be my wife.' He looked down solemnly into the girl's wide-eyed, unbelieving gaze. 'And she has consented to do me that honour,' he added defiantly.

CHAPTER FOUR

WITH his arm closely across Sabrina's shoulders, Alexander guided her from the room and outside into the night. Neither of them said a word to each other as they walked rapidly towards the car, each fired up inside at what had just happened at the crowded dining-table.

Alexander could scarcely believe his mother's attitude and rudeness—but why was he so surprised? he asked himself. She'd never been one to consider the feelings of others, and older age was certainly not improving her in that respect.

As for Lucinda, and what she'd said, he shrugged inwardly. He didn't want to think about the woman at all. As far as he was concerned, she was a non-person, a nobody, a distant character from his past.

But Lydia could never be that distant; the blood tie was there, and couldn't be changed or ignored. He bit his lip. Even though he had made so many allowances for her behaviour when he was young, it still hurt Alexander to witness his mother's hurtful lack of concern for others. She wasn't an evil person, he thought helplessly—just impossibly egocentric.

They reached the car, and as he handed Sabrina into the passenger seat he could see that she was quietly furious with him. He raised one hand submissively, then closed the door and walked around to his side and got in, pausing for a moment before inserting the key into the ignition.

'Sorry,' he said briefly. 'It was the only thing I could come up with.'

'What? To get yourself out of the party you never wanted to come to anyway? Or were you hiding behind me to give your *lady friends* the final brush-off?' Sabrina clasped her hands together tightly, trying to regain control of her anger. It wasn't just anger she was feeling, it was acute anxiety. How on earth was this going to affect her job, her precious job? Could she possibly go on working with Alexander McDonald? Surely they'd both be horribly embarrassed in each other's company? Sabrina knew very well what she *should* do—she should give him her notice now! But did she have the strength of mind, could she afford, to walk away from that salary he was paying her?

Trying desperately hard to make some sense of this mind-boggling turn of events, she felt a surge of anger well up inside her. For his own ends, she thought, he had taken complete advantage of her, of her situation, saying the first stupid thing that had come into his head. She swallowed, keeping her voice deadly calm.

'Alexander,' she said quietly. 'I promised to be your secretary, your personal assistant, and to do everything in my power to help you with your present project. I did not expect to join you in a total and very public lie.'

'Yes. I thought you supported me very well,' he said. 'The booking you'd made for our dinner—what time did you say it was, nine-thirty?—sounded utterly convincing.' He paused and Sabrina saw his eyes twinkle maddeningly as she looked across at him. 'I'm beginning to feel quite hungry, actually,' he added.

Now he was teasing her, and this made Sabrina feel so annoyed she could have hit him.

'This isn't funny,' she said flatly. 'Because of who you are, our fictitious engagement is sure to get in the papers. What were you *thinking* of?'

He waited before replying. 'I was thinking of you,' he said quietly. 'And how you must be feeling. I was so incensed at my mother's behaviour that I decided to put the cat amongst the pigeons.' He looked across at Sabrina for a moment, thinking how unspoilt and defenceless she looked, and so appealing, even though she was clearly very angry with him. He shifted in his seat. 'And, by the way, I never hide behind anyone,' he said. 'If this does become public, we'll deny it, simple as that. It won't last more than one edition of any newspaper.' He put the key in the ignition and started the engine, glancing across at her again. 'And don't worry. You're quite safe with me. I don't intend marrying anyone—ever.'

Back at the party, with the deafening noise fuelled by drink louder than ever, Lydia looked around at the handful of her guests who'd been witness to Alexander's announcement. Determined not to let the staggering incident spoil the atmosphere, she said gaily, 'All that was total nonsense, of course! It'll never happen. My son is a writer. He's always making things up—makes his living at it!'

She paused, fixing each of them with an intensely steely gaze. 'And I do not expect a word of this to be breathed by anyone. Anyone at all.' She stared, almost glared, at the bewildered faces looking back at her. 'I hope I've made myself clear,' she added.

The four or five women concerned, looking back

fearfully at their majestic hostess, had no option but to agree that they'd all keep mum.

Sitting beside Alexander as he drove the car smoothly along the country roads, Sabrina began to calm down a bit. Although it had seemed a very impetuous thing for him to do, she couldn't help believing him when he said it had been his way of defending her feelings, of standing up for her. It certainly wasn't in his own interests to have said such a thing. Sabrina breathed a long, deep sigh and glanced across at him, at the chiselled features and strong chin, at the strength of his thighs clearly visible beneath the fine fabric of his trousers. She decided to offer an olive branch.

'I'm quite hungry too,' she said.

At once, the handsome face creased into a broad grin, and without looking at her he said, 'Wonderful. I know just the place.'

Twenty minutes later, still long before they'd reached the motorway, Alexander turned left into a narrow road. Half a mile along it they could see a sign which said 'The Woodcutter'. Almost immediately he pulled into a wooded car park and brought the car to a halt, glancing briefly across at Sabrina.

'I hope you're going to like this,' he said. 'I don't manage to get here very often, but it's certainly one of my favourite places to eat.'

Sabrina was still gazing up at the inviting-looking building, which she could see was almost completely surrounded by fir trees and holly bushes. The rosy lighting which shone from every latticed window added to its welcoming appearance.

'Well, at first glance this is a delightful place,' she

said. 'And rather remote. I didn't know it existed. How did you find it?'

He smiled at her, feeling upbeat and optimistic for a second—not only because he'd successfully extricated them both from his mother's party, but because he was here with Sabrina. He realized, with a jolt of surprise, how quickly she was melding into the fabric of his life. How, from almost the first day, she'd seemed to know exactly what was required of her without any fuss or unnecessary querying. Just his sort of woman, he thought, counting himself lucky that she'd accepted the post.

'Oh, I chanced upon it several years ago after visiting my parents,' he said in answer to her question. 'I haven't been here for a while, but the chef—if it's the same one—has a fine reputation.'

Sabrina waited for him to come round and open her door, thinking that whatever was on tonight's menu she'd enjoy it, because by now she was starving.

As they walked up the short path to the entrance, a comfortably happy sound of chatting and laughter reached their ears. Sabrina felt overwhelmingly thankful that she was here and not at Lydia's party. From nightmare to nirvana, she thought instinctively.

Almost at once, the man serving drinks at the crowded bar looked up and smiled, raising his hand in greeting.

'Hi, Alex!' he called over. 'Where've you been? Hiding yourself away again?'

Alexander moved towards the bar, his hand on Sabrina's waist for a second as he guided her slightly in front of him. 'Hello, Grant. Yes, sorry, I've been out of touch for a while.' He paused, noting the man's questioning glance in Sabrina's direction. 'I've brought my secretary, Sabrina, with me tonight for a well-deserved supper. Have you still got a table available?'

Grant nodded affably. He'd make sure he'd accommodate Alexander McDonald, his most famous customer. He finished pulling a pint for the man he was dealing with, then came from behind the bar to join Alexander and Sabrina. 'Sit over there by the window just for ten minutes, Alex,' he said. 'I'll send someone to take your drinks order, and a table will be available in the restaurant at nine-thirty. Is that OK?'

Sabrina and Alexander exchanged smiles, and he said, 'That suits us perfectly, doesn't it, Sabrina? Thanks, Grant.'

Sitting at their discreet table for two, Sabrina looked around her appreciatively, realizing just how much she'd missed this kind of occasion. As she looked up into the solemn gaze of Alexander's black eyes, studying her intently, she had to admit that she wasn't going to complain at being here. To be with such a handsome and attentive member of the opposite sex had a certain palpable magic, so she might as well enjoy it, she thought. Enjoy this evening which seemed to be turning into a theatrical production.

As the light from the candle flickering on the table in front of them lit up Sabrina's features, and her thoughts, Alexander sensed again that there was an unusual depth to her character—a depth which he'd like to delve into.

He suddenly remembered her telling him at the interview that she had a sister, so casually he enquired, 'How is your sister at the moment? I think you mentioned that she didn't enjoy the best of health.'

Brought back abruptly from her lingering thoughts, Sabrina put down her glass and looked across at him.

As her wide and moist eyes looked into his, Alexander had difficulty in not gently putting his fingers beneath her chin and tilting her face closer to his. Instead, he put down his own glass and waited for her to reply to his question.

'I sincerely hope that Melly is very well,' she said lightly. She paused. 'She flew to Spain this morning, on a teaching contract for a couple of weeks. I'm hoping that the complete change will do her good, cheer her up.' Sabrina sipped her drink. 'It's a music-and-dance school,' she explained. 'She's already texted to let me know they've arrived safely and are settling in.'

Alexander hadn't taken his eyes off her as she spoke. 'Melly is younger than you?' he asked, guessing that this was the case, because Sabrina's whole attitude told him that she obviously felt responsible for her sister.

'Only a couple of years,' Sabrina said. 'But she's sometimes rather vulnerable when life seems to get the better of her, and I do have to pick up some pieces occasionally.' She looked away for a moment. Melly was hundreds of miles away tonight, and must look after herself, but Sabrina was here sitting opposite the man who earlier this evening had taken it upon himself to inform anyone listening that she was about to become his wife! Another sudden wave of hot embarrassment swept over her as she remembered. That she was about to calmly eat supper with Alexander McDonald, and make inconsequential conversation with him, seemed absurd. She cleared her throat; she had to say something more about it, she thought.

'I know you made light of what happened at Lydia's party,' she said carefully. 'But I don't feel as convinced as you seem to be that no more will come of it.' She hesitated, lowering her voice. 'I still can't quite believe you said all that,' she added. 'I nearly dropped through the floor.'

'Well, you covered your discomfort very well,' he said smoothly. 'No one could have guessed that you weren't totally aware of—and happily in accordance with—the announcement.' He grinned suddenly, disarmingly. 'Forget it, Sabrina. It was an unexpected one-off, an unforeseen circumstance which we dealt with perfectly. And nothing has changed between us,' he said, leaning forward. 'You are my PA, and I am your somewhat demanding employer who expects you to rise to any occasion that may present itself. Which you did, with flying colours.' He sat back, as if that was the end of the matter. 'Ah, good, here comes our supper,' he said cheerfully.

To her surprise, Sabrina knew that she was going to be able to eat every morsel of the delicious food put in front of them, even though she admitted to feeling slightly traumatized at what had happened still. To hear herself discussed so publicly and so unpleasantly had been a horrible experience, and she knew she wouldn't forget it for a long time. Then, even worse, for Alexander to have announced that she'd accepted his proposal of marriage still left her feeling shattered. It was like a silly dream, the sort of thing which she and Melly sometimes told each other about as they chatted at breakfast time—though Melly's dreams were always more highly coloured than her own.

Sabrina shrugged inwardly. She and her boss would really have to forget that the wretched business had ever taken place, even though she knew, whatever he said, that she was going to feel awkward when she turned up for work tomorrow morning. How could she help it?

But now, as far as he was concerned, Alexander

seemed completely unfazed as he tucked into the rare steak he'd ordered. He glanced across at her.

'I thought you said you were hungry,' he said casually. 'You're not eating anything.'

Sabrina smiled quickly, then picked up her knife and fork. From the first mouthful her lamb cutlet and salad proved to be as mouth-watering as it looked.

'I was just thinking,' she said. 'That's all.'

'And apparently you can't eat and think at the same time?' he enquired, reaching for more mustard.

Sabrina didn't bother to answer that. Then she asked curiously, 'Why do you call your mother by her Christian name?'

Alexander didn't look up as he replied. 'Because that is what she told us to do when we were kids, my brother and I.' He picked up his glass of wine. 'Lydia never took kindly to motherhood, I'm afraid,' he went on, 'so as long as we didn't call her Mother—or, perish the thought, Mummy—she could forget she was one.' He looked thoughtful for a moment. 'Not long after I was born she got herself sterilized to avoid the fatal mistake of conceiving any more little brats.' His mouth twisted briefly. 'Makes you wonder why she bothered in the first place.'

Sabrina kept her eyes on her plate as she listened, her professional mind already forming familiar patterns. 'And your father—what about him?' she asked lightly, trying not sound as if she was interviewing a patient.

'Oh, no such hang-ups for Dad,' Alexander said. 'Even though Lydia wanted us to call him Angus. But he wouldn't hear of it, and we never did.'

'Was he at the party tonight?' Sabrina enquired innocently, realizing that she was developing an almost clinical interest in the McDonald family.

'Well, I didn't see him,' Alexander replied. 'But then, my mother's parties were never his thing. And as he works for an international bank he's seldom at home. Which gives him the perfect excuse,' Alexander added wryly.

By now, the good food, wine and enveloping warmth of the place were filling Sabrina with an overwhelming sense of contentment, so that everything that had happened earlier was actually beginning to slip comfortably into the background. Perhaps the news wouldn't get out and nothing would come of it, as Alexander had said, she thought. Then everyone, including herself, could forget the whole thing.

'You're thinking again,' Alexander accused her lightly. She smiled across at him now, the candlelight making her eyes more sparklingly green than ever as she trapped his gaze, holding him spellbound for a second.

'Sorry. I do rather a lot of it,' she said. 'Part of my training, I'm afraid.'

Suddenly, abruptly, he said, 'Is there a man in your life, Sabrina?'

The unexpectedness of the question almost threw her for a moment, then she smiled crookedly.

'Not any more,' she said quietly.

There was a long pause, during which neither of them spoke.

'Stephen—my fiancé—was killed in a tragic, bizarre accident eighteen months ago.'

'I'm sorry.'

Sabrina shrugged briefly. 'Time passes. One has to accept what life throws at you.' She drained her glass. 'I don't expect ever to marry now,' she went on casually. 'For one thing, my sister comes first. And for another…' Sabrina looked wistful as she looked across at Alexander. 'I don't intend placing myself at the mercy of fate a second time. It's just not worth the risk. Or the agony.'

Much later, after he'd dropped Sabrina back home, Alexander sat in his study, his legs propped up on the desk, and stared pensively into his glass of whisky. That had been quite an evening, he thought, and it hadn't turned out as badly as he might have expected.

To his own enormous surprise, he realized that he had really enjoyed being off-duty with Sabrina Gold, that he had not wanted the evening to end. His new secretary didn't fall into the normal category of womankind he'd been used to—all of whom had very quickly bored him to death. Which was probably all his own fault, he reasoned. So, what? What was bugging him like this at gone one o'clock in the morning? He frowned briefly as his thoughts ran on. Why would such a young, beautiful woman declare herself out of bounds for the rest of her life? Why was she so negative about her possible future?

He drained his glass, then swung his legs from the desk and stood up. What the hell was it to him, anyway? he asked himself. His mouth twisted. At least there was one good thing about it—with no man on the scene, there wouldn't be any occasional stupid, romantic emotional problems to deal with, to hold things up here. His work was the only important thing to be considered.

He stared down at the shadowy garden below, at the street lights casting their gentle beams across the grass, then turned abruptly and strode from the room.

Alexander McDonald knew exactly what was getting to him. For some reason, he was suddenly feeling emotionally out of his depth where his secretary was concerned. But why? Well, he'd soon put that right, he thought irritably. Tomorrow morning it would be Cinderella time—business as usual!

CHAPTER FIVE

AMAZINGLY, Sabrina managed to feel fairly normal when she arrived for work the next morning, even though she'd found it very difficult to get any sleep.

Once again, Maria was just leaving the house, and the two women smiled at each other.

'Hullo, dear,' Maria said. 'My, you do look smart. What an unusual-colour top you've got on: what do you call that?'

'I think it's taupe,' Sabrina replied, thinking that she didn't feel very smart this morning. She'd woken late and grabbed the first thing that had come to hand in her wardrobe. But she was glad of the compliment.

'I'll just pop along to the shop and get Mr McDonald his newspapers,' Maria said as she went past. 'I'll leave them all in the kitchen, as usual. He's already working in the study,' she added over her shoulder.

The mere mention of newspapers made Sabrina's tongue go dry; there couldn't possibly be anything in them about Alexander yet, surely?

She tapped lightly on the door of the study before going in. Alexander looked up, angry at the rush of pleasure he felt at seeing her again, especially as he'd given himself a good talking-to last night before he'd eventually got to sleep. His unusual interest in his new secretary was totally unexpected, totally unlike him, and if he wasn't careful it was going to intrude on his work plans. He was not interested in Sabrina Gold's past life and loves or her future, he told himself. The only thing which concerned him was the present and her presence here as his personal assistant.

'I'd like all this typed up ASAP—and then I want to hear you read it out,' he said, deliberately keeping his tone formal. He sighed. 'I think I'm getting there, at last, and not before time,' he added, handing Sabrina a thick sheaf of papers.

Sabrina couldn't help smiling inwardly. As he had said would be the case, today and from now on it would be business as usual. She was his secretary and he was the boss. Could it only have been a handful of hours ago that they'd sat opposite each other, drinking wine, letting their hair down, telling each other things?

She avoided looking at him again, immediately setting to work, and before long she found herself engrossed in the writing she was typing out. He was an outstanding author; she really must find time to read one of his books for herself. Even from the fragmented chapters she'd so far seen, she'd felt completely immersed in the lives of his complex characters. No wonder he sometimes looked as if he was in another world, she thought.

It was almost twelve before Sabrina was satisfied that she'd got everything typed up accurately before printing it out. She stretched back, raising her arms above her head and flexing her tense shoulder muscles. She and her boss had not exchanged a word for almost three hours, and had not even been disturbed by the phone ringing for once. Sabrina realized, with a slight pang of guilt, that she hadn't made them any coffee yet, either.

She glanced across at Alexander who was sitting with

his back to her, staring thoughtfully up at the ceiling. She cleared her throat.

'Sorry; I've been so engrossed, I forgot all about our coffee.'

He turned his head slowly to look at her. 'That isn't important,' he said. 'Anyway, isn't it nearly time we thought about something for our lunch?'

Suddenly the telephone rang, and Sabrina automatically reached out to answer it, colour flooding her cheeks as Lydia's familiar voice reached her ears.

'Hello? This is Lydia. Is that you, Alexander? I have been trying all morning to reach you on your mobile, but you seem to have switched it off.'

'Um, just a second; I'll see if Mr McDonald is available,' Sabrina said faintly, trying not to sound panicky. 'It's Lydia,' she mouthed to Alexander.

He raised his eyes briefly, but picked up his extension.

'Good morning, Lydia,' he said casually.

'Why on earth aren't you using your mobile, Alexander? I do not expect to have to ring the office in order to speak to my son.'

'There are certain points in my working life, Lydia, when I need to be unavailable—to all-comers.' He paused. 'Anyway, how can I help? There's nothing wrong, I hope?'

'Of course there's nothing wrong. Not with me, anyway!' Lydia sighed heavily. 'I really rang to find out how *you* were this morning. It was strange that you went home so early last night. I hardly had time to speak to you at all.' There was a moment's pause. 'I suppose you had to get back to your writing.'

Alexander smiled slowly to himself, catching Sabrina's eye for a second. This was obviously a fishing phone-call, he thought, for his mother to find things out. Of course, he knew that his mother was not going to sully her lips by referring to the engagement announcement. She was certainly not going to bring his secretary into the conversation, nor to even mention her by name. It was obvious that Lydia was going to pretend that the incident had never taken place—so he would play her game, which would be convenient for all concerned.

'Oh, my work is always *much* more important to me than socializing, Lydia. You know that,' he said. 'And, as a matter of fact, I have exactly four weeks to meet the deadline for my current novel and I still haven't completed the penultimate chapter. So, as you can imagine, my time is precious.'

There was more silence as Lydia battled with her thoughts. Then she said, 'Well, just so long as you're feeling OK, Alexander. I did wonder, you know, last night, whether you may have been overdoing things a bit—losing your grip on reality,' she added through pursed lips.

Alexander couldn't help a slow smile creasing his mouth. 'Whatever would give you that idea, Lydia?' he said. 'No, I assure you that I'm perfectly well and in full possession of all my faculties. You really mustn't worry about me.'

He could almost see his mother shake her head in total perplexity, and he was enjoying every moment of her confusion.

'So, if there's nothing else, Lydia, I must fly.' He shuffled some papers and yawned volubly. 'And now my lovely secretary is about to make me a nice sandwich for my lunch before a meeting with my editor later this afternoon.'

They ended the call, and he looked across at Sabrina.

'You no doubt got the gist of all that, I'm sure?' he said casually. He paused. 'My mother has always been very good at sweeping anything which she doesn't like under the carpet.' He stood up. 'That is why she deliberately did not mention our *exciting* news.' He grinned suddenly. 'I'm sure she was hoping for some further information on the matter—hopefully a denial or, heaven help her, a confirmation. And I had the greatest pleasure in not providing either.'

He looked at Sabrina solemnly. 'So there you have it, Sabrina. Least said, soonest mended. You can forget the whole thing.'

Sabrina looked at him doubtfully. 'But what about Lucinda...and the others?'

Alexander walked over to the door. 'Oh, I'm quite certain my mother would have given them all precise instructions to keep their mouths shut... Anyway, by the end of yesterday evening, they would all have been very much the worse for wear. Probably don't remember anything at all today.'

Although Sabrina wasn't entirely convinced at that, she realized that Alexander was probably right. He clearly understood his mother and her friends very well. In any case, perhaps what had happened last night wasn't all that unusual. Maybe he had done this kind of thing before—after all, she knew nothing about the details of his personal life and loves. He might have had many fleeting relationships that no one took seriously, that came to nothing.

She followed him as they went downstairs into the kitchen. As usual, Maria had brought plenty of food in, and soon Sabrina was filling fresh slices of bread with succulent ham and some grated cheese while Alexander made their coffee.

Presently, sitting side by side on the tall stools by the kitchen bar, he glanced across at her.

'I've told you all about my parents,' he said between mouthfuls. 'What about yours? Are they still...?'

'Oh, Philippa, my mother, moved to Australia over ten years ago with her new husband,' Sabrina said. 'My father walked out on us when I was seven. I hardly remember what he looked like,' she added casually. 'My sister was only five then, and as my mother had to go out to work to support us it fell to me to look after the house, always to be there to take care of Melly.' Sabrina paused, picking up her mug of coffee. 'Anyway, some years later—I was sixteen—my mother met David, an Australian. After a whirlwind affair they married and went to live in Sydney.' She sipped from her mug. 'We hear from them. Occasionally,' she added.

There was silence for a few seconds. 'I imagine you had to grow up pretty quickly, Sabrina, having to take responsibility for your sister from such a young age after your father abandoned his family.'

Sabrina smiled quickly. 'I never really thought about it like that,' she said. 'But, yes, I suppose I did grow up almost overnight. Anyway.' She nibbled at her sandwich. 'Melly and I were always close, even as small kids—it sort of came naturally to me to take care of her,' she added.

'Do you go to Australia much to see your mother?' Alexander wanted to know.

'We've been twice,' Sabrina said. She hesitated. 'Time and distance eventually alienates you even from close relations,' she said simply. 'My mother has a new life, new friends. She can well do without us hindering her plans.' Sabrina's mouth twisted briefly. 'I got the distinct impression that she was relieved to wave us off back home last time.'

Alexander looked solemn for a moment, an unexpected rush of compassion filling him as he considered what Sabrina had just told him. She hadn't exactly had an easy life, he thought, yet she'd never demonstrated even a hint of self-pity in her attitude—except, perhaps, when she'd spoken about her fiancé last night. No, not self-pity, he amended, just sadness—genuine sadness.

Suddenly Sabrina smiled brightly. 'But the good news is that my sister seems to be on cloud nine at the moment. We had a long, long phone-call early today, and all the signs are very positive. The people she's with are very friendly and helpful, and she loves the place they're staying in. In fact, she sounded happier than she's been for a long time. Apparently work starts in earnest tomorrow, and she can't wait!'

'That must be a real relief for you,' Alexander said, feeling glad for Sabrina's sake. Well, anyone would feel sympathy for another human being who'd had more than her fair share of life's custard pies, he thought. He couldn't help comparing Sabrina's lot with his own and his brother's. Although Lydia had always been a non-parent, he and Bruno had never wanted for any material thing, had never known hardship of any kind. Angus was a loyal and affectionate father, even though he was so often away from the UK. And there had always been others on hand to supply their every need.

But what of his relationship with *his* sibling? Alexander asked himself. The two boys had always been grimly competitive, that was a well-known fact. It was fortunate that the famous brothers had each been so highly successful in their different careers. But they certainly did not enjoy the warmth and closeness that

Sabrina and her sister so obviously did, and for the first time in his life Alexander felt regretful about that. He stared out of the window for a second as he finished the last of his coffee. It must be good, it must be brilliant, to be so deeply loved by anyone, he thought. Loved selflessly, with no regrets and with no expectation of anything in return. Just love for its own sake.

Sabrina got down from her stool and turned to Alexander. 'More coffee?' she asked, and he shook his head.

'No thanks, I'm fine for now.' He glanced at his watch. 'I'll go and pick up the printout you did this morning and take it with me to the editor. I'm due in town shortly.' He paused. 'There's all the scribbles I did earlier relating to my final chapter for you to decipher, Sabrina,' he said, and paused. 'I should be back by five-thirty, but if I'm going to be delayed I'll give you a ring.'

'Fine,' Sabrina said as she drew water into the sink to wash up their things, privately making up her mind that with Alexander safely out of the way she would find time to clean up the study a bit. Working amongst dust and disorder put her teeth on edge. She'd already spotted where Maria kept all the dusters and polish.

As Alexander was about to leave the room, his mobile rang and he glanced over at Sabrina as he clicked it on. 'I knew this morning had been just too peaceful,' he said. 'Hi, Bruno!'

It suddenly struck Sabrina as weird that she was finding herself caught up in the lives of the famous McDonald brothers. As she glanced briefly over at Alexander, she saw him make a face.

'I'm honestly too caught up here with my own stuff to offer you any time, Bruno,' he began, then stopped as Bruno interrupted. After a couple of minutes he said, 'Oh, OK, then. Look, why don't you send the script over for me to have a look at first, then perhaps we could have a bite out somewhere on Sunday at lunch time.' He paused. 'We haven't got together for a long time, Bruno. It'll be a chance to put that right.' Even as he spoke, Alexander was surprised at his own suggestion, but knew that Sabrina's influence had something to do with it. Perhaps he and Bruno should make time to see each other now and then. Neither of them made any effort in that direction, he thought, but it was never too late to change things.

There was another pause as he listened to his brother again. 'OK, fine. And if I'm not here my secretary will be, and you can give it to her. What? No, no, it's not Janet. She's retired and I've got a new PA now. Sabrina. Yes, Sabrina! And yes, yes…' Sabrina saw Alexander make another face. 'Yes, Bruno, have no fear of that… And she's competent as well,' he said flatly.

The call ended and Alexander glanced back at Sabrina as he went towards the door. 'Someone will be calling by to drop an envelope in at some point—could be this week, it could be next,' he said. 'Anyway, see you later,' he added briefly as he left the room.

That was the trouble with Bruno, Alexander thought irritably as he went up the stairs. He only ever thought of women in terms of their sex appeal. His brother had immediately wanted to know what Sabrina looked like, whether she had a good figure…. Alexander had far too much respect, especially since Sabrina had been listening!

As he went into his bathroom for a quick wash and brush-up, he looked thoughtfully at himself in the mirror for a second. How *would* he describe Sabrina to someone who'd never met her? he thought. Well, there was no difficulty there. She was small, with small hands and feet and a heart-shaped face, a slightly tip-tilted nose and desirable, full lips; she had long, fair hair almost down to her waist but always immaculately groomed. But the colour of those eyes, those magical eyes… They were a translucent green, like the deepest part of a placid ocean.

But… She wore no make-up, no nail varnish, no heady, sickening perfume; no pretence of any kind.

Not Bruno's type at all, Alexander thought with some satisfaction.

Later, armed with a floor cloth, disinfectant, polish and some dusters, Sabrina went upstairs to the study. Through the partly open door of a large cupboard along the landing, she'd seen a vacuum cleaner and brushes. Good; that should all be quite sufficient to sort out Alexander McDonald's mess, she thought.

The first thing she did was to open all the windows in the study and let in some fresh air. Then, turning, she went across to the *chaise longue*, filled her arms with all the cushions and went over to bang them furiously together out through the window. The dust flew out in clouds, causing her to sneeze three times in quick succession. That hadn't been done in a long time, she thought—but no blame could be attached to Maria, who wasn't even allowed in this room.

A sudden thought struck Sabrina for a moment and she went over to the small pile of dusters, selecting one which had obviously not been used, because it was still neatly folded, and tied it around her head. At least that would be some protection.

Then she started to tackle the floor. Masses of dust

had gathered along the skirting boards and in the corners; picking up a broom, she began sweeping it up carefully, collecting it in the dustpan she'd found. The vacuum cleaner could do the rest, she thought, going over to switch it on.

As she moved the machine briskly over the huge Persian rug, she soon began to see the colourful design beneath. Although it clearly wasn't new, it was a beautiful piece of soft furnishing which must have cost a fortune. When she'd finished that, she got down on her hands and knees and polished the dark-oak flooring until it shone, realizing that she was actually enjoying doing all this. She'd never minded house work in any case, but doing it in someone else's place was slightly more interesting, or so it seemed just then. When she was satisfied that the whole area resembled something other than a receptacle for grime, Sabrina stood back and surveyed it critically. Well, that would do for a start.

But there was still a long way to go, and for the next two hours she took down and wiped clean all the books from the shelves, polished the oak doors of the fitted cupboards and worked a damp sponge along the window frames.

She decided to leave Alexander's desk until last. Then she suddenly realized that there was still the old granite fireplace to deal with, almost hidden by a couple of high-backed chairs standing in front of it. With almost wild abandon, she scooped up all the bric-a-brac from the mantelpiece: old post cards, a torch which didn't work, a box of matches, a nail file, a cork screw, a box of tissues, another one of plasters and some cough sweets. She shook her head as she put it all to one side. *How can anyone—how can Alexander McDonald—live like this?* she thought. But then, he didn't live here, this was where he worked. And none of this disorder registered with him. He only had eyes for the words taking form in front of him.

Standing in front of the chimneypiece was a huge jug of dried flowers long past their sell-by date, so that they had mostly disintegrated into a powdery heap. Well, she'd dump those and replace them with some fresh greenery from the garden. She'd spotted plenty of bushes down there that had some colourful leaves on one or two of them.

When she finally got round to tidying his desk, Sabrina realized that here she must not take liberties. This was Alexander's domain, and he wouldn't like anything put back differently.

Sitting herself in his chair for a moment, it gave Sabrina a genuine thrill as she stared at everything in front of her. There were countless pens, pencils—most of them chewed at the top—rubbers, sticking tape, directories and reference books. Not many people had the chance to sit here where all the imagination flowed, all the expertise, culminating in Alexander's books, which sold in their millions. Almost reverentially, Sabrina cleaned the dust from every corner of the desk, wiped over the computer and telephone and tidied the books, before replacing everything she'd moved back to where it had been before.

Suddenly, a small snapshot fell to the floor; it had obviously been tucked inside a page somewhere. Picking it up, Sabrina saw that it was a picture of a somewhat younger Alexander on a beach somewhere, tanned and wearing a brief pair of swimming trunks, his arms clasped tightly around the waist of a dark-haired young woman in a bikini. She was gazing up at him adoringly, and the whole scene told its own story. Those were two people very much in love.

Sabrina put the snap back into one of the books, wondering who that girl had been. Someone who was once very special to Alexander, she thought.

Then she shrugged. There were no doubt plenty of other photographs like that, of other women in his life—why did it bother her? And of course it didn't, not a bit.

Decisively, Sabrina finished what she was doing before putting away all the cleaning stuff she'd been using. Then, letting herself out of the back entrance, she slipped outside into the garden to pick an armful of foliage to put in the jug. It cheered that black grate up no end. Looking around at her afternoon's handiwork, she felt satisfyingly gratified. The whole room looked pleasant now, almost habitable.

Glancing at her watch, Sabrina saw that it was already five-thirty—and she hadn't done a scrap of that typing he'd left for her! *Help!* He would be back soon, because he hadn't rung to say he was delayed.

Suddenly feeling quite exhausted, Sabrina moved over to the *chaise longue* and without thinking collapsed down on to it, lying down and resting her head back, closing her eyes. Just for a few moments, she thought. Just a few moments to recover.

Alexander looked down at the sleeping form of his secretary, a strange expression on his face. His gaze swept around the room, taking in the shining floorboards, the amazingly bright rug, the books on his shelves standing to attention, the smell of polish and fresh air and the casually elegant display of greenery in the fireplace. A slow smile touched his lips as he stood, motionless, for a few moments. Well, she'd asked permission to clean up and he'd agreed. He had to admit that an unusual sense of well-being came over him as he looked around. It was a very pleasant experience to see his study—which somctimes felt like his prison—so *cared-for.*

Then his eyes softened as he looked back at Sabrina. Even with a bright-yellow duster tied around her head and a dark smudge of dust on her nose, she looked, well, wonderful, he thought. Wonderful, vulnerable… He turned abruptly to leave the room just as her eyes flickered open, and shc struggled to sit up.

'Heavens! What's the time?' she faltered, looking up at him. 'I only meant to sit down for a momcnt. I must have dozed off…'

'Well, from what I can see all around me, I'm not surprised,' Alexander said, reaching his hand out to raise her up. 'It's six. It took me a bit longer to get back, I'm afraid.' He paused. 'Sabrina, you've transformed the study. Thank you—thank you very much.'

She smilcd up at him. 'I quite enjoyed doing it, but I haven't done any of the rather more important work you left for me, Alexander…'

He placed his hand briefly on her shoulder. 'There's always tomorrow,' he said. 'And now I'm going to take you home. You've had a long, long day.'

CHAPTER SIX

ON THURSDAY, two weeks later, Sabrina was feeling so involved with Alexander McDonald's work and life-style, she felt she'd known him for ever. They seemed to have developed a rapport so quickly that any dread she might have felt about working for such an important man—who'd left her in no doubt at the interview that a lot would be expected of her—had disappeared almost overnight. But she did concede that her own qualifications had been an advantage because she had learned to read his mindset straight away, and knew when it was wise to say something or when to keep quiet. And she took it as a great compliment that he sometimes asked her opinion about something he was agonizing over as he wrote. She realized, with some surprise, that even great writers seemed to need constant reassurance and encouragement. The fact that he ran something by her occasionally made her feel ridiculously proud.

To her relief, the penultimate chapter of his current novel had been approved, and now they were well into the final moments, the denouement of the story. How on earth was he going to bring it all together? she asked herself.

As she typed up the first draft of the last chapter, she felt herself completely caught up with the plot, as if this total fiction of his mattered, really mattered. She would buy his books from now on, she decided, all of them. Because now she had an intensely personal interest in anything and everything that concerned Alexander McDonald.

Of course by now his dreadful scrawl had become as plain as day to Sabrina. What she'd found so difficult to make out on that first day was not difficult any more. He seemed amazed at how quickly she was able to pass him the most recent printout.

Sabrina's present feeling of being so upbeat had a lot to do with Melly's experience in Spain. They'd only had three phone conversations since she had left, and each one had been full of how well everything was going over there; how Melly was being complimented on her work and attitude; how much fun she was having. Sabrina could barely recognize the voice at the other end. Her sister was usually the one whose pint was always half-empty rather than half-full, but there was no hint of pessimism now. She was having a ball, and although Sabrina was careful not to mention anything about health it was quite obvious that her sister was feeling on top of the world, with no talk of her being depressed or anxious about anything at all. A hasty text this week had informed Sabrina that the tour had been extended, possibly for two or three weeks.

At around midday the front-door bell rang and Sabrina stopped typing and looked up in surprise. They seldom, if ever, had any visitors.

Going downstairs, she opened the door to see the instantly recognizable figure of Bruno McDonald standing there, casually dressed in black trousers and blue rugby-shirt. He was tall and broad-shouldered, and although there was an obvious likeness to his brother it was clear at Sabrina's first glance that it was Alexander who'd been especially endowed by nature. For one thing, Bruno did not possess the same spectacular jet-black eyes, the same magnetic, searching expression…

His smile was friendly, and more than interested in Sabrina as he looked down at her.

'Ah, you must be the new secretary—the lovely Sabrina,' he drawled lazily, his glance sweeping from Sabrina's face, down the entire length of her body and back again, making her feel as if she was standing there with nothing on.

'Yes, I'm Sabrina, Mr McDonald,' she said hesitantly. 'I'm afraid your brother is not here at the moment. He goes to the gym on Thursdays.'

Bruno waited a second before answering. 'Yes, I know, and I realized he probably wouldn't be back yet. But I was in the area and thought it worth dropping in. I want to talk to him about something he's looking at for me.' He smiled slowly. 'I'll come in and wait for him.'

Sabrina stood back at once for him to come inside. 'Of course. Can I make you a coffee?'

'That would be most kind, Sabrina.' The words which anyone might use, but spoken in that particular way, made Sabrina feel distinctly uncomfortable. She hoped Alexander wouldn't be long.

Bruno followed her along the hall into the kitchen, and presently stood idly leaning against the wall, his hands in his pockets, watching Sabrina as she filled the kettle.

'So, how long has…Sabrina been working for my brother?' he enquired.

'Oh, just a few weeks,' Sabrina replied, not looking at him, not wanting to make eye contact.

'Well, now, and what's he like as an employer?'

Bruno said. 'Of course, the other woman—Janet—was with him for absolutely ages, put up with him for years, so I suppose she was used to his ways. But—' he paused '—I imagine that Alexander can be difficult—a bit of a brute at times.'

Now Sabrina turned and looked at Bruno squarely. 'On the contrary,' she said coolly, 'I have never found Mr McDonald to be anything other than entirely businesslike and professional.'

How dreadful was this? she thought. Discussing Alexander under his own roof with a complete stranger, even if it was with a member of the family. She was beginning to heartily dislike the man standing there beside her. If his manner and approach were anything to go by he couldn't be less like Alexander. Even at the very beginning Sabrina had always felt relaxed and comfortable with her boss, which was not how she was feeling at the moment.

'Well, well, perhaps you're a good influence on him,' Bruno said languidly. 'Maybe a fresh face…and a fresh figure…was what he'd needed all along,' he added with heavy emphasis.

By now, Sabrina's nerve endings were really beginning to tingle. Any minute, Bruno McDonald was going to make a pass at her, she thought.

As she busied herself with preparing his drink, she turned and glanced back at him, changing the subject.

'I think we're having what they call an "Indian summer",' she said casually. 'For October it's really warm today, isn't it?'

'It certainly is,' he agreed. 'And I, personally, *love* warm weather because it encourages all you lovely girlies to dress in your scantiest, most revealing clothes.' He paused, deliberately staring at Sabrina again; she cringed, wishing that she'd not chosen to wear her rather low-cut top this morning. But it was the coolest one she owned, and it was sometimes rather hot working upstairs in the study.

'Of course, in winter,' he went on, 'you all insist on covering yourselves up in layers and layers of thick things. Which is such a shame for all us susceptible males lusting in the wings for a glimpse or two of the female form.'

If he doesn't shut up, Sabrina thought, irritated, *I'm going to tell him where to go.*

She was moving across to the cupboard where they kept the biscuits, standing on tiptoe to reach the tin, when Bruno immediately came up behind her. With one hand on her shoulder, he leaned across her and took the biscuits down from the shelf. With his face close to Sabrina's now, he looked down at her solemnly, and she could smell alcohol on his heavy breath.

'Now, Sabrina, if you had eaten up all your greens when you were a little girl, you would have grown a bit taller,' he said reprovingly.

Then, unbelievably, he slipped his hand from her shoulder and cupped it deliberately over her breast, squeezing it gently for a second. To which Sabrina's immediate response was to dig her elbow hard into the most vulnerable part of his solar plexus so that he staggered back, only just managing to stifle a painful, 'Ouch!'

For a few moments, Sabrina stood and glared at him, her eyes like jewelled daggers ready to strike, when thankfully the door opened and Alexander stood there. He looked first at Sabrina, then at Bruno, then back at Sabrina—and he could see straight away that something wasn't right. The atmosphere was undeniably charged, and he'd never seen an expression on Sabrina's face like that before.

Standing there in his shorts and T-shirt, his hair damp and tousled, he said, 'What's going on, Sabrina?'

'Oh, it's all right…it's nothing, really,' she began, her voice clearly unsteady.

But that tremulous remark of hers only confirmed Alexander's understanding of the situation, and for a dramatic moment he had difficulty in not punching his brother squarely between the eyes. *Bloody Bruno!*

'Alex, dear boy!' Bruno said, totally unfazed by his brother's arrival, or indeed by the thunderous look on his face. 'I thought I'd chance my luck that you might be able to see me for half an hour,' he said. He looked back at Sabrina. 'Your delightful secretary is just making me a coffee, which is sweet of her.'

But Alexander McDonald was nobody's fool, and he knew his brother. He went over to stand between Bruno and Sabrina. Putting his arm lightly on her shoulder, he could feel her shaking. 'Get out, Bruno,' Alexander said in a way that brooked no argument. 'I'm busy.'

'Oh, but I was hoping to show you this latest thing I'm interested in,' Bruno began. 'Hoping for your…input, Alex.'

'I repeat—get out,' Alexander said, keeping his voice calm with great difficulty. 'And please do not expect to just drop in any old time without letting me know first,' he added.

For the next few moments, Sabrina really thought she was going to faint. Where had she landed *this* time? Although she could see that Alexander guessed that his brother had behaved inappropriately, just how was this going to affect her chances now, her position here? Might Bruno McDonald even accuse her of leading him on, if Alexander demanded an explanation? She shuddered as she recalled his podgy hand mauling her.

But, feeling Alexander's protective grip on her shoulder, Sabrina knew that he had assessed the situation straight away, and she began to relax a bit. For her part, she would never tell her boss exactly what had upset her just now, she thought. In any case, it had hardly been the most mind-shattering thing to have taken place. But, still, it had taken her completely unawares and all she wished now was that she was out of here and safely back at home.

Alexander strode across the room and opened the door wide. 'Allow me to show you out, Bruno,' he said bluntly. 'And I repeat—next time, have the courtesy to inform me that you're going to call in. It's the least anyone should expect,' he added.

Bruno raised his arms helplessly, as if he didn't know why he was suddenly so unwelcome in his brother's house. 'Oh, deary me,' he said laconically. 'I have obviously hit a nerve or two this morning, haven't I?' He looked across at Sabrina whose cheeks had gone from rosy to almost deathly pale in the last few moments. 'You must understand, Sabrina, that we creative types can be difficult, prone to moodiness from time to time, and today is clearly one of those times. My brother doesn't seem to be a very happy boy, does he?'

Bruno sauntered over to leave the room, glancing back for a second. 'I wish you the best of luck, my dear,' he added. 'Enjoy the rest of your day.'

Then he was gone, and presently Alexander came back into the kitchen and looked down at Sabrina, who was still rooted to the spot.

'I...I won't ask you to elaborate, Sabrina,' he said quietly. 'All I will do is to apologize, profusely, for any inconvenience my brother put you to while I was out. Because clearly he had.'

Sabrina managed to smile faintly. 'I don't want to say anything about it, Alexander—as I said, it was nothing…not really. It was just a silly man behaving like silly men do. It's not the first time I've experienced it, and it won't be the last. Unfortunately,' she added.

But not from Alexander, Sabrina thought; never from him. Despite Bruno's ridiculous parting-shot, she had always felt comfortable, secure and totally at ease alone with her boss. How could two brothers be so unalike? Perhaps the touchy-feely theatrical world was to blame, she thought, glad that Melly had never been exposed to Bruno's sickening advances for more than a few moments at those auditions she'd attended. If she herself was ever put in that position with the man again, she thought savagely, she'd find an even more tender part of his anatomy to make her point.

'Well, anyway,' Alexander said, still clearly ruffled. 'Let's not ruin the rest of our day by thinking about my brother any further.' He paused. 'Do you feel like making us a sandwich while I pop up and have a quick shower? We've an afternoon's work ahead of us.'

'Wilco,' she said, touching her forehead in a mock salute.

As she prepared some toasted sandwiches for their lunch, Sabrina's thoughts centred on Melly for a moment. It seemed such a long time since her sister had left for Spain—and the girl didn't seem in any particular hurry to return! Although Sabrina was missing her a lot, she admitted to feeling carefree for the first time in ages. *Well, I'd better enjoy it*, she thought, *because when Melly returns nothing much will really have changed and there'll be the inevitable sense of anti-climax to deal with.*

But she mustn't think of all that now, she thought. She was looking forward to this afternoon, when she'd be reading aloud all the stuff she'd typed so far in this final chapter of Alexander's novel. Knowing all his characters by now, she felt she knew exactly how it should sound. How she would make it sound, bring it all to life.

Soon, now wearing dark, well-cut trousers and a fine, light-grey shirt, Alexander sat in his chair facing away from Sabrina, staring out of the window as she settled down to read the printout.

Keeping her voice firm and modulated, Sabrina began to feel something like an electric thrill coursing down her spine. This wasn't work, this was total, utter pleasure, she thought gratefully. As the simple yet masterful prose began to take shape as it was spoken aloud, Sabrina felt honoured again to be the first one, apart from the author, to hear it. It was like marking out the first footsteps on an expanse of freshly fallen snow. It was a privilege.

Alexander listened intently. She knew he wouldn't interrupt her, but once or twice she was aware of him bending his head to write something briefly on the pad on his knee.

So intensely did Sabrina feel her emotions being stirred as the story developed that, as she came to a particularly poignant section in which the two main protagonists were having a terrible, violent quarrel, her voice rose and fell in anguish at the impossible situation they were in. Why would people say such dreadful things to each other? she thought, her own thoughts silently interrupting the plot. How could anyone be so vicious? And further on, when it seemed unlikely that anything could ever be resolved, she felt such a degree of helplessness that her voice actually broke as she read out the plaintive dialogue, the longing in the sentiments expressed. It was magical writing, leaving her almost breathless.

It took more than half an hour for Sabrina to get to the end, and when she'd finished she stayed quite still, looking down at the script, not wanting to break the spell which Alexander McDonald had put her under. That long, last passage had been so full of heat, of passion, that she felt physically exhausted. And when she finally looked up Alexander had swivelled his chair around and was gazing down at her, a strange expression on his face.

'Thank you, Sabrina,' he said quietly, his eyes almost melting as he saw a large tear slip down Sabrina's cheek. She was such a sensitive woman, he thought, so readily in tune with what she'd been reading.

There was a long pause. 'I just wish that everyone who read my books—read any writer's books—would take the time to engage as you've just done,' he said. 'So many people skim-read, don't give true value to all the blood, sweat and tears which go into fiction. But you, Sabrina—you just brought all that alive, even to me, who knew what was coming!' He smiled. 'In fact, I learned something fresh about my characters and their motives just listening to you.' He hesitated. 'Have you—have you ever done stage work…any acting?' he asked.

Sabrina shook her head, suddenly feeling embarrassed that she'd had difficulty restraining her tears, knowing that he'd seen them. 'No, that's not my thing,' she said, wiping her nose with a tissue. 'That's my sister's domain.'

Alexander cleared his throat. 'One or two small points did strike me which I'd like us to discuss.'

He identified the parts he was referring to, and for the next hour they picked over his doubts together, tossing ideas back and forth between them. Sabrina could never have dreamed in a million years that she'd ever be asked to do such a thing. Alexander seemed to take on board every suggestion she plucked up the courage to make.

Finally, Sabrina stood up. 'I'm in need of a strong cup of tea, Alexander.'

'I think we could both do with a break,' he said. 'That was quite a marathon. But useful, very useful.'

After she had gone downstairs, Alexander sat staring into space for a while, still hearing Sabrina's sweet voice lingering in his ears. He admitted to a feeling of disquiet suddenly, because he realized that his new secretary was making herself so indispensable to him it would be an almost impossible task ever to do without her. But one day he would have to; he knew that. With her qualifications, it was obvious that she would want to return to her own profession at some point, and he would never try to dissuade her. That would be unfair; wrong. It wasn't just the fact that her work was so neat and meticulous, it was everything else which any employer yearned for in an employee—an attitude, a readiness to comply, to take the rough with the smooth, to be flexible and still keep a smile on her face.

He sighed heavily. The thought that one day she wouldn't be sitting there in his study filled him with an acute depression. Depression, something that hit him from time to time, had been blissfully absent since he'd taken her on. Then he squared his shoulders. For heaven's sake, she hadn't resigned—not yet—and it could be well into next year before the economic situation improved and she was offered her job back. Until then, she was his. He was paying good money—and he'd pay more if necessary to keep her by his side.

Later, as they sipped their tea in comparative silence, each with their own thoughts, Alexander said, 'I think it's time to call it a day, now, Sabrina. We're both tired.'

He looked down at her, for the first time noticing how some loose fronds of her hair had escaped from the band she was wearing and were falling prettily either side of her face and across her forehead. It made her look child-like and, to him, utterly adorable. He wished he had the courage to gently put those wavy fronds back in place, to trail his fingers over her cheeks for a moment as he did it, a familiar act like a lover or a husband might do.

He dragged his gaze from her. 'I'm going to take you home now,' he said.

'No, honestly, Alexander. There's no need. It only takes an hour for me to get back,' Sabrina said, but he interrupted.

'I do have an ulterior motive,' he said. 'If we go now, it'll give you a chance to freshen up before I take you out to supper.' He paused, looking down at her. 'I think you deserve a hearty meal—and the other day when I dropped you home I spotted a very nice-looking Italian place nearby…'

'Oh yes, that's Marco's,' Sabrina said. 'It's good. Melly and I go there sometimes.' *After I've been paid*, she thought. 'And we might discuss the next steps in chapter forty,' she suggested. 'Only if you want to,' she added hastily.

'Um, yes, we might,' he agreed. 'Or, there again, we might not. We might well feel we've had quite enough of that for one day. Besides,' he said as they left the kitchen together. 'I have another, slightly different, proposition to put to you. If it fits in with your personal plans,' he added enigmatically.

CHAPTER SEVEN

SABRINA had to admit that being driven home in Alexander's swish car could hardly be compared with her usual trek, involving walking and being squashed in the tube after a long day. As usual, the traffic was heavy, and it had gone six o'clock by the time they pulled up at the house. Sabrina's car was outside in its allotted parking space, but for once there was a spare slot opposite for Alexander to leave the Aston Martin.

He glanced across. 'Do we need to book a table at the restaurant?' he asked, and Sabrina shook her head.

'I don't think so, as it's Thursday. Weekends are always the busiest.'

Before he could get out, Sabrina opened her door and was already making her way up the short front path before he joined her. As they went inside, she looked up at him quickly.

'Do you want the TV on while I have a shower?' she asked, thinking that after the day she'd just had the thought of soaping herself under some nice, warm water was just what she needed.

'You carry on—don't worry about me,' he said casually, following her into the sitting room. 'Anyway, there's no rush, is there?'

Sabrina paused by the door for a second. 'Would

you like something to drink?' she asked, then thought, what could she offer him? She certainly didn't have a well-stocked cellar to choose from. But then Alexander came to her rescue.

'No, I'm all right, thanks. But why don't I make us a cup of tea?' he suggested. 'While you're freshening up.'

'OK, let me introduce you to the kitchen,' she said.

Although Alexander had driven her home once or twice, he had never come into the house before. As he followed Sabrina along the hallway it was no surprise to him to see how well-kept everything was. He was beginning to know her by now; the recent transformation she had made to his study told its own story.

'This is due for a refit,' Sabrina said, glancing around the kitchen, slightly embarrassed. 'I've been looking at home-improvement brochures to get some ideas.'

'It looks fine to me,' Alexander said. 'And perfectly adequate for two people.' He went over to the glass-panelled back door and stared out at the garden. 'Who keeps this tidy?' he asked, observing the rectangular piece of neat lawn accompanied by small groups of flowering bushes.

'Oh, we do. But it doesn't take long, not with the size it is,' Sabrina replied, taking down the tea bags and opening the fridge for some milk.

Leaving Alexander to it, she left the room and went upstairs, knowing straight away what she was going to wear. It would be a dress for a change, she thought, a special dress.

The item she took from her wardrobe was the one she knew suited her perfectly—a simple cream number, its flimsy, floaty skirt just reaching the knee, with a somewhat dramatic gold pattern slashed across it at random intervals. Sabrina smiled as she remembered how Melly had described her in it: that it looked as if she'd been struck by lightning.

Soon, luxuriating under the shower, she leant backwards, letting the hot water drench her from head to toe. She remembered suddenly what Alexander had said earlier—that he had a proposition to put to her. What had he meant by that? Sabrina wondered. He hadn't taken it any further, and she hadn't asked him to explain. But she hoped it would be something that her circumstances could cope with; Melly was due home soon. But, still; Sabrina shrugged. She must try and co-operate with Alexander's requirements, she thought, because she was not going to give up this job with him for a long time yet. There was more money going into her bank account than she'd ever known before. Plus, she was getting used to seeing Alexander every day.

Sabrina bit her lip for a moment. During their telephone conversations, Melly had not once asked how Sabrina was getting on, how the new post was turning out for her. The talk had all been about Melly and how her life was going. But then, her sister had always been a bit like that, Sabrina admitted as she stepped from the shower and reached for a towel.

Downstairs, as Alexander sat idly watching the news with his mug in his hands, he suddenly heard a tremendous crash from above followed by an agonized shriek from Sabrina. Without hesitating for a second, he put down his tea and raced up the stairs, wondering what on earth he was going to find.

Sabrina was standing at the top clutching a huge white bath-towel around her, obviously very upset about something.

'What's going on?' he demanded. 'Are you OK, Sabrina?'

He swallowed hard. Her hair was streaming wet around her shoulders, making her look like a winsome nymph who had just emerged from a deep lake. He knew very well that she was naked and vulnerable under that towel. For a fraction of a second Alexander struggled with a natural impulse to pick her up in his arms and make love to her there on the floor at the top of the stairs…

'What's happened, Sabrina?' he repeated.

Without a word, she turned. He followed her into the bathroom, where he saw that a large mirror, still steamed up, had fallen from its place on the wall and had crashed to the floor, a huge, ugly crack right across its surface. Glancing at her quickly, he could see that she was visibly upset about it.

He stooped to examine the damage at the back of the mirror. 'There's the problem,' he said. 'The cord holding it up on the wall has frayed, that's all.' He glanced up at her. 'I'm afraid you'll have to buy another mirror, Sabrina, this one's had it.'

She shivered, her teeth chattering for a second. 'That's going to be seven years' bad luck, isn't it?'

'Rubbish,' Alexander said emphatically. 'You don't believe that stuff, do you?'

'Not really,' Sabrina said doubtfully, thinking that she and Melly didn't need any more wicked fairies planning unpleasant surprises for them. She smiled apologetically. 'Sorry to give you a shock, Alexander, but it certainly gave me one. I thought the roof was coming down on my head!'

He raised one eyebrow slightly. 'It was one hell of a

noise,' he agreed. 'I wondered what on earth could have happened.'

Suddenly, the position she was in caused Sabrina to flush to the roots of her hair. It seemed weird enough that her boss was here at all in their simple little home, but much worse was the fact that he was standing in the bathroom next to her, knowing that she had absolutely nothing on under the towel.

He bent down again and picked up the cumbersome mirror in his arms. 'This one's probably for the tip,' he said casually, noting the considerable damage to the frame. 'But fortunately the glass hasn't shattered, so there are no splinters for us to pick up.' He glanced back at her as he left the room. 'I'll bring up your tea,' he said briefly. 'It's getting cold.'

In her bedroom, Sabrina towelled herself as quickly as she could. It had never struck her that she should check the cords holding up all their pictures and mirrors, and she still felt unnerved by what had happened. She was especially unnerved because during probably the one and only time her boss would ever visit the house he'd had to witness the whole sorry thing.

Well, what was done was done, she thought. Now, slipping into her underwear, she switched the dryer to fast, brushing her hair out at the same time. It would just have to stay damp, she thought. She'd leave it loose to dry by itself, because she couldn't keep Alexander waiting any longer. Then she smoothed a trace of foundation onto her face and neck, adding a slick of eye shadow and a touch of blusher to her cheeks, before thrusting on her gold heels and going downstairs.

Alexander was lounging on the sofa, his long legs stretched out in front of him. Hearing her come in, he turned his head to gaze at her and for a second neither of them spoke. Then, 'You look beautiful,' he said briefly. He knew that he'd paid that same compliment to plenty of women in the distant past, but there'd never been a time when he'd meant it more.

Sabrina did look *divine*, he thought. That dress could have been made especially for her, and her hair—clearly still damp and floating loosely around her shoulders—made her look more seductive than she herself could possibly know. That was one of the things he liked about the woman—she seemed totally unaware of the effect she had on the people around her. Well, had on him, anyway, he admitted. And how had he allowed that to happen? he asked himself. He'd always held that mixing business and pleasure was a no-go area, well known to cause more trouble than it was worth.

They left the house and Alexander glanced down at Sabrina as they wandered along side by side, not touching.

'Won't you need a wrap of some sort?' he enquired casually, covertly admiring the creamy smoothness of her bare arms and neck, the glimpse of her delicate cleavage. 'I know we're having a phenomenally warm October, but it's bound to get cold later on.'

'No, I'll be OK—it only takes a couple of minutes to get to Marco's. And it's always pleasantly warm in there,' she replied, a little ripple of pleasure running through her at what he'd just said. It was so good to have someone—a drop-dead-gorgeous man like Alexander McDonald—be considerate of her in that way. It felt comforting, reassuring, and she suddenly felt more elated than she had for a long time. She realized just how much she'd missed going out on a date—if you could call tonight a date, she thought. Tonight was merely her boss's way of saying thank you for this afternoon's reading. But wasn't that what he was paying her for anyway? Perhaps this was by way of a bonus.

She knew that she was enjoying her present employment more than she could have dared to hope—and she had the distinct impression that Alexander wasn't finding her constant presence too intolerable. It might have been so different, she acknowledged, if he had turned out to be a creep like his brother. Well, that would have brought matters to a very rapid close. But thankfully, in that way, and probably many others, the two brothers could not be less alike.

As they entered the restaurant, the young, dark-eyed manager came forward.

'Hello, Signorina Sabrina!' he exclaimed effusively. 'We have missed you!' He was thinking that one of their favourite clients never came in with a man these days.

'Hi, Antonio,' Sabrina said. 'Um, this is Alexander—a friend,' she added, glancing at the two men in turn.

'Signor,' Antonio murmured, bowing his head deferentially.

'Buona sera,' Alexander said casually. Of course Alexander probably spoke the language fluently, Sabrina thought, and many others.

Antonio led the way to a candlelit table by the window. Alexander said, looking around, 'So, this is your local, is it, Sabrina?'

Sabrina smiled quickly. 'We don't come here all that regularly,' she replied. 'Probably once every couple of months or so. They're always so welcoming, though.'

It was on the tip of Alexander's tongue to say that Antonio could hardly be blamed for his flattery, with Sabrina looking as she did tonight. But, wisely, he kept quiet.

'I'm going to choose something rather good for us

this evening,' Alexander remarked, running his finger down the wine list. 'To celebrate the fact that we've kick-started chapter forty. I feel optimistic that with a bit of luck I can get it finished by the end of the month. Which is what the publisher expects,' he added.

Sabrina looked down for a second. *Did he say* we've *kick-started chapter forty?* she thought. Was that a slip of the tongue, was he being overly kind…or was she really that important to him? Either way, it gave her a thrill to hear him say it.

It didn't take them long to make their choice from the large menu, though Sabrina let Alexander lead the way. Well, he was paying, and she didn't want to select anything too pricey.

He decided they'd have Antipasto Misti to start, followed by Saltimbocca alla Romana—escalope of veal braised in Marsala wine, with ham and eggs.

'Does all that sound OK with you?' he asked, glancing across at her.

'Perfect,' she said, realizing that in all the time coming to Marco's she usually stuck to pizza or lasagne, which were the less expensive things on offer.

As they started on the second course, she glanced up at Alexander, suddenly feeling shy. He was incredibly handsome, she thought—not for the first time. He had such strong features, almost perfectly outlined, the firm chin already forming a fine stubble of dark, seductive hair…. But the mesmerizing feature had to be his eyes. Not just their intense, dramatic colour but the way he quite often used them to look at her. His thoughts behind that magnetic expression were unknowable, but it added to the delicious sense of mystery about Alexander McDonald which she'd been painfully aware of from the beginning.

Sabrina sighed inwardly as she picked up her fork again. No wonder he'd apparently spent half his life holding the female sex at bay, she thought. He could afford to pick and choose. For a second she felt almost sorry for Alexander McDonald. Too much choice became no choice at all, in the end. And what about that lovely girl in the snapshot who he'd been holding so closely, so intimately? What had happened to her? She obviously hadn't matched up to his expectations. Sabrina wondered whether there was a woman alive in the whole world who he could ever commit himself to. Somehow, she doubted it—anyway, hadn't he assured her after his mother's party that he intended to remain single for ever?

Sabrina put another morsel of veal into her mouth as her thoughts ran on. She didn't think that Alexander McDonald ever changed his mind about anything. Not once he'd declared it.

Briefly remembering that awful evening at his family home, Sabrina couldn't help comparing it with how she was feeling at the moment. Their supper afterwards at The Woodcutter had been good, and Alexander had been charming and conciliatory about what had happened. But this was different. She felt unexpectedly confident and happy to be here with her boss; she was enjoying every second of this occasion. And if he wasn't sharing her feelings then he was putting on a pretty good show, she thought. He seemed more relaxed than she'd seen him before. After all, this was his idea; there'd been no need for him to take her out and buy her dinner.

Interrupting her thoughts, Alexander said as he picked up his wine glass, 'I'm curious about something, Sabrina.'

She looked up. 'Oh? What's that?'

'You're the first woman I've ever been with—honestly, the first woman—who never wears any jewellery. Well, I've never seen you with any,' he added.

Sabrina smiled quickly. 'I do have some,' she said. 'And I used to wear some, now and then. But I made it my own unwritten rule never to have any on when I was on duty…in my other life,' she added. 'When in the company of patients, it seemed more appropriate to keep a low profile, to be sort of anonymous, to avoid distractions. The only noticeable person in any session should be the client—well, that's my opinion,' she added apologetically.

He nodded slowly. 'I take the point,' he said, thinking he should change the subject—quickly. He didn't want Sabrina—or himself—to think of her professional career; there was still so much *he* needed her for. But he knew the time was bound to come when she'd want to take off again.

And he wasn't going to tell her that, even as a small child, he was suspicious of anyone over-dressed. He'd never liked all the bangles and beads his mother was never seen without, nor the suffocating smell of the scent she insisted on spraying all over herself.

'What about perfume?' he ventured, instinctively thinking that Sabrina Gold was quite fragrant enough without it anyway. 'Does that come in the same category?'

'It does,' Sabrina replied, putting down her fork at last and sitting back.

It was dark by the time they left the restaurant, and as they walked back along the streets they could hear the sound of loud, gaudy music.

'Where's that coming from?' Alexander asked curiously.

'Oh, that must be the fairground—it's right over there in the municipal park,' Sabrina said. 'I'd forgotten that it always arrives in time for the half-term school break. Perhaps the warm weather has encouraged them to come earlier this year.'

'I haven't visited a fairground for ages,' Alexander said almost longingly, and Sabrina looked up at him in surprise.

'I can't imagine it would be your kind of thing,' she said.

'Well, you're wrong there,' he said. 'Let's go over and take a look…just for a few minutes?'

It didn't take long to reach it, and Sabrina could see at once that Alexander was like a boy again as they wandered amongst the crowds. The place was buzzing, with all the usual rides at full tilt; the nostalgic smell of the generators filled their nostrils.

'Fairgrounds have been around for generations,' Alexander said, drinking in the atmosphere. 'I hope they never go out of fashion. They're part of our history.'

At the far end was the ferris wheel. Suddenly Alexander took hold of Sabrina's hand, pulling her alongside him towards it.

'Come on, let's be daredevils.' He looked down at her. 'Are you game?'

Sabrina could hardly believe this. Was this her *boss* here with her, helping her into the seat, securing the safety straps around them both? But she was having fun, she thought to herself, feeling ridiculously child-like. And, noting Alexander's expression as he gazed out into the night, as the giant machine took them ever onwards and upwards, she knew that he was having fun too.

They reached the highest point, and as the wheel paused briefly to take on more customers, they could see the city's lights spread out beneath them like a magic carpet of stars. For Sabrina, it seemed an intoxicating moment, and she took a deep breath.

Then, just as they began moving again, a strong breeze caught them unawares, momentarily lifting Sabrina's dress right up, making her shiver. Immediately, she felt Alexander put his arm around her shoulder and pull her towards him. She instinctively responded, nestling into him, feeling her body ache for something more…

'I told you you'd need a wrap,' he shouted above the din of the music, still not letting her go.

'I didn't expect to be this far up in the stratosphere!' she shouted back, trying to pull her skirt down again. But she knew he'd seen her naked thighs, the edge of her underwear, and she bit her lip. This whole day was turning out to be surreal, she thought.

They eventually came back down to earth, and started to stroll back, neither saying much. Alexander looked down at her.

'Are you OK, Sabrina?' he asked.

'I'm fine,' she assured him at once. But she knew she wasn't fine at all. Despite having had a fantastic evening, she was full of guilt. She'd been enjoying herself with her boss far too much, and when he'd drawn her into him up there in the night she'd realized how much she loved the feel of him close to her, loved the masculine scent of him teasing her nostrils. And she knew this was wrong, wrong, wrong! How was she allowing such thoughts to intrude on her official status as his secretary? This could be a dangerous game, she thought, because she knew that her time with Alexander McDonald was going to be short—and inconsequential.

As they got back to the house, he said suddenly, 'Oh, I forgot to talk to you about something, Sabrina…'

This was obviously going to be the proposition, she thought, not looking up.

'Oh?' she said.

'Yes. I think I'm overdue for some respite time,' he said. 'At my place in France. It'll still be nice and warm there, and I'd like you to come with me. I'm already starting to think about the next project, the next big idea, and fresh surroundings might provide some fresh inspiration.'

They arrived back to where he'd parked the Aston Martin. 'We could leave at the end of the month,' he went on. 'It takes less than a day to get over there. We'd be away for perhaps two weeks… How does that grab you?'

Sabrina sighed inwardly. She'd never heard anything before about his home in France. She hesitated before replying.

'I'm not sure I could agree to that, Alexander,' she said. 'My sister will be back soon.' Sabrina crossed her fingers as she spoke. Making her sister an excuse could be a convenient ploy sometimes—because that was what it was. Sabrina's immediate reaction, not wanting to go to France, was less to do with Melly and much more to do with not wanting to be alone with Alexander away from work. Especially in *that* romantic part of the world. Her emotions tonight had been sufficient warning, surely?

'Well, give it some thought,' he said casually. 'I shall be going in any case. And I would hope that you *can* come,' he repeated.

They made their perfunctory goodnights, and Sabrina let herself into the house, her mind in turmoil. Everything had been going so well, she thought, until Alexander had insisted on them riding on the wheel. How could she have let Alexander's unexpected touch cause such a titillating thrill of erotic excitement run through her? Because he *had* excited her. For those few, brief moments her body had ached for him. She shook her head angrily. Was she really that susceptible?

As the Aston Martin sped through the now almost-deserted streets, Alexander felt a sudden burgeoning sense of optimism. He admitted that he did enjoy the company of lovely women, something he'd deprived himself of for a very long time. And his secretary had shown him just how much he'd missed it.

He tapped his fingers on the steering wheel as he waited for the lights to change. Although Sabrina hadn't seemed particularly enthusiastic about his request that she should go with him to France, he knew that his powers of persuasion would probably win her over. She was so genuinely eager to help him with everything he asked of her, he could probably convince her that the trip would be good for both of them. One of his reasons for taking her was to give her a holiday, to give her a treat, to give her the chance to relax and enjoy the peaceful surroundings which he himself always found so therapeutic. And if anyone deserved a holiday, both from emotional and business ties, then surely it was Sabrina Gold.

And who better to spoil her and give her a really wonderful time than Alexander McDonald?

CHAPTER EIGHT

SABRINA woke early the next day. As her eyes flickered open, she saw that the hands on her bedroom clock pointed to six a.m. and she snuggled back down for a minute, smiling to herself, remembering. She had dreamed the most wonderful, colourful dreams for most of the night, it seemed.

Then she sat up slowly, hugging her knees, a slight frown knitting her eyebrows. That off-duty time with Alexander had added a whole new dimension to what they had, she thought. She wasn't going to think of it as a relationship, because that word embodied something far too significant, too meaningful. But neither could she deny that a sea change had happened—at least to her. For the very first time since he'd been her employer, Alexander had shown her something of his very personal self.... Could she ever forget his touch, his caress?—that intimate caress? That was what it had been. As that fairground ride had swung them slowly backward and forward in the night-time breeze, he had held her to him possessively, keeping her warm and safe, not wanting to let her go. Another memory which would last her for a lifetime.

But what about this morning, when they came face to face? Would she be able to act casually, noncommittally? And would Alexander even remember the incident which had given Sabrina such erotic dreams?

One thing she had already made up her mind about: she was definitely not going with him to France. It was not only about leaving Melly by herself; it was because Sabrina could not afford her plans to be altered in any way, and she knew that being alone with her boss in one of the most romantic countries in the world could spell danger. How easily she had allowed her mind to wander last night. How easily she had succumbed to the briefest expression of physical contact with a man! Her frailty of determination had surprised her, and she shook her head briefly. She must see that she continued to remain single-minded, looked out for herself and Melly, and did not let any interruptions rock their boat.

Getting out of bed, she went across to the window and drew aside the curtains. There was another working day ahead of her; she bit her lip thoughtfully. She would tell Alexander straight away that she would not be going with him. How was he going to take that? And would he still pay her if she wasn't by his side? That was a worrying thought… But, then, she'd be here, wouldn't she? To answer the phone, check the Internet, maybe send any additional stuff over to the publisher if necessary, be a general dogsbody and keep the place ticking over… And Alexander could always send her any instructions he might have for her by email. Distance was no deterrent to progress these days.

By the time she got to number thirteen, Sabrina felt rational, cool, calm and collected—even though she was dreading having to tell Alexander her decision.

She waited a few moments for someone to answer the door; Maria had clearly already left, and presumably Alexander was out too—or maybe still asleep! Then she opened her purse for the key she'd been given, and let herself into the house.

She was beginning to feel almost as much at home here as in her own place, she thought as she went up the stairs, though she'd only ever seen the kitchen, bathroom and study. Pausing briefly, she glanced along the landing. There were three or four doors to other rooms on this floor, and presumably the same number on the one above. What a place for Alexander to rattle around in all by himself.

Did he ever feel lonely? she asked herself, before dismissing the idea. Alexander McDonald was a complete entity. He'd never need anyone to keep him company. The only reason she'd been asked to go with him to Lydia's party a couple of weeks ago had been made very clear at the time. And now his wish that she should go with him to France was for the same thing: he would find her useful to him. Any need was purely self-centred and work-oriented.

Shrugging briefly, Sabrina went into the study and as usual went straight over to open the windows. It didn't take her long to realize that Alexander must have been working late into the night—the unmistakable litter on his desk said it all. Glancing at her own, she saw a pad with his familiar scrawl on it; obviously the next part of chapter forty, she thought. Great! Because she was longing to know how the convoluted plot was going to unfold…

By now it was obvious that she was alone in the house. Alexander must have left very early—probably an extra gym-session. He hadn't bothered to open the mail, so for the next twenty minutes Sabrina checked what was in the post, then booted up their computers and made a note of the emails she knew Alexander would want to follow up. He was so selective in who he agreed to correspond with, she thought, it was surprising he had a friend left in the world. But he obviously did have, because there seemed to be so many who never gave up trying to contact him.

Suddenly, starting to feel over-warm, Sabrina went back downstairs to get herself a drink. For some reason, she hadn't wanted any breakfast earlier, having made do with a mug of tea, but it wasn't coffee she needed now—it was water. Cold, cold water. She went over to the tap to fill a glass, realizing that she was suddenly desperately thirsty. She drained it almost immediately, then reached over for a refill….

Now Sabrina knew that something strange was happening to her. Instinctively, she clutched the edge of the sink to steady herself, aware of her heart beating at a furious rate. She felt odd; her head was swimming, and the room seemed to be shifting under her feet…perhaps she was still at the fairground! But this wasn't funny, and she wasn't amused as panic began to set in. Things were not normal and she was no longer in control. She tried to take deep breaths, hoping she wasn't going to be sick in Alexander's immaculate kitchen.

With her legs now decidedly shaky, Sabrina went across to sit down carefully on one of the high stools…. Cross that; within just a few seconds her life seemed to be out of her own hands. Gently, she placed her forehead down on the granite surface of the unit, grateful for the momentary respite it gave her.

Then she heard the door open and from a very, very long way away she heard Alexander's voice.

'Sabrina! What… What is it?'

Raising her head carefully, she looked up to see him

striding over towards her. He was so unbelievably tall today, she thought, like...like a giant...

Then, just before he could reach her, Sabrina lost it completely and she began to slip from the stool, falling gracefully towards the floor. But before she actually hit the ground Alexander's strong arms were around her. She felt him lift her up towards him, felt the reassuring strength of his body enfold her, heard him call out her name urgently again and again, until, in a wonderful dream-world of unreality, Sabrina slowly drifted into unconsciousness.

Presently, when she finally came to her senses, Sabrina found herself flat on her back, gazing up at an unfamiliar ceiling. It took at least ten seconds before she realized what had happened to her and where she was.

She was on Alexander's king-size bed—well, she presumed it must be his—and he was leaning over her anxiously. As her eyes focussed on his, he gave a slightly awkward grin of relief.

'Ah, good. You've decided to return to the land of the living,' he remarked.

'What on earth...? What on earth happened?' Sabrina began, struggling to sit up, but he restrained her gently.

'Lie still. It's OK, Sabrina.' He paused, resting his hand on her forehead for a moment. 'I think you're beginning to cool down a bit.' He stared at her solemnly. 'Does this sort of thing happen to you very often?'

'What *did* happen?' Sabrina demanded. 'I was only...I remember getting myself a drink of water—and then I don't remember anything else.'

'Well, you collapsed fairly dramatically, that's what happened,' Alexander said. 'I came back just in time to catch you.' He shook his head briefly. 'You gave me the fright of my life.'

'Why? Were you afraid I was going to die before we'd finished the book?' Sabrina said, attempting a shaky smile. He didn't smile back.

'Why did you come in this morning, if you didn't feel well?' he said.

'But I *was* feeling well!' Sabrina protested. 'There was nothing wrong with me at all. And I can't remember if I've ever fainted before.' She swallowed, aware that her head was beginning to thump painfully. 'The only thing was, I didn't want any breakfast this morning, that's all. And then upstairs in the study I started to feel very thirsty…and the rest you know.'

But what she'd really like to know was how she'd managed to get up the stairs. Alexander read her thoughts.

'I'd thought you were coming round, once or twice, in the kitchen,' he said. 'Then I'd lose you again. So I thought I'd better get you up here to lie down for a bit.'

'How did you…?'

'I carried you, of course. You certainly weren't going anywhere under your own steam,' he replied flatly.

Sabrina let her thoughts dwell on the scene for a moment. She knew she didn't carry any excess weight, but still it couldn't have been an easy task for Alexander to lift her bodily and take her up that long flight of stairs. Or perhaps it was no problem at all for someone with his strong frame and wide shoulders, his muscular biceps…

'I'm going to take you home straight away,' he said. 'And you're not to come back in to work until you feel absolutely OK again.'

'But I'm sure I'm going to feel OK *now,*' Sabrina protested. She hated being ill; she wasn't used to it. And, anyway, there was only room for one patient in any household, and it had never been her.

He looked down at her thoughtfully for a moment. 'I hope we… I hope I haven't been expecting too much of you lately, Sabrina—not working you too hard,' he said. 'I can go on for hours without a break and sometimes forget that others might need to take things at a slower pace. Sorry, but you really should tell me if you're feeling tired.' He hesitated. 'I've never thought of myself as a slave driver—the only head I've ever beaten with a stick is my own—but maybe I am and haven't realized it.'

Sabrina smiled wanly. 'This is not your fault, Alexander,' she said. 'And you're not a slave driver. If I'd thought you were, I would probably have given you a sign of some sort.'

In a minute or two, Sabrina attempted to sit up again, then began to have the horrible suspicion that there was more to her situation than she'd thought. The glands in her neck were beginning to feel stiff and painful, and there was a strange, unfamiliar taste in her mouth.

'Oh dear,' she said faintly. 'I don't feel so good after all, Alexander.'

'No, and you don't look it,' he replied bluntly. He paused, gazing down at her, unfamiliar feelings of tenderness rippling through his body. He came to a sudden decision.

'I'm not going to take you home after all,' he said. 'You're going to stay here—at least for the weekend.'

As Sabrina started to protest, he went on firmly, 'Everyone's talking about this horrible virus that's going around like wildfire. And although I'm no medical genius it looks to me as if you might have it.' He put his fingers gently either side of Sabrina's neck 'Does that feel tender?' he asked.

Sabrina sighed. 'It does,' she admitted reluctantly. 'But honestly, Alexander, it's better if I go home.' She paused. 'I'm quite used to looking after myself, and you don't need me around.'

Oh, but I think I do, Alexander thought.

'Why go home to an empty house?' he demanded. 'Your sister won't be there, so you won't have her to worry about. Why turn down the chance for someone to look after you, for a change? Someone to make you hot drinks, maybe even bring you scrambled eggs in bed?' he added.

But he knew he wasn't thinking only of her. He was thinking of himself. He wanted to look after Sabrina, wanted to take care of her. Why had he never felt like this about a woman ever before? What had stopped him having those feelings?

In spite of not really wanting to fall in with his plan, Sabrina did suddenly feel drawn to the idea. He was probably right about her having picked something up. She looked at him, her eyes huge now in a face which looked pale and wan.

'But if I *have* caught this virus, wouldn't it be better for me to make myself scarce? Aren't you afraid of catching it?' she asked.

He grinned properly now, sensing that he was going to get his own way.

'Not a chance of that happening,' he said cheerfully. 'For some reason, I always manage to remain impervious to bugs of all kinds.'

But, rather worryingly, not impervious to the winsome charms of my present secretary, he thought.

Sabrina bit her lip. She obviously had nothing with her, no night clothes or toothbrush, and she hated being unprepared. Once again, Alexander read her thoughts.

'Sorry I haven't anything in the way of female attire to offer you,' he said. 'But you're welcome to borrow my T-shirts—which will reach your knees, I should think, so they shouldn't be too uncomfortable And there's a new pack of toothbrushes in my bathroom cabinet. Anyway,' he added, 'there's enough of everything for you to make do.'

By now, the idea of not having to go back home was becoming more attractive by the second. Sabrina knew without any doubt that whatever she had was not going to go away easily. She sighed, smiling up at him briefly.

'Well, if you're sure I shan't be, you know, interrupting your creative flow, Alexander, or be in the way…'

'Let's forget my creative flow for five minutes,' he replied firmly. 'Let's think about you, just you, for a change.'

The next twenty-four hours passed in a blur of semi-misery for Sabrina as she alternated between spells of uncomfortable sleep and fits of coughing that made her chest hurt. She felt very hot and very cold by turns, her subconscious mind an outrageous mix of noises and disruptive sounds. And all the time she was barely aware of Alexander silently coming and going into the room to place fresh water by her side, and to gaze down at her almost ghost-like appearance.

He had decided not to move her from his bed, and had used one of the spare rooms for himself. But he'd been so concerned about Sabrina that he'd hardly slept at all, tiptoeing in and out to check up on her.

At three o'clock on Sunday morning, he went in to find her sitting up, mumbling incoherently, her face flushed and her hair in damp tangles around her shoulders. Suddenly Alexander was angry with himself, really angry, that he hadn't called for his doctor to visit—though he could well imagine what Sabrina's reaction would have been to that suggestion. But what if she had something much more serious than they thought? What if this was the dreaded meningitis, or something else equally as dangerous? He would never, ever forgive himself if the worst possible scenario should take place under his roof—and to someone like Sabrina…all because he'd neglected to get professional advice.

Without saying a word, he picked up the glass of water by the bed and gently encouraged her to take a few sips. Then he laid her back down gently and went into the adjoining bathroom to rinse out a wet cloth to place on her forehead. Catching a glimpse of himself in the mirror, he thought *he* didn't look too good, either. His face appeared unusually tired and careworn. But then, he reminded himself, this was the first time he'd ever had to look after someone who was sick; he had never experienced these surprisingly deep feelings of closeness, of compassion, this longing to wave a magic wand and make someone better.

At least he was thankful that he'd managed to persuade Sabrina to stay here. It was unthinkable that she should be in this state alone at home.

Going back in with the cold, damp flannel, he placed it gently on her forehead, holding it there for a few moments. He realized that she seemed to be calmer now, her breathing less rapid, and he began to relax. Perhaps he was panicking unnecessarily; from everything he'd heard about the present infection, that was apparently decimating the population, Sabrina's symptoms were classic. And, if it was true to type, by the morning she should be over the worst.

That was how it turned out, because he went back in to find Sabrina breathing peacefully—having actually managed to sleep himself for a couple of hours—the hurtful coughing no longer punishing her slight body.

Sensing she wasn't alone, she opened her eyes and smiled up at him. Alexander was so relieved to see that she was definitely so much better, he could have rushed across and clasped her to him. It was the best possible feeling in the world, he thought, to know that someone you cared about was no longer in danger.

He sat carefully on the edge of the bed and took hold of her hand. 'Hello, Sabrina,' he murmured.

'Oh, Alexander. Where have I been?' she said. 'What day is it?'

'It's Sunday—at eight a.m. And I think you've been on an unexpected journey to No-Man's Land. But you're better now, or you will be soon.' He squeezed her hand more tightly and she sat up then, leaning her head on his shoulder for a second. The sight of Sabrina in his huge T-shirt—which had slipped off one side, exposing a smooth, tender curve of her breast—made Alexander's heart almost burst with tenderness. What power did this woman possess to give him such feelings? he asked himself. Was she a witch?

Later, after he had brought her tea and a thin slice of toast and marmalade, Sabrina felt sufficiently recovered to have a leisurely shower and wash her hair, which had become an unruly mass of tangles as she'd tossed and turned. By now she was just beginning to appreciate the position she'd landed herself in—albeit through no fault of her own. She had spent the weekend in her employer's bed, had apparently been watched over by him for many hours, and had sat up to obediently eat the first solid food she'd had for a couple of days while he'd just sat there, watching until she'd finished every crumb.

How on earth had all that come about? she asked herself. How had he persuaded her to stay here overnight—over two nights? It felt both strange and amazing at the same time. Alexander McDonald had taken care of her in a very personal way, while she'd been completely unable to do that for herself—something she never could have imagined in a thousand years! She shook her head briefly.

Life was so full of surprises, she thought, some ghastly, some exciting and pleasurable. Despite the fact that she'd been feeling so utterly wretched for two days, this latest episode in her life could easily be placed in the latter category! For her boss to stand over her in his dressing gown—as she'd been aware of from time to time—looking unusually unkempt and unlike himself was something she'd never expected to see. But all she knew was that it had made her feel grateful that someone else had taken control.

It was mid-morning by the time she'd dried her hair and got dressed, and although she still felt as if she was walking slightly above the ground Sabrina knew that she was well on the way to recovery. She also knew that she must go home soon and recharge her batteries in her own surroundings. She could get used to being here, she thought, glancing around at Alexander's luxurious bedroom. Unlike his study, everything was immaculate, from the expensive drapes at the window and the cream, fitted carpet on the floor, to the tasteful prints on the wall. And his bathroom was to die for, she admitted, thinking of her own—and shuddering at the memory of him standing there the other day beside her. Chalk and cheese was about it, she thought.

Then she squared her shoulders. Such thoughts were not allowed. It was useless to wish for something you knew could never be yours. She and Melly had enough of everything they needed. And they had each other.

She went downstairs; the smell of coffee coming from the kitchen was starting to wake up her taste buds. Alexander turned and smiled at her.

'Ah, that looks more like you, Sabrina,' he said, looking down at her approvingly. How could he have dismissed her appearance as irrelevant on that first morning in September? he asked himself. Sabrina Gold could never be thought irrelevant—in any way at all.

She went over to stand next to him as he made the coffee. 'Do you mind taking me home in a minute, Alexander?' she asked, wishing she felt strong enough to get back under her own steam.

'Why go back straight away?' he asked casually, not looking at her. 'I was thinking that after I've impressed you with my scrambled-egg dish we might have a run out in the country for an hour or so. It would do you good to have some fresh air—perhaps a stroll for ten minutes or so?' Now he did look at her. 'Unless there are urgent things for you to attend to, of course,' he added.

Sabrina knew that there wasn't anyone or anything urgent waiting for her at home, and in any case she still felt very fragile. What Alexander had suggested was suddenly very appealing.

'Well, that does sound rather attractive…' she began.

'Good. Then that's settled. The newspapers are in my

sitting room, next to the bedroom. Take your coffee up, and I'll start constructing the eggs.' He grinned down at her, thankful that Sabrina was obviously so much better—and pleased that she was ready to fall in with his plans for their day.

Sabrina did as she was told, finding that Alexander's sitting room was much as she would have expected. Again, beautifully, expensively furnished—but not without the tell-tale signs of someone who found that being tidy was an irksome task. But it was cosy, lived-in and lovely, Sabrina thought as she settled herself back down in the enveloping cushions of one of the large, deep-green sofas.

For the next few minutes she tried to read the newspaper, but found that she couldn't concentrate long enough to take anything in. She picked up her mug of coffee and sipped thoughtfully for a moment.

When was she going to pluck up the courage to tell Alexander that she was not going to France with him—after he'd just been so kind, so thoughtful? She could repeat what she'd already said—that Melly couldn't be left on her own for long. She could hardly tell him the truth. She could hardly say, *sorry, Alexander, you're becoming far too important to me. I am beginning to like you too much, to need you too much. And this is not the template for my life. You're cutting across my plans. And I must somehow put a stop to it before it's too late, because I believe that it won't take much for me to be seduced by you. To be seduced by my employer. And that's not good for business, is it? Not good for you, with your career to think of, and not good for me, who has vowed never to be emotionally involved with a man ever again.*

She would tell him later, when he took her home,

Sabrina decided—get it over with before she changed her mind.

Soon, she heard his voice from below. 'Breakfast is served, my lady!'

Smiling, she got up and went downstairs. As she reached the bottom, the front-door bell rang, and without hesitating she went to see who it was.

The smile on her lips died in an instant—Bruno was standing there. And, as their eyes met, his sly expression said it all.

'Well, well, well...' he drawled. 'I didn't think you were expected to work on *Sundays*, Sabrina.' He moved forward to come in. 'I told you he could be a demanding brute, didn't I?'

Almost at once, Alexander was behind them, and he didn't bother to couch his words as he stared at his brother with distaste.

'Didn't I make myself clear the other day, Bruno?' he said flatly. 'Didn't you get the message that I do not welcome unexpected visitors—whoever they are?'

Bruno smiled slowly, looking from Sabrina to his brother and back again.

'I can quite see why not,' Bruno said suggestively. 'And I'm sure it *is* a surprise, Alex, old boy,' he said. 'I've obviously come at a *very* inconvenient time.'

'Yes, you have. We're just about to eat our breakfast,' Alexander said, unsmiling. 'Even so, I would ask you to join us—but, sadly, I've used up all the eggs.'

'Oh, don't worry about me, Alex,' Bruno replied, totally unperturbed. He paused. 'Have you two been working all hours, then? You...you must have had quite a night.'

'Bruno, you wouldn't believe the night we've had,' Alex said solemnly. 'Which is why Sabrina and I need some nourishment to upgrade our energy levels. So I'm sorry to rush you away, but please have the grace to inform me the next time you're likely to call, won't you?'

And, with the briefest of goodbyes, Bruno was gone.

'Well, you know what *he* was thinking!' Sabrina said, following Alexander into the kitchen.

He looked down at her, with the heart-stopping twinkle in his eyes that sent delightful shivers right down her spine to her toes.

'What—that you spent the night in my bed?' He paused. 'Well, you did, didn't you?'

'Yes—but you know what I mean, Alexander. He's sure to jump to all the wrong conclusions.'

Alexander raised one eyebrow. 'Who cares?' he said. 'Now, come and eat your breakfast.'

CHAPTER NINE

THANKFULLY, the virus which had invaded Sabrina's body disappeared within two or three days, so Alexander's novel could progress unhindered.

He had been more than usually preoccupied with bringing his latest masterpiece to a successful end, and as they continued to work almost silently together in the study Sabrina made a point of keeping her head down and not intruding on his thoughts. She had learned by now when to keep quiet, when to make herself invisible, when sometimes not even to distract him by making them coffee or tea. And once or twice, when she'd arrived in the mornings, she'd been aware that he'd almost certainly been up most of the night, scribbling, crossing out—and no doubt cursing. But there was always the latest manuscript waiting for her to sort and print out, and he was keeping the promise he'd made—that it would all be completed by the end of October.

Now, as Sabrina saw the plot unfolding before her eyes as she typed, she had to admit that the conclusion was completely unexpected, with a totally amazing, unbelievable twist that brought a smile of satisfaction to her lips. This, then, was why Alexander McDonald's books never failed to impress—or to sell in shed loads.

She'd hardly seen him at all today, but now as she

handed over the final printout for his inspection she couldn't resist telling him how she felt.

'Alexander,' she said quietly. 'This is an amazing piece of work—and I loved the end. Just loved it! I'd had no idea how it was going to work out. How…how did you do it?'

He shrugged. 'Thousands of hours of practice,' he said. 'But thanks for the compliment, Sabrina.'

He looked down at her as he spoke, remembering just how ill she'd been ten days ago and how little fuss she'd made about it. He'd wanted her to have time off to recover properly, but she'd had none of that—and he didn't persuade her to change her mind. Because he needed her—wanted her—by his side. He could never have envisaged how indispensable this woman would become to him. How he looked forward to every day, just to see her, be close to her.

He had decided not to mention France again until after the novel was complete, but he was pretty certain she'd be coming with him despite her reservations about her sister. And it would do them both good to get away from here for a spell, breathe different air, he thought. Surely she'd see that?

He stood up and pushed back his chair. 'This is great, Sabrina,' he said, indicating the pile of papers in his hand. 'I'm going to take it over to the editor right away, and when I come back—I shouldn't be long—we might even open a bottle of champagne.'

Sabrina smiled up at him, pleased that he was so happy, so obviously content with all the hard work he'd put in over the last months. And, when he was happy, it made her happy too.

He turned to go. 'Oh, by the way, make some enquiries about flights to Carcassonne…say towards the end of next week? That would suit me, if it suits you.'

Sabrina paused before answering. 'I don't think I agreed to come with you, did I, Alexander?' she said carefully. 'Though it's very kind of you to include me in your arrangements.'

'It's got nothing to do with me being kind,' he said flatly. 'It's all to do with us both having a brief period of renewal. You've been putting in nearly as many hours as I have and you're due for a break. Especially after that bug you picked up.'

Sabrina stood up, pushing a stray frond of hair from her forehead. 'No. The thing is, Alexander, my sister texted me last night to say the group are due back on Sunday—a bit earlier than was expected. So I do need to be around for her for a while.'

'That's OK,' Alexander said, not to be put off. 'We can leave when we like—Wednesday or Thursday next week—and that'll give you three or four days to settle your sister back home, won't it? And it's still lovely in the Languedoc area in early November.'

Sabrina looked at him squarely. 'I really cannot say with any certainty that I can come,' she said. 'I've already told you, I need to be here for my sister's return.'

'Well, she certainly seems to have done all right without you in Spain,' Alexander said bluntly.

'So it would appear,' Sabrina retorted. 'But I would still like to see her.'

'And that's understandable,' Alexander said, trying to sound reasonable, even though he couldn't see why someone of twenty-six couldn't be left in her own home for a couple of weeks without her big sister holding her hand. 'And you *will* be there—for several days—to make sure everything's OK.' He paused. 'I'm sure your sister would like to think of *you* having some time away, too.'

Sabrina looked at him for a moment, biting her lip. This exchange between them wasn't going too well at the moment, she thought—especially as she couldn't give Alexander the other rather important reason why she didn't want to go to France.

'Well, all I can say, Alexander, is that my instinct is that you will be going to France without me. But,' she said quickly, seeing the handsome face darken, 'I will think it over. And, anyway, I'll still be here when you get back. In the meantime, I'll see that everything ticks over—check the post and the web. I might even do a bit more cleaning up in here!' she said, trying to keep things light for a second. Alexander McDonald was used to having things all his own way, to not having his plans upset, and she could see from the expression on his face that he was annoyed with her.

'Well, in my opinion, I think you should give your sister the opportunity to stand on her own feet for once,' he said. 'It seems to me you've been a kind of crutch to her for too long—always dependable, always there to sort out her life. From the little you've told me about her Spanish assignment, she's been doing very well, thanks. Sometimes, Sabrina, love is shown in the letting go—so I've heard. Are you sure this isn't more about you than her?'

That hurt! And Sabrina had been listening to what he was saying with growing anger and dismay. How dared Alexander McDonald interpret her life like this? What did *he* know? Well, he'd blown it now, she thought. She was damned well not going with him—anywhere! Who did he think he was? Let him stick to his fictional characters and their problems, and leave her and Melly out of it.

She managed to keep her voice calm. 'I'll bear your opinion in mind,' she said coolly. 'And I'll come to my decision about France in due course. And you'll be the first to know,' she added.

And with that she left the room, shutting the door with an unnecessary bang, and went downstairs to make herself a cup of tea.

Later, alone in the study, Sabrina felt somewhat at a loose end now that the novel was finished. She'd almost felt the tenseness lifting from Alexander as he'd come to the end of it—but he'd already stated that ideas for the next one were beginning to boil in his head; she knew it wouldn't be long before it was a case of *déjà vu*.

After busying herself with the filing, which had been woefully neglected of late, she took some invoices from his personal file and started to write out the necessary cheques for him to sign later. She was just finishing the last one when the phone rang. It was Alexander.

'Sabrina,' he said. 'I'm afraid I'm going to be held up here for a bit because we're waiting for the publisher to put in an appearance.' He paused. 'You go on home. And, look—have tomorrow off. That'll give you a nice long weekend to prepare for your sister's homecoming.'

Was he being sarky? Sabrina thought.

'Oh, OK, then,' she said coolly. 'Thanks.'

'No—thank *you*, Sabrina,' he said. 'The final draft has been approved, so it's all smiles here. I think we can congratulate ourselves.' He paused. 'Sorry about the champagne, but I'll keep it on ice. Oh good—they've just arrived, so I'll have to ring off. So, see you Monday,

Sabrina—and I hope you find your sister in good spirits on her return.'

Sabrina put the phone down, biting her lip. His hurtful remarks earlier had cut into her deeply—but was he right? Had she assumed for far too long that Melly couldn't survive without Sabrina being on hand all the time? And most awful thought of all—one which had only just taken root in her mind—had Melly in fact been a surrogate child, the child Sabrina had always longed for?

The possibility that Alexander might have a point made a considerable impact on Sabrina; wasn't she supposed to be the psychologist? Wouldn't she have worked out the true position for herself by now? But maybe perceptions were dimmed when you were too close to a situation, she agonized; objectivity could often take a back seat when it concerned you and yours.

With her thoughts running in all directions, Sabrina rested her head on her hand. Why not forget what Alexander McDonald said, just for a moment? she told herself. Melly would be back home in three days—and how was she really going to be? It was true that she'd given no indication that anything might be wrong, or that she was unwell, but Melly was a clever actress, and could be confusing sometimes. She would have realized that, even if she had been unhappy, there'd have been nothing Sabrina could do about it. Maybe her apparent enthusiasm had all been a sham because she didn't want to worry her sister. The two girls had never been apart for this long before; how would Melly have survived this totally new dimension to her life?

With her head beginning to ache now, Sabrina stood up suddenly. It was all very well for Alexander McDonald to offer his illustrious opinion, but his own family values were hardly creditable. They were feeble, in fact. He didn't know what he was talking about.

In his editor's office, as they uncorked a good bottle of wine, Alexander's mind was only half on the discussions going on around him. He wished he hadn't said all that to Sabrina, about her and her sister. The moment he'd uttered the words he could see the hurt spread across her features. And she was an intelligent woman; she didn't need him butting in. Especially as he knew very well that the real reason he'd done it was because he'd been angry with her. Angry that, for the first time, he'd almost put his heart on the line, and Sabrina had said No. He'd been silly, childish and unfair, and he wished with all his heart that he could rewind the tape. The thought that he'd made her unhappy—even for a second—was unbearable.

One thing was certain, he thought grimly. She'd never agree to come abroad with him now. And much, much worse—what if she decided she didn't want to work for him any more? What if she gave in her notice?

With yet another stab of genuine surprise at the intensity of his feelings towards her, Alexander realized that being without Sabrina Gold in his life was unthinkable.

Early on Saturday morning, the telephone by her bed rang and Sabrina sat up to answer it, rubbing her eyes. It was Melly.

'Sabrina? *Hello!* Oh, Sabrina, I've had the most marvellous time, and there's so much I have to tell you!'

Sabrina couldn't help smiling. Her sister was on cloud nine, obviously. 'Won't it wait until tomorrow, then?' she asked mildly.

Without a pause, Melly said, ‘No, not really. Well, let’s just say that *I* can’t let it wait until tomorrow!’

‘Go on, then,’ Sabrina said. ‘Fire away.’

And Melly did fire away, her words coming out in a rush. For the next twenty minutes, she gave Sabrina a blow-by-blow account of everything that had happened on the trip, hardly stopping for breath. She was deliriously excited; a transformation had taken place.

‘I’ve never had such a brilliant time in all my life, Sabrina. And the thing is, well, I—me and Sam—remember you met Sam?—we’re not coming back tomorrow with the others. Not for a couple more weeks.’

Sabrina sat up properly then, utterly bewildered at this sudden change of plan.

‘Perhaps you’d better explain,’ she said.

Melly took an audible, deep breath before going on.

‘It’s Sam and me—that is, well, Sam has just been wonderful the whole time, Sabrina. I think I’m in love with him.’ She paused. ‘In fact, I know I am. I’ve never felt like this about a man before; I’ve never met anyone like him before. And I know you’re going to say it’s a passing holiday-type thing that has no future, but I know differently. And so does Sam. We like the same things, we laugh about the same things…we’re just on the same wavelength! All the time! And, well, I hope you won’t think I’m being stupid, but…’

Sabrina got out of bed, clutching the phone more tightly in her hand. Spain had certainly had a very dramatic effect on her sister.

‘I’m not thinking anything,’ Sabrina said. ‘You’re twenty-six years old, Melly. It’s time you began to interpret your own emotions and not rely on me to do it for you all the time.' She paused. 'What has Sam said to you, exactly?'

'He said that he wants us to get to know each other better, spend more time together. And not only that—he can almost guarantee me permanent work with his team. And, the thing is, he needs to stay on here after the others have gone back home—there's more work for him—and he wants me there as well. By his side,' she added. She paused. 'He really is lovely, Sabrina, and I know we love each other. Really I do. And you're going to love him too, when you get to know him.'

For a few moments, Sabrina felt almost bowled over by all this. Melly had had one or two minor relationships in her life before, but had never expressed her feelings in such extravagant terms.

'You don't think I'm being silly, do you, Sabrina?' Melly repeated earnestly. 'And—do you believe in love at first sight? Sam does, so he told me. And I think I do, because he's on my mind all the time. I just want to be with him.'

Thinking over what her sister had just said made Sabrina feel envious…just for a second. 'No, I don't think you're being silly,' she said slowly. 'And I…do believe in love at first sight. But I don't think it happens every day—and when it does it should always be treated with a certain degree of caution.'

'That's exactly what Sam said! We won't rush things; we'll value each day as it comes. And I've been managing everything fine so far, making the clothes I brought with me last—well, there are laundry facilities here, of course. And I've also bought a couple of T-shirts. And because I've been paid my wages I don't need to ask you for any more money—which I'm sure you're glad about!' she added.

Suddenly, Sabrina felt completely anonymous, as if she wasn't there at all, as if she was hearing everything from a long way off. She recognized that, through Melly, she was experiencing again the euphoric joy of being in love. She could only hope that her sister's expectations wouldn't be dashed to the ground—for whatever reason. Life could be so unfair, so unpredictable. What if Sam wasn't all that Melly thought he was? He wasn't exactly young—probably nearly ten years older than her sister—and would have known plenty of women. He was an attractive man. She sighed inwardly. The last thing Sabrina needed was to have to pick up the pieces of Melly's life again if this all came to nothing.

Neither of them spoke for a few moments after that; Sabrina wondered when her sister might be interested enough to ask about what had been going on here at home, or how Sabrina was getting on with *her* job.

Presently, Melly said, 'Oh, how's your life—your job—going, Sabrina?'

'Ticking along,' Sabrina replied carefully. 'In any case, it's only pro tempore, as you know, until I get back to my proper job. I'm not really sure how long this one's going to last—it could end at any time—but the pay is more than enough to cover the mortgage and all our other bills at the moment, and that's a very comfortable feeling.'

'Well, it looks as if I'll be able to add to our coffers myself as soon as I get home, Sabrina,' Melly said. 'Because Sam's promised me plenty of work, so I'll be earning good money for a change.'

Suddenly, rather like she were witnessing a warm sun emerge from behind a cloud, Sabrina said, 'By the way, Melly, I'm going to be away myself, just for a short while. It's a work thing,' she added. 'I think we're leaving for France on Thursday—probably back mid-November. So I may not be here when you eventually get back. Is that OK?'

'Of course. And how lovely for you, Sabrina! Have a great time, won't you? But don't let them work you too hard, will you?' Melly giggled suddenly. 'Something else I forgot to say—do you know, Sam only lives a mile away from us? He told me he's been jogging past our house every morning for the last year! Isn't life amazing?'

'Oh yes—it certainly is amazing,' Sabrina said faintly.

CHAPTER TEN

ALEXANDER paid the driver of the cab which had brought them to the airport, then he and Sabrina trundled their cases towards the entrance. He glanced down at her, noting that she'd pulled her long, fine-wool cardigan closer around her.

'Yes,' he said. 'There's definitely a colder feel to the air now. But don't worry; where we're going it's still lovely and warm. I checked it out last night.'

As he guided Sabrina in front of him through the revolving doors, he was still amazed and elated that she'd agreed to come with him, almost at the last minute. But, after all, she *had* promised to be his PA, hadn't she? His right-hand woman in every way? Though, taking her abroad had never been on his agenda… He rarely invited anyone to the Barn, relishing the peace and solitude of the place, his escape route from everything and everyone.

But Sabrina was different. She was the only woman he'd ever known who he'd not quickly grown tired of, who'd never, ever, got on his nerves. And as that thought struck him, he realized that surely he must be partly to blame—that he was the one out of step, not womankind in general. It was just that so many of those he'd met all seemed to fit into the same mould as Lydia—taking everything for granted, never satisfied for long, restless. There *had* to be women who were different, who shared his values, his perspective on life. Well, of course: wasn't she here, right next to him?

They made their way through the crowded aisles and were shown into the lounge for business-class passengers. In spite of all her earlier reservations, Sabrina couldn't help feeling upbeat. It *would* be good to have a change of scene, even though she'd had second thoughts after telling Alexander on Monday that she'd go with him, mostly because, judging from her latest phone call, Melly had been unstoppable, incorrigible, in her new-found euphoria. Sabrina was waiting for the bubble to burst, for the girl to come back down to earth.

For his part, Alexander had been wise enough not to show undue surprise that Sabrina was coming with him—and not to look smug, as if as usual he was going to have his own way.

'Oh, fine,' he'd said, noncommittally. 'Let's go Friday, shall we? And why don't you have Wednesday and Thursday off, so you'll have time to get ready.'

Her sister was, apparently, not coming home just yet—which fitted their—his—plans perfectly.

Now, as they took their places in the aircraft, Sabrina had to admit that Alexander always managed to surprise her. He exuded such power and confidence, he almost gave the impression that he could take over from the captain. Sabrina found herself basking in the comforting warmth of being with someone who was taking control of everything, who was planning out every move ahead. All she had to do was to sit there and enjoy it. She could get used to this state of affairs! she thought.

As the plane droned its way towards their destination, Alexander glanced across at Sabrina, feeling proud to have her sitting by his side. She was wearing black, slimline trousers and a white scoop-neck top which exposed the tantalizing smoothness of her skin. With her hair coiled up on top of her head, she managed to look both smart and casual at the same time. It was the first time he'd seen her in high heels; her black patent-leather shoes completed her stunning appearance. How did she always manage to look just right? he wondered. Was there ever a time when she was caught unawares, or at a loss? Then Alexander smiled to himself, remembering her reaction when her bathroom mirror had crashed to the floor.

'Have you done much travelling? Have you been to France?' he asked her casually.

She turned from gazing out of the window to look up at him. 'Yes, to Paris,' she replied. 'Melly and I had a five-day break there a few years ago, and we went to Brittany once or twice when we were young. But we know home shores better than foreign ones.'

'Well, it'll be great to show you the part of France that suits me best,' he said. 'Still basically unspoiled, and the perfect place to unwind.' He smiled. 'We do have a few neighbours, but no shops, I'm afraid—so, if you'd hoped for some retail therapy while we're away, you're going to be disappointed.'

'I'm not a great shopper,' Sabrina said. 'So that won't be a problem.'

She didn't bother to add that earlier in the week she had gone into town for a couple of new things to bring away with her. Having agreed rather reluctantly to come on this trip, she'd made sure she wouldn't run out of clothes before the end of it.

The flight only took a couple of hours or so, just long enough for them to enjoy the wine and the light lunch which was served to them. Only ever having flown economy class before, Sabrina couldn't help comparing the two. There seemed so much less hassle, she thought, and the extra space made all the difference. Especially to someone like Alexander, who had no difficulty in stretching out his long legs and relaxing.

'I've packed my laptop in my case—' she began, and he interrupted her.

'Why? This is supposed to be a holiday.'

'But—but I thought it was partly about your next novel. That's what you said, Alexander,' Sabrina replied. 'You said you were hoping to find fresh inspiration…'

'Oh, did I? Well, maybe I will, maybe I won't—with an emphasis on the latter,' he said breezily. 'I intend to be thoroughly lazy and drink a great deal of wonderful wine—and I hope you're going to join me,' he added, smiling slowly into her upturned face. 'And we'll take it in turns to rush out for fresh baguettes every morning, because at exactly nine-fifteen Claudette arrives in her little white van with fresh supplies for the locals—and she doesn't hang around. Three sharp beeps on her horn, and you've got about two minutes to join the queue before she makes a fast getaway.'

Picturing the scene, Sabrina couldn't help smiling. 'Are there really no shops—even food shops—then?' she asked.

'Nope. The nearest supermarket is five miles down the road, where we can restock everything now and then,' he said. 'But we'll be OK for the first few days because two of my neighbours, Marcel and Nicole, will have made sure we won't go hungry. They're a great couple—you'll like them. They look after my place for me when I'm away, and stock up the fridge to greet me when I come back.'

'It sounds an ideal arrangement,' Sabrina said. 'You're lucky that they're around to do it for you.'

'It is,' he agreed. 'And I am. And I bet they'll insist we have dinner with them tonight—they know I'm bringing someone with me this time.'

Sabrina looked away as he spoke. Who did he usually bring with him? she wondered. Was there a special female that no one knew about? She kept remembering that beach photograph; when, and where, had that been taken? Then she shrugged inwardly. From Alexander's youthful appearance on the snap, it was clearly taken rather a long time ago.

But Sabrina admitted that she was curious about her employer's personal life. Although he'd stated that he intended to remain single—for ever, he'd said—there were bound to have been many other women. Someone with his masculine appeal could have the pick of the bunch. Whatever he'd said to her, it certainly didn't mean that he never enjoyed the full company of a female when he felt like it. And where better to do that than in an isolated place in rural France? There wouldn't be any photographers popping out from behind bushes to catch him unawares and provide gossip for the media. Was this his real purpose in asking her along? If so, she'd make sure she wasn't another notch on his bedpost!

As she dwelt on all this, Sabrina wondered whether she'd made the silliest mistake in her life by coming with him. His apparent reason for inviting her had been that it would not only be a chance for a rest, but that they might do some work in relative peace. But now, apparently, he'd changed his mind about doing any writing.

The flight was smooth and uneventful, and as they came into land Sabrina stared down in fascination at the medieval city of Carcassonne. Alexander touched her arm. 'We'll spend a day there before we go back home,' he said. 'It's something not to be missed.'

At the airport, Alexander had made arrangements to hire a car, and as they fastened their seat belts he said, 'It takes about forty-five minutes to get to the Barn, so sit back and enjoy the scenery.'

The roads were blissfully uncluttered, and from the effortless way Alexander negotiated the twists and turns it was obvious that he must have made this trip scores of times.

'Where is everybody?' Sabrina asked, staring out of the window, and Alexander chuckled.

'That's just the point—there isn't anybody,' he said. 'That's why I come here.' He glanced across at her briefly. 'Though that's not strictly true, of course. We'll be going through some little villages in a minute, and nearer the Barn you'll see the huge hypermarket on the horizon.'

In almost exactly the forty-five minutes Alexander had said it would take them, Sabrina could see a cluster of buildings ahead, and soon they arrived at a small hamlet of about half a dozen dwellings. 'This is it,' Alexander said briefly.

As he drove slowly up the poorly maintained road, Sabrina couldn't help feeling rather surprised. It was hardly the most inspiring scene in the world, she thought, noting that the heavy door of every building they passed looked as if it hadn't seen a coat of paint for years, and almost all the walls seemed to be flaking and unkempt. *Hardly Alexander McDonald territory*, she thought.

He pulled in and switched off the engine. 'Welcome,' he said.

Inside, what a different world, a magnificent conversion from what had once been a farming necessity!

It was spacious and airy, with polished hardwood in evidence everywhere. As Alexander showed Sabrina around each room it was obvious to Sabrina that, for him, this was home from home.

There was a huge dining area with a refectory table large enough for at least ten people, and at the end was a fully fitted kitchen. On the same floor were two *en suite* bedrooms and a wet room, and tucked in one corner was a sizeable, partly obscured area for a television and a sophisticated sound-system.

Alexander led Sabrina up the beautifully crafted oak staircase to two more *en suite* bedrooms. At the end of the landing a pair of full-length windows opened out on to a balcony, from which the patio and swimming pool beneath could be seen, and ahead in the near distance was an uninterrupted view of rows and rows of vine trees and olive groves.

Almost lost for words, Sabrina looked up at him. 'Alexander,' she said slowly. 'What an absolutely lovely place.' She thought, *never judge a book by its cover!* How could she ever have guessed what lay beyond that rather scruffy front door?

'I had a feeling you might like it,' he murmured.

Then, they went down to the lower floor and made their way through the games room, complete with table tennis and snooker tables, and out on to the patio.

'I usually swim most mornings,' Alexander said casually. 'And, if it's hot, several other times of the day as well.' He smiled down at her. 'I told you it would still be warm here. Marcel told me on the phone that it's been a good year for weather.'

If she'd had any worries about coming here, those worries had suddenly disappeared! This was a magical place; who couldn't be happy here just for a couple of weeks? *I'm going to enjoy every minute of this totally unexpected holiday*, she thought. *And I have no fears where Alexander McDonald is concerned, either... I know exactly how to take care of him, if I have to!*

'What a lovely surprise that Alex has brought...a *friend* with him this time,' Simone said, pouring another glass of wine for Sabrina and pushing it along the table towards her.

Alexander had been right when he'd said there would be an invitation for dinner from the French couple, and Sabrina had to admit that Simone and Marcel LeFevre were everything he'd described.

The pair were in their fifties, Sabrina guessed, Marcel a dark, swarthy, good-natured man, his wife a rather round-figured woman with light-coloured, frizzy hair and shrewd blue eyes.

Their home was a pretty, ancient farmhouse with swimming pool—obviously not as grand as Alexander's. But their table groaned beneath delicious, unusual cheeses, a massive langoustine soufflé and salad, and home-made pastries straight from the oven to eat with crème fraîche and sweet almonds. And there was wine, and more wine, and rich, sensuously aromatic coffee. Would she need another thing to eat ever again? Sabrina asked herself.

It was getting late, and the two men had gone out onto the patio to chat, Marcel puffing happily on a cheroot. Simone leaned forward conspiratorially, her perfect English prettily laced with her own accent.

'Alex told Marcel on the telephone that he was bringing someone with him this time, but we never thought it would be a beautiful woman,' she said. She paused, unashamedly looking Sabrina up and down. 'I feel so glad, because as soon as I saw him today he looked different. Not so…sad, as he usually does.'

'Sad?' Sabrina said curiously.

'Oh, *mais oui*! Yes, sad, *chérie*,' Simone said emphatically. 'We have talked about it many times, Marcel and I, and always thought it was to do with the writing—his head always in another world, he has no time to think much about the one he's living in.'

Sabrina thought about that for a moment.

'His home—the Barn—is very big, just for him, isn't it?' she said. 'Doesn't he ever bring anyone here with him?'

'Never. Always alone,' Simone said. 'He has lent it to one or two friends in the past—and his brother came here once with a woman—but Alex seems to like being here alone. Which doesn't seem *natural* for a man, not natural for someone like Alex.' She smiled quickly. 'Have you known him a long time?' she ventured curiously.

Sabrina smiled back, not minding the question because it was obvious that the woman had a real liking for Alexander, cared about him.

'About six weeks,' she replied. 'I'm his secretary.'

'Ah, *ça va*? His secretary…' Simone said, nodding her head slowly.

'And the only reason I've been invited,' Sabrina went on, 'is because we've had a very busy time of late. Alexander has only just completed the latest novel and things have been a bit tense recently. So he thought we both needed a break—and, as it happened, my own circumstances allowed me to accept his suggestion.'

A slight frown crossed the knowing features. 'You—you have someone…?'

Sabrina smiled. 'No—at the moment, I'm quite free,'

she replied, wilfully misunderstanding Simone's enquiry. 'For a little while, I'm fun and fancy free!'

Simone's expression cleared. 'I am so happy to hear that,' she said. She stood up to fetch more coffee from the stove, and turned to look at Sabrina. 'I hope you will have a really good time here,' she said. 'You and Alex… together. He deserves someone to teach him one or two things.'

'I'm not sure what you mean by that,' Sabrina said, smiling.

'To teach him how to be a living person—a man,' Simone said firmly. 'And to open his heart.'

Only a French person could have said something like that, Sabrina thought, shrugging inwardly. She wondered how much of Alexander's past Simone and Marcel knew—about his parents, of the rather strange relationship Lydia had with her sons.

'Oh, I don't think we need worry about Alexander,' Sabrina said lightly. 'I'm sure there have been many women in his life.'

'Ah *oui*, of course!' Simone agreed firmly. '*Affaires*…naturally! But, love?' She nibbled thoughtfully on another almond. 'I am talking about the sort of love that only happens in sound relationships: family ties—commitment.'

'I've the feeling that Alexander would rather have a fit than a family!' Sabrina said, smiling at the thought. 'I'm sure he could never tolerate children getting under his feet. In that respect, he's the typical loner, I'm afraid,' she added.

Simone sipped at her wine. 'You're wrong, Sabrina,' she said. She put her glass down and leant forward, her elbows on the table. 'Our first grandchild was born a couple of years ago, and she was about six months old when Alex saw her. My daughter brought her over for a visit, and he was here. And he was—how shall I say?—*enchanté*! He could not take his eyes off her! And he has showered her with gifts ever since. In fact, he is godfather to our precious baby.'

Sabrina could hardly believe this. Alexander and… *babies*?

'I hope he didn't drop her at the font,' she said only half-jokingly, and Simone threw her hands in the air.

'Drop her? He handled that child as if he'd had six of his own! It was difficult for anyone else to get a look in, because he wanted her all to himself!'

If Sabrina had just been told that Alexander McDonald had beaten Edmund Hillary to the top of Everest, she couldn't be more surprised at what Simone had just told her. But before any more discussion could go on, the two men came in from the patio.

'I'm suddenly beginning to feel rather tired,' Alexander said, smiling down at Simone. 'Thanks largely to that magnificent meal, Simone. Thank you so much; as usual, we shall be returning the compliment before we go back home.'

Simone stood up and put her hands on his shoulders. 'You know how much we love your visits, Alex,' she said fondly. 'You don't come nearly often enough. And it has been a great pleasure to have a lady to talk to this time.'

'Well, if you want to keep good staff you've got to treat them well,' Alexander said, smiling briefly at Sabrina. 'Sabrina and I have been keeping our heads down for too long lately.'

After making their goodnights, Alexander led Sabrina the short distance between the two properties. Sabrina admitted that she, too, was looking forward to some sleep. Earlier, she'd been more than relieved to be shown her own room on the first floor; Alexander apparently always slept on the one above. She'd been prepared for the possibility that he might have expected her to share.

As they let themselves into the Barn, Sabrina glanced up at him.

'Why do you go in for such massive properties, Alexander?' she asked casually. 'This is huge. And so is number thirteen, of course.'

He paused outside her bedroom, looking down at her thoughtfully for a second. 'Because I like space, that's all,' he said. He waited a moment before murmuring, 'Goodnight, Sabrina. Sleep well.'

Then he turned and went upstairs, and Sabrina heard his tread on the wooden stairway. Slowly, she went into her room and closed the door.

Snuggling down under the luxurious duvet, she tried to imagine which room Alexander was sleeping in. Was it directly above her own, or the one further along? She hadn't quite got a handle on the geography of the place yet.

It had been a rather wonderful day, she thought sleepily. There was not a single thing she could complain about, anyway. The journey had been pleasant, and Alexander had acted the perfect gentleman the whole time, making her feel comfortable, unthreatened, and for some reason sublimely happy. She smiled faintly in the darkness, remembering everything Simone had told her. Alexander McDonald cuddling a baby in his arms! What a preposterous thought!

The other slightly less preposterous thought was that, if he'd wanted to seduce her, it wouldn't have taken him too much effort, she admitted!

* * *

In his own room, Alexander glanced at himself in the mirror as he brushed his teeth vigorously. Despite Sabrina's initial reluctance to come with him, he knew that she was happy to be here…happy to be here with him. And he also knew that he felt happier than he had for a very long time. She was the first person he'd ever invited to have a break here with him; he'd never wanted to share that solitude he so valued. But, for once, he *wanted* to share—and, if he'd been presented with a vast selection of other human beings to consider, Sabrina would have been his first, his obvious choice.

CHAPTER ELEVEN

THE first thing that Sabrina was aware of the next morning was the sound of three short blasts from a horn outside in the road. Of course: the van bringing fresh bread for breakfast. Well, she'd never make it in time to buy any! She hoped Alexander didn't expect her to take first turn, anyway—even though she must remember that she was still his secretary, his Jill of all trades.

But the next moment, after listening to several excitable voices raised in spirited greetings outside, she heard the heavy door slam and Alexander's swift tread coming towards her room.

Not bothering to glance at herself in the mirror, Sabrina shrugged on her dressing gown, opened the door—and came face to face with Alexander, who was clutching two large French sticks and a paper bag of something or other.

'Your turn tomorrow,' he said, smiling down at her in one appraising glance. The flimsy dressing-gown she had on revealed the tantalizing shape beneath, and her hair—tousled untidily and loose around her face, which was still pale from sleep—caused his senses to spin in mad circles for a second. He swallowed.

'Did you sleep well?' he remarked casually.

'Like the proverbial top,' Sabrina replied. She hesitated. 'You've clearly been up some time?'

He was bare-footed, his muscular legs brown and glistening, and he was wearing white shorts and a navy T-shirt. His hair was wet and plastered to the sides of his face which was unshaven, a strong line of dark hair shadowing his chin.

'I've been in the pool for half an hour.' He paused. 'But I wasn't going to wake you; we had a long day yesterday.' He turned to go. 'I was just coming to tell you it's nine-thirty already, so let's have breakfast.' He turned to go. 'And don't bother to get dressed now,' he added over his shoulder. 'You can take your time later. All this'll be ready in five minutes.'

Doing as she was told, Sabrina went back into her bedroom to sponge her face and hands and brush her hair quickly, before going through to join Alexander in the kitchen. The glorious smell of percolating coffee drove her tastebuds crazy.

He had cut the baguettes into generous slices, and laid out butter, jam and honey. Sabrina realized that she was feeling really hungry by now. Especially when she saw the two still-warm pastries he'd bought as well.

'After that wonderful supper last night, I didn't think I'd ever want to eat again,' she said, sitting down at the table and watching as Alexander poured the steaming coffee into two huge, wide cups. He passed her some milk and sugar and sat down opposite.

'Ah well, that's what French air does for you,' he said. 'Plus being totally relaxed and with no pressures.'

He was right, Sabrina thought as she spread butter onto a slice of bread. She did feel relaxed, had never felt more relaxed in her whole life. She suddenly seemed to be inhabiting a whole new world where nothing really mattered, quietly amazed at how quickly she and her employer had somehow adapted their relationship. She had that strange feeling once again that they'd known each other for ages. She shrugged inwardly. Perhaps that had something to do with the nearly three days spent ill in his bed.

Later, choosing to wear her dark-green cut-offs and an ivory, loose-fitting top, Sabrina slipped on her flip-flops and went downstairs.

'I think I'll show you the area, drive you around a bit this morning,' Alexander remarked, glancing across at her briefly. She was wearing her hair in one long, thick plait down her back; however she did it, it always seemed to suit the contours of her fine features perfectly—and to leave those intriguing green eyes room to express themselves in a way which fascinated him as much now as it had on the first day he'd met her.

'Sounds great—whatever you say, Alexander,' she replied, going over to the window and gazing out. 'I am in no position to argue about anything,' she added, smiling, thinking just how much she was enjoying the present situation.

'I can't imagine a time when you wouldn't be prepared to put your point of view, Sabrina,' he said, coming up to stand alongside her. 'But in this instance I shall take complete control of our day—and you can complain later if you haven't enjoyed it.'

The rest of the morning was spent idling through the local countryside. Although it was pretty deserted, as Alexander had said it would be, they did pass along a few clusters of dwellings, and the occasional small garage.

'Do you, um, do you ever bring other friends here?' Sabrina asked casually, not looking at him.

'Certainly not,' he said as if she should have known that without asking. He clicked his teeth, irritated for a second as he recalled the hundred and one hints Lucinda had made in the past about wanting to visit the Barn with him. 'I've just remembered something. Lucinda—you will recollect having met her, Sabrina?' This was said with a sardonic twist to his mouth. 'Lucinda is about to celebrate a rather important birthday soon, I believe. I received my gilt-edged invitation to what will be a ghastly event just before we came away.'

'That should be fun,' Sabrina said noncommittally.

'Probably not,' he replied. 'But, as I shan't be going, it's irrelevant.'

'I know where I'm going to buy you lunch,' Alexander said. 'It's a pretty little place, and the village has a rather interesting *château* on the hill.' He turned to smile at her briefly. 'The French are big on *châteaux*,' he added. 'But the restaurant right by the canal is the one I've used before—food's good.'

As they meandered along lazily, Sabrina could easily see why Alexander loved this area so much. You couldn't get much further away from civilization, at least as they knew it. But it was interesting scenery, vastly populated by olive trees and vine groves, separated now and then by a narrow river. Suddenly they came upon a small village which, surprisingly, had quite a large shop in the middle of the street they drove along. It had paintings in the windows, and various items of craftware displayed outside. Noticing her leaning forward, Alexander immediately slowed down.

'Do you want to look?' he asked.

'I'd love to,' Sabrina said at once. 'I suppose somewhere like this is bound to attract artists,' she said, and he nodded.

'Oh, there are several forms of cottage industry around and about,' he said. 'And the French have a formidable eye for business, as I'm sure you know.'

He parked the car and they wandered along, browsing curiously as they went and passing one or two interesting-looking cobble-stoned alley ways before coming to the shop.

'It's a surprising place—and there's lots more to see inside,' Alexander remarked. After they'd looked at the paintings in the window, they went through to be greeted effusively by a young Frenchwoman.

'Bonjour, monsieur, mademoiselle...' She smiled, indicating that they should come inside.

'*Bonjour*, Colette,' Alexander said easily. He glanced down at Sabrina. 'I know you said you were no shopper, but this could well lead you astray, Sabrina,' he added, before wandering off by himself to look further inside.

Sabrina had to admit that he had a point. It was a fascinating place, much larger than it appeared, and opening into other, smaller areas. For the next half an hour she enjoyed herself picking things up and putting them down again, studying everything that was on sale and wondering whether to buy or not to buy...

As well as quite expensive water-colours, there was a rack of woven scarves and shawls, a display of hand-painted plates, vases and pots of every description. There was a section for local jars of honey, of garlic bulbs in oil, of cherries in syrup, and rows and rows of home-baked biscuits in polythene wrapping. And in a corner by the window there was a display of brightly coloured, hand-made jewellery, all glistening in the pale sunlight.

She'd been so engrossed in looking around that she'd only been dimly aware that Alexander was further in the shop, having a lengthy conversation with the owner. But just then he emerged, smiling, and glanced at what Sabrina had in her hands.

'Have you made your choice, then?' he enquired, and Sabrina handed a scarf and bangle to the French woman.

'Yes, thanks,' she said. She looked up at him. 'Have you bought anything?'

He nodded briefly. 'Oh, just a small present I needed to get, but it's rather bulky to take back with us so Colette's arranging for it to be shipped home later,' he said.

Well, that was obviously some little gift for Lucinda's birthday, Sabrina thought. He might not intend to go to her party, but the woman would certainly expect a decent present from someone as rich as Alexander McDonald.

Colette wrapped Sabrina's gifts carefully before handing them to her, and Sabrina took some euros from her purse. 'You have a lovely shop,' she said, and the woman smiled, darting a quick glance at Alexander.

'Merci, mademoiselle,' she said. 'Please do come again soon.'

They went back to the car, and just after one o'clock, they arrived at the other, slightly larger village which Alexander had told Sabrina about. He pulled up outside a restaurant which had a few tables outside standing under brightly coloured canopies which were moving gently in the breeze.

Across the road and through the trees, Sabrina

could see a canal glinting in the sunshine with a well-maintained longboat idling on the water and one or two small craft floating nearby. She was struck again by the whole atmosphere of stillness and quiet. She thought, *I could get to love this place, too.* Time really did seem to stand still.

They strolled over to the restaurant and took their places at one of the tables outside. There were one or two other people already eating, and immediately a waiter came up with a menu. Soon, Alexander and Sabrina began to enjoy the fluffy omelettes they'd ordered, complemented by a bottle of good wine and some cheese.

Leaning back in his chair and watching Sabrina finish the last of her food, Alexander wondered, not for the first time, what lucky chance had sent his current secretary into his life. He hadn't found a single fault with the way she did her work, or with her attitude at all times. But best of all, he realized, he loved her company.

They left the restaurant a little later and began to walk up towards the *château* Alexander had talked about. This once-beautiful residence, resembling those constructed during the Renaissance, had been built by a noble family but was now largely in ruins. It was a somewhat austere, turreted building standing right on the cusp of the hill, and suddenly the sun went in and Sabrina felt a chilly breeze around her bare arms. She reached into her bag and took out the scarf she'd bought.

'I think I'm going to need this sooner than I thought,' she said, coiling it around her neck and shoulders, and Alexander nodded briefly.

'Well, it is November, and it can get cool quite quickly,' he said. 'I hope you came prepared for all weathers.'

'I most certainly did,' Sabrina replied, thinking of the thick sweater she'd brought with her.

There was only a small party of French schoolchildren there as well, and Alexander and Sabrina wandered mostly uninterrupted through thick, stone entrances and gaunt passageways, before deciding to go back to the Barn.

'I think I feel ready for my swim now,' Sabrina said as they drew up outside.

Alexander smiled across at her. 'And I'll join you,' he said. 'After I've made us a cup of tea.'

Later in her room, as she slipped into her black one-piece bathing suit, Sabrina admitted to feeling worried about everything—about Alexander, and about herself. Because, heaven help her, she knew that she desired him… She'd have had to be made of stone not to want him to touch her, to make love to her—and she had to keep reminding herself over and over again not to get carried away. She did not want, did not need, any emotional turmoil or entanglements with him, or with anyone, that could lead to more disaster in her life.

She went barefoot into the bathroom to fetch a towel to take downstairs, her mind still darting every which way. The good thing was, Alexander had behaved impeccably, almost impersonally, since they'd left the UK. They'd barely brushed against each other at all, she realized, hardly made any physical contact. So, if she'd thought he had an ulterior motive in asking her to come with him, she was obviously mistaken. But every instinct told her that for her part she'd better keep any romantic notions—and her emotions—well under control.

Unfortunately, over the following few days the weather deteriorated considerably. But Alexander and Sabrina were still able to enjoy their morning swim in the warm water of the pool, and go for long walks; Alexander was clearly intent on showing her this part of the country he loved so much. They also drove to the coast on the one afternoon when the sun reappeared. There was certainly no talk of any writing being done.

They'd been there for more than a week when Sabrina's mobile rang. That could only be Melly, she thought, who'd rung a few days ago to say that she and Sam were back in the UK.

But it wasn't Melly; it was Emma, one of Sabrina's past colleagues who'd been lucky enough to be retained, telling her that an opportunity was coming up which Sabrina should apply for.

'It's a new thing they're initiating,' Emma explained. 'And they've actually got the funding this time, surprise surprise. And it's just up your street, Sabrina. As soon as we were told about it, your name was on everyone's lips. But you'll have to apply formally. Shall I get the stuff for you and send it over to your house?'

It took Sabrina a few seconds to get her mind into gear. She hadn't given her own profession a thought lately. 'I'm on holiday in France at the moment, Emma,' she said. 'But we'll be home at the end of next week.'

'Who's *we*?' Emma asked.

'Um, I'm here with my employer, actually—it's a sort of working holiday. Look, I'd be really grateful if you would send me the application form,' she added quickly.

'Course I will. Final date for submission is thirty-first of December.' There was a pause. 'And I'm glad you're having a break, Sabrina,' she added. Emma had known Sabrina for several years, knew about the problems with her sister and about Stephen's dreadful accident.

Alexander and Sabrina had been reading and listening to music, and now he looked across at her as she snapped her phone shut.

'That was one of my old workmates telling me about a post coming up that I should apply for,' she said briefly, picking up her book again.

Alexander resumed reading his magazine. 'Oh? And…are you going to?' he enquired, as if it was the last thing in the world that interested him.

'Oh, I shan't know until I've learned what it's all about,' Sabrina replied. She turned a page casually. 'Shall we have that steak we bought yesterday for our supper?'

'Sure,' he said, though wondering whether he'd have any appetite to eat it. His spirits had dramatically plummeted at the thought that Sabrina might even be *thinking* of leaving him—leaving him to pursue a different path, which would mean he wouldn't be seeing her every day, that she wouldn't be there any more.

Much later after supper, as they were sitting under the heater by the pool, Sabrina turned to glance at Alexander. 'I don't want to spoil your well-earned rest, Alexander,' she said. 'But have you given any thought to the next blockbuster? I told you I'd come prepared to do some work.'

'I haven't thought about it at all,' he said. *No—all I've been doing is enjoying myself here with you, Sabrina, with someone who feels like a part of myself.*

'Well, I just thought it my duty to mention it,' she said lightly.

It was past midnight before they left the poolside and climbed the stairs to the first floor where Sabrina slept. Before going up to his own room, Alexander paused briefly.

'Sabrina, thank you for another perfect day,' he said softly, and she turned to look back at him.

'Alexander,' she said. 'Any thanks are due to *you*. And…you're giving me such wonderful memories to take back with me.' She smiled tentatively. 'They're going to last me a lifetime.'

Silence between them hung in the air like a question waiting to be answered. Then, totally unable to stop himself, Alexander moved slowly over to Sabrina. Bending his head, he parted her lips with his mouth and kissed her fully, expertly, aware of a surging tide of passion tightening his groin. And, with her eyes closed against the intensity of the moment, Sabrina felt her senses exploding into a state of helpless longing….

Then, gently, he released her and without another word went upstairs. Sabrina heard his bedroom door close softly.

With her heart beating violently in her chest, she went in and sat on the edge of her bed, watching her knees trembling uncontrollably.

That was a *terrible* thing to have happened! she told herself, knowing that she should never have let it take place. To allow her boss to kiss her, really kiss her, in an unbelievably heart-stopping way, was pure madness! Their relationship—association; whatever the word was—was going somewhere neither of them wanted. Well, she was sure *he* didn't want it, and she couldn't *afford* to want it! They could never have a business arrangement now, after that, surely?

After a few moments, Sabrina felt her heartrate lessen and she stopped trembling, a feeling of quiet resignation sweeping through her. She knew that those erotic few moments just now had ruined all her good intentions, put paid to her common sense. She knew just how much she'd wanted it to happen deep down, had longed for it. To be held in Alexander's arms and feel his body press against hers had been bliss, pure bliss, proving once and for all that she must face up to things, to the inevitable. She was tired of running away; she'd been doing it for too long.

After a few moments, she got up and left the room—not even stopping to close her door—and slowly climbed the stairs towards Alexander's room. Without bothering to knock, she went inside, closing the door behind her.

He was standing by the window, and when he heard her come in he turned and looked down at her, a slow smile touching his seductive lips.

'Alexander,' Sabrina said, her voice cool and steady. 'Would you mind helping me undo this little hook at the back of my neck?'

CHAPTER TWELVE

AFTER a few seconds of complete silence, Alexander came over towards Sabrina, his arms outstretched. As he reached her she collapsed against him, automatically resting her head on his neck, a long sigh escaping her lips. They stood there, motionless, not uttering a word, letting this first breakthrough in their unspoken need for each other take them over.

Then with casual ease he picked Sabrina up, carried her over to the bed and sat down alongside her. Sabrina dropped her head forward so that he could undo the hook of her top, and as she felt the warmth of his hands on her skin a raging tide of feeling surged through her, making all her senses crawl erotically, making her whole body limp with surrender.

With infinite patience, Alexander slipped off her top and released the clasp of her bra, cupping his hands under her aching breasts and dropping a tender, lingering kiss on the back of her neck, making Sabrina want to cry out with desire.

Slowly he began to undress her, then laid her down on the bed before removing his own clothes until he, too, was completely naked.

For several breathless moments, he gazed down at her, drinking in the beauty of her tender curves, the smooth creaminess of her skin, and his eyes glittered like granite, glittered bright with heady anticipation. With wide and misty eyes, Sabrina looked back at him, the open, tender curve of her lips inviting him to take her…

Then Alexander lay down beside her and, taking his time, began to slowly explore her body with gentle, thrilling caresses, before his mouth, hot with passion, travelled from her lips to her neck, to her breasts and the flat plane of her stomach…. Their hearts raced in tandem as they trembled on the edge of fulfilment.

In a state of dizzy euphoria, when time seemed to stand still, Sabrina felt herself drifting on a cloud of pure ecstasy as Alexander's expert, unhurried love-making made every nerve in her body deliciously painful. Then he raised himself up and over her, and she felt the hardness of his muscles tight against her until, with irresistible grace and confidence, he slipped inside her. She clung to him with desperate exhilaration, her whole world seeming to explode into a vast display of star-studded emotion.

For a long, long time they lay clasped in each other's arms, neither wanting this magical experience to come to an end, but eventually he eased himself away and lay down beside her again. Then he brought her head onto his chest, holding her to him protectively, and gave a long sigh of emotional revelation.

As a pale moon shafted its gentle beam on to the lovers, they gave themselves over to a glorious sleep, a sleep which was filled with colour, wonder and total release.

When Sabrina awoke, dawn had barely broken; realizing that she was alone, she sat up, rubbing her eyes. Then she took the huge duvet which had covered them all night and wrapped it around her, before hobbling over to peep out of the window. It had been the sound of water being thrashed about which had roused her, and she smiled faintly as she saw Alexander, half-submerged, thrusting forcefully towards the far end of the swimming pool directly beneath the window. Then he turned and swam back, his powerful stroke covering the distance in a matter of seconds, before swimming back again and again… Perhaps all this activity was to make up for his lack of gym sessions, she thought.

He swam to the side, treading water for a second. Sensing that he was being watched, he glanced up and smiled, waving briefly before resuming his powerful overarm stroke.

He knew he had needed to do this, to energize, to be on his own to think about what had happened last night. Because where should he go, what should he do now? he asked himself. Although Sabrina had left him in no doubt that she had welcomed his ardour—and had returned it with a passionate lack of inhibition—he had no idea what to do next. What, if anything, did she expect would happen now? When they got back to the UK, would the situation be what it had been before—business as usual? But for him that would be unthinkable. He could not bear to be near her and not be able to hold her in his arms; he didn't have *that* much will power! But Sabrina had told him that no other man would ever claim her as his own, that that part of her life was over.

He cursed inwardly. Had he taken her by surprise, was it something which she might already be regretting?

And, worse, would she feel in the cold light of day that he'd taken advantage of her?

He lessened his pace for a few moments, his brow clearing slightly as he remembered. After all, it was she who had come to his room last night. Yes, it had been supposedly for him to help her with that hook on her top, but she'd never asked for his assistance before. And the hook was a simple enough one to undo; she could have done it easily by herself.

Well, he had taken it as an invitation, and he hadn't waited for a second one. There was less than a week before they returned home. Had he spoiled the remainder of their holiday together? He was feeling as insecure as a teenager after a first date. Still deep in thought, he swung himself out of the pool.

From her vantage point, Sabrina saw him walking towards the door to the games room. He was without swimming trunks, and her helpless gaze was riveted to his bronze, muscular body, the powerful strength of his physical being ravishing her senses once again.

Turning quickly, Sabrina remembered that she, too, was naked and should get back to her own room. But almost before she could reach the door he had opened it, and they stood looking at each other. Then, as if making a sudden decision, he went over to her and kissed her gently, once, on the mouth.

'You should have joined me—the water was perfect this morning,' he said lightly, as if what had happened last night had never taken place.

Sabrina swallowed, then said shakily, 'Do you mind if I borrow this for a minute?' pulling the duvet more closely around her.

'Feel free,' he said, going towards the bathroom to

shower. 'And I'll take your turn to fetch the bread this morning,' he added.

Picking up the clothes she'd had on last night, Sabrina turned and made her way down to her own room, feeling dizzy with mixed emotions. She hadn't known how he would treat her this morning, but one thing was crystal clear: his incredible love-making was par for the course. Today he'd barely looked at her—not properly, not meaningfully—and that swift kiss just now was merely a little acknowledgment that they were on slightly more personal terms than they'd been before; that well, hey, casual love-making was what people did, what grown-up, sophisticated people like him and the women he knew did.

As she showered and got dressed, Sabrina suddenly felt a huge wave of depression flow over her. Last night had been a wonderful miracle cure for all ills, but today she was completely downbeat, a state she rarely allowed herself to sink into. And it didn't take long to work it out.

Alexander's need for her was purely superficial and meant nothing to him. And why should she be surprised? He liked women well enough—he'd admitted that a long time ago—but only up to a certain limit. And that limit had been reached in the privacy of his room last night. So, having known all that, why had Sabrina allowed her own need to lead her astray? She had walked right into it, had walked uninvited into his room, and her not-so-innocent request that he undo the hook on her top had had the result she'd hoped for. So what was the problem?

She knew the problem. She was not needed by anyone in the emotional sense. Not by the man she was hopelessly in love with and now, apparently, not by her sister either.

For the first time in both their lives, Melly seemed to be standing perfectly well on her own two feet without Sabrina there to support, encourage and patch up.

Stepping out of the shower, Sabrina reached for a towel and began to dry herself. Pausing reflectively for a second as she caught a glance of herself in the mirror, she remembered Alexander's rather hurtful words the other day about her relationship with her sister. Perhaps he'd been right after all—perhaps it was a specific need, that she'd made herself more or less indispensable to Melly when it was being proved that she was not indispensable at all. But, what she really was, was guilty. Guilty of being over-protective, of stepping forward when she should have stepped back sometimes.

Well, Sabrina thought, she was beginning to see the light. About everything, about everyone. She was wising up, mostly about herself. And she might as well accept it: emotionally, she was not essential to anyone. They could all do without her, thank you very much.

Sabrina straightened her shoulders. She'd faced up to reality many times before in her life and she was good at sorting herself out. She'd do it again. There was still plenty of world out there waiting for her.

And, as far as her employer's future professional needs were required, he'd be able to find someone else, some other PA, easily enough when the time came. Just as he was going to have to do when—fingers crossed—she secured that post on offer.

On the last night in France, Alexander invited Marcel and Simone over for supper.

Sabrina had decided on her menu—chilled prawn

bisque to start, followed by blanquette of veal with fresh vegetables, and a Victoria sponge-cake with cherry sauce and cream for dessert. And, as Alexander was no cook, he'd been only too happy to let her get on with it and confine himself to selecting the wine.

For Sabrina, spending some time shopping and cooking was a welcome break from having had rather too much free time. She'd never been this long without having things to do.

Now, as she spooned the sponge mixture into the tins carefully, she felt relieved that they were going home tomorrow. It wasn't that she hadn't enjoyed herself, but ever since their fateful love-making things had been different between her and Alexander. He had seemed to be deliberately careful not to touch her much, and hadn't made a single move that could be interpreted as amorous. And she certainly hadn't invited herself into his room again. It was hard to actually describe the position between them, she thought. Their attitude towards each other was warm enough, and once Alexander had put his arm around her waist briefly. But she did feel that a sea change had taken place, that the waters had been temporarily ruffled and were now flat and calm again—with nothing to show there'd been any disturbance at all.

Yes, it was time to go home, she thought as she slid the pans of cake mixture into the oven to cook. But what was she going to find when she got there? Melly's new man might be sleeping under their roof for all she knew—how long might that be for? If he was, would Sabrina feel like an intruder in her own home?

Much later, with Sabrina's menu exclaimed over, and after every last morsel had been eaten, Simone and

Marcel made moves to go home. Simone put her arms around Sabrina and hugged her tightly.

'It has been good, *très bon*, to meet you, *chérie*,' the Frenchwoman said. 'And so good that the Barn has been occupied—even for a short time.' She paused, darting a quick glance at Alexander. 'You will bring Sabrina back again soon, won't you, Alex?' she said. 'Your lovely home needs to be lived in, and we love having you as neighbours. So…why not come for Christmas? We do Christmas very well here. Our little hamlet looks like fairyland with all the lights, and we all go carol singing, and eat and drink far too much! Do say you will come, *mon ami*?'

Alexander grinned down at Simone. 'I'll give it some thought, Simone,' he said. 'But I don't know whether Sabrina would want to come with me; she has family at home who need her, would expect her to be there at that time of the year.'

Sabrina looked away, not bothering to respond. She had no doubt that as far as Melly was concerned this year it would be two's company, three's a crowd.

'Well, anyway, before Christmas comes Sabrina and I have some serious work to do,' Alexander said. 'Two weeks off are as long as I can afford.'

After the couple had gone, Alexander and Sabrina cleared up the supper things together, and as he wiped the last of the wine glasses he glanced down at her.

'You've made a definite hit with those two,' he said. 'Marcel couldn't keep his eyes off you, and Simone has taken a real fancy to you as well.' He paused. 'I shall be got at now, and nagged every time I ring them, to bring you back here.'

Sabrina smiled at his words but said nothing, and in a minute he went on.

'I've never spent Christmas here myself, but from what Simone said it sounds as if it might be OK. Maybe I'll give it some thought.' He paused. 'But I suppose you'll be needed at home to cook the turkey, Sabrina?'

'I have a feeling that there could be a distinct change in routine this year,' Sabrina said casually. 'But I don't want to think about Christmas…not yet. Christmas is a long way off.'

'Not all that long,' he countered. 'And before that I've got to get started on the next novel. And I always crack on pretty well with the first section, so you'll be kept busy too.' He deliberately avoided mentioning the phone call from Sabrina's ex-colleague about a possible appointment. Let sleeping dogs lie, he thought.

'So I'm needed at my desk on Monday, then?' Sabrina asked, thinking that that would give her less than forty-eight hours to collect her thoughts, do some washing and assess the situation at home.

Alexander put his hands firmly on her shoulders and looked straight into Sabrina's eyes.

'You are,' he said flatly. 'And for as far into the future as it is logical to expect.'

CHAPTER THIRTEEN

AS THEY took their seats in the plane at Carcassonne, Sabrina didn't know whether she was glad or sorry to be leaving France.

She had to admit that Alexander had gone out of his way to see that she relaxed and enjoyed herself, showing her all around the area he loved so well. And she had enjoyed herself. He had been the perfect escort and companion—and, yes, the perfect lover, she thought. Their one romantic night together would stay in her memory for ever. But the thing which had made Sabrina feel dismal ever since that poignant time was that no words passed between them to reassure her, to tell her something. Physically, he had expressed his ardour—wasn't that enough? For her, it was not enough and never would be. He hadn't said, in the heat of their coupling, *I love you, Sabrina*—words she'd hoped he might say. But it had been a vain hope; she realized that. It was not Alexander McDonald's way, and never would be.

She sighed briefly. The uncomfortable conclusion had to be that on that magical evening he had needed her—they had needed each other—and that need had been fulfilled. Totally. And that was that. Now, it was back to reality, work and the status quo.

Yet, even if their love-making had been a superficial

event for him, Sabrina didn't regret a thing. How could she regret being made love to by someone like Alexander McDonald, who had proved himself passionate, thoughtful and tender? Glancing up at him now, as he was putting their in-flight bags in the locker, she wondered if he'd actually thought about it at all afterwards. There'd certainly been no indication that he had.

Sabrina decided to get a grip on herself, on reality. She would consign the whole experience to her precious box of memories and get on with her life. She'd had a wonderful holiday; she'd met the lovely LeFevre couple, and for the first time ever she was expecting to go home and not have to worry about her sister.

They were waiting at the carousel for their cases when Alexander's mobile rang. He raised his eyes at Sabrina as he answered it; he'd left it switched off for most of the holiday, but now it was possible that his publisher might appreciate a word.

It wasn't his publisher, it was Lydia.

'Alex! Oh, thank God! I've been trying to reach you for two days.'

'Sorry, I've been having a bit of a break, Lydia. What's the matter?' It was obvious that something was wrong.

'It's Angus. He had a heart attack on Thursday and he's still in Intensive Care and…'

'Where is he—where are you?' Alexander demanded. Looking at him as he spoke, Sabrina could see the shock on his face.

For a few moments she heard Lydia's near-hysterical voice at the other end.

'OK, Lydia, I'll be with you in—' he paused to glance at his watch '—about an hour. We'll come straight over.'

There was another pause. 'Tell Dad… Tell Dad I'm on my way.'

He snapped the phone shut just as their cases appeared in front of them, and grabbing his and Sabrina's in his strong grip, he looked down at her.

'My father's had a heart attack,' he said briefly, and for the first time since she'd known him Sabrina saw a look of real fear, real concern, on the handsome features. 'We need to get to the hospital—now,' he added briefly.

Sabrina had to trot alongside him to keep up as they made for the exit, and as they reached the taxi rank she said, 'I'll find my own way home, Alexander.'

'No, you won't. I want you to come with me…please,' he said bluntly. Sabrina thought, well, yes; maybe there was something she could do to help.

It took less than an hour to get to the hospital, then they quickly made their way up the flight of stairs to the private room which had been allocated to Angus. As they almost ran along the corridor, Sabrina felt her stomach lurch with dread. She hadn't visited a hospital for a long time….

Almost immediately they were shown into the darkened room, and Lydia got up from her chair, her face a mixture of torment and despair. 'Oh, Alexander, I'm so glad to see you…' The words came tumbling out. 'It's been such a terrible shock—Bruno came to the hospital with me when it happened, of course, but he's got a raging flu and they've instructed him to stay away.' Clearly overwrought, she put her hand on the edge of the bed to steady herself for a second. 'Naturally, I haven't left Angus since he was brought in here, but…'

Alexander led his mother gently back to sit down. 'Now, Lydia, start from the beginning,' he said quietly.

Feeling slightly as if she was intruding on a personal family affair, Sabrina stood listening as Alexander's mother told him what had happened.

For several moments he let Lydia tell him the details—how Angus had come back from one of his regular trips abroad, hadn't felt very well after supper and had collapsed.

'I thought I'd lost him then, Alexander,' Lydia whispered. 'I couldn't pick him up from the floor and he looked so…so awful. He's come round once or twice, but he doesn't know me, Alexander. He doesn't know me….'

Now the tears began to flow, and Sabrina frowned slightly as she watched the scene in front of her. From what Alexander had said, it was not a particularly loving marriage, yet his mother was clearly distraught at the thought she might lose her husband of so many years.

Alexander went silently over to the bed where his father lay, and for several long moments just looked down at the inert figure. Then he caught hold of Angus's hand in both of his and started rubbing it gently.

'Hello, Dad,' he whispered. 'It's Alex…. Can you hear me, Dad?'

Just then, a young nurse came in followed by the doctor, and for several minutes they had a subdued discussion with Alexander, while Lydia sat like a crumpled bundle of clothes in the corner, just staring into space. Gone was the extravagant make-up, the ostentatious clothes; she was dressed in a plain navy skirt and jacket, and she didn't seem to have registered that it was Sabrina who'd come with Alexander. But then, she thought, she'd been invisible to Lydia that other time, and obviously still was.

The nurse and doctor left the room, and Alexander

beckoned to Sabrina to come over as he spoke to his mother.

'They're still waiting for more results before they can give us much idea of the prognosis,' he said quietly. 'But you must go home, Lydia, and get some rest. I'll stay tonight, and for as long as I'm needed.' He glanced across at Sabrina. 'You remember my secretary Sabrina, don't you, Lydia?'

Lydia turned listless eyes to Sabrina. 'Yes—yes, I remember.'

'Well, we'll take over for now. I'll get them to call a cab for you—and try not to worry too much. They tell me that all is not lost.'

Lydia got slowly to her feet, obviously thankful that someone was there to take over, her tears starting again. 'I feel so wretched, Alexander…' she began, and he interrupted.

'Of course you do—you're worn out. And you've had a shock. You must try and hold on, Lydia.'

'No—no, I mean I've not been a good wife to Angus. I know I'm selfish and have always put myself first when I should have thought more of him—and of you two boys, too…'

Alexander held his mother away from him for a second, a look of puzzlement crossing his features. Was this Lydia talking?

'I owe Angus so much—I owe him everything. He was the only one who understood me, understood everything about me,' Lydia whispered.

'What do you mean, Lydia?' Alexander asked quietly.

Lydia let several moments pass before she went on. 'He's the only one who ever knew the truth about me…about my upbringing.' She swallowed, but now for a moment her eyes were dry. 'My parents—your grandparents—didn't die in a car crash as I'd always told you. They gave me up for adoption to a couple who never really wanted children after all. They liked the idea, but not the reality. And a few years later—I was about ten—they divorced. My adoptive mother had to bring me up alone. I learned all about life from her… Oh yes—how to make men notice me, to always put myself first, not to let family get in my way… To stand up for myself because no one else would do it for me.'

Still holding her, Alexander rested his chin on the top of his mother's head as she spoke, unable to believe what he was hearing.

'I was very young when I met Angus, and when he asked me to marry him I couldn't believe my luck,' Lydia went on calmly, as if she was giving a recitation. 'He was everything I was told I should try and catch—a good-looking man with money. But he was so much more than that. He was kind and generous, and he always forgave my failings and promised he would never leave me. And I couldn't bear life without him. We…we understand each other, you see. Although he's away such a lot, he's always there when I need him.'

Lydia stared into space for a moment, as if she was in another world. Then, in a monotone she said, 'If Angus dies, I shall want to die too.' Her eyes filled again. 'I mean it. I couldn't bear the thought of life without him.'

She took a tissue from her pocket and looked up at Alexander.

'And the very best thing he ever did for me was to give me my two wonderful sons—sons I've been proud of all my life. Sons I've never been worthy of,' she added sadly.

* * *

Later that night, as Sabrina lay down on the bed in the private room which Alexander had arranged for her to sleep in, she felt as if she was part of an unfolding television drama. It was so unreal, she thought, so unexpected. By now, she should be at home, unpacking her clothes and reliving her holiday. Instead of that, she'd not only become part of a crisis, she'd seen a different side to Alexander McDonald—a deeply caring side. His love for his sick father was touchingly transparent, and an emerging softness towards his mother was obvious.

After he had seen Lydia safely off in the taxi, he and Sabrina had gone down to the hospital café to have something to eat. Although Sabrina had felt rather embarrassed at being party to everything Lydia had spilled out, Alexander seemed only too anxious to talk about it.

'Today, I think I met my mother for the first time,' he'd said slowly as they drank their coffee. 'She has never spoken of her past before.' He'd paused. 'I have learned one or two things…. It shows that you can't possibly know what makes people who or what they are,' he'd added.

Now, Sabrina pulled the unfamiliar duvet around her shoulders. At least the fact that they'd come straight from the airport meant they had their clothes with them, and that she could clean her teeth and wear a nightdress in bed. Though whether she'd get a wink of sleep was another thing—especially as she would rather have stayed by Angus's bed with Alexander and shared his anxiety. But he had been insistent that she should rest.

'Goodness knows what I might need you for tomorrow,' he'd said as he dropped a light kiss on her cheek. 'Sleep well. I'll wake you if there's any change.' He'd hesitated, pulling her towards him. 'And thank you for coming here with me, Sabrina.'

She'd gestured helplessly. 'If only there was something I could do,' she'd said.

'But you're doing it,' he'd replied softly. 'You're here.'

For the next thirty-six hours it was touch and go with Angus.

When Lydia returned to the hospital on Monday morning, she found Sabrina sitting alone in the ward. As the older woman came in, Sabrina stood up quickly.

'I—I've taken over for a couple of hours, Mrs McDonald,' she explained. 'Alexander is tired out, so I made him go and have a rest.'

Lydia smiled, still looking wan and distressed. 'That is very kind of you, Sabrina,' she said. 'Thank you.'

Well, that was another surprise, Sabrina thought. She'd half-expected to be met with resentment that she, a comparative stranger, was here at all during this sensitive family time. Especially as she was only a secretary.

At that moment a nurse came in and, going over to the bed, she made a little exclamation.

'Ah, Mr McDonald, you're looking a bit better,' she said gently. 'Look—your wife is here to see you. How are you feeling?'

And amazingly, after a few seconds, Angus croaked, 'I'm feeling…f-f-fine. Thank you.'

The next few moments passed in a blur as the doctor was called urgently. As Lydia stood cradling her husband's head, Sabrina slipped away to fetch Alexander.

When she got to the private room, he was standing by the window, his hands in his pockets, and Sabrina went over and touched him gently.

'You're needed, Alexander,' she said. 'I think you should go now.'

He turned quickly. 'My father hasn't…? He's not…?' he said almost savagely, and Sabrina smiled.

'No. He's just told everyone that he's feeling fine.' She paused. 'I'm sure you'd like to hear it too.'

After he'd gone, Sabrina began to finish packing the few things she'd taken from her case, ready to go home.

'Obviously, you must stay at home until I get in touch with you, Sabrina,' Alexander had said when she'd told him she was going. 'I don't know when I'll be back at work—I'll stay here for ever if necessary—but as soon as the situation becomes clearer I'll ring you.'

As she collected her few things from the bathroom and zipped up her wash bag, Sabrina paused for a moment. She had never met Angus McDonald before—not in the proper sense—but she knew she liked him. And she really, really wanted him to get better. For Alexander's sake—and, yes, for Lydia's too.

One evening, ten days later, Sabrina arrived home to find Melly and Sam had also returned. Before they got their greetings underway, the doorbell rang. Immediately Sabrina got to her feet and went to answer it. Alexander stood there, holding a large parcel wrapped in brown paper.

'Alexander!' she exclaimed, not bothering to hide her pleasure in seeing him again. 'What…? Why…? I mean, sorry—come in!'

Alexander grinned down at her and followed her into the house. 'Oh, well, I was just passing,' he said. They both knew he was not 'just passing'. 'And thought it was a good opportunity to drop this off.'

Sabrina didn't know what he was talking about, but they went inside where Melly and Sam were having coffee. Sabrina said brightly, 'You haven't met my sister, have you, Alexander? Um, Melly, this is my...my boss, Alexander McDonald. I don't think I ever actually mentioned his name.'

Alexander put the heavy parcel carefully down against the wall, stood up and went over, holding out his hand.

'Hello, Melly,' he said easily. 'I've heard a great deal about you.'

Melly smiled up at the handsome face, clearly impressed at meeting the famous Alexander McDonald.

'I am so glad that your father is making such a good recovery,' she said, thinking that, if she had to listen to one more word about her sister's employer's troubles, she'd go mad.

'Thank you. Yes, it's an enormous relief all round,' Alexander replied.

Melly glanced down at Sam. 'And this is my partner, Sam Conway,' she said.

The two men shook hands and Sabrina said, 'You'll have some coffee, won't you, Alexander?'

'Thanks—yes,' he said.

Sabrina passed Alexander his coffee. Glancing at Melly, she wondered if her sister was comparing him to the other famous brother she'd met once or twice. Well, there was no comparison, Sabrina thought. Not in looks, style, manner—anything at all.

Alexander stood up. 'Now,' he said. 'I have something to fix upstairs.'

Sabrina stared at him. 'What do you mean?' she said.

'I have a small task to undertake, that's all.' He smiled down at her slowly. 'You can come and help me.'

Together, the pair went out into the hall and Sabrina helped to tear the brown paper from the parcel. When she saw it, she gasped in admiration.

'Alexander! Is this…is this for us? You shouldn't have! It's gorgeous… It's absolutely fantastic!'

'I knew you'd like it,' he said. 'I asked Colette to pack it with tender, loving care.' He lifted the ornate, heavy mirror and began going up the stairs, Sabrina following. 'As soon as I saw it, I could imagine it hanging where the other one had been,' he said over his shoulder. 'My problem was in keeping it a secret from you—but you were far too busy with your own purchases, fortunately.'

It was mid-December before Alexander asked Sabrina to return to work. Now, as she made her way along the familiar street to number thirteen, she felt glad at last to be getting back into a routine. She certainly hadn't wasted the time at home, but being paid to be away from her desk had begun to make her feel useless.

The time alone had got Sabrina to thinking. Seeing how happy Melly and Sam were, and the little ways the two had demonstrated their deep feelings for each other while Sam had been staying with them, Sabrina felt a familiar, small stab of envy. They were so obviously in love, she thought. They could have been made for each other.

While Sabrina was thrilled and happy for them, deep down she recognized another less comfortable feeling: that the umbilical cord between Melly and her had been severed once and for all.

But all this introspection was nothing compared to

how she was feeling about her employer. Her employer. Her boss. Someone who *did* need her. Oh yes, he needed her all right…for now. He'd told her so, several times. She had fulfilled all her secretarial duties to the very best of her ability—staying late or coming in early whenever he'd asked, making him countless coffees and lunches, and one or two suppers too. And she'd gone with him to France, because that was what he'd wanted at the time. She'd allowed him to make love to her because that was also what he'd needed. Then he'd needed her to be a consoling presence in that hospital ward. So what? He was paying her handsomely for all her efforts, wasn't he?

Sabrina slowed her steps for a moment. Be honest, she told herself. He might need her, but she needed him too—because the hard fact was she knew she loved him deeply. She'd fought against it, not wanting to risk a passion that might end in yet more pain. But it was a lost cause. Useless. Because he didn't love her—not in the way that her heart yearned for. And she doubted that Alexander McDonald could ever profess his love for her, or any woman. It was just not in his nature.

Sabrina let herself into the house with her key, then made her way upstairs. It seemed a long time since she'd been here, she thought as she went into the study. So much had happened…

There didn't appear to be anyone else around. Maria had obviously already gone, and there was no sign of Alexander. As she went over to her desk, Sabrina suddenly spotted the large, leather-bound book lying there; immediately knowing what it was, she picked it up eagerly: it was their novel. Its weight in her hands made her realize just how much work had gone into it—not that she needed telling.

Carefully, almost reverentially, she opened the first page of *Symptoms of Betrayal, by Alexander McDonald.* Sabrina's hands almost shook as she looked down at it, a feeling of personal pride entering her consciousness. She had been there while this famous writer had fashioned a lot of this; had watched him covertly as he'd wrestled with the difficult parts; had shared his relief when that final chapter had come together…

As she continued staring at it, Sabrina read the first couple of pages which contained the author's imposing list of previous publications. There were the usual acknowledgements, together with the usual disclaimer about all characters being fictitious, and then… Hardly believing her eyes, she had to sit down for a moment.

On the page immediately preceding chapter one was the dedication—just two words, dead centre, saying simply:

For Sabrina

That was all. Sabrina's first sensation of shock was followed by one of incredulity and choking emotion. There had never been any discussion about a dedication, and seeing her own name there had almost taken her breath away.

She sat back for a moment, her eyes still fixed to the page. Well, of course; that had to be his way of expressing his gratitude, she thought. A little pat on the back for her loyalty—perhaps by now he was running out of friends to include.

Whatever his reason, Sabrina was overcome, and she had to fight back her tears. It was a privilege, and she did feel honoured.

As she reached for a tissue from her bag, a piece of

paper fell out and fluttered to the floor. It was the application form for the new position which Emma had rung her about. Sabrina had kept putting off filling it in, but maybe now was the time. Maybe her duties here had run their natural course and now, with Alexander's novel safely under wraps, she should call it a day. Because she loved being here too much, and was beginning to forget that she was a highly qualified psychologist with another life out there, another world that did not include Alexander McDonald.

In his sitting room two doors along from the study, Alexander sat brooding silently, staring into space. He had heard Sabrina come in but had wanted her to see the book—their book—before they came face to face this morning. He had delayed her return to work until now because he'd needed some time away from her to see whether he could face the future without her. To convince himself, one way or the other, whether she really had become as indispensable to him as he thought. But he knew the answer to that. He'd known it for a long time.

Suddenly, he stood up, strode purposefully along the landing and thrust open the door to the study. This had to be the moment of truth, he told himself. He couldn't bear to wait another day, another hour…

Sabrina looked up and smiled quickly, indicating the novel in front of her.

'Oh, Alexander,' she said. 'Doesn't this look good? Doesn't it look lovely? It's great to see the finished product.' She paused. 'You must be very proud of it.'

He shrugged. 'Well, aren't you?' he asked bluntly. 'I seem to remember there were two of us on the project.'

So, she'd been right, Sabrina thought. He clearly thought he'd pay her the compliment of adding her name.

'And thank you—so much—for the dedication.' She swallowed. 'I could hardly believe it.'

He came over and glanced down at the application form which Sabrina had begun filling out.

'What's that? What are you doing?' he asked frankly.

Well, she supposed he had every right to ask; he was paying her for her time here.

'Oh, this is the application for the post my ex-colleague rang me about when we were in France,' she said casually. 'And don't worry; even if I'm successful—which is by no means certain—the post isn't open until the end of March, so we'll have plenty of time before that to concentrate on your next novel.'

'Don't!' he said harshly. 'Don't do this. I don't want you to go.'

Sabrina's shoulders sagged slightly. She knew that he needed her skills, and it was undeniably true that she seemed to fit in with all his requirements, tick all the necessary boxes. Of course he didn't want her to go. What else had she expected?

But Sabrina knew that she must think more of herself and less of him on this occasion. And as she looked up at the impossibly handsome face, at those eyes which had always seemed able to read her innermost thoughts, she knew she must put a stop to it now. She could no longer bear to be close to him—and not be loved by him.

'I'm sorry, Alexander,' she began. 'But I feel it's right that we should part company soon.'

'Why?' he demanded roughly. 'Why is it right? I

thought we were good together, you and I, Sabrina. We could go on being good together, couldn't we?'

'What exactly do you mean by that?' she asked.

'Well, what I mean is, I want us to be together—properly. To commit to each other.' He shook his head irritably. 'I mean, I want you to marry me, of course! What's the problem?'

For a second, Sabrina felt almost amused at the question; now was the moment. 'You're the problem, Alexander,' she said, surprised at her own coolness of tone.

'Why? Explain!' he demanded.

Looking up at him, her bewitching eyes moist and full of emotion, Sabrina said, 'I agree that we are good together.' Would either of them ever forget their one passionate night together? 'But I don't think you understand me, Alexander. I am more than aware of *your* needs—your wants—but I don't believe that you're aware of mine. You simply have no idea,' she added quietly.

'But, if you leave me, I'll never find out what your needs are, what you're talking about!' He thrust his hand through his hair. 'If it's about wanting to return to your own profession one day, well, of course I fully understand. I'd never stand in your way. You could set up your own consulting room here, if you wanted—there's plenty of space. And you could still go on working for me. We'd sort it between us somehow. But don't leave me, Sabrina. You'll have to give me time… That's all I'm asking for—time…'

'Time is not what you need,' Sabrina said slowly. 'What you lack, Alexander, is the ability to utter the one thing I—or any woman—would expect to hear you say. Well, three things, actually.'

'Which is? Which are?'

After a long moment, staring straight in front of her, Sabrina said slowly, 'I want you to tell me that we should be together, that we should commit to each other, simply because *you love me*—and for no other reason. I want you to force yourself to say it—to say, "I love you".' She swallowed, quietly amazed at her own temerity. She was giving her boss instructions! How had she found the courage to do that? But she was forcing him to give her a reply now. It would be his only chance; she knew that. And after a moment she repeated what she'd said. 'I want you to tell me that you love me, Alexander. Is that such a hard thing for you to do?'

In the complete silence which followed that remark, the two were like solemn players in a momentous production which was about to reach its climax; the intensity in the room was palpable, and painful. Then Alexander walked slowly over to stare out of the window, his hands thrust in his pockets.

'Perhaps I should explain something,' he said. 'About Angelica.' After a few moments he went on. 'I met her at one of my book signings. Or, rather, she was in the long queue of people which the organizers were trying to hurry along.' He paused. 'On these occasions there are always those who want to engage in conversation and chit-chat, and the whole procedure can drag on a bit. This particular day did seem endless because hundreds had turned up.'

Alexander waited before going on. 'Anyway, I'd glanced up once or twice and I'd seen this tall, raven-haired, beautiful girl… Well, you couldn't miss her. She never actually got to where I was signing. But eventually she was the last one, and we exchanged pleasantries as she gave me her book.' He paused. 'She asked for the entry to read "for Angelica"—and "never give up". Which I thought was a bit strange at the time,' he added.

Alexander turned to glance back at Sabrina briefly. 'Then later, as I left the building to go the car park,' he went on, 'there she was. She'd somehow managed to park her car right next to mine—she must have been there very early in the day to do that.' There was another long pause.

'She asked if she could buy me a drink. Well, it'd been a long day, and suddenly the thought of spending an hour in the company of a very attractive woman seemed…enticing. So I bought us some dinner and it was midnight before we parted company. We exchanged phone numbers…you know how you do…and I thought she'd been good company: intelligent, and a good listener. She hung on my every word, and I suppose I had my head turned a bit.' Alexander turned to stare out of the window again. 'Well, this was all a very long time ago,' he added defensively.

'For the next two or three months we saw quite a lot of each other—and I even began to wonder whether she'd be the one I'd marry and settle down with…' A derisive snort left Alexander's lips.

At this point, Sabrina got up and came across to stand next to him, knowing that he wasn't enjoying telling her all this, but he went on.

'One evening, I was invited to go with her to someone's twenty-first birthday party. It was at a wine bar in town, and very crowded. Plenty of bright young things there, a lot of excitable noise and merry-making and plenty of drink to go with it. I knew it wasn't my kind of thing, but anyway…' He shook his head slightly. 'Unfortunately—for both of us—I enjoy very keen hearing. Later in the evening I overheard Angelica talking to two friends.' Alexander grimaced to himself. He could recall the incident without difficulty.

'The long and short of it was that Angelica's purpose in making herself known to me was to get to Bruno. To get to my famous brother. She apparently had great ambitions for herself in the theatrical world—something she'd very skilfully kept from me, by the way. My brother's name had barely been mentioned between us. Up to that point I'd been listening to everything she was saying with only half an ear, but when Bruno's name cropped up I immediately took more interest and it all became clear. Especially when I heard Angelica's final remark.' Alexander's mouth twisted as he remembered.

'"As soon as my feet are fully under their family table, who knows what'll happen for me? Alexander could be my fast track to success at last…perhaps even stardom! And then telesales can take a run and jump!"'

'That's what she said,' Alexander went on flatly. 'It wasn't me she was interested in at all—it was Bruno, who could maybe give her the chance to progress her stage career. And, looking back, I had to give her full marks for her enterprise. She'd made me feel that I was the only man on the planet that she had eyes for.

'But her final words to her friends were, "I'll do whatever it takes… You know me. Persistence is all—and I never, never give up—not when I really, *really* want something".

'Then I remembered what she'd asked me to write on the book, and it left me in no doubt about her true motive in hanging around to speak to me.'

There was complete silence for a few moments as Sabrina took in everything Alexander had told her. How dreadful that must have been, to be used as a tool in someone's ambitions—and especially to get to a close relative. How hurtful and how degrading for him. Being degraded was something Alexander McDonald would not have experienced before, and something he would never tolerate again.

'So our wonderful "relationship" ended that night—and I've never seen her since,' Alexander said noncommittally. 'Neither have I seen Angelica's name in lights either,' he added.

Gently, Sabrina put her arm around Alexander's waist and rested her head on his shoulder. 'I'm sorry that you had to tell me that, Alexander,' she said. 'But I'm glad that you did because it does answer my question. To be treated in that way is unforgivable—well, I wouldn't be able to forgive it if it happened to me,' she said bluntly. 'But I can understand your reluctance to actually tell someone—tell a woman—that you love her…'

At that, a slow smile spread across Alexander's features and almost hungrily he gathered Sabrina up in his arms, virtually crushing her to him.

'Sabrina,' he whispered, his lips lingering over her hair and her neck. 'I have never said those words to anyone because, I suppose… Well, because…' He frowned briefly. 'I have never heard them actually said to me. They are words which have always seemed unreal, belonging to another world, just out of my reach.' He gazed down into her eyes, making Sabrina almost melt with longing and tenderness.

'But since I met you I have found myself whispering those words, Sabrina, whispering them to myself. And now I'm going to say them out loud. For the first time in my life, I'm going to tell someone that I love them. *I love you, Sabrina Gold. I love you.* With all my heart, my soul and mind.'

And as he uttered the words, Alexander felt the

loosening of a lifetime's tension, felt the unbelievable magic of laying his soul bare to someone he knew he would trust and adore for the rest of his days—if only she would have him.

Leaving him in no doubt about that, Sabrina wound her fingers around his neck, drawing him even closer to her. She tilted her head back, offering him her parted lips, all her senses swimming with emotion and happiness. Because she knew that he had unlocked that part of her she'd thought she'd lost for ever. For her, there was to be no more running away.

Today was the beginning of the rest of her life—of their lives.

And she knew it was going to be wonderful.